Romantic Suspense

Danger. Passion. Drama.

Colton's Dangerous Cover
Lisa Childs

Peril In The Shallows
Addison Fox

MILLS & BOON

Lisa Childs is acknowledged as the author of this work
COLTON'S DANGEROUS COVER
© 2024 by Harlequin Enterprises ULC   First Published 2024
Philippine Copyright 2024   First Australian Paperback Edition 2024
Australian Copyright 2024   ISBN 978 1 867 29962 2
New Zealand Copyright 2024

PERIL IN THE SHALLOWS
© 2024 by Frances Karkosak   First Published 2024
Philippine Copyright 2024   First Australian Paperback Edition 2024
Australian Copyright 2024   ISBN 978 1 867 29962 2
New Zealand Copyright 2024

MIX
Paper | Supporting
responsible forestry
FSC® C001695

Published by
Harlequin Mills & Boon
An imprint of Harlequin Enterprises (Australia) Pty Limited
(ABN 47 001 180 918), a subsidiary of HarperCollins
Publishers Australia Pty Limited
(ABN 36 009 913 517)
Level 19, 201 Elizabeth Street
SYDNEY NSW 2000 AUSTRALIA

Cover art used by arrangement with Harlequin Books S.A.. All rights reserved.

Printed and bound in Australia by McPherson's Printing Group

Colton's Dangerous Cover

Lisa Childs

MILLS & BOON

Dear Reader,

I am thrilled and honoured to be part of **The Coltons of Owl Creek** continuity series. My book *Colton's Dangerous Cover* is the second in the series, with things definitely heating up in Owl Creek between Detective Fletcher Colton and DJ Kiki Shelton. But of course, their "relationship" is just a cover to catch a serial attacker. Or is it?

I loved writing this book. While I've written about a lot of officers of the law over the years, this is my first time writing about a DJ. This is probably because I have no musical ability myself. Per my elementary school music teacher, I am definitely tone-deaf. When tested on which musical instrument I should play, I was told, "No. Just no." While I can't tell which note is which, I do love music and dancing, so writing Kiki's character was a joy.

I also enjoyed writing about the puppy she's fostering for Crosswinds Training. Fancy, the little shepherd mix, reminded me so much of the shepherd-mix dogs my family had while I was growing up. They were all loving, loyal, protective and so very smart.

And as always, Colton books are about family. Those sibling and cousin connections I know so well because I have so many of both.

Hopefully you'll enjoy reading my contribution to the continuity as much as I enjoyed writing it.

Happy reading!

Lisa Childs

DEDICATION

With great appreciation for the talented authors also contributing to this Colton continuity—it's been an honour and a pleasure!

Chapter 1

The music was loud, even in the alley. Pulsating. Throbbing. It was alive. Like the rage burning inside the Slasher.

After the third assault a couple of years ago, that was what the media had named the attacker: *The Slasher*.

The Slasher smiled, enjoying the name and the attention. That attention was finally being paid for the right reason. For the power. Not the weakness. *This* was all about taking power back, about taking it away from them.

He would have found the note by now. The invitation for this tryst in the alley. He wouldn't know for certain who'd left it for him, but he would think he was going to get lucky. He had no idea...

A door creaked open, letting some light and louder music seep into the alley. "Hello?" a man's voice called out. "Are you out here?"

Still deep in the shadows, the Slasher called out in a husky whisper, "Over here..."

The guy chuckled, low in his throat, and stumbled away from the door, letting it click closed behind him. Darkness enveloped the area again, but for a thin sliver of moonlight slicing between the tall buildings on either side of the alley.

That thin sliver provided just enough light for the Slasher to see the victim, and for there to be a glint off the sharp blade as the Slasher swung the knife toward the head of the next victim.

Fletcher Colton was dealing with his last case with Salt Lake City PD before he would head home to Owl Creek, Idaho. It was another slasher case. He hoped this job wouldn't cause him to postpone his start date for the position he'd accepted with Owl Creek PD as lead detective.

This case was getting a little personal for him. This was the second time the Slasher had struck in Salt Lake City. Fletcher hadn't worked the first case; he'd already been working a homicide, which had taken priority over an assault. So far, the Slasher hadn't killed anyone.

But the wounds across the victim's face and chest were so deep that the man was going to have to spend some time in the hospital while they healed to make sure they didn't get infected. These wounds were even deeper than the ones the last victim had received. The violence seemed to be escalating.

So it was just a matter of time before someone died, Fletcher thought. And even if they didn't, the Slasher's victims were going to be scarred for life—physically and mentally as well. The Slasher had to be stopped. These two cases in Salt Lake weren't the only assaults. Over the past few years, there had been random attacks outside nightclubs in LA and Vegas. And now Salt Lake City. The randomness made it impossible to figure out where the Slasher would strike next.

Fletcher wanted to make sure that it was nowhere. He'd already interviewed the victim at the hospital. Now he was at the scene, watching as the techs collected evidence. Or at least he hoped they were collecting something that could be used as evidence. Lights had been set up in the alley so that nothing would be missed. The light illuminated the spatters and pools of blood from the attack that had been violent and vicious.

And somehow personal…

But the victim had no connection with the last one. At least none this victim, Eric Holt, was aware of. Fletcher couldn't find any association to the victims in the other states.

What the hell was the motive?

Maybe there wasn't one.

Was this just some psycho who randomly picked victims to disfigure?

"Not much here, Detective Colton," one of the techs said. "Not even footprints, and given the amount of blood, I would have expected to find something."

Fletcher pushed a hand through his dark hair, which probably needed a cut, like usual, and sighed. "The victim wasn't able to give us any useful info either. Everything happened so fast. He couldn't even tell if it was a man or a woman who attacked him." The guy had been vague about all the details, but then he was pretty drunk—with a blood alcohol level that was twice the legal limit.

That was the one thing all the victims had had in common. They'd been drinking. A lot. This guy had been at his bachelor party. So had one of the other victims…

But the others had just been at the club as far as Fletcher knew. He had to find something else. Another lead. "I'm going inside to do some interviews," he told the tech. "Let me know if you find any—"

His cell rang, and he pulled it out of his jacket pocket. The contact information read *Uncle Buck*. In the middle of interviews, he would have ignored it…if not for what had happened recently with his sister Ruby, for how close they had come to losing her forever. But that case had been closed and the deranged guy was locked up. She should be safe, especially with Sebastian Cross so determined to make sure she and their unborn child stayed out of harm's way.

Still, Fletcher was concerned enough that he swiped to accept the call. "Uncle Buck, what is it? I'm at a crime—"

"It's your dad, Fletcher. He's had another stroke. It doesn't look good. He's been life-flighted to Boise Medical. You need to get there as soon as you can."

Fletcher cursed. His relationship with his dad was complicated, but Robert Colton was still his dad. Fletcher loved him even though he got frustrated with him, like he was now. "After the last stroke, he was supposed to quit the drinking and smoking…"

And whatever the hell else he'd been doing that he shouldn't have been doing, that he wouldn't have been doing if he'd cared about anyone but himself.

"Fletcher, it's too late for all of that now," Buck said, his voice gruff with emotion.

A twinge of guilt struck Fletcher. He shouldn't have been thinking about that, let alone voicing his thoughts aloud. He shouldn't have been thinking about anything but his dad's health and about his family. Buck's relationship with his brother hadn't always been the easiest either, but they were brothers. If his dad didn't recover from this stroke like his last one, it wasn't going to be easy for anyone to handle, especially not Fletcher's mother.

"I'll be there as soon as I can," Fletcher assured his uncle.

He had already turned in his resignation to leave Salt Lake City PD for Owl Creek. Someone else would have to take over this case. Someone else would have to catch the Slasher before anyone else got hurt.

Kiki Shelton's hand shook as she scrolled through the messages and posts popping up on the screen of her cell phone. *Oh, no…*

Not another one…

She had to call, had to make sure everyone she knew was all right. She glanced toward the closed door off the kitchen that was dark but for the dim glow of the under-cabinet lighting. Soft snores emanated from behind that door. Her grandfather had gone to bed a while ago, but he was a light sleeper, especially when they were fostering a puppy for Crosswinds.

Fancy was a little two-month-old shepherd mix with tan fur everywhere but her muzzle, which was as black as Kiki's hair. Except for her deep auburn tips. The puppy bounced around Kiki's bare legs, excited that someone else was awake at this hour. Kiki wanted the two of them to be the only ones, so she opened the patio door and stepped onto the deck attached to the back of the cottage.

She didn't want her grandfather to overhear her talking on the phone. He already worried about her too much. He didn't need to know that there had been another attack. In addition to the texts and calls sent directly to her, news of the slashing had also popped up on all her social media accounts.

Thank God Jim Shelton still refused to pay attention to any of them. But he would probably catch it on the news. He never failed to watch the network broadcasts every morning and every night, flipping from channel to channel to get different takes on the same story.

There was only one take on this one. There was a maniac brutally attacking people.

Concerned that someone else had been hurt, she made the call she'd been anxious to make.

"Kiki!" the male voice cracked with the exclamation of her name.

"Are you okay?" she asked Troy. He was usually her assistant, but she'd loaned him out to another DJ since she hadn't had a gig this weekend.

He'd been there. In Salt Lake City. At that very club where the attack had happened...

"It's messed up, Kiki," he said. "I stepped outside to smoke and saw the guy lying there..."

"I'm so sorry, Troy," she said, her stomach churning over the thought of what her friend had found, had seen. And that poor man. "That's horrible. Are you okay? Is he?"

"Yeah, I'm okay. It was way worse for him, but I think he'll live. But it was so bad..." His voice cracked again, and she could hear his shudder through the home. "It's just messed up, Kiki..." He slurred a bit; maybe he'd had something to drink or maybe he was just tired.

It was late. But Kiki was used to staying up late; so was Troy. "You need to get some rest," she suggested.

"Every time I close my eyes I see him there, all cut up and bleeding..." She heard the shudder again.

"Take some time off for a while," she said.

"If I'm not working, I'll just keep thinking about it..."

"Then join me early in Owl Creek," she said. She had some gigs set up for them in the area in a few weeks. "It's safe here. Nothing much happens."

She wouldn't tell him about what had happened at Crosswinds—how she could have lost a good friend. But that criminal had been caught, so Owl Creek was safe again.

Like it had always been...

Kiki's safe haven. After she'd lost her parents in a horrific car accident when she was six, she had come to live with her grandfather along the shore of Blackbird Lake. She leaned on the deck railing and stared out at the surface of the lake, which reflected the night sky and the stars twinkling in it along with the big crescent moon.

It was beautiful here and so quiet, just cicadas chirping in the night as fireflies flitted around like sparks, appearing and disappearing. Fancy tore around the yard, chasing after them, her little teeth snapping as she tried to capture them in her mouth. But it was still quiet, despite the antics of the puppy.

So quiet and so beautiful that it always seemed to recharge Kiki, especially after a long winter and spring of playing clubs in LA and San Francisco and Salt Lake City. But the money she was saving and the reputation she was building was worth all the hard work.

She should have been working the club in Salt Lake this weekend, but she'd wanted to stick around Owl Creek to make sure Ruby was okay and that her grandfather could handle the new puppy. Every time she came home, it seemed like he'd aged while she was gone. And she didn't want him being alone so often, even though he insisted he was as spry as he ever was. And the truth was, he probably preferred to be alone. Either working with puppies from Crosswinds, at his tackle shop or his favorite place, out on his boat on the water, fishing.

"You sure, Kiki?"

She had pretty much forgotten Troy was still on the line. "What?"

"You sure it's safe there?"

She thought of what Ruby Colton had just gone

through. But that was over now. "Yes, it's safe here, Troy. Come to Owl Creek."

But as she clicked off the cell, a strange shiver chased down her spine. Maybe it was just the night breeze. Maybe it was foreboding. After what had happened with Ruby, was Owl Creek as safe as Kiki had always believed it was?

Or maybe that just proved that something bad could happen anywhere...

Chapter 2

The past week had passed in a blur of hospital vigils and now this: the funeral.

Fletcher's dad hadn't survived this stroke like he had the last one. After days in a coma, Robert Colton's body had given up the fight. He'd slipped silently away from them.

"Are you sure you don't want to say anything?" Fletcher's older brother asked him.

He shook his head, uncertain what he could say about his father. Sure, he'd loved him, but he'd also sometimes wondered how well he'd really known him. Robert Colton had spent more time at work than with his family.

"No, Chase," Fletcher said. His older brother, who'd worked with his dad at Colton Properties, knew their father far better than Fletcher had. Fletcher just wanted to make sure that Mom was all right and made it through this day. To find her, he moved through the crowd of family and friends and Owl Creek residents who'd gathered in the funeral parlor to mourn or at least to support the mourners.

Every one of his siblings had someone standing beside them, offering their condolences and probably memories of his father. He'd heard his share already, during the hospital vigils, and at the visitation the night before. He really just wanted this to be over, for his sake, and for his mom's.

Over the past week Jenny Colton had been strong and loving, as she always was, comforting her *kids* instead of letting them comfort her. Maybe that was because she was a nurse and was just used to taking care of others. Maybe that was just because she was an amazing person.

She'd raised not just her own six kids pretty much on her own while Dad had worked crazy long hours, but she'd also helped Uncle Buck raise his four kids after Aunt Jessie, Mom's twin, had abandoned her husband and family. They were all adults now, but Jenny Colton still always put them first, before herself.

But she always made time to take care of her physical health. Fit and active, the only indication of her age were the streaks of gray in her short, dark blond hair. Fletcher breathed a little sigh of relief that she was all right, that she was healthy.

But how was she doing emotionally?

It had been a long week for him. He couldn't imagine how it had felt for her. He found her with Ruby and Sebastian, which he totally understood after they could have lost Ruby. Instead, they'd lost Dad.

Mom wasn't the only one standing near them. An older man with thick white hair, Jim Shelton, stood beside Sebastian. He'd been running a bait and fishing business on Blackbird Lake for as long as Fletcher could remember. And the woman standing next to him looked nothing like his little orphaned granddaughter who'd come to live with him so long ago.

Kiki Shelton, with beautiful, thick black hair and ample curves, had certainly grown up over the past twenty years. She seemed to get more beautiful every time Fletcher saw her, but that hadn't been very often recently. He'd been working his way to detective in Salt Lake City, and she'd been working clubs in LA and Vegas and San Francisco. She'd even worked some in Salt Lake City. Ruby had let him know a few times when Kiki was DJing, but going to a club, with the noise and the crowds, wasn't his idea of a good time. At least on the few times he had ventured out, he'd only wound up with a headache, though, not scarred for life like those other guys.

The wounds across Eric Holt's face flashed through his mind along with the blood spattered and pooled in that alley. He wondered how the Slasher case was going back in Salt Lake, who'd taken it over and if they had found any leads.

It was easier to think about that case than about this day, about the funeral, about his dad's senseless death.

If only he'd taken better care of himself...

* * *

Kiki hated funerals because of the flood of memories they brought back. Of her parents' funeral. Of losing them both so suddenly and shockingly as she had in that traffic accident.

Fortunately, she didn't remember much about that, even though she'd been asleep in the backseat. They'd been on their way to Grandpa's for Christmas. A pang struck her heart, as it always did, when she thought of them. She still missed them so much, nearly twenty-one years later.

But Grandpa had taught her that attending funerals was the right thing to do, to pay your respects to the deceased and to offer your sympathy and support to their survivors. Robert Colton had a lot of survivors. The Colton family was big.

Ruby Colton was the one Kiki knew best because the veterinarian owned Colton Veterinary Hospital and took care of the animals for Sebastian Cross's Crosswinds Training. The two had an even closer relationship now. Sebastian's arm wrapped tightly around the blonde. He was definitely supporting her.

Ruby had three older brothers, two younger sisters and four cousins, too. A pang of envy struck Kiki. She'd always wished she had siblings. She probably had some cousins on her mother's side, but they were back in Mexico and she hadn't heard from any of them. Her grandfather had reached out, sending letters and pictures over the years, but they'd been returned as undeliverable.

Grandpa had always done his best for her. She

wrapped her arm around him, knowing that it was getting harder for him to stand for long periods of time with the arthritis he had in his back. The funeral was due to start soon, so they would be able to take a seat then.

Right now, they stood talking to Sebastian and Ruby and Ruby's mother. Jenny Colton was a strong woman. Although she was a little pale, her eyes were dry and clear. But her second oldest son must have been worried about her because he'd clearly been looking for her when he'd walked up.

Fletcher Colton. He wore a dark suit for the solemn occasion, but his hair was a little long, a little unkempt. A little sexy.

His broad shoulders strained the seams of that suit, and his eyes... They were a deep, vivid green. And his gaze was focused on her right now.

Kiki's pulse quickened at the intensity of his stare, but she tried not to take it too seriously. Fletcher Colton just seemed like an intense guy. A detective.

Detectives probably checked out everyone the way he was checking her out.

"You remember Kiki," Ruby said to him, and her lips curved into a slight smile as if she thought he had another reason for staring at her friend.

"Yes, of course," Fletcher said.

"I'm sorry for your loss," Kiki told him, repeating the words she hadn't understood when she'd been six and standing in this very room. She hadn't been able to comprehend why people were apologizing to her like they were responsible for that crash. She hadn't even known what happened for sure, since she'd been sleeping, but Grandpa had said that it was weather. No one's fault.

But now, since losing them, she had a lot more empathy. She understood how it hurt to lose a parent.

Having probably heard those words a hundred times, like she had back then, Fletcher just nodded.

"Your father did a lot for this town," her grandfather said. "He will be missed."

"Thank you, Mr. Shelton," Fletcher said. "It's great to see you."

"Don't know how long you're sticking around Owl Creek but come by if you'd like to do some fishing," Grandpa told him.

"I'm moving home," Fletcher said.

And Kiki's pulse quickened even more.

"He's taken the position of lead detective with Owl Creek Police Department," Jenny said, beaming with pride in her child.

Fletcher shrugged. "Probably won't be as busy as it was in Salt Lake City, so I'm sure I'll have time for some fishing, Mr. Shelton. Thanks for the invitation."

Since Kiki helped Grandpa with the tackle shop and fishing excursions, she would probably be seeing Fletcher around, too. That thought unsettled her for some reason.

Or maybe this uneasy feeling she had didn't have anything to do with him and it was just because he'd mentioned Salt Lake City, as it reminded her of the Slasher's recent attack outside the nightclub where Troy had been working.

Her assistant was still shaken over finding the victim, over what he'd seen. But he'd come to Owl Creek. Troy had even found a place to stay since Kiki was going to be here for the summer, helping her grandfather while doing gigs in the area. She'd booked a job at a nightclub in Conners for this upcoming weekend.

Conners was just outside Owl Creek and was just as safe. Well, just as safe since the deranged man who'd gone after Ruby had been caught.

Music began to play, signaling the beginning of the service. Mrs. Colton, Ruby and Sebastian started off toward the chairs nearest the casket. Fletcher hesitated for a moment before following them, probably dreading this.

She could totally relate.

But then he glanced at her, and there was some question in his green eyes as if he wanted to ask her something. But then he blinked, and the look was gone. He just nodded at Kiki and her grandfather, in some kind of acknowledgement, as he headed off after his family.

She and Grandpa found chairs near the back of the service, since they would have to leave right after it to check on Fancy. So Kiki probably wouldn't see Fletcher again for a while unless he actually took her grandfather up on his fishing invitation.

If he did, she'd probably make herself scarce. She had no interest in getting involved with anyone. Her career was really taking off, and when she wasn't busy working, she wanted to help Grandpa as much as she could.

She had no time for romance. No matter how good-looking Fletcher Colton was.

Not that he was interested in her. He probably just wanted to fish.

* * *

Flyers had gone up around town. Hot LA DJ Kiki Shelton was going to be spinning at Conners Club this weekend. This was an event not to be missed.

The poster had a picture of Kiki on it with her black hair, the ends dyed deep red, and her killer body. A lot of men would probably show up to watch her spin and dance.

A lot of men who would drink too much. Who would get careless.

Who might step into a dark alley.

The Slasher smiled in anticipation.

This attack was soon after the last one. The closest together of the attacks yet.

But this urge burned inside the Slasher. This urge to act again.

To lash out.

To get the attention and the revenge they deserved. And to make sure that some man in Conners got exactly what he deserved, too.

Chapter 3

As if the funeral hadn't been bad enough, Fletcher, his mom and siblings had had to meet with the estate lawyer the next day. Fortunately, he'd come out to the house and Fletcher had been able to slip out of the meeting early. Leaving the others upstairs in the great room, Fletcher slipped downstairs to the walkout level where he'd been staying in his old bedroom.

None of what the lawyer had told them had been a surprise. Jenny got the house and whatever money they'd had in their accounts. Each of the kids got an equal share of Colton Properties while Chase was named the new CEO.

It was pretty much what Fletcher would have expected, probably what they'd all expected. If they'd ever thought about their dad dying...

Even after the first stroke, Fletcher hadn't thought about it. Hadn't considered it was possible.

He'd recovered so quickly and completely from that first stroke. And even though the doctor had warned him to change his lifestyle, it hadn't really seemed possible that Robert Colton would die before he even hit sixty years old. It just hadn't seemed like it could happen.

But it did.

He was gone. But he'd been gone a lot while Fletcher and his siblings were growing up. He'd been away so much that the house didn't even feel different without him being here. Fletcher was staying with Mom, just to make sure that she wasn't alone.

Eventually he would look for his own place. But for now, it was comforting to be home, if not for Mom then at least for him. He'd already lost his dad. He didn't want anything to happen to her, too.

Kiki Shelton had lost both her parents suddenly when she'd been just a kid. When she'd said sorry at the funeral, like so many other people had, it had meant a little more because he knew she knew.

She knew even better than he did about loss.

Maybe that was why she'd intrigued him so much, why he hadn't wanted to stop talking to her even as the service started. No. That was because he'd wanted to ask her about the Slasher.

Or at least that was the idea he'd had at the time. But he realized now it was a reach. Sure. She was a DJ who worked at nightclubs. But there were a lot of nightclubs. And even if she had been at any of the ones where an attack had taken place, she would have already been questioned. She probably wouldn't have any new information to give him no matter what he'd asked her.

And that case in Salt Lake City wasn't his anymore since his dad's stroke had compelled him to cut his two-week notice short. He was glad that he'd been here, though. Glad that he'd been here for his mom and his family.

But now that the funeral was done and the will was read, it all felt so anticlimactic. So strange and surreal.

He had to get back to real life. Fortunately, he was starting at Owl Creek PD in the morning, a week earlier than he'd been scheduled to start. But he needed to get back to work. He needed to help people since he hadn't been able to help his father.

Not even the doctors had been able to help his father.

Knuckles rapped against his door and then it creaked open. He turned away from the window that looked out over Blackbird Lake, surprised to see it was Chase who'd sought him out. "Everything okay?" he asked.

"I was just going to ask you that," Chase said. "You slipped out of the meeting so quickly."

"I thought it was done," Fletcher said.

Chase arched a light brown eyebrow over one of his green eyes. While he and Fletcher had the same color eyes, Chase's hair was lighter brown, and he kept it conservatively cut. And even though this meeting had been at their home, Chase wore a suit. He'd probably come right from the office, though.

Fletcher felt a pang of envy that his brother had had something to keep him busy over the past week.

"Are you upset?" Chase asked.

"About what?" Fletcher asked.

"That I was named CEO."

Fletcher chuckled and shook his head. "You were born CEO, Chase. Everybody knew that was going to happen someday."

"It happened too soon," Chase said, his voice gruff.

And Fletcher knew that even though he'd kept busy, Dad's death had probably affected his oldest brother the most. He'd certainly spent the most time with him. He closed the distance between them and pulled his brother's lean body into a brief hug. "I'm sorry..." he murmured.

And as he said the words, he thought of Kiki Shelton. Of how she'd said them.

Yeah, it was good he started his job tomorrow. Then he could get his mind off not just his dad's death but off Kiki Shelton, too. He had too much going on to even allow himself an attraction to anyone right now.

He was starting a new position with a new police department while helping his family deal with his dad's death. He didn't need any other distractions.

A couple of days had passed since the funeral, but Kiki hadn't been able to get that image of Fletcher Colton out of her mind. The way he'd looked at her...

What had he wanted to ask her?

Not that she really cared. Or had any time for it.

She needed to stop thinking about him and focus on everything else she had going on in her life. She glanced across the console of her SUV to where Fancy sat, her harness secured to the seat. The puppy whined and quivered.

"You have to get used to riding in vehicles," Kiki told her. If she went into service as a scent dog like Sebastian had predicted for her, she was going to have to travel a lot. Like Kiki did.

But a drive up toward the mountains wasn't a sacrifice at all. She loved coming out this way to Crosswinds Training Center, with the enormous sparkling blue of Blackbird Lake on one side of it and the mountains behind it.

Her heart stretched with love for this place where she'd grown up. Owl Creek was beautiful. And there was actually a creek—well, more of a river—by that name, too. It curved around and through town and emptied into the lake.

Kiki had to steer her SUV around those curves on her way up to the training center. Fancy needed a checkup, and Ruby was working out of the medical offices there today.

Kiki had been a bit surprised that she was working at all. She couldn't even remember much of that time immediately after her parents had died. Just the funeral and Grandpa.

He'd gotten a puppy then as if it would make her feel better. And somehow it had worked.

Fancy, with her tan fur and black muzzle, reminded her of that dog. Buster. Even now, years after he'd passed, Kiki remembered Buster. He'd helped her through a rough time. Just like some of the dogs that Sebastian

Cross helped train were used as PTSD dogs to help veterans, like him, through a rough time.

Maybe that was why Ruby had chosen to work, to take care of the animals she loved so much. But, remembering how closely Sebastian had stuck by Ruby's side during the funeral, it wasn't just the animals that the veterinarian loved at Crosswinds. Or that loved her.

A wistful sigh slipped out of Kiki's lips. Not that she was jealous or anything. She liked her life exactly as it was. Focused on Grandpa and growing her brand as a DJ and building her nest egg.

Fancy whined again.

"And you…" Kiki murmured. She enjoyed volunteering with these puppies as much as her grandfather did. A veteran himself, he liked helping out with the ones who were trained to assist with PTSD. But Fancy was special.

Sebastian thought so, and so did Kiki. But probably for different reasons.

"Hang in there, sweet thing," she said as she steered her SUV down the last part of the private road and onto the Crosswinds property. In addition to the big brick and wood training center, there were indoor and outdoor kennels and the medical building. "We're here," she said as she pulled up next to the medical building.

Sebastian also had a cabin on the property that he'd renovated some time ago. He had transformed it from the family getaway it had once been into his home now. Crosswinds was an ideal place with the view of the lake below and the mountains behind it, but Kiki preferred to be on the water.

When she had a gig in Owl Creek or nearby, she often went "home" to the houseboat her grandpa had on the lake instead of back to his cottage. That way she didn't risk waking him up. Maybe she would stay there tonight when she came back from the club in Conners.

She parked the SUV, then went around and opened the passenger's door. As she leaned inside to release Fancy from her seat harness, the puppy's furry body quivered with excitement, and the little dog licked Kiki's hands and then her face.

Kiki chuckled and helped the puppy down from the vehicle, holding tightly to her leash so she didn't run off. That wasn't a really big concern, though, since Fancy tended to stick close to her. "Checkup time," she said as she led the little dog toward the medical building.

Maybe Fancy understood what she'd said because she tugged against the leash, as if trying to head back toward the SUV. Maybe she remembered being here in the kennels and preferred Grandpa's cozy cottage. Kiki had been spoiling her a bit.

She'd also been working with her, though, on commands. "Heel," she said.

The puppy tensed for a moment.

"Walk."

And Fancy trotted along beside her.

"She's coming along," Sebastian said as he opened the door for her.

Kiki smiled. "She's very smart, so it doesn't take much to train her." But she still had a few bad habits, like chewing things she shouldn't. This time it had been one of Grandpa's favorite slippers.

"I really appreciate you and your grandfather helping out, though," Sebastian said. He crouched down and let the puppy sniff his hand, her little black muzzle wrinkling as she smelled the scent of other animals on him. "She's going to be good to go soon."

Kiki felt a little pang. Sure. She knew scent dogs were necessary for a variety of things, for sniffing out drugs or explosives or for tracking missing persons. But she didn't want to think of the dog ever being in harm's way because of her abilities.

Through the open door behind Sebastian, another person stepped out. Della Winslow was a couple of years older than Kiki, with long, light brown hair and brown eyes. She was a K9 search and rescue tracker, and her black lab, Charlie, was close by her side as usual.

Fancy yipped at the lab, either with excitement or fear. Kiki tugged on her leash as the puppy tried to clamor around the bigger, male dog.

"I'm sorry," Kiki said.

"Charlie is used to it," Della assured her with a smile.

"This is the pup I've been telling you about," Sebastian said. "The one out of Sable's litter."

"I remember the litter," Della said. "But you placed them with foster families so quickly, I didn't get to know any of them very well."

In addition to her job with Search and Rescue, Della also worked as a trainer at Crosswinds. She crouched down to pet the puppy, looking her over, and nodded. "I see the potential." She glanced up at Kiki. "You and your grandfather always do such a great job socializing the pups."

"You'll have to choose one to keep one of these days," Sebastian suggested.

Kiki shrugged. "I'd love to, but I travel so much. I'll mention it to my grandfather, though."

Sebastian chuckled. "He always says that he fosters them for your sake, but I think he enjoys having them, too."

Or he remembered how much Buster had comforted her and thought she still needed comforting for some reason. "He really does do a lot for my sake," Kiki said.

And she could never repay him enough for all the love and support he'd given her. So she wouldn't ask him to keep a dog for her if it really would be too much for him.

"I think it's mutual," Sebastian said. "You would do anything for him. You could still be working out in LA or Vegas, but you always come home to help him in the summer."

She shrugged again. "I enjoy playing some of the smaller venues around here."

"I saw your flyers up around town for the Conners Club tonight," Della said.

Troy had put up all the flyers. It had given him something to do, to get his mind off that attack in Salt Lake City. "Come out if you can," Kiki encouraged them.

Della gave her a noncommittal nod. But then she probably couldn't commit, never knowing what might come up that would require her help as Search and Rescue.

Sebastian grinned. "Ask Ruby—"

"Ask Ruby what?" the veterinarian asked. She stood in that open door behind Della.

Della smiled and said, "I better get going. Thanks for checking Charlie out for me. He's just been a little off lately."

Kiki could relate. She'd felt a little off since seeing Fletcher Colton at the funeral. Why did she keep thinking about him? It was good that she had a gig tonight, something else to think about besides him and how good-looking he was.

She knew there was a bachelor party that would be stopping in because the best man had messaged her some special song requests. Based on a couple of those requests, she might suggest the groom pick another best man.

"I know you were concerned that Charlie has been sleeping so much, but he's fine," Ruby assured Della. "Might just be a little bored."

That was probably Kiki's issue as well. The reason for her giving Fletcher Colton a second thought—just boredom. Once she was playing and the crowd was dancing, she would forget all about Fletcher.

Della smiled. "Well, in our business, being bored isn't a bad thing."

"It is in mine," Kiki said.

The others chuckled, and Fancy jumped up with excitement over the mood. "Down," Kiki said.

And the little dog immediately dropped down to all fours.

"Yes, she is going to be good," Della agreed with a glance at Sebastian.

Kiki wondered for a moment if they were talking about Fancy or about her. But Della rushed off and so did Sebastian, leaving Kiki alone with her friend.

"So, what was Sebastian telling you to ask me?" Ruby asked as she led the way back to an exam room.

Kiki lifted Fancy onto the table and let the nervous pup lick her face again. "About coming to the club in Conners tonight."

Ruby smiled. "I've been a little tired lately."

"After everything you've been through, that's totally understandable," Kiki said. "I'm sorry again about your dad and that whole…"

"Madman trying to kill me because he thought I was preventing him from getting this land away from Sebastian?" Ruby finished for her. "It's all over now. And it worked out." She touched her stomach and smiled again.

Kiki gasped. "Are you pregnant?"

Her smile widened, and her green eyes sparkled with happiness. "Yes."

"You and Sebastian…?"

Ruby nodded. "Yes, I've actually moved in with him."

"I'm happy for you," Kiki said, and she felt that traitorous little jab of envy again. Not that she wanted a baby or even a significant other. But sometimes, even in a crowded club, she felt so alone. That was another reason she loved to come home to Grandpa in Owl Creek. But then she shouldn't have had that feeling here.

"What about you?" Ruby asked.

Kiki patted her stomach and hips. "I'm not pregnant. Just curvy."

Ruby snorted. "You're perfect, and you know it. I meant what about your love life?"

Kiki snorted now. "What love life?"

"Exactly. How can someone like you not have a significant other?"

"I do," Kiki said.

And Ruby's eyes widened.

"My grandpa," Kiki said. "And this little nugget of cuteness here." She pressed a kiss to the top of Fancy's furry head.

Ruby chuckled. "This little nugget isn't going to stay little long. She's growing like crazy. What was your concern about her?"

"She ate part of one of Grandpa's slippers."

Ruby took out a stethoscope and listened to the puppy's belly. "How long ago was this?"

"Had to be sometime during the night. The only time Grandpa takes them off when he's in the house is when he's in bed. He didn't notice until he went to put them on this morning."

"Did she go out this morning?" Ruby asked.

Kiki nodded. "I let her out before I knew about the slipper. But I think she passed it. I just want to make sure that she's all right."

"Everything sounds fine," Ruby said. She pulled a small puppy snack from her pocket and held it out for Fancy who gobbled it up. "She has an appetite, too."

The little muzzle wrinkled as Fancy's nose sniffed the air and then Ruby's pocket. The vet chuckled and gave her another treat. "That's your reward for sniffing it out. She does have a natural talent."

"Sebastian does, too, because he already figured she'll be a scent dog," Kiki said. "He really knows what he's doing."

Ruby smiled. "Yes, he does."

"Guess I didn't have to tell you that," Kiki said with a chuckle of her own.

"Nope. We're going to be getting married soon," Ruby shared. "After what happened with us and with Dad, it just proves how short life can be and how very precious." She touched her stomach again.

Kiki laid her hand over Ruby's. "I'm so happy that something good came out of everything you've gone through recently."

Ruby blinked and smiled at her. "Of course, you'll have to be at the wedding."

"I'd love to DJ it," Kiki assured her.

"I meant as a bridesmaid," Ruby said. "I didn't expect you to work it. I'm not even sure how big a wedding we'll have. There has been so much going on here."

"Too much for you," Kiki said.

"Too much for Owl Creek," Ruby said.

"Hopefully everything will quiet down now," Kiki said.

Ruby nodded heartily in agreement but then added, "But not so much that you get bored and head back to LA early. Or that Fletcher heads back to Salt Lake City. He's used to being a lot busier than he'll be here, even with Owl Creek PD covering some of the surrounding areas."

Kiki hadn't considered that—that Fletcher might not stick around Owl Creek. She felt another strange twinge. "Do you think he'd leave?"

"Not anytime soon," Ruby said. "He's worried about Mom. We all are. But she's doing really well."

"That's good."

"Good that Mom's doing well or that Fletcher will be staying?"

Heat rushed to Kiki's face. "I don't even know Fletcher." She sighed. "Don't be one of those happy brides-to-be that tries matching up all their friends now."

Ruby held up her hands. "I promise I won't. I'm really busy. It was just the way you two looked at each other at the funeral…"

Fletcher wasn't the only one in his family who'd been intensely studying her then. Ruby must have been, too. But Kiki had only noticed Fletcher. Despite the warmth of the June day, a little shiver raced down her spine.

"Your pregnancy must be causing hallucinations," Kiki teased. "I doubt Fletcher is any more interested in me than I am in him. And now I better get this little fur ball back to Grandpa and start loading up my equipment for my gig tonight. Sure you won't come?"

Ruby yawned. "Maybe another time."

Kiki nodded. "Sure. Take care."

"You, too."

And Kiki felt that little shiver again. She was safe. Wasn't she? It wasn't as if anything would happen at the Conners Club that had happened at those other clubs.

Those had been in bigger cities, more dangerous areas of town.

Conners wasn't much bigger than Owl Creek, so hopefully it was just as safe as Kiki had assured Troy that it was. Nothing bad was going to happen here.

This music was so much better than what had played in Salt Lake City. It was more alive, more melodious, and made the Slasher feel as if it had been mixed to choreograph to their movements, to the swing and swish of the blade cutting through the air and then cutting through the next victim.

He screamed and lifted his hands to his bleeding face. And the Slasher cut through those as well.

And when the hands fell away and the victim dropped to the asphalt in the alley, the Slasher slashed some more…

Chapter 4

His first few days on the job had been uneventful. Despite being lead detective, Fletcher hadn't had many investigations to lead. A stolen vehicle. A suspected driving under the influence incident. The most exciting thing had been a possible embezzlement of a school's booster fund by one of the parents.

With as close as the police department was to his sister Frannie's bookstore café, Book Mark It, at least he'd been able to stop in and visit her a few times. Check on her. They'd always been super close growing up. Not that he had liked books the way she had, but they'd both loved a good mystery.

After some of the things he'd seen in Salt Lake City, like the latest victim of the Slasher, Fletcher should have been relieved that, despite what had happened with

Ruby and Sebastian, his hometown was relatively safe and quiet. He *was* relieved for the sake of his family.

But for himself…

Fletcher loved working. Maybe he'd gotten that from his dad. But unlike his dad, Fletcher knew that his overwhelming love of his job meant he was better off single than trying to have a wife and family. He didn't want to miss all the things that his father had over the years. But not working wasn't an option for him.

He had to work. Had cases to solve, criminals to catch and put away even in Owl Creek. So he'd focused on the car thief, the drunk driver and the embezzler and had closed those cases. At least Owl Creek PD covered Conners as well, but nothing had come up yet there that they hadn't been able to handle on their own.

Until Fletcher's phone rang in the early morning hours of Saturday. His cell vibrated across the surface of the bedside table and he reached out for it, answering with a groggy, "Colton."

"Fletcher?"

It was the chief, his boss, so Fletcher roused himself. "Yes, sir."

"You've been requested to help out with an assault that just happened in Conners."

"Requested? Me specifically?" he asked. How did anyone in Conners even know he'd accepted the job at Owl Creek PD?

"You're needed at the crime scene there," the chief continued.

"Needed? Requested? I'm confused, Chief," he admitted.

"Conners PD know there've been some cases like this in Salt Lake City when you were there," the chief explained. "So they need you out at the crime scene ASAP."

Fletcher went from groggy with sleep to wide-awake and tense. "Cases like what?"

"Where a guy is found in an alley behind a club and he's been viciously attacked—"

"The Slasher."

Here? In the Owl Creek area?

Not the big clubs in the big cities.

It didn't make sense, but that made it even more interesting. "Is the guy all right?" He asked the most important question.

Had the attacks escalated, like he'd been worrying they were? Had it become more than assault?

"He's alive," the chief said. "I don't know any more about his condition or what happened. Just that they'd like you to advise." And he gave him the address of the crime scene.

"I'll be there." Fletcher rolled out of bed and dressed in a rush, desperate to get to the nightclub in Conners before it was too late, before all the witnesses were gone. But as fast as he'd dressed and drove, he still arrived too late to interview the victim. And most of the guests had left the club.

Fletcher got an almost dizzying sense of déjà vu. The location was so similar to the last crime scene where he turned up in the alley as the techs were processing it. The blood pools and spatters were the same. "Let me guess," he said. "No footprints? No evidence?"

One of the techs looked up at him, her eyes narrowed with suspicion. "We're not giving interviews."

"That's good," Fletcher said. "Because I think the Slasher is getting off on the notoriety."

Why else had the perp stepped up his attacks? If their victims were really random, then the only reason would have been for more attention. For more media coverage.

The reporters had been out front, but Fletcher had slipped through them unnoticed and then flashed his badge at the officer guarding the entrance to the alley. He flashed it now at the tech. "I'm the lead detective with Owl Creek PD."

The young woman nodded. "I heard they were sending somebody over since we're short-staffed. Right now, we're processing everything. Hopefully we find something."

"If you don't, you won't be the only techs who couldn't," he assured her.

"You've worked these cases before?"

"Not like I've wanted to," he admitted. The first one he hadn't been assigned as he'd had other cases to close first. And the second...

His dad had had the stroke, and Fletcher had been called home early to Owl Creek. And he'd thought then that he wouldn't have the chance to work the Slasher case again.

But the Slasher had come here, too. Maybe.

"Are you sure this case matches the profile of the other ones?" he asked the tech. He couldn't imagine that, if the Slasher wanted publicity, they would choose here for their next attack. Wouldn't they go back to LA or Vegas where there was more of a media presence?

"The victim was slashed up bad across his face, hands and chest," a man said as he stepped out through the back door that was open to the interior of the club. He extended his hand toward Fletcher. "You must be Detective Colton. I'm Sergeant Powers." The man had thin gray hair and a lot of lines in his face.

Fletcher shook his hand and nodded. "I appreciate you calling me in on this."

"I appreciate you pitching in. This kind of a case is above my pay grade, especially since I'm semiretired." He yawned. "I have another officer conducting interviews with the last of the people who actually stayed in the club and didn't take off the minute the police were called."

"Sounds like that wasn't many," Fletcher remarked. That had appeared to be the same situation in Salt Lake City, too. Nobody wanted to get involved, or maybe they were worried about public intoxication or some other charge, depending on what they'd been doing in the club.

"Wrapping up now," the sergeant remarked, and he stepped away from the door so that Fletcher could see inside the club. The lights had been turned up, the harsh fluorescent bulbs illuminating the nearly empty space.

And he saw her.

She wore black, like she had when she'd attended his dad's funeral, but it wasn't a dress. She wore tight leather pants and a cropped top. And her voice was even huskier than it had sounded in the funeral parlor as she replied to the officer's question. "There's really nothing I can tell you about what happened in the alley. I was behind the turntables the whole night, usually with my headphones on."

"So you didn't see or hear anything. You can go," the uniformed officer that the sergeant had assigned to take statements told her.

While they'd called in Fletcher to help, they weren't letting him do very damn much. He'd wanted to conduct the interviews. But he wanted more than that.

He had an idea. With Kiki's help, he might have a way that he could work the case. Maybe he would actually be able to solve it and catch the Slasher.

But when he started toward the door, the sergeant stepped in front of him. "I need to pick your brain about these cases," the older man said. "See if you have any idea where we should start."

He had a damn good idea.

With Kiki Shelton.

She hadn't been lying to the officer when she'd answered his questions just moments ago. Kiki hadn't heard or seen anything. She'd had her headphones on, as she always did, while mixing the tracks. Hell, she'd even had her eyes closed, moving to the music. Feeling her own vibe.

And during that time, someone had been getting attacked in the alley.

She shuddered in horror. The same horror Troy must

have been feeling, because he'd disappeared sometime during the night, too.

She wasn't even sure when. One minute he'd been there and finally, when she'd noticed the commotion in the club, she'd also noticed he was gone.

Had he found this victim, too?

She'd thought it was one of the bachelor party guys who had discovered the injured man because he'd been waving his arms around, his hands smeared with blood.

And she'd taken off her headphones to hear him screaming for help and to hear other clubgoers yelling when they saw the blood on the man.

Everything had descended into chaos after that, with people running and shouting. And Kiki had pretty much been trapped behind the turntables, unable to get out and even look for Troy. She'd expected he would show up.

But he hadn't.

Even after the police cleared the club of whoever had actually remained behind to talk to them. While she had stayed as well, she hadn't been any help to the police. And now she had no help herself.

"Troy, where are you?" she whispered into the darkness of the back parking lot. Her SUV was out here, one of the shadows in the night. She would have clicked the fob to turn on the lights, but her hands were wrapped around the handles at the top of the speakers she rolled across the asphalt.

In addition to her turntables and mixers, Kiki always used her own sound system. Sometimes she patched it in with the club's system, but most of the time hers was better. Because she preferred her own setup, she had a lot of things to schlep from club to club.

That was why she needed an assistant. Even though she was strong enough to carry the equipment on her own, if she was working alone, she had to take more trips for set-up and breakdown. And breakdown, at the end of a long night, needed to be faster because by that time all she wanted to do was go home, shower and drop into her bed and sleep.

That probably wouldn't be possible tonight, not when she was worrying about that poor man. There had been all that blood just on his friend.

How much had there been on the victim?

She didn't want to think about it, but her maudlin mind kept circling back there, to the alley where he'd been found. She'd done her best to keep to the other direction, which was thankfully where she'd parked.

Before the attack, the club owner had offered to let her and Troy unload and load up their equipment in that alley, but Troy had shuddered and refused, saying that he never wanted to set foot in another one after the last.

She'd promised him then that nothing like that would happen around Owl Creek. She'd promised him it was safe here. That the Slasher wouldn't attack anyone here.

Had it been the Slasher?

Maybe it had just been some random mugging.

Not that it made anyone any safer.

In fact, it probably made them less safe because then there were, potentially, two dangerous people out there: a mugger and the Slasher.

No. Not here. Not this close to home.

She shivered despite the warmth of the June evening and hastened her pace across the parking lot. But footsteps echoed hers. She glanced over her shoulder, but nothing was visible in the dark but darker shadows.

What had happened to the streetlights out here? Were there any? It had been light when she and Troy had parked out here, his truck next to her SUV.

She turned back to where they'd parked, but it looked like only one vehicle was still out there. Hers.

Troy had left.

So who was behind her?

She heard the footsteps again, the scrape of shoe soles against the asphalt. Her pulse quickening with fear, she released the handle on the speaker and reached inside the bag slung over her shoulder. She wasn't looking for the key fob. She was looking for her pepper spray.

Nobody was getting close enough to slash her.

Chapter 5

Where the hell was she?

He could hear something in the darkness, something like wheels rolling over asphalt. Like someone was moving a suitcase or something...

Curious, he'd followed the noise. But in the darkness, he couldn't see anything. He'd considered turning on his light and calling out. But what if it was the Slasher?

He uttered a short, derisive snort at the thought. The Slasher hadn't avoided getting caught all this time by hanging around the crime scenes. They probably moved on to the next city shortly after an attack.

But why here?

"Don't try anything! I have pepper spray!" a voice called from the darkness.

"Kiki, it's me," Fletcher said as he turned on the flashlight on his phone. The beam illuminated her standing in the middle of the dark parking lot, a small canister clutched in her hand, her finger ready to press the sprayer.

"It's Fletcher," he clarified. Since he was still in the dark, she probably couldn't see him. So he moved the light closer to his face.

"What the hell..." She released a shaky breath. "Why didn't you say anything? You scared me!"

"I'm sorry," he said. "I couldn't see who was out here either."

"What are you even doing here?" she asked. "You weren't in the club tonight."

Maybe it hadn't been that busy then, since she sounded so certain that she hadn't seen him there. Or maybe she just assumed, correctly, that he wasn't the type to go to clubs. They were too loud. Too crowded. Too full of drunk, obnoxious partiers that he dealt with all too often already as a detective.

"After the person was found in the alley, the Conners Police Department called us in to assist."

She released another shaky breath. "Oh, that makes sense."

Apparently, more sense to her than him being at the club having a good time.

But she wasn't wrong. Fletcher couldn't actually remember the last time he'd had a good time. Certainly not since his dad's stroke and...

"Did you think it was the attacker out here?" she asked and shuddered.

"I didn't know what to think," he said and pointed

to the canister in her hand. "Evidently neither did you." But he was glad that she'd been prepared to defend herself had it been necessary.

"This is so damn scary," she said. "People getting attacked like that so viciously." She shuddered again.

"You were prepared with the pepper spray," he said. "But you really shouldn't be out here alone in the dark like this. It's too dangerous. And I'm not just talking about the Slasher. Anyone from the club could have followed you out here."

Her lips curved into a faint smile. "You're the only 'anyone' out here besides me. And you sound like my grandfather."

"Jim Shelton is a very wise man," Fletcher said.

"He worries too much. And after this…" She sighed. "He's going to worry even more."

Fletcher had an idea.

A solution to her problem and maybe to his as well. "Maybe we can figure out a way to allay his fears," he said.

"We? What are you talking about?" she asked.

He glanced around that all-enveloping blankness. Anybody could be out there, hiding in the dark. Even the Slasher.

"Let's talk about it somewhere else," he said. "What are you doing out here?"

She thumped her hand against the top of what looked like a speaker on wheels. "Putting my equipment in my vehicle."

"You parked way out here?" he asked.

She sighed. "It didn't seem that way out when it was still daylight."

"And you're moving all this equipment on your own?"

"I have an assistant."

Fletcher swung the beam of his cell flashlight around the area. But he only saw the two of them. "Where is your *assistant*?"

She sighed again, and this one was heavy. "I don't know. I haven't seen him since the lights came up and the police were called."

"He just took off?"

"A lot of people did," she said. "It was chaos."

"Why?" he asked.

"A man was attacked," she said. "People were screaming. There was blood." She shuddered now, more violently than she had before.

"You saw the victim?"

She shook her head. "No. The guy who found him, his friend, had blood on his hands and shirt and he was screaming for help." Her voice cracked with emotion, with empathy.

"So instead of helping him, people took off," Fletcher pointed out. "Including your assistant, leaving you to move all your equipment on your own."

"I'm sure he was just shaken up like everyone else," Kiki said. "They didn't know how to react. They were just scared, especially Troy. I assured him it would be safe here after Salt Lake City."

"What do you mean?" Fletcher asked. "Just because of what happened there with the Slasher? Or were you there?"

"I wasn't," Kiki said. "But Troy was. He found that victim, and it really freaked him out. I promised him that it was safer here, that nothing would happen."

This Troy had been at the scene of two of the attacks.

Fletcher needed to find her assistant. "When did you last see Troy?"

She shrugged. "I don't know. I was so busy with special requests and people coming up. I don't remember when I saw him last."

So he could have slipped into the alley before the attack.

"Did you try calling him?" Fletcher asked. "Texting him?"

"Yeah, of course," she replied. "But I didn't get any reply or even his voice mail. It's like his phone is dead or off or something."

Fletcher suspected the *or something*. Like the man took his cell apart so that nobody could track him. And Fletcher could think of one reason why.

So no one would find out he was the Slasher.

Instead of a police escort, Kiki had had just one lawman tailing her home. Why?

She doubted he was concerned about her safety; she didn't fit the profile of the Slasher's usual victims. She wasn't male. And she was pretty sure, from the way he looked at her, that Fletcher Colton was well aware of that. Just as she was well aware of how very male he was.

Her pulse quickened, but that had to be because of what had happened that night.

She hadn't seen the victim, but she'd seen all that blood on his friend. That poor man.

Who would do such a thing to someone? Attack them so viciously?

Kiki turned her SUV into the driveway of her grandfather's cottage. Lights shone in her back window as a vehicle pulled in behind hers. Fletcher's. He got out of his SUV at the same time she stepped out of hers. "You didn't need to follow me home," she told him.

"You have all that stuff to unload," he said, waving his hand at the rear hatch of her SUV.

He'd helped her load up the rest of her equipment at the nightclub.

"I leave it in there," she said. "There really isn't any room for it in the cottage." Her grandfather's house was small, so she had more storage space in the back of her SUV. With the tinted windows, it was hard to see the expensive equipment stored inside so she didn't worry about it getting stolen.

She hadn't thought she needed to worry about those Slasher attacks here in Owl Creek either, though. Maybe she needed to be more careful. "I should grab my laptop, though," she said, clicking open the hatch.

As it rose, the front door of the house opened and the yard light flashed on, illuminating the driveway while leaving the man standing in the doorway in the shadows.

Jim called out, "You okay?"

She sucked in a breath, worried that he might have heard about the attack already. "I'm fine, Grandpa."

Fancy pushed past him in the doorway and ran out to the SUV, bouncing around Kiki's and Fletcher's legs.

"I heard a man's voice," Grandpa said, "and I wanted to make sure you were all right."

"Fletcher Colton is out here with me," she said, though her grandfather could probably see that for himself now.

"I was just making sure she got home safely, sir," Fletcher called back to Grandpa.

"Something happen?" the older man asked.

Kiki smothered the groan trying to slip out of her throat. Before Fletcher could say anything about the attack, which would upset her grandfather and keep him awake, she grabbed his hand, squeezing it to shut him up and also to make her grandfather think that they were together. "No. He was just being a gentleman, Grandpa."

"Few of them left nowadays," Grandpa said. "I'll leave you two alone then." He chuckled. "Well, except for that little furry chaperone."

Fancy still hopped around on the driveway but her interest appeared to be more in the back of the SUV than in them, since her little muzzle wrinkled as she sniffed. She was so focused that she didn't even react when the door closed behind Grandpa.

"What's she smelling?" Fletcher asked, and his long body seemed to tense next to Kiki, reminding her that she was holding his hand.

She jerked hers away, her skin tingling in reaction. "I don't know. Sebastian thinks she'll be a scent dog. I think he's right."

"Drugs?"

She tensed now with righteous indignation. "What are you saying? You think I have drugs in my vehicle?"

Fletcher held up his hands. "I was just asking what he was training the dog to sniff out."

"Nothing yet," Kiki replied. "Fancy has to get socialized first and learn basic commands. Like Sit." And she turned toward the puppy, held her hand out—palm up—at waist level and then raised it toward her shoulder.

Fancy whined and danced around for a moment.

"Sit." She repeated the gesture and finally Fancy planted her little squirmy butt on the ground. The dog was smart. They'd only been working together a couple of weeks, and she was already beginning to master the basic commands. Kiki reached into the back of the SUV and pulled out her laptop bag. In the front pocket was a small packet of puppy treats. She rewarded Fancy with one. "That's what she was sniffing out. Her treats. Not drugs."

"You're a little defensive."

"I hate that people assume, just because I work in nightclubs, that I'm either a user or a dealer." She groaned her disgust at that all too common assumption. "There are a lot of people who go to nightclubs to listen to music and dance and just have a good time."

"That guy tonight—in the alley—he didn't have a good time," Fletcher said. "The other victims of the Slasher, disfigured for life, didn't have a good time."

She flinched. "I know. But that had nothing to do with the music or the nightclub."

"Those attacks have only happened outside night-clubs," Fletcher said. "So they definitely have something to do with nightclubs. So does your assistant."

She sucked in a breath. "You suspect Troy?"

"You don't?"

A laugh bubbled out of her, but it cracked a bit with nerves. "God, no. I can't believe you do. He was devastated when he found that body in Salt Lake City. And tonight."

"Yes, what happened to him tonight?" Fletcher asked. "Where did he go?"

She shrugged. "I don't know. I'm sure he just got freaked out that it happened here after I promised him it was safer in Owl Creek. I told him things like that didn't happen here."

"Things like that can happen anywhere," Fletcher said.

As a detective, he probably could have given her examples, but he didn't need to. She knew what had nearly happened to his sister Ruby here.

She just sighed. "I know. And I shouldn't have made him a promise I couldn't keep. He's probably angry and disillusioned—"

"Or guilty," Fletcher interjected. "I need to talk to him. Tell me where he is."

She shivered at his tone and his intensity. Now she knew why Fletcher had been hired as lead detective. He could probably get a confession out of anyone with that look, that edge to his voice.

Probably even out of an innocent person, which was

what she believed Troy was. But Troy was also a bit flighty at times, emotional, reactive.

That had to be why he'd taken off like he had. He was scared. And Fletcher interrogating him would scare him even more.

"I've known Troy for four or five years now," she said. "He's a good guy. He works hard and is very helpful."

"Helpful to whom?" Fletcher asked with a pointed glance into the back of her SUV.

"He would have helped me with this equipment, but that attack, so soon after the last one, must have scared him," she said, her voice heavy with concern for her friend and for the victim. "That's why he took off like he did."

"Without a word to you," Fletcher said. "Without checking to make sure you were okay."

"I'm okay," Kiki said. "I was in the club the whole time. I was never in danger."

Fletcher nodded. "No, you weren't. You're not the Slasher's usual victim." His gaze flicked down her body in her leather pants and cropped top. "You're definitely not male."

And despite the warmth of the June night, Kiki shivered a little with goosebumps, not of cold but of awareness, rising on her skin. "Are you flirting with me, Detective?" she asked.

His lips curved into a slight grin. "Just making an observation."

She smiled and mused, "Strange observation to be making during the course of your investigation." Then, because she'd been wondering, she asked, "Why did you follow me home?"

Fletcher chuckled and his grin widened. "You definitely aren't in any danger," he said. "You're too perceptive to have anyone sneak up on you."

"Are you trying to sneak up on me?" she asked. "Just as I was never in any danger, I wasn't the danger either, in case you consider me a suspect. I was behind the turntables in front of a hell of a lot of witnesses when that attack must have taken place. And I was here when the man in Salt Lake City was attacked."

She'd been in some of the same cities for those other attacks, but she wasn't about to point that out to him. Not when he clearly considered her assistant a suspect.

"Troy was there," he said, confirming his suspicion. "And I need you to help me find him so I can question him. Will you do that?"

She sighed and nodded. "Only because I know that once you question him, he'll be able to provide alibis and prove his innocence to you."

"Let's hope that's the case," he said.

"Liar," she said. "You'd probably like it to be Troy, so that you can close this case."

"You are perceptive," he said. "The Slasher needs to be stopped. What he's doing to these victims is so cruel, and eventually one of them will probably die from their injuries."

She shivered again with revulsion and dread. "You're right. I'll help you find Troy. But what happens when you realize he's not the Slasher? How will you catch this person then?"

He looked at her again, his forehead furrowing beneath the strands of his overly long hair. And that intensity was back in his green eyes.

The intensity that unsettled her for a lot of reasons.

"I have an idea about how I can do that," he said.

"Why do I feel like that idea involves me?" she asked uneasily.

His grin widened even more, and his green eyes glinted in the light from the porch. "Because you are perceptive."

His idea definitely involved her.

Chapter 6

Fletcher was certain that Kiki wasn't in danger from the Slasher, which was the only reason he'd considered the idea he'd had to be able to investigate from the inside of the nightclub scene. But before he shared that plan with her, he wanted to find out if it was even necessary or if the first real suspect in the case was the Slasher.

Her assistant. Troy.

"You really don't know his last name?" he asked with suspicion as he glanced across the console to the passenger's seat of his SUV. Fancy rode in the back, her harness strapped to the seat.

"No, I don't," she said, her voice a little sharp with either irritation or maybe embarrassment.

"You said you've known him for four or five years."

"I have."

"And he's your assistant. Don't you have to have his full name to put on his paycheck?"

"He just takes a share of the tips. He doesn't want a paycheck."

"He doesn't want to pay taxes," Fletcher concluded.

"You have to pay taxes on tips." Kiki said it so matter-of-factly that it was clear she would never consider not declaring them.

He doubted that Troy was as conscientious about that as she was. The man was either avoiding income taxes or child support or maybe both. What else was he running from? Fletcher doubted that it was really the Slasher.

Every one of the victims had been a clubgoer, not someone who worked at the club. But someone like this Troy, who went from club to club… He made a very interesting suspect.

By that line of thinking, so did Kiki. He would have to double-check her story that she had been working the entire evening. That she hadn't taken a break at all.

And he had an idea of how he could check her story. If it was necessary.

But if this mysterious Troy was really the Slasher, then Fletcher had no reason to spend any more time with Kiki Shelton. A pang of disappointment struck him at the thought.

But that was ridiculous, just as flirting with Kiki had been silly. She was Ruby's friend, and Ruby had already been through too much even before they'd lost their dad. The last thing his sister needed right now was Fletcher creating any awkwardness with her friend, who was also someone who fostered dogs for Ruby's soon-to-be husband Sebastian.

And Fletcher was pretty certain it would end in awkwardness, as most of his relationships had. Either he got ghosted—like his girlfriends believed he was ghosting them when he was simply busy—or he got cheated on because someone else gave them more time and attention than he was able to.

No. He had no business flirting with Kiki Shelton. But he couldn't stop glancing across the console at her. She was so beautiful, and the way the black leather clung to the curves of her body had his body tensing with desire for her. He had to ignore his attraction to her, though, and focus on the case.

The Slasher could not claim any more victims.

He slowed his SUV and turned into the driveway for the seasonal RV park where Kiki said that her assistant had parked his van. He drove past some high-end travel trailers and motor homes toward the outskirts of the RV park where the woods had begun to claim back the cleared areas. In a section of weeds, someone had parked a vintage VW bus.

"That's it," Kiki said. "He's here!"

The van was dark, like the other vehicles parked around it. "How do you know?" he asked.

"He drove that to the club tonight," she said. "It wouldn't be here unless he'd driven it back."

So he was here. This close.

The Slasher?

Fletcher reached for his weapon as Kiki reached for

the door handle. "No," he told her. "You need to stay here. Wait until I make sure he isn't a threat."

"He isn't," Kiki insisted. "Not to me."

"But if he considers you being here a threat, he's going to be one, too. Somebody dangerous is hazardous to anyone who gets in their way," Fletcher said.

In denial or defense of her friend, she shook her head. But she didn't open the door.

Fletcher stepped out into the darkness and listened. Gravel crunched. Twigs snapped and there was a subtle shift in the air, indicating movement around him. It could have been other RV residents or animals. But somehow, he suspected it wasn't.

He drew his weapon and his flashlight and aimed his beam around the area as he approached the van. Tree limbs rustled. Something was definitely out there.

Or someone.

"Police," Fletcher called out, identifying himself even though he really didn't want to, just in case he needed to fall back on his other plan. The one he had yet to bring up to Kiki.

But whoever, or whatever, was out there didn't come out of the trees. More branches rustled but the sounds were farther away now and getting fainter as the person fled. So when Fletcher shined his light into the van, he wasn't surprised to find it empty.

Troy had taken off again.

The passenger's door opened, and Kiki stepped out. "He's gone?"

"Yes."

Fletcher touched the handle of one of the back doors

of the van, and it easily opened. Troy had run off in such a hurry that he'd left it unlocked.

Another door opened and then Fancy rushed up next to Fletcher. The van was lower to the ground, so the puppy easily jumped inside, sniffing through the bedding and belongings tossed about the back of the van.

Then she yipped and pulled something from the bedding and brought it toward Fletcher. He shone his light through the clear plastic to the collection of different colored capsules inside it. The puppy's sharp teeth were already tearing through the bag.

And Kiki gasped with concern. Then she pointed toward the ground. "Drop!"

Fancy whined.

"Drop!"

And the little teeth released the bag, dropping it onto the threadbare carpet next to Fletcher. "Some little pharmacy he has here," he mused.

"These could be his," Kiki said, but even she sounded doubtful now. But she scooped Fancy up in her arms and lifted her out of the back of the van.

"Troy has a medical condition?" he asked.

She sighed. "Not that I know of."

He shone his light over the van, watching for it to glint off metal. And it did. Off beer cans. Not a knife blade.

She tensed and turned toward him. "Don't you have to have a warrant or something to search his premises?"

"Nobody has seen him since the attack," he said. "I have probable cause to make sure that he's all right."

"You can't take those pills," she said. "What if they are medically necessary?"

Fletcher snorted in derision at that, but he didn't have a warrant, as she'd pointed out. He really shouldn't have even opened the door to the van.

And he had no right to open the glove box either. So he shut the door. Then he made a note of the license plate number. He'd run that, see if he could find out Troy's last name and if the van was actually registered to him.

Instead of releasing the puppy, Kiki snuggled it against her as if she needed comforting.

"You're not so sure of your assistant's innocence anymore," Fletcher remarked.

"I know he's not the Slasher," she insisted. "But the drugs…" She sighed again. "Sometimes he seems a little out of it. I thought maybe he drank too much."

"There were a lot of beer cans in the van," Fletcher said.

"And that bag of all those drugs."

"So maybe some of those people who approach you for drugs do it not because of your working in a night-club but because of Troy?" he asked.

A little breath of air hissed through her teeth. "I don't want to think that."

But she clearly was thinking it now.

"So from his disappearing act, it looks like you're going to need a new assistant," he said.

"I'll be able to find someone here in Owl Creek," she replied. "I know a lot of people willing to help me out."

"You don't have to look any further," Fletcher told her.

"What do you mean?"

But instead of answering her, he just opened the back door of his vehicle for her to buckle Fancy back inside. Then he opened her door too before heading around the hood to his side. He glanced around him again, feeling someone out there. Watching them.

Listening to them.

So he wasn't going to ask her here.

Kiki knew that Fletcher had a plan that somehow involved her. But he didn't share it with her that night. Or that early morning.

He just dropped her and Fancy back at Jim's and drove away, leaving her wondering. Awake. And worried.

He must not have slept either because he returned a few hours later, pulling his SUV into the driveway behind hers. Fortunately, Jim had already left to take out a fishing charter on the lake. He had a boat docked near where the houseboat was. After last night, waking her grandfather up when Fletcher had followed her home, she probably needed to stay out on the boat, at least on the nights that she DJ'd.

Fancy barked and jumped on the door, trying to get outside to greet Fletcher before he even got out of his vehicle. "Someone's smitten…" Kiki murmured as she got up from the table where steam rose from her mug of coffee. Then, through the screen door, she watched Fletcher walking toward the house. The wind ruffled his overly long dark brown hair and plastered his shirt against his broad shoulders and muscular chest. She didn't have to be a detective to conclude that this detective worked out and that Fancy might not be the only smitten one.

But when he got up to the house and the wind was no longer blowing his clothes against his body, she could tell that they were a little oversize and wrinkly, like Grandpa's favorite TV detective that he watched reruns of nearly every day no matter how many times he'd already "solved" the case.

She pushed open the screen door and let Fancy out to bounce around his legs, pawing at his khaki pants.

He leaned down and scratched behind the puppy's ears, and the shameless mutt dropped and rolled onto her back, giving him her belly to rub. He chuckled as he scratched that fur, too. "She's seriously cute," he said, and he glanced up at Kiki, his green eyes warm with affection for the pet.

He was seriously cute, too.

She'd thought so every time their paths had crossed in the past. But with him working in Salt Lake City and her working in so many other cities, they hadn't seen each other often over the years. Not even when she came home for the summers to help Grandpa.

Because Fletcher hadn't lived in Owl Creek for a while.

"What are you doing back here?" she asked him, the curiosity overwhelming her.

He tensed for a moment. "I have an idea about how I might be able to catch the Slasher."

She shook her head.

"You're not going to hear me out?"

"No, I meant why did you come back to Owl Creek?"

she asked. "It had nothing to do with the Slasher because you probably didn't think the Slasher would show up here any more than I did."

"I came home when Ruby was in danger, and I liked how Owl Creek PD handled the case."

And they'd liked him enough to offer him the job of lead detective. "I know that. But why did you really want to come back? You could have stayed in Salt Lake City or gone somewhere else where there would be more crimes to solve."

"There are crimes here to solve," he said.

She sighed. "Not usually. I can't believe that was the Slasher last night."

"You don't want to believe it," Fletcher said. "But the MO and the wound patterns match the other victims. It was definitely the Slasher."

She sighed again, but it was ragged. And her chest ached. "You still didn't answer my question, you know."

He flashed her a grin. "Maybe you should be the detective. You're good at this interrogation thing."

She laughed. "It's one question. I'm not interrogating you. I'm…"

"What?" he asked. "Interested?"

"Curious," she corrected him. Interested implied something more like attraction, like desire…

And she actually felt those, too, but she didn't want him to know that. He and his family had already been through too much lately. And she…

She had too much going on for a serious relationship. And to her, the Coltons were serious people. At least Fletcher seemed to be with that intensity of his in the strained cord in his neck, in the twitch above his square jaw and in that stare he fixed on her.

"So, are you going to satisfy my curiosity?" she asked.

"If you'll satisfy mine sometime," he said, negotiating with her.

She smiled and shrugged. "Sure." She wasn't sure what he would ask her, but she had nothing to hide. "So…"

He shrugged now, those broad shoulders pulling the wrinkles from his oversize cotton button-down shirt. "I was worried about Ruby and noticing how much older my parents were getting. And Hannah is raising Lucy all alone." He shrugged again. "I felt like I needed to come home. I just wish I'd realized that sooner, before my dad had another stroke."

She reached out for him then, grabbing his hand to squeeze in hers. "I'm sorry."

"You offered your condolences at the funeral," he reminded her.

"But it doesn't hurt just that one day."

He turned his hand in hers and squeezed back. "You would know. I'm sorry about your parents."

She shrugged off his sympathy. "That was a long time ago."

"It doesn't hurt just that one day," he said.

She smiled at him repeating her words back to her. "So it's your turn," she said. "You can satisfy your curiosity now."

His gaze slipped then, to her lips, and his thumb rubbed across the back of her knuckles.

Saliva filled her mouth, and she had to swallow hard

so she didn't start drooling over the man. He wasn't thinking about kissing her. That wasn't the curiosity he wanted to satisfy. She was sure of that.

But then she remembered how he'd looked at her in her black leather outfit, his gaze sliding up and down her body like a caress. She wasn't wearing leather now. She was wearing very old and ragged jeans with a light cotton T-shirt. But the material was soft enough that it did cling to her curves, and the holes in the jeans revealed her tan thighs and knees.

His gaze dipped down over her again like it had the night before, and his green eyes darkened, the pupils dilating. Maybe he did want to kiss her.

She wouldn't protest. She was curious about his mouth, too. But then she reminded herself how bad an idea it was to get involved with anyone right now, least of all a Colton. He was mourning. She smiled again and stepped back, breaking the contact of their hands.

And she was busy. She had to help Grandpa with the fishing business and Fancy and...

"I need your help," Fletcher said.

"With what?" she asked slowly, reluctantly, because she'd already suspected he'd wanted to ask her to do something, something she probably wasn't going to want to do. Like when he'd asked her to show him where Troy lived.

"Did you find Troy?" she asked. Maybe he wanted her to talk to her assistant and encourage him to answer Fletcher's questions.

He shook his head. "Not yet."

"He couldn't have gotten far," she pointed out, "without his vehicle."

"I know. I have someone watching it. An APB out for him to be picked up for questioning. Hoover. That's his last name. He's Troy Hoover."

She shrugged. "I didn't know. Like I told you, it never came up."

"You didn't know his last name. Or that he's had a previous arrest for drug possession and that he owes back child support? That didn't come up either?" he asked, and he was definitely doing the interrogating now.

She shook her head. "He helped another DJ I knew, and when that DJ retired, Troy just started helping me out. It wasn't like I had him fill out a job application and checked his references."

"Or even got his last name."

"I knew him for a while—through the other DJ, through the clubs." She sighed. "But yes, I should have asked him more about himself." She couldn't deny that now, especially since he apparently had a record. "When were those arrests?"

"The drug possession was a while ago," Fletcher admitted. "And the child support is just outstanding. No arrest warrant for that yet."

"I didn't even know he had a child," she murmured.

"Two."

Two kids that he wasn't helping to support. She cursed. "I shouldn't have let him take his wages from the tips."

Fletcher shook his head. "No. That helped him evade garnishment of his wages and taxes."

She released a ragged sigh. "Well, I still don't believe he's the Slasher. But I won't let him work with me ever again either." Guilt pulled at her that she, however inadvertently, had helped him avoid his responsibilities. "I really thought I knew him better than that."

"Some people are hard to get to know," Fletcher said.

And she suspected he was one of them. Although he had eventually answered her question about his return, he had yet to tell her what his plan was and how it involved her.

"Yes, they are," she agreed with a pointed look.

He chuckled. "I'm an open book."

"So read the chapter heading to me about why you're here then," she urged him.

"You need an assistant," he said.

She narrowed her eyes and studied his face. "I have managed on my own." But it was work.

"You don't need to. I know someone you can use as your assistant," he said.

"Really? Who is that?"

"Me."

She closed her eyes and tried to picture him—in his wrinkly business casual khakis and button-down cotton shirt, standing behind the turntables with her—and a laugh bubbled out of her at the image. "Everybody would know you're a cop."

He shook his head. "No. I just started the job, and I didn't interview anyone in Conners last night. Only a tech and the sergeant saw me. And I haven't been around much since I moved away from Owl Creek, so most people won't recognize me."

"People might not recognize you as Fletcher Colton, but they'll make you for a cop right away."

He glanced down at himself. "How? I'll hide my holster."

"It's not the gun," she said with another laugh.

"What then? How can I not pass as your assistant?"

"Do you dance?" she asked.

He grimaced.

And she laughed again. "Have you ever gone to a nightclub—" she held up a hand when he started to open his mouth "—that hasn't been a crime scene?"

"Not for a while," he admitted.

Her curiosity piqued again. She asked, "Why not?"

"I've been busy," he said. "With work, with my family."

She sighed. "I understand being busy, but in my business that's a good thing." It meant she was in high demand, that people wanted to come where she was spinning. "Not so much in your business."

He shook his head. "No. It's not. That's why I really need to catch the Slasher."

"And you're right, then, that you need my help," she said. He wasn't going to pass as her assistant without it. "Do you have anything in your closet that isn't khaki and or button-down?"

"I have jeans," he said.

She pointed at hers. "Like these?"

"I throw them out before they look like that," he said. But the way his gaze moved over her skin that the holes exposed, he didn't seem to mind that she hadn't.

She smiled and stepped closer to him and touched

the buttons on his chest. "And something that doesn't button down?"

"I will need the button down to hide my gun," he said.

"Hiding your gun is less important than hiding that you're a cop," she said. "Just your presence alone will scare the Slasher away."

Which wasn't a bad thing. She would rather not have another attack happen here. But she didn't want them to happen anywhere else either.

"I have to catch this person," he said. "Whoever it is, they're so dangerous. Their victims will be disfigured for life, and eventually…eventually…" His throat moved as he swallowed. "Someone is going to die."

Fear clutched her with the knowledge that he was right. Eventually someone was going to die. She didn't want that someone to be him, though.

Where was the news coverage? The Slasher scrolled through their phone, trying to pull up stories about the latest attack. But the only one that came up was the last one. In Salt Lake City.

Not this one in Conners, near Owl Creek, Idaho. The area was pretty.

With the lake and the river and the mountains in the distance. It was so idyllic that something bad happening here should have been big news.

Should have incited a panic.

And it had at the club. Once the victim had been found, everyone had been screaming and running in fear, afraid that they might be next.

And maybe they would be.

Because the Slasher was going to stick around town and make damn sure that Owl Creek acknowledged how powerful they were. And how very dangerous...

Chapter 7

Fletcher hadn't wanted to admit it, but Kiki was probably right about his ability to fit in at a nightclub. His cover wasn't going to be effective if *anyone* suspected he was a cop. Because rumors would spread, and nobody would talk to him.

And the Slasher would just move on to another nightclub and find their next victim elsewhere.

So he'd agreed to go shopping with Kiki for some clothes that would help him go undercover as her assistant. But first he'd stopped by the hospital in Conners to check on the Slasher's latest victim. Some of the guy's wounds had gotten infected, so he was receiving IV antibiotics. He also needed more surgeries to try to limit the scarring he was going to have.

The guy had a long road ahead of him to heal. Physically and emotionally. But when Fletcher walked up to his door, he heard laughter behind it. A man's and then a woman's familiar, raspy laugh. He pushed it open to find Kiki standing next to the man's bed, smiling down at him. Today she wore shorts so short that the bottoms of the pockets hung out of them, and a T-shirt that was so short that it showed off her belly button and the piercing in it.

Fletcher's pulse quickened.

Kiki glanced at him, and her smile faded. "I should leave now and let you get your rest."

The guy glanced at Fletcher, too, and emitted a soft sigh. "Don't think that's happening. Another cop with questions, I presume?"

Fletcher swallowed a groan and nodded. Kiki had been right about people pegging him for police. "I'm Detective Colton." He identified himself, flipping his badge out to show it. "I just have a few questions."

"I should go," Kiki said. "I have a date to go shopping with someone." She glanced at her wrist. "In just a little while."

"You have a date," the man said, and he didn't swallow his groan.

"You're engaged," Kiki reminded him.

"Yeah, but you came to visit me, and she hasn't."

"Are you two friends?" Fletcher asked. And if so, why hadn't Kiki mentioned that to him before?

"I wish," the guy replied. "Her helper never lets anyone through to talk to her."

"I just came to check on him," Kiki said, "after finding out what happened at the club."

"That damn Slasher…" the guy murmured, his voice cracking.

"Did you see them?" Fletcher asked.

"I just saw that damn blade coming toward my face and then…" He shuddered. "I didn't see anything."

"What were you doing in the alley?" Fletcher asked. "Why'd you go out there?"

The guy glanced at Kiki who stood near the door, and as if she'd realized he was reluctant to admit it in front of her, she waved and popped out of the room.

The guy groaned again. "It was stupid."

"What was? Why were you out there?"

"I found a note in my pocket. Someone must have shoved it in there on the dance floor. I thought…"

"What did the note say?"

"Meet me in the alley for some fun." The guy lifted one of his bandaged hands to his bandaged face. "Some fun…"

"Do you have the note?" Fletcher asked.

The guy shrugged. "I don't know. They took all my stuff when I got to the hospital."

It wasn't with his things. The techs had all that stuff now—had already processed it for DNA, fingerprints, whatever they could find to help find the Slasher.

"We'll keep looking for it," Fletcher assured him.

"I hope you find it before my fiancée does." His voice cracked again with fear. "Oh, God, maybe she already found it and that's why she hasn't been here."

Fletcher doubted that, but he would check with her, too. "She wasn't at the club?"

"No, it was my bachelor party. We just stopped in

because we knew the DJ was hot." He glanced toward that closed door, as if trying to see her through the solid wood.

"You came there for Kiki?" Fletcher asked.

The guy nodded. "A lot of people follow her around the club circuit. She's good."

"And hot," Fletcher added.

The guy chuckled a bit, then flinched, wrinkling the bandages on his face.

"You need your rest," Fletcher told him. "But please, if you think of anything you haven't already shared—"

"I know," the guy replied. "I know. I should have told the police everything."

"That was it?" Fletcher asked, double-checking.

"Just the note," the guy replied. "That was it. I didn't mention it before because I didn't want my fiancée to know."

But since she wasn't the woman who'd visited him right now, Fletcher had a feeling she'd already figured it out even without the note being found with his stuff.

Where was the note?

"Hope you heal quickly," Fletcher told him before turning to reach for the door that had closed behind Kiki such a short while ago.

"I got a question for you, Detective," the guy said.

Fletcher looked back over his shoulder. "What?"

"Why?" the guy asked. "Why me? Why would anyone do this?"

Fletcher shook his head. "I don't know. But I'm going to work hard to get those answers for you and the other victims and to put this person away."

Tears rolled down the guy's face, wetting his bandages.

And Fletcher felt a jab to his heart. The guy hadn't been a great fiancé, but he hadn't deserved this.

Nobody did.

Fletcher opened the door, and he felt that jab to his heart again. But this was for another reason, for the woman leaning against the wall across from him.

She was definitely hot.

And Fletcher couldn't help but think, as he stepped into the hall to join her, that this undercover assignment was going to be far more dangerous than he'd ever considered. And not just because of the Slasher.

Kiki fought the smirk that was trying to curl up her lips. "Hey, what's keeping you?" she called from her place outside the door of the men's dressing room.

Since there was only one clerk in the store, and she was planted behind the register, Kiki had been playing sales associate, picking clothes for Fletcher to try on. After meeting up at the hospital in Conners, Fletcher had followed her to the outlet mall there since all the shops in Owl Creek were a bit higher end. The outlet mall was cheaper with a wider variety of stores—so many that this one wasn't at all busy. They were also the only customers in the store, so nobody would mistakenly think she was calling out to them. Fletcher should also have no doubt that he was the one she was talking to, yet he wasn't replying. Or coming out.

"Fletcher!"

"What's keeping me?" the question bounced back at her from the dressing room. "I can barely move in these pants." He pushed open the door and stepped out, wearing the skintight jeans and silk shirt she'd picked for him. The emerald green made his eyes sparkle even more and the silk molded to his chest and arms like the denim molded to his legs.

"It's either go for this look or the tattoos and piercings," she said. "That's what Troy looks like."

"I'm looking *for* Troy. I don't want to look *like* him," Fletcher said.

"You don't want to look like a cop," she reminded him.

He raised his fingers to his lips, trying to shush her like his undercover assignment had already started.

She laughed and pointed at the teenage clerk. "She has earbuds in."

He relaxed a bit, and when he did, the seams of the shirt strained at his broad shoulders and along his arms. To be built like that, he had to work out. A lot. The guys Kiki knew who worked out like that usually wore clothes to show off the result of their efforts, not hide them.

"You need some better fitting clothes," she insisted.

He reached for the top button of the shirt. "Yeah, and these aren't it."

"They fit better than your usual clothes," she pointed out, "which look like they're two sizes too big."

"I have to be able to run in case I have to chase a suspect down, and I need to be able to hide my weapon."

"Not everybody in the club hides their weapons," Kiki said. "If they have a permit to carry, some bouncers let them in with them."

Fletcher groaned. "Alcohol and guns. What could go wrong?"

"The Slasher isn't shooting their victims," Kiki said. "And not everybody that comes into the club drinks. Some just come for the music."

"Not the Slasher."

"You don't even know if that person comes inside the club. Maybe they just wait out in the alley until someone steps out for a smoke break or something."

He shook his head and glanced toward that clerk again. The girl wasn't even looking their way. She was focused on whatever video was playing on her phone. And nobody else had come into the store yet. "The Slasher doesn't wait for their victims to come to them."

Kiki tensed with dread. "But I've never seen anyone getting attacked like that happening inside." Fights. Sure. There were often fights. Sometimes someone even waved around a gun that Fletcher, with good reason, seemed to disapprove of them carrying while they were clubbing.

"Most of the victims have admitted to getting a note slipped into their pocket without them even realizing it." He tried to shove his hand into the pocket of his jeans, but they were too tight for him to fit more than his fingertips inside. "These aren't going to allow for that."

So he wanted the Slasher to slip him a note? To try to lure him into an alley?

She resisted the urge to shiver as a sudden chill chased down her spine. He wasn't just going undercover then. He was setting himself up as bait. She'd agreed to let him act like her assistant as his cover, but she hadn't realized how dangerous it was going to be. And she really didn't want him getting hurt like that man she'd visited in the hospital earlier today.

"And I thought it was cool to wear baggy pants and flannel jackets right now," he persisted.

She smiled at his persistence and his language. "Cool?"

"Hip, fly, whatever the words are that you kids use nowadays," he said, his green eyes twinkling with amusement.

"So are you trying to sound like my grandfather?" she asked, her smile widening. "Because he sounds more hip and fly than you do." And a giggle slipped out. "But then I guess you are older than I am." Probably five years at the most, but she couldn't help but tease him.

He glared at her, but his eyes were still twinkling. "I am not that old. I am just not that…"

"Cool?" she asked. He certainly wasn't now. Not in those clothes. He was *hot*, and she was getting hot as he undid another button and revealed some of the dark hair on his chest. Her heart beat faster and faster. Then she took a step back and whirled around. "I'll get you some hoodies and other things so you can hide your weapon."

But she wasn't necessarily talking about his gun. His weapon was how damn sexy he was.

He chuckled as if he'd realized he'd affected her. But maybe that was only fair. She'd purposely worn a pair of her shortest shorts just to get to him.

When she came back with an armload of hoodies and flannels and some looser jeans and Timberlands, he opened the door to his dressing room. The clerk hadn't even looked up from her phone while Kiki had flitted around the store picking out more clothes for Fletcher to try on. She wasn't paying any attention to them at all.

And Kiki kind of wished she was because she had no excuse not to step inside the dressing room with Fletcher to dump her armload onto the bench behind him. But when she would have ducked out again, he stepped between her and the door.

"What did you bring me now? Jeans I'm going to have to lie down on the floor to get on?" he asked.

She chuckled. "Bed. People usually lie down on the bed to get their jeans on. But for me." She patted her hips. "It's easier to get them on if I bounce up and down while I'm standing." And when she bounced to demonstrate, his gaze slipped down her body again.

A groan slipped through his lips. "Wouldn't you rather go shopping for you?" he asked.

"No. This is fun. And I already have all the clothes I need for the club." She kept a separate wardrobe of things that fit with the brand she'd built as a stylish and trendy female DJ whose music got people moving. "You need something you can wear this weekend, something that will help you fit in with the club scene."

He rolled his eyes.

"You really don't like clubs?" she asked.

"What's to like? They're loud and hot and crowded and really damn dangerous lately."

She couldn't deny that, not after she'd checked in on the Slasher's latest victim at the hospital. "That's why you need to fit in," she said. "If you want to catch the…"

She glanced around him to where that clerk stood at the register, watching her phone. The buds were still in her ears. "Slasher."

Fletcher walked toward the pile of clothes she'd dumped on the bench. "What do you want me to try on next? And why do I feel like a life-size Barbie doll right now?"

"Ken," she corrected him. Then shook her head and corrected herself, "G.I. Joe."

"That's my brother Wade," Fletcher said with a sigh of his own. Wade had been hurt, badly, on his last deployment, so it was no wonder that Fletcher was probably worried about him. His whole family had to be.

"How is he doing?" Kiki asked.

"He's healing," Fletcher said, his voice a little gruff with emotion.

He clearly loved his family very much.

"It was sweet of you to check on the Slasher's latest victim," he said, his green gaze fixed on her with that unnerving intensity.

"I feel bad it happened while I was spinning, and I never noticed..." That someone was getting disfigured while she played. There had been so many bandages on the man, so much pain in his face. She shuddered.

"The music is loud. The place is crowded. There's no way you would have noticed," Fletcher said.

She was touched that he was defending her or at least trying to make her feel a little less guilty that someone had been hurt while she'd been playing.

"So how is this cover going to work for you so that you'll notice what's going on?" she asked.

"Do I have to stick by you all the time or just help with setup and takedown of your equipment?"

"Setup and takedown only," she assured him. "Troy only hung out with me for a couple of songs, usually. We had a little dance thing." She smiled as she considered teaching it to Fletcher.

He shook his head and backed up. "No dancing."

"Nobody will guess you're a cop if you do," she assured him.

He shook his head and some of his hair fell across his eyes. "I should get this cut," he grumbled as he shoved it off his face.

"No!" she gasped, and she reached up to put her hands in it as if the scissors were heading toward it as he spoke. His hair was so soft that her skin tingled from contact with it. "This is the one thing that makes you look less like a cop."

"You say that like it's a bad thing to look like a cop," he said.

"If you want this undercover thing to get the results you want, it is a bad thing," she pointed out. "Otherwise…"

"Otherwise what?" he asked.

"I have no problem with the way you look," she admitted, and she knew she should pull her hands from his hair, but it was just so soft. And he was so good looking with his chiseled features and vivid green eyes.

His mouth curved into a slight grin. "Really?"

Standing in that dressing room with him, trapped between the bench and his long, muscular body, she might have felt a little uneasy. But she didn't particularly want to escape right now. She enjoyed flirting with him entirely too much. And touching him.

"Well…" she murmured. "There is one thing that you could use…"

And he arched a dark brow over one eye. "Are you going to suggest a tattoo or a piercing again?"

She shook her head. "No. What you could really use…" And she leaned a little closer to him, her mouth near his ear, her chest almost touching his.

His body tensed, and he audibly sucked in a breath. "What?" he asked, his voice a rasp.

"You could really use—" she said, her voice all breathy "—an iron."

He chuckled. "Is that why you're picking out all tight clothes for me?" he asked. "So there will be no wrinkles?"

She glanced down his body the way he'd glanced down hers. He still wore those tight jeans, molded to his muscular thighs. "Yeah, that's the reason…" she said with a laugh, her particularly naughty-sounding laugh.

"Are you flirting with me, Ms. Shelton?" he asked.

"Don't take it personally," she advised him. "I flirt with everyone. Occupational hazard."

He laughed. "I'll try to remember that."

And she would have to try to remember that he was only helping her out as part of his cover in the club. He didn't really want to spend this time with her. He just wanted to catch the Slasher.

Chapter 8

Club Ignition was just outside the city limits of Owl Creek in what had once been an abandoned warehouse. It was all metal and brick with a big open ceiling. And it was also loud and hot and crowded with sweaty bodies. All the things Fletcher hated about nightclubs.

But there was also Kiki.

She lit up the place, shining brighter than the strobe lights flashing around the club. One flashed now, nearly blinding him. How the hell was he supposed to spot any potential suspects when he could barely see at all?

The lights kept rhythm with the music, flashing in time to the beat. So not only was she managing the sound, but the light show, too.

And the sound, while loud, was also rich. Thick and heavy like cream and just as smooth. How did she do it all? He'd had no idea how much was involved with being a DJ. In addition to the expense of buying and maintaining all the equipment, there was also the physical labor of moving and unpacking the equipment. But the work didn't end with setup or takedown.

In addition to the lights, she also worked four turntables, mixing songs and adjusting bass, and as she turned and mixed, she moved. Her body swayed to the slower songs, jumped to the faster ones and Fletcher wasn't the only one who couldn't look away from her.

Everybody in the club was as fascinated as he was. The men tried to get close to her, but she had a short barricade separating her DJ booth from the crowd. Knowing Kiki like he was starting to, she probably used it more to protect her equipment than herself.

But whatever her reasoning was, Fletcher was glad she had it, that she wasn't vulnerable to that crowd that could include the Slasher. Or just some men that might not respect her boundaries.

Even a group of women jumped up and down near that barricade, screaming her name with excitement on their flushed faces. "Kiki! Kiki! Play our song!"

Despite the headphones she wore, she must have heard them. Because when the song "Where My Girls At" started pumping out of the speakers, those women lost their minds, screaming louder and jumping up and down even higher, their arms waving wildly over their heads.

He'd planted himself near the booth, but closer to the floor so he could watch it. Too close to the floor, because one of the women from that group tried pulling him out with them to dance. He shook his head.

"Come on, Fletcher!" Kiki called out to him over her microphone. "Dance with my girls!"

"Then you gotta dance with us, Kiki!" a guy yelled out, pointing to the floor.

"With me!" another guy yelled.

As the men hollered at her, and she ignored them or just shook her head, the women tugged Fletcher out onto that floor. He knew how to dance; he'd grown up with three younger sisters who'd needed practice partners for prom and other school dances. But those dances had been a while ago, so he didn't know how to do half the stuff these women were doing.

Even then, he might have stayed out on the floor if he'd thought it would give the Slasher an opportunity to slip a note in his pocket. But while the women were rubbing up against him and touching him, he didn't feel anything being put inside his pockets. And given the damage to the victims, he wasn't sure that a woman could have inflicted it.

Some of the victims had been big guys. Wouldn't they have been able to fight off a woman?

No. It was more likely a man who'd done the damage. A left-handed man, according to the medical examiner who'd studied the wounds of all the victims. So he studied the guys who called out to Kiki, wondering if it was one of them.

And he broke away from the women and leaped over the barricade to join Kiki in her booth that was already overcrowded with equipment. If he was going to dance with anyone, it was going to be her. Hell, he'd rather do more than dance with her.

But he was here to find a killer.

Not a good time.

Fletcher could dance. First with the women.

She would have been concerned that he was getting a note slipped in one of his pockets, but she knew those women well. They really were her girls. They came out to the clubs because they loved to dance.

"You've been holding out on me," Kiki said when he joined her in the booth. "Making it sound like you didn't even know how to…"

"I never said I couldn't. Just that I don't because I don't want to," he explained. But he was moving with her, against her, grinding up on her.

Instead of being offended, she giggled. And she'd thought he was uptight.

Fletcher Colton was full of surprises. And damn, he looked good. He wore a tight white T-shirt that changed color with every flash of the strobe lights. To hide his holster and his weapon, over the T-shirt he wore a light checked button-down shirt, but she had insisted that he leave it unbuttoned. And he had.

The jeans were loose and baggy but with enough holes to show off the hair on his muscular legs. And to make her heart race a little every time she looked at him. Or felt that brush of hair against her bare legs. She wore leather again, but shorts and a vest. And instead of black, she wore red—nearly the same color of the tips of her hair that swung around her shoulders as she danced.

Music filled her. Lifted her.

It had always been like that, ever since she was a little kid. She moved to it as if it was inside her, guiding her arms and legs. Her heart thumped in perfect tempo with the beat, just as heavy and deep. Except for now.

With Fletcher dancing with her.

Now her heart beat faster and faster with every touch of his body against hers.

She twirled in his arms and leaned close to his ear, whispering, "Aren't you supposed to be investigating?"

"I'm making sure my cover works," Fletcher said, grinning as if he knew how badly he was getting to her.

How much he was making her want him.

Like in the dressing room earlier this week, when she'd touched his hair and had wanted to keep on touching it. She'd touched it earlier when he'd showed up at the club to help her unload the equipment. She'd put some mousse in it, played with it, all on the pretext of making him look the part of her assistant.

Troy had never looked like this. While some women had probably found him attractive and danced with him, the crowd hadn't reacted to him like they had Fletcher.

And, while she had danced with other people before, she hadn't reacted to anyone like she was reacting to dancing with Fletcher. Because she wanted to do more than dance.

Her heart pounded so hard that she struggled to breathe. She needed air and some distance from her sexy assistant. "You can man the turntables while I take a bathroom break, then," she told him.

"What?" His green eyes widened with shock and fear.

She wasn't really leaving him to play anything, she explained. She'd already put a set of songs in order, including the requests from some bachelor party attendees. The music would keep pumping from the speakers while she caught the breath she'd lost, that her lungs ached to find again.

She wasn't out of breath from the dancing or from the spinning but from the closeness of Fletcher Colton. Of how he looked and of how he made her feel...

So damn attracted to him.

She slipped past him and down the couple of steps to the barricade that she vaulted herself over. As she moved through the crowd, guys called out to her and tried to dance with her like Fletcher had been. But she didn't stop moving until she pushed her way into the crowded bathroom.

Women moved aside and applauded while they chattered at and around her.

"Kiki, you're the best!"

"Kiki, what a huge improvement over Troy."

"I liked Troy."

"Yeah, we know why."

"Who is he?" one of her usual crew asked. Claire was a blonde who always wore bright red lipstick.

"He's hot!" Janie said. Her hair was dark like Kiki's but wildly curly, even a little frizzy tonight—probably from the heat.

"He yours?" Amy asked. She was a redhead, but probably about as natural a redhead as the tips of Kiki's hair were natural.

Kiki's pulse quickened even more at the thought of that. Of Fletcher being hers.

But she didn't want anyone. Not really. At least not for keeps. That would make life too complicated. She was committed to traveling from club to club, building her brand so that she could get a record deal like so many other DJs she knew.

She shook her head. "He's just an old friend."

Janie snorted. "Looks like more than that."

"Is he?" Amy asked with a trace of disappointment.

Feeling a pang of jealousy that these women were so interested in Fletcher, she smiled slightly, smugly, as if she was claiming him. "Now, ladies, I need to use the bathroom so I can get back to the turntables."

As she slipped into a stall, voices called out to her, requesting songs. Someday, maybe, the song they requested would be one of hers.

That was the dream, one she'd had since she was a little girl and had felt that music moving inside her. But the music wasn't the only thing inside her tonight.

Tonight, she had that overwhelming attraction to Fletcher. And all these women talking about him, drooling over him, only made him more attractive to her. As if he hadn't already been attractive enough.

But he was only here because of the case. She had to remind herself of that, of the Slasher. Detective Fletcher Colton wasn't here to dance with her or to drive her to distraction over how damn attractive she found him.

He was here to catch someone before that person hurt anyone else. That was what mattered most. Making sure nobody else got hurt, or worse.

A little flicker of fear shortened her breath for a moment as she worried that she might be the one getting hurt if she wasn't careful. Not by the Slasher.

But by Fletcher, if she acted on this attraction she felt for him. She couldn't do that for so many reasons. She had her friendship with his sister Ruby, her busy schedule, her life goals…

Their careers were going to take them in different directions. His was going to take him into dangerous places.

And she'd already lost people she'd loved. She couldn't fall for Fletcher.

The Slasher needed another victim. The police wouldn't be able to keep another attack from the media. Wouldn't be able to keep the story from spreading, from going national like the other attacks had.

The Slasher needed another victim because they needed the attention, the fear, the respect.

So they were at their usual hunting ground. A crowded club.

There were so many men to choose from.

Even Kiki had brought someone new tonight.

Someone to help her with the equipment. Or was he her boyfriend? The way they'd danced together, the way they'd looked at each other…

They definitely knew each other well. There was an

intimacy between them. If not, the Slasher would have been concerned that this man was something else…

Like a police officer.

Would one go undercover to catch the Slasher?

Were they that important?

How many different police departments and agencies were trying to catch them?

Trying to stop them?

Nothing and nobody would. And if anyone tried to get in their way…

They would wind up being the next victim of the Slasher, and maybe that person would lose more than their looks.

Maybe they would lose their life…

Chapter 9

Fletcher wanted nothing to do with the turntables or with all the requests being shouted at him while Kiki was gone. Where had she gone? Just the restroom?

Not the alley.

His pulse quickened as he thought of that—of her becoming a victim of the Slasher. The serial attacker hadn't gone after women before, but that didn't mean that the person wouldn't, especially if Kiki stepped into the alley at the wrong moment. As he started across the dance floor toward the bar and the door behind it through which they'd dragged all her equipment, he got distracted by the sound of a familiar, raspy voice.

"Let go of me," Kiki said with indignation and determination.

"You danced with that loser but you won't dance

with me?" The man sounded indignant as well. "It's my bachelor party. Come on."

"I know, and I've been playing your favorite songs," Kiki replied. "And to keep doing that, I need to get back to my booth."

"Just one dance. Or a drink. I'll buy you a drink. I can buy you a lot of things, pretty Kiki."

"I am not for sale," she said. "Now let me go!"

"Let her go!" Fletcher growled as he pushed through to where some guy, just a little taller than Kiki, was holding tightly to one of her bare arms.

Kiki tried wrestling free, but the man's grip tightened to the point her skin was turning red.

"Oh, here's your lapdog now," the guy remarked with a disparaging smirk. "Come on, Kiki, give up losers like this for real men. Men with means."

"I don't—"

Fletcher didn't interrupt her. He just grabbed the man and jerked his arm behind his back so that it fell away from hers. With the abrupt release, she stumbled back a step into the crowd that had gathered around them.

The guy wrestled in Fletcher's grasp. "How dare you! Get your hands off me!"

"I will break your arm," he threatened. He raised the man's arm a little higher behind his back until he cried out. "Don't you ever touch her again."

"Let me go!" the guy said again, but it was more of a frightened whine than the condescending demand it had been earlier.

Fletcher twisted the guy's arm just a little harder before he released him. The minute he did, the guy swung his fist toward him. Fletcher ducked and swung back, striking him just enough to knock him into the man's friends who'd gathered behind them. "Now get the hell out."

Finally, the bouncers arrived, dragging the man from the crowd, as he hurled insults and protestations. "This is my bachelor party! Do you know who I am?"

Nobody cared. The mocking laughter of the crowd followed the guy out along with a few of his friends.

"You're going to be sorry!" was his last pitiful proclamation.

The laughter got louder.

Nobody was.

But the way Kiki looked at Fletcher, glaring as she rushed past him toward her booth, he figured he might be sorry later when she had time to talk to him. What had she wanted him to do? Let the guy hurt her?

The thought wrenched his guts, making him feel sick. While she might have been annoyed with him, nobody else was. They all patted his back and shoulders. "Way to protect Kiki!"

"Let me buy you a drink," someone offered, and he was swept up with the crowd gathered around the bar until he was up against the long peninsula of granite and glass.

"Drink's on me," the bartender said when cards and money were extended toward him.

"Just coffee," Fletcher told him. He couldn't drink on the job, especially this job. He needed to be alert to deal with the Slasher. And if he had alcohol, tired as he was, he wouldn't be able to stay awake. Unless he watched Kiki.

"Everybody, get back on the floor!" Kiki's command echoed from the speakers. "I need you all out here. I need you to…" Her voice trailed off, replaced with the upbeat music and song, "Dance, dance, dance!"

The clubgoers shrieked and headed back out, jumping and yelling along with the lyrics. With Kiki.

She wanted the drama involving her forgotten. She wanted to focus on the music, on other people having a good time. That seemed very important to her.

The bartender leaned over the bar, that was a whole lot less crowded now, and said, "Thanks for getting rid of that entitled ass. Too many rich guys come in here thinking they can have whatever they want."

Fletcher focused on the bartender. With dark blond hair and stubble on his pointy chin, he was probably a little younger than Fletcher—maybe late twenties, like Kiki's age. But there was a jadedness to him already, despite his youth.

"Must get sickening," Fletcher agreed with him. "Having to listen to them spout off about how important they are."

The bartender nodded. "You have no idea. Just because they have money, they think they can treat everybody like dirt." He snorted. "Money doesn't buy class or manners, that's for damn sure."

Fletcher was glad that when he'd met the bartender earlier that evening, when he and Kiki had been bringing in her equipment, he hadn't shared his last name. Thanks to his dad's real estate investments, the Coltons had money. Fortunately, thanks to how their mom had raised them, they also had class and manners.

But this guy seemed to lump all rich people together and equate them with rudeness and entitlement. He'd probably had some bad experiences over the years, but it looked like his bitterness about rich guys ran pretty deep.

Had all the Slasher's victims had money?

Fletcher made a mental note to follow up on that. Wanting to show camaraderie with his new acquaintance, he grinned and picked up the mug of coffee. "Thanks," he said. "And cheers to getting rid of entitled jerks!"

The bartender grinned.

"Cheers," another voice chimed in.

Fletcher glanced down the bar to where an older man sat alone, his glass lifted toward Fletcher. With iron gray hair and several deep lines in his face, this guy had to be in his sixties. He didn't look like the other clubgoers. Maybe he owned the place.

Fletcher leaned across the bar and asked the bartender, "What's his story? Owner?"

The bartender snorted. "No. Just a regular customer. He comes around a lot."

"Really?" Fletcher asked. The guy didn't seem to be into the music, but he kept looking at the dance floor.

"Yeah, I thought he was a cop at first, but he's actually just a dad looking for his missing daughter."

A pang of sympathy for the distraught father struck Fletcher. "Oh…"

"Yeah, sucks. He hasn't seen her for a few years.

Don't know why he thinks he's going to just happen to run into her in a club someday." He shrugged. "But whatever..."

"Bart! Bart!" a male customer called from the end of the bar.

"Gotta go," Bart said. "Don't wanna keep these entitled jerks waiting."

When the bartender walked away, Fletcher approached the older guy. "Cheers," he said to him again.

Unlike the bartender, who wore a black uniform that was fading to gray from age and frequent washing, this guy wore a suit that looked tailored and expensive. He also wore an expensive watch on his right hand, which probably made him a lefty. He could have been one of the entitled jerks that Bart and Fletcher had been talking about.

Hell, with the shares of Colton Properties that Fletcher had just inherited, he could probably be one of those entitled jerks. But he hadn't even stuck around for the reading of the will to find out what the value of those shares were. It had been too hard.

Losing someone sucked.

"Cheers," the stranger repeated. "Better enjoy your drink because I think you're in a little bit of trouble."

"How's that?" Fletcher asked. "Think that guy is going to call the police?" It would be funny if he did.

But Fletcher didn't want to blow his cover.

"Kiki doesn't seem too happy with you," the guy said with a slight grin.

Fletcher groaned. "Yeah."

"She can take care of herself."

The way she'd whirled on him with that pepper spray last weekend, she'd proved that she could. But with the Slasher on the loose...

And the way that jerk had been squeezing her arm...

She would probably have bruises, and that infuriated Fletcher. "I actually showed some restraint," Fletcher insisted. He hadn't thrown the first punch, and he hadn't broken the guy's arm like he'd been tempted to for hurting Kiki.

The man chuckled. "I doubt Kiki's going to see it that way, especially since it was the guy's bachelor party."

"So, you know Kiki pretty well," Fletcher remarked. And he also paid a lot of attention to what was going on in the club since he'd known that the guy who'd hit on her was the guest of honor at his bachelor party. Was this stranger so observant just because he was looking for his daughter?

The guy shook his head. "No, I don't know Kiki all that well. I've just been at some clubs while she's playing the music."

He definitely wasn't part of the club scene, despite how often he must frequent them. Fletcher could relate.

"You haven't been with her before," the gentleman observed. "She usually has some skinny, tattooed guy with her. Where's he tonight?"

Fletcher shrugged. "Good question. He took off on her last weekend and hasn't been seen since."

Fletcher saw him flinch and regretted that he'd probably reminded the older man of his missing daughter. Had she run away from home? Was that how he'd lost track of her?

Fletcher wanted to ask these questions, but appearing too interested would risk his cover, too. He narrowed his eyes and studied the guy. "Are you a cop?" he asked.

The man grimaced. "No. I don't have much use for the police."

"Why's that?" Fletcher asked.

The stranger sighed. "They don't give some things, some people, the attention they deserve."

The Slasher was all about getting attention, but Fletcher hadn't been able to figure out why yet. Was this it? Because the man wasn't getting the help he wanted to find his daughter?

"I'm sorry," Fletcher said.

"Why?" the man asked, narrowing his blue eyes. "Are you a cop?"

Ignoring the jab of concern that he had risked his cover, he laughed heartily. "That's funny," he said. "Me? A cop?"

"So then you're more like her other assistant?" the man asked.

And Fletcher wondered now if the man was looking for his daughter or for drugs. "No. I'm nothing like Troy either," he assured him. "Kiki and I are old friends. I just stepped in to help her out."

Until the Slasher was caught.

And Fletcher needed that to happen soon, before anyone else got hurt. Or worse.

Kiki should have been relieved that Fletcher stayed away from her booth. She was annoyed that he'd felt the need to step into that situation on the dance floor.

Like she'd needed his help.

Like he thought she couldn't take care of herself.

She'd been handling jerks like that for a long time on her own. She knew how to get rid of them. A few sharp words cut up their egos like the Slasher.

No. Nothing compared to what the Slasher did to their victims. Nothing.

She couldn't get over the sight of the victim she'd visited in the hospital. And she hadn't seen him until after he'd been treated. She couldn't imagine what Troy must have seen when he'd found that victim in the alley behind that Salt Lake City club. No wonder he'd taken off when he'd heard about another attack.

Though apparently, he had other reasons to avoid the authorities. She felt a pang of guilt over that, over helping him evade his responsibilities. But she'd had no idea he had children. And just because he was a deadbeat dad, it didn't make him the Slasher like Fletcher clearly suspected he was.

But why?

What would his motive have been?

What was the Slasher's motive for hurting people so horrifically? For disfiguring them like that?

She shivered despite the warmth of the crowded club. And she tried to peer through that mob of people to catch sight of Fletcher.

Where had he gone?

Was he still wrestling with that creep who'd hit on her? Or was he wrestling with someone far more dangerous? Trying to get a better view, she climbed onto one of the speakers in the booth. She danced along with the music she played while searching the crowd.

She caught sight of him, his dark hair mussed despite the mousse she'd put in it for him—or maybe because of it, since she'd kept playing with the soft strands. Or had one of the women who'd danced with Fletcher messed it up? Or maybe it had happened during his tussle with that boor of a bachelor who had acted like his money could get him whatever he wanted from any woman.

She snorted at the thought. She would play song requests, but those were the only requests she fulfilled. And most everyone who came to her shows knew that.

Did Fletcher know that? And if he did, why hadn't he let her handle that creep on her own?

She'd done it plenty of times. She hadn't asked for his help. She didn't need him, but she damn well wanted him. He was so attractive.

From her vantage point on her speaker, she peered around the club, trying to find him. He was at the bar talking to Mr. Sullivan. She'd met the guy a couple of years ago, and every time she saw him, her heart ached for his sadness and desperation.

He'd shown her a picture of his daughter, asking if Kiki had seen her. If she had, she wouldn't have recognized her as the girl wearing a school uniform, her hair pulled back into a tight ponytail. If Kiki had ever seen her, the girl had probably looked like so many others who hung around the clubs, desperate to have a good time.

Some were a little too desperate.

Desperate to look older, prettier, more desirable. So desperate that they sometimes made bad choices. Kiki didn't know for sure if that was what had happened to Dan Sullivan's daughter any more than she knew for certain if she'd ever seen her before.

She'd disappointed the older man because she couldn't help him. Fletcher could. But was that why he was at the bar talking to the man?

Or did he wonder if he was the Slasher, just like he'd suspected Troy, too?

Fletcher's head turned from the bar toward her. Across that crowded room, she couldn't see his eyes, but she could feel the intensity of his gaze.

That look he'd been giving her every time they came into contact. Lately, they'd connected a little too often for unfortunate reasons.

His father's funeral.

The attack at the club in Conners.

But every time they saw each other, they had this bizarre connection. He found her as attractive as she found him. But neither of them could afford a distraction right now, not with that dangerous attacker out there, probably prowling clubs for another victim.

Was that Fletcher's real reason for going undercover at the club? Not just to find clues to the Slasher's identity but to get the Slasher to try to attack him?

He'd wanted the loose jeans—loose enough to chase after a suspect, but also loose enough for a note to be slipped into his pocket.

That was why she'd been so desperate to find him in

the crowd. To make sure he was still inside the club and not out in the alley.

Because ever since their shopping trip, she'd had the horrible feeling that Fletcher was using himself as bait for this vicious person. That he was setting himself up to be the Slasher's next victim.

Chapter 10

Fletcher had avoided Kiki since he'd saved her from that drunk because, like the man at the bar, Fletcher doubted that was how she'd seen it. That he'd saved her.

She probably just figured he'd interfered. And he had no doubt that he would hear about it when the night was over, and when he was alone with her. Despite knowing he would probably get told off, he couldn't wait for the night to end. And not just so that he could be alone with her.

He was so damn tired. It wasn't for lack of sleep. He was used to working late, sometimes even around the clock, when he had a case to solve. He was tired because of the noise and the music and the definite attraction he felt for Kiki.

She was amazing.

The way she worked all that complicated equipment left him in awe. The sounds she made…

Especially when she sang along with some of the lyrics. Her voice was amazing. Sexy and vibrant and hauntingly beautiful. Just like her.

When she danced, she moved like the music was inside her, pouring out of her every pore. She was so captivating it was nearly impossible to look away from her. Like everybody else in the club, he watched her now, dancing away behind the turntables.

She'd even been on top of one of the speakers earlier tonight. As if she'd been looking for him—and maybe she had been, because once their gazes had met, she'd jumped down. And he'd felt a little flicker of excitement that she might have been concerned about him.

With the way she kept distracting him, just by being her, how the hell was he going to catch the Slasher?

Sure, he'd been working, subtly interviewing that distraught father and the bartender. He'd gotten Dan Sullivan's name and his daughter's name. Caitlin.

He'd gotten the bartender's full name, too. Bart Taylor. Fletcher had even managed to sneak one of the glasses the man had touched beneath his shirt and then into the duffel bag he had slipped in with Kiki's equipment. He would run it for prints. Check out the man's past.

Find out why he hated rich guys so damn much.

If only the Slasher had ever left prints at the scene— something to match them to. But while several prints had been found at every scene, in every alley, none of them had been the same. The wounds and the weapon that had made them had all matched, though, so the Slasher must be just one solitary person committing every assault.

A left-handed person. A coroner had studied the wounds and determined that from the depth and direction of the cuts, a left-handed person had swung the blade.

The bartender was left-handed.

So was Dan Sullivan.

Fletcher hadn't realized there were so many left-handed people until he'd started looking for them in the club. The bartender and Sullivan hadn't been the only ones. The way other patrons had waved at the bartender to order drinks or some of the women had waved at Fletcher to draw his attention had shown they were probably left-handed, too.

What about Troy?

Kiki's former assistant was still high on his list of suspects. Where was he? The bartender had mentioned to Fletcher that he'd thought he'd seen him earlier. Someone else had said the same, but Fletcher had searched the crowd and hadn't caught any sight of him. He'd even searched the alley, too. Hell, he'd made a point of going out there at least once an hour to see if the Slasher was lying in wait for someone.

Or if they'd already attacked.

Did Kiki have any idea where her assistant was? She hadn't even known the guy's last name, or about his drug possession charge and back child support. Fletcher doubted she knew anything else about the man that would help locate him. But maybe she would know if he was left-handed or not.

If she would talk to him…

So far all she'd done was glare at him since he'd pulled that drunk off her on the dance floor.

Fletcher had wanted to check on her, to see if her arm had bruised from how tightly the guy had been gripping it. But the one time he'd gotten close, when he'd slipped that glass into his duffel bag, she'd given him such a look, all tight lips and lowered brows.

He was probably in more danger from her than from the Slasher right now. Nobody had tried to slip him a note. His pockets were empty. And the night was nearly over.

No. The night was over. It was early morning now.

Kiki had shouted "last call" and the songs were winding down in tempo while the lights gradually got brighter.

And the crowd thinned out.

Dan Sullivan had left a while ago.

The bartender had slipped away after fulfilling the last call orders. He was probably in the back, washing dirty glasses. Or maybe looking for one.

No. He wouldn't miss the one that Fletcher had tucked into his duffel bag. He wished he'd managed to get Dan Sullivan's glass, too, but the guy had only had one drink and he'd kept his hands around it the whole night, as if he'd been worried that someone would slip something in it.

Was that what he'd thought happened to his daughter?

While Fletcher had gotten him talking about his daughter, the man had just showed him his picture and said that she'd always liked going to nightclubs, even when she wasn't really old enough to get in.

So maybe he blamed nightclubs for her going missing. And the attacks on clubgoers was his way of getting revenge.

Because the viciousness of those attacks made them feel so personal.

Like someone was after something.

Notoriety or revenge?

Or both?

Fletcher sighed, which turned into a yawn so big that he closed his eyes and leaned against the barricade he'd been standing near, just outside Kiki's booth.

"Hey, old man, try to stay awake," Kiki chastised him, her voice soft and close to his ear.

Realizing that her voice was the only sound he heard but for a buzzing echo, he opened his eyes and blinked against the brightness of the lights. "Is it over?" he asked, letting his eagerness slip out. Maybe it hadn't been the eventful night he'd hoped it would be, but while he hadn't had a note slipped in his pocket, he had found some more potential suspects. Besides Troy.

The bartender had mentioned seeing him in the club, but when Fletcher had looked around, he hadn't seen anyone who'd matched the description he'd had of the man. Had he been there? Maybe he'd intended to help Kiki after all.

And then he'd seen Fletcher. Too bad Fletcher hadn't seen him.

"Yes, it's over," Kiki said, "and I have a lot of equipment you need to help carry out, since you're so help-ful and all…"

Fletcher flinched. "I figured I would pay for that."

"For making a scene? For embarrassing me?"

"The scene was already being made," he said. "That guy was a jerk."

"He was drunk and acting like a bigshot in front of his friends," she said. "It was his bachelor party."

"That doesn't give him the right to harass you," Fletcher said, appalled. "I'm glad I decided long ago to never get married."

"You don't want to get married?" she asked.

He shook his head. His parents had not had the ideal marriage. He wasn't sure if it was just because of how much his dad had always worked but knowing how his own relationships hadn't withstood his work sched-ule, he wasn't going to risk anything more permanent. "Nope. And really, I don't think that guy should either. What a dick."

Those lips, which had been tightly drawn together, twitched up into a smile. "Yeah, he was, but I would have handled him so that I didn't ruin his evening."

"I doubt his evening was ruined. I'm sure he went on to another bar," Fletcher assured her. "Or maybe a strip club."

She sighed. "He did kind of act like that was where he thought he was."

"I'm sure their bouncers would toss him out, too, if he tried anything," Fletcher said, and he was smiling now at the thought.

"You are not a bouncer, though," she said, and she

reached over the barricade, poking him in the chest. "You didn't need to rush to my rescue because I am not some damsel in need of saving."

He tried to fight his widening smile so that he wouldn't infuriate her even more than he already had. But she was so damned beautiful when she was feisty like this. Hell, she was always so damned beautiful. He nodded. "I know. But I didn't want you to get hurt."

He looked at her arm now. The bright lights illuminated the mark on her skin that was still red from how tightly the man had gripped her. And Fletcher wished he'd hit the guy a little harder.

She glanced down at where his gaze was focused and shrugged. "I get bigger bruises than that hauling this equipment around," she said. "That's nothing. And if he'd not let me go, he would have gotten an injury that would have had a terrible effect on his wedding night."

Fletcher chuckled. "Okay. Remind me not to piss you off again."

She nodded. "Oh, I will," she promised.

He chuckled again. "Oh, I have no doubt that you will."

"You're kind of pissing me off right now," she said.

"How's that?"

"You're stalling when we have work to do," she pointed out. "Let's get this equipment out to the SUV."

He tensed. "Are you going to come around to the alley again like when we unloaded it?"

"You're too tired to schlep it out to the parking lot?" she asked with a teasing smile.

"No," he said. "We can do that. But first, I do need to check the alley."

Especially since all his suspects had disappeared a while ago.

What if one of them had attacked someone else while he'd been in the club, drooling over Kiki? He would never forgive himself for getting so distracted.

But he would also never forgive himself if something happened to her. "No. I'll check the alley after I walk you out to your SUV."

She narrowed her eyes and glared at him. "If I thought I needed a guard dog, I'd bring Fancy to work with me."

He chuckled. "Fancy is pretty young to be a guard dog."

"She's feisty."

"Like her owner."

"I'm not her owner," Kiki said with a trace of regret. "Just her foster mom."

"You never get attached to these puppies you foster and want to keep one?" he asked.

She shook her head. "No. I travel too much to have a pet or a relationship."

Was she warning him off? She probably couldn't miss how attracted to her that he was. But it was just attraction. Nothing more.

Attraction and concern.

"We'll carry out some of the lighter things to your vehicle," he said. "Then you can drive it back to the alley and we'll get the heavier stuff."

She sighed but nodded. "Okay."

He was going to make her wait until he checked the alley before she pulled her vehicle into it, though. He didn't want her to find another victim, either with him or without him.

Kiki's irritation with Fletcher slipped away the minute they stepped outside the club. The parking lot wasn't very well lit, like the one in Conners.

And the night was eerily quiet. Not even a cicada sang or a cricket chirped.

Apprehension raced over her like a cold breeze, and she shivered.

"Here," Fletcher said. "Take my shirt." While holding one of her turntables, he managed to pull off his shirt and drape it over her shoulders.

She would have refused, but it was warm, and it smelled like him—like soap and man. "Aren't you worried about someone seeing your holster and gun?" she asked.

"If they're out here in the dark, it might be a good thing if they do," he said.

The Slasher hadn't ever attacked an armed man. So it was definitely a good thing, especially since she suspected Fletcher was going to insist on checking the alley alone once he'd walked her to her vehicle.

Her grandfather would have been charmed by Fletcher's protectiveness and chivalry. Kiki kept trying to tell herself that she was annoyed.

But she might have been just a little bit charmed as well. Not that she was taking it personally. As a lawman, Fletcher had taken that whole oath to protect and serve or serve and protect... Whatever it was.

He was really undercover to protect any more men from being attacked by the Slasher.

Even though she was happy that she wasn't out here alone in this eerie and all-encompassing darkness, she felt compelled to say, "You really don't need to walk me to my vehicle. I'm not in danger from the Slasher."

"We already talked about that," he said. "If he or she feels threatened..."

She snorted. "I'm not carrying the gun, and I have no idea who would do something like that." She certainly hoped she didn't know someone that vicious and evil.

"I'm not just concerned about the Slasher," Fletcher said. "I don't entirely trust that bachelor party groom wouldn't come back after the club closed."

"Then once again, you're probably in more danger than I am," she said. She'd considered that, though, and her pepper spray canister was hooked to one of the belt loops of her red leather shorts. Just in case.

Kiki believed in being better safe than sorry, which was why she wanted to ignore this attraction she felt for Fletcher. But the heat from his shirt, and the scent of him in the fabric, titillated her senses.

"Why'd you park so far out?" Fletcher asked. Clearly, he was more annoyed than titillated.

"I parked out here because I couldn't leave my vehicle in the alley where we unloaded," she reminded him. "And by the time we unloaded it, the lot was already starting to fill up so I had to park out here."

Fletcher groaned.

"We're almost there," she assured him, clicking the key fob so that the lights on her SUV blinked on. "Despite all that coffee I saw you drinking, you're still tired. Not used to staying up so late?"

"It's more these boots you had me buy. As expensive as they were, I expected them to be more comfortable," he grumbled.

"You need to break them in first," she said.

"I thought I was…with the dancing." He did a couple fancy cha-cha steps.

Kiki laughed. She clicked to open the back of her SUV, setting her stuff inside the hatch.

"You've been holding out on me, Colton. You're going to have to salsa with me." She reached out and grasped his hips, trying to move them back as she took a couple of steps toward him. But he didn't move, and suddenly she was flush against his long, hard body. "You're supposed to dance."

"I don't know how to salsa," he said, his voice a little gruff. And even in the dim light from the hatch of her SUV, his eyes glittered as he stared down at her.

The intensity of that stare moved inside her like the music did, making her want him so damn badly. With her heels on, she wasn't that much shorter than he was, so his face wasn't that much above hers. Her gaze moved to his lips, and yearning filled her, making her stretch just a bit until their mouths were so close that there was only a breath between them.

Fletcher groaned.

And Kiki smiled. "Feet still hurting from those new boots?"

"It's not the boots that are bothering me now," he admitted in a husky whisper.

"What's bothering you?" Kiki asked. But as close as she was to him, she could feel his body's reaction to hers.

"You are," he said, and his breath whispered across her mouth.

She parted her lips, breathing him in before releasing a shaky, wistful sigh. "Fletcher…" She couldn't remember the last time she'd been this attracted to someone. And they hadn't even kissed.

She stretched up a bit and brushed her mouth across his. And heat swept through her body.

"This is a bad idea," Fletcher murmured.

"What?" she asked, playing coy.

"I can't afford any distractions right now, not with this investigation, and my cover…" But then he kissed her back, as she'd kissed him, just brushing his mouth across hers before pulling back.

"What's the distraction?" she asked.

"You are," he repeated. "So damn distracting…" And he kissed her again. Deeply. His mouth settling firmly against hers.

She parted her lips and deepened the kiss even more. Their tongues touched, flirted, teased and, again, desire coursed through her like music, making her body want to move with his.

But then that eerie silence broke, something smashing against something, like the sound of glass breaking. They jerked apart, Fletcher reaching for his weapon.

"What? Where…" she murmured.

"Stay here," Fletcher whispered, and he moved back toward the club, disappearing into the darkness.

Had the sound come from the alley? The way it had echoed, it probably had.

Maybe it was just the bartender or someone else who worked at the club dumping something into the trash behind the building. Or…

It was the Slasher attacking another victim, and Fletcher was either going to stop it or put himself in danger as well. Her heart pounded fast and hard with fear.

For him.

Then she heard something closer. And she was scared for herself.

She'd parked so far out that the SUV was near a field. Something moved in the grass, making it rustle softly. It was probably just an animal.

The real threat was in that alley, where Fletcher had rushed off to.

He was the one in danger.

She had no reason to be afraid, except for worrying over him. Maybe she was also afraid over that kiss.

Another sound emanated from the field, something low and forlorn.

Maybe that animal she'd heard was in pain. Hurt.

She took a few tentative steps away from the SUV. Fletcher hadn't meant for her to stay exactly where he'd left her. He just hadn't wanted her to follow him.

She understood that. She had no gun. And she didn't want to be a distraction to him, like he'd already accused her of being. She didn't want him to get hurt because of her.

And she didn't want any other living creature in harm's way either. Peering into the darkness, she walked closer, until she stood just inside the tall weeds of that field. She tilted her head and listened.

Not just for that sound she'd heard but also to the soft rumble of Fletcher's voice. He'd found something in the alley. But he hadn't fired his weapon.

Maybe everything was fine. It had just been what she'd thought: an employee throwing trash into the dumpster. Fletcher was fine.

But then something reached out of the weeds and darkness and grabbed her, and she knew she was the one in danger. As she fumbled for the pepper spray on her belt loop, she opened her mouth and screamed. But if it was the Slasher who'd grabbed her, help would probably come too late to save her.

Chapter 11

One minute Fletcher had been talking to the bartender, Bart Taylor, in the alley where the man had dropped a crate of empty bottles, and the next that scream had rung out.

Kiki's scream.

God, he'd thought she was safe. Safer out there than if she'd followed him into the alley. Fear gripping him, he ran back toward the lot, toward where he'd left her.

But he didn't see her standing near her SUV. The dome lights casting a glow out of the hatch didn't illuminate her. "Kiki?" he called out, his voice cracking a bit with his concern for her.

"Here!" she yelled. "Over here! Call an ambulance!" Her voice was high with fear or adrenaline or both.

"Are you hurt?" he asked, that alarm gripping him still, squeezing his heart.

"Not me. But…there's another victim…"

Fletcher found her standing in a field just beyond her vehicle. She seemed fine, just slightly shaky as she pointed down at the ground.

"I don't want to move him."

Fletcher holstered his weapon and pulled out his cell. The light from the screen illuminated the area and the body lying in the weeds, blood pooling all around it. He was facedown, the back of his head bloodied with maybe a cracked skull.

Fletcher dropped to his knees next to the man, reaching for his wrist to check for a pulse. "Is he dead?"

"No," Kiki said. "He—he grabbed my ankle…"

And Fletcher could see now that the man's arm was outstretched toward Kiki. And there was blood smeared on her skin.

The man's hands and arms were cut. But there was a pulse, albeit faint and slow. Fletcher called in to dispatch, requesting an ambulance and a police response. He glanced around, making sure the bartender wasn't close enough to hear, then he identified himself, gave his badge number and added, "Make sure no one acknowledges me. I'm undercover so question me like any other witness."

But he wasn't like any other witness because he hadn't seen a damn thing. He'd been distracted, just like he'd told Kiki, with her. While he'd kept checking the alley for the Slasher or for another victim, he hadn't thought to check out the parking lot. Hell, he hadn't even noticed anything when he'd walked Kiki to her SUV, and given the blood, the guy had been lying here for a while.

"Should we do something?" Kiki asked. "Roll him over? Make sure he's breathing?"

"With his head wound…" Fletcher was hesitant about moving him. "I don't want to hurt him any worse than he already is."

"But he could be dying."

Fletcher touched the guy's wrist again, and that thready pulse was gone now. His skin even slightly chilled. He hated to move the guy, but in order to administer CPR, the victim had to be on his back.

Fletcher slowly rolled him over, being so careful of his head, and even he gasped while some strangled sound slipped through the hand Kiki had clasped over her mouth.

"Oh, my God…"

There were deep slashes across the guy's face, but despite the wounds, Fletcher recognized him. He was the groom with whom he'd tussled on the dance floor.

"Oh, my God…" Kiki murmured again.

Fletcher didn't know if she recognized him, too, or if she was just horrified by the injuries, the deep lacerations across the guy's face and chest and arms.

He leaned closer to him, listening for breath, watching his damaged chest to see if it was moving, and he heard a soft rattle from it. He was still breathing, but his lungs were filling, probably with blood. "He doesn't need CPR," Fletcher said.

He needed far more help than Fletcher's first aid

training had covered. Sirens whined in the distance, gradually getting louder and louder as the ambulance and police approached. And Fletcher let out a little breath of his own—of relief that help was arriving.

He wasn't sure, though, if they would be able to save the guy either, not with how badly he was wounded. He was by far the most seriously injured of the Slasher's victims.

Just as Fletcher had feared, the level of violence was escalating. And it was only a matter of time before an attack became fatal and claimed a life.

Kiki was shaken. Too shaken to sleep. Too shaken to stay at Grandpa's cottage and not accidentally wake him up while she paced. So she just stopped at his house, picked up Fancy and drove around the lake to the marina where the houseboat was docked.

She wouldn't disturb anyone else here. She'd left a note for Grandpa just in case he had heard her drive up. Knowing how light a sleeper he was, he probably had.

That was why she'd rushed around to get out of the house, with Fancy and a bag of clothes and toiletries, before he came out of his bedroom. She hadn't wanted to talk about what had happened that night.

What she'd found.

The latest victim of the Slasher.

What a maniac. A monster, really, because how could one human being do that to another?

She shuddered despite the fact that she still wore Fletcher's shirt. The cotton was pretty thin, though, and it had lost the warmth of his body that it had when he'd first given it to her.

He'd lost his warmth, too, when the ambulance and the police had arrived. He'd been all business, talking to everyone else almost furtively, probably because he hadn't wanted to blow his cover.

And another officer or detective had questioned her. Kiki had been so shocked by what she'd found, by that hand reaching out of the darkness and the weeds to grasp her ankle.

The scream had been instinctive, but her throat burned a little from how loudly she'd uttered it. And she trembled again from the terror she'd felt in that moment.

Fancy whimpered. Either the puppy had picked up on Kiki's fear, or she was nervous walking down the dock toward the houseboat.

Water lapped against the boats they passed and against the posts of the dock, swirling around them in the faint light of the sliver of the moon overhead.

Where had that moon been earlier?

She could have used that in the parking lot. Then maybe she would have found him sooner.

The way the EMTs had looked—from how furiously they'd been working to the way they'd sped away, lights flashing and siren ringing out loudly…

It hadn't looked good.

She didn't know if he was going to make it. And she felt a pang of guilt for how she'd felt about the man earlier that evening, when he'd grabbed her arm.

It had been him, hadn't it?

Another groom-to-be celebrating his bachelor party

like the last victim of the Slasher. What the hell did that person have against men like that?

Sure, this guy, whoever he was, had been a jerk. But the other man...

The victim she'd visited in the hospital hadn't seemed arrogant like that one. He'd even managed, despite his injuries, to laugh with her.

She wondered if tonight's victim would ever be able to laugh again. She wondered if she would, after finding him.

No wonder that Fletcher always seemed so intense. This was his life, the career he'd chosen for himself. To investigate crimes like the one that Kiki had literally stumbled across tonight.

The body.

No. The person. He had to live.

"Oh, Fancy..." Kiki murmured, her heart heavy with dread. With regret.

Maybe if she and Fletcher had done things differently...

Maybe if the man hadn't been evicted from the club...

Maybe he wouldn't have been hurt so badly.

Maybe he would be...

He had to be fine.

She wasn't sure that she would be again, after what she'd seen. She needed a beer and some soft music. Grandpa kept beer in the fridge in the galley on the boat. And she always had music with her. Either on her phone, or just inside her.

Maybe if she sang to herself...

People had said she was singing when she'd been found, in the wreckage of the crash that had killed her parents.

The wreckage she had escaped without a scratch on her. She didn't remember any of that. Maybe wiping the memories from her mind had been her childlike way of dealing with that horrific tragedy.

But she wasn't a child anymore. And she doubted she would be able to forget anything about tonight. About finding that man.

Or about that kiss she'd shared with Fletcher. If not for whatever had happened in the alley, maybe they would have…

No. Not in a parking lot. She wasn't some wild teen-ager. She never had been. She'd been tempted in that moment to act like a hormonal teen, though, to give in to her desire for Fletcher.

Thinking about that kiss should have been better than thinking about what had happened after it, but her pulse quickened even more. And the adrenaline was rushing through her again.

That kiss had been dangerous to her.

But why?

Fletcher had said he wasn't ever getting married, that he didn't have time for relationships either. And she certainly understood why. His work was definitely more important. Catching the Slasher was absolutely more important.

That was why, after answering the officer's questions, she'd left. The club had been pretty much sealed off, probably as a crime scene, so she trusted that her equipment would be safe there overnight.

She had another gig there this weekend, if the club was allowed to reopen, so it made sense to leave it there anyway. It was just so expensive, though, that she usually preferred to keep it with her.

But after what had happened to that man, she'd realized how inconsequential material things were. People mattered more. Maybe she should have stayed at Grandpa's.

But he was safe. Nothing was going to happen to him.

He was long past the age when he used to come to the clubs to watch her. She didn't have to worry about the Slasher attacking him.

But she still worried about him.

He'd always been there for her. She couldn't imagine a world without him in it.

Fancy whimpered again, reminding Kiki that she'd just stopped on the dock. She was near the houseboat, but her thoughts had been weighing so heavily on her that it seemed hard to step across the side and onto the boat deck. As if she might slip and fall between the boat and the dock.

Fancy probably feared that, too, because the puppy whimpered again.

"It's okay," Kiki assured her, and she bent over to scoop the puppy up in her arms. She held her close for a moment, burying her face in the dog's soft fur. Instead of reassuring the puppy, she was looking for comfort.

Maybe she should have woken up Grandpa. He had

always been so good at comforting her. At making her feel better about everything.

But he was getting older, and she didn't want to burden him with things like this, things that would make him worry more about her than he already did.

And he already worried too much.

She understood, though, because she worried about him, too. She didn't want to lose him like they'd already lost her mother and father. She didn't want to lose anyone else she loved. Another reason she needed to make sure this attraction she felt for Fletcher didn't go any deeper, didn't become real feelings.

After tonight, she realized all too well just how dangerous his job was. That could have been him bleeding out in the blood-soaked, overgrown field.

She shuddered. And Fancy bristled in her arms. "Sorry," she murmured to the puppy. She was definitely not making the little dog less nervous.

"Here," she said. And she passed the dog over the side of the boat before stepping onto the deck herself. The boat rocked a bit on the softly lapping water.

Then Fancy headed toward the door to the cabin. The open door.

It should have been locked. Kiki had certainly locked it the last time she'd been here. What about Grandpa? Had he forgotten?

He certainly believed Owl Creek was safer than anywhere else, which was why he preferred it when she was home. He had no idea how dangerous this place could be.

But after tonight, Kiki knew.

And she wondered if that danger had found her here.

Chapter 12

"Where the hell is she?" Fletcher asked.

But the night had no answer for him as he stood outside Jim's cottage. Her SUV wasn't parked in the driveway like it should have been, like he'd hoped it would be.

Sometime after she'd been questioned, she'd slipped away from the club. From the crime scene.

She'd even left her equipment behind, which had alarmed him. Why wouldn't she have waited for his help to load it up? Why would she have taken off without it?

While her equipment had been there, his duffel bag had gone missing. With that glass inside.

The bartender had stayed to answer questions, though, as had a couple of the waitresses, bouncers and dishwashers. They had all made certain to share that the last time they'd seen the victim had been when he'd been fighting with Fletcher over Kiki.

Was that why she'd taken off?

Did she suspect him of being involved like the club employees had?

No. The officer who'd questioned her had assured Fletcher that she'd alibied him. Even if the officer hadn't known that he was a detective, the young woman would have ruled him out as a suspect then.

Not that she was running the investigation. He was.

He told himself that was why he needed to find Kiki. But even he knew he was lying about that. He needed to find Kiki to make sure that she was all right. That she wasn't too upset about finding the latest victim of the Slasher and that the Slasher hadn't followed her from the crime scene.

Could they have been worried that she'd seen something?

Was that why they'd attacked the latest victim so far from the alley? So it would be harder for anyone to see the attack? Or to find the body?

This assault had been far more vicious than the others. And the blow to the head…

That was new. None of the other victims had had a wound like that, none had been hit over the head so hard that it had rendered them unconscious.

The wounded man hadn't regained consciousness after the paramedics had arrived either. Would he? On his way to Kiki's house, Fletcher had called the hospital in Conners where the man had been taken since there was only an express medical clinic in Owl Creek.

After identifying himself, Fletcher had asked for an update on the victim's condition.

From the wallet found on him, with all his money and credit cards in it, Fletcher knew the guy's name was Gregory Stehouwer. Stehouwer was in a coma. His head injury had been that severe, and they weren't sure he would wake up. Maybe he'd seen the Slasher. Could that be why he'd been hit so hard in the head? Maybe the Slasher had tried to kill him so that this victim wouldn't be able to identify them.

From the extent of that blow, Fletcher was beginning to lean toward a male assailant or a very strong female. The only thing Fletcher knew for certain about the Slasher was how dangerous they were.

So dangerous that he'd needed to make sure that Kiki had gotten safely home. But she wasn't home. Where the hell was she? And had she gone there on her own or had someone forced her to go where they'd wanted her to?

Or was he just overreacting because he'd been so damn shaken when she'd screamed?

He sighed, uncertain of whether or not he should knock. If he woke up Jim and alarmed him and she was fine, she would be furious. But if something had happened to her and he'd done nothing to find her...

"Who's out there?" a gruff voice called from the darkness within the house.

"Mr. Shelton?" he called back. "It's Fletcher Colton, sir."

A bright light flashed on, momentarily blinding him. He squinted and turned slightly away from the porch light.

"It is you," Jim Shelton said as he pulled open the interior door and peered at Fletcher through the screen. "Has something happened? What are you doing here?"

Fletcher's tongue stuck to the roof of his mouth for a moment as he considered his answer. Then he cleared his throat and said, "I saw Kiki at the club earlier tonight, and I had to follow up about something she saw."

Shelton released a heavy sigh. "Something happen again like that one in Conners and the other in Salt Lake City?"

Those weren't the only places where the Slasher had attacked, but those were the most recent. Fletcher gave a noncommittal shrug. "I don't know for certain, sir." And as he said it, he realized that it was true.

The whole MO of this felt so different than the other attacks and not just because of how severely the victim had been injured, but because he'd been so far from the club. The other victims had been left in the alley, where someone would almost certainly find him when they were cleaning up after the club closed.

This victim had been left out in a field beyond the parking lot, as if nobody had wanted him to be found. Or, at least, maybe not with enough time to save him.

"And you think Kiki will know what happened?" Shelton asked, and he stared intently through that screen.

Fletcher shrugged. "I don't know." Then, because he was being honest, he added, "Probably not."

Instead of being concerned, the older man chuckled. "Thought there was something-something between the two of you even at your daddy's funeral. Sorry about that, son. I really thought that Robert was too tough to die, at least so damn young."

To a man in his late seventies or early eighties, fifty-nine was young. Hell, to Fletcher, fifty-nine was young no matter how hard his dad had lived those years. Working too much, drinking, smoking and eating too much.

"How's your mama doing?" Shelton asked.

While not everybody had been a fan of his dad's, they all loved his mom. "She's doing well, sir," Fletcher replied. "More worried about the rest of us than herself."

"Sounds like your mama," Shelton said with a smile. "My Kiki is a lot like her—always worrying about me when she should be worrying about herself."

Fletcher was worried enough about her right now for the both of them. But he didn't want to concern her grandfather too much. At least not until he knew where and how she was.

"Have any idea where she might be, sir?" he asked.

Shelton chuckled. "Of course. She left a note when she picked up the puppy."

Fletcher should have realized that he hadn't heard the little shepherd yet. And if it had been here, the puppy probably would have been jumping on him. "Where did she go, sir?" he asked.

"The houseboat."

Blackbird Lake was so big that there were a few marinas on it as well as many, many private docks. Obviously, the houseboat wasn't docked at the cottage, or Kiki's vehicle would have been parked in the driveway where Fletcher had been hoping to find it.

"Where is that, sir?"

The older man pushed open the screen door and stepped onto the porch with Fletcher. "I'm not sure I should tell you since she didn't leave you a note."

Fletcher smiled. "I think she figured I was busy, so she didn't bother saying good-bye when she left." At least he hoped that was reason she had.

"And you really want to say good-bye to her?" Shelton pushed. The older man was shrewd. He obviously knew Fletcher was interested in his granddaughter.

But Fletcher didn't want him to know how worried about her he was. "I need to ask her a few questions, too."

Like if she regretted kissing him now. Or if she regretted it having to stop, like he did.

Most of all, he just wanted to make sure that she was safe.

"What the hell happened tonight?" Shelton asked, his voice sharper now as if he was irritated. "You know I'll hear about it."

Fletcher had made certain that there had been no reporters at the club tonight, and the ones who'd shown up in Conners had been denied a story. Nobody had answered any of their questions, and he'd also taken steps to protect the investigation from the Freedom of Information Act for now. Since it was an ongoing investigation, no reports could be shared with the public. He wanted to starve the Slasher of the very thing he or she seemed to crave most: fame.

But maybe that was why the Slasher had struck again so close to the last attack. Maybe he or she was chasing headlines, trying to get into the news again. Trying to get attention.

And if so, maybe Fletcher was to blame for that man's attack tonight. Not directly, like the bartender and other club staff had seemed to imply, but indirectly.

And when he'd thrown the man out of the club, he'd just about delivered him to the Slasher. But the guy hadn't left alone. Some of his entourage had left with him. Had he returned on his own?

For Kiki? Maybe that was why he'd been attacked near her vehicle.

"I really can't say, sir," Fletcher said. "You know how quickly gossip spreads in Owl Creek."

"But would it be gossip?" Shelton asked.

Fletcher sighed. "Not exactly gossip…but not exactly fact either. Until an investigation is complete, it's all pretty much just speculation."

Fletcher had been doing a lot of that because he'd had no real leads to the Slasher until now. Now he had many leads to follow. The bartender. The distraught father.

And Kiki's missing assistant.

He just hoped none of them had followed Kiki from the club and then to wherever this houseboat was.

"You're about as slippery as that minister from that strange, fairy-tale church."

"Fairy-tale church?"

"You know. The Ever After Church."

Fletcher tensed. That was the church that the guy who'd gone after Ruby had been obsessed with, so much so that he'd been trying to get Crosswinds for them. Supposedly unbeknownst to the pastor, though.

Or was it?

"Markus Acker?" Fletcher asked.

"What?"

"The minister you're talking about," Fletcher prodded him.

"Yeah, that's probably it," the older man said with a shrug. "I've only seen him a couple of times, usually running around the countryside." Then Jim Shelton yawned.

Fletcher had been so tired himself earlier, but once he'd kissed Kiki...

All hell had broken loose in more ways than one. "Sir," he prodded the man. "I really need to talk to your granddaughter."

Shelton sniffed as if he was smelling a load of bullshit. And he kind of was.

Fletcher wasn't being entirely honest with him. And even the old man must have realized that Fletcher wanted to do more than talk to her. What had he called it? The something-something between them?

Fletcher grinned.

And the old man chuckled and shook his head. "You can go see her." He gave him the name of the marina and the slip number. "But don't say I didn't warn you."

"Warn me? About what?"

"Kiki's not settling down anytime soon," Shelton said. "She only comes here as much as she does out of obligation for me."

"Love," Fletcher corrected him.

And Shelton grinned. "Yeah, she's a sweetheart. But she's also as stubborn as..." His grin widened. "As her grandfather. Nobody's going to tie that girl down or tell her what to do."

"I don't want to tie her down," Fletcher assured him. But now...

He shook his head to clear those kinds of *something-something* thoughts from it.

He just wanted to make sure that she was all right.

"I know," Shelton said with another yawn. "You want to *talk* to her."

Fletcher nodded. "Thanks for telling me where she is." And he hoped like hell that the old man was right that she was at the houseboat.

Safe.

But a sudden chill rushed over him, and his fear returned. And he felt like he had when he'd heard her scream.

Like she was in danger.

Kiki may have stood there for seconds, frozen on the deck as she stared at the open door. But it wasn't just open. The glass in the door had been broken; shards of it littered the deck, sparkling in the faint glow of that crescent moon.

Grandpa hadn't forgotten to lock the houseboat. Neither had Kiki.

Someone had broken in. Were they still there?

She'd stood there, frozen, wondering what to do. Call the cops? Grab her pepper spray? But Fancy hadn't stayed beside her. Instead she'd walked over that glass and into the cabin area of the houseboat.

Now she barked and then yipped, like she'd been

hurt. Thinking of that man, how badly he'd been injured, Kiki charged forward, her pepper spray clasped tightly in her hand. She wasn't even scared. She was furious.

"Don't hurt her!" she yelled. "Don't you dare hurt her!" With her free hand, she fumbled for the switch inside the galley kitchen. Light flickered on over her head and spilled into the living area of the boat and onto the man who lay on the couch, the dog nipping at his worn jeans. "Troy!"

"I'm not hurting her," he said, as he pushed the dog back.

The puppy nipped at his hand.

"Fancy!" she called. The dog turned toward her, and she made the gesture of her hand at her side, palm up, and then bent it toward her opposite shoulder. The shoulder of her hand that still held the pepper spray. "Come."

The dog glanced back at Troy, as if still uncertain of him, before finally obeying Kiki's command. She planted her bristling little puppy body, her hair raised, between Kiki and Troy. Her protectiveness was as instinctual as Sebastian considered her "scent" skills. Maybe Fletcher's need to protect was just as instinctual.

If only he could have protected her from what she'd seen…

Did she need protection now? From Troy?

"What the hell are you doing here?" she asked. "The police are looking for you."

"I know," he said. "That's why I'm here. You showed me this place when I first got to Owl Creek."

On the way to show him the campground where he'd rented a space, she'd stopped off at the marina to check on the boat. He'd been nervous around the water, though, as nervous as he'd been around the club.

She'd thought he'd just been on edge after what he'd seen in Salt Lake City. After finding that victim...

Was Fletcher right? Was that too much of a coincidence?

But then she'd been working the club in Conners and then tonight...

She resisted the urge to shudder over the memory of what she'd found, of how that hand had wrapped around her ankle and she'd thought it was the Slasher that grabbed her, not the Slasher's latest victim.

"I didn't intend for you to use this boat, especially not to hide out from the authorities," she said.

"I'm not... I can't..." he stammered.

"They just want to talk to you about what happened at that club in Conners last weekend," she said. Had he been here all week?

He swung his legs down from the couch and sat up.

She tensed, worried that he was going to jump up, that he was going to come at her since she was between him and the door. The door that he'd broken to get inside.

Could she trust him? She knew now how very little he'd told her about himself.

But instead of getting up, he leaned forward and put his head in his hands. "That's so messed up, Kiki."

"Yes, it is," she agreed.

"I'm sorry I didn't get there in time to help you tonight," he said.

She tensed. "You were at the club tonight?"

"Yeah. I showed up late, though, and you had someone else there," he said, with a hurt tone, almost as if she'd betrayed him. "Who is he?"

The lawman who considered him the prime suspect in his Slasher case.

"An old friend," she said. "I've known him for years." That was true. But she'd left out important details, just like Troy had about himself. Troy had left out that he was a criminal. She'd left out that Fletcher was a cop. "I thought you were a friend, too, Troy, but then I realized how little I know about you."

He looked up at her then. "You know me, Kiki. We've known each other for years."

"Yes," she said. "But how is it possible that I didn't even know your last name?"

"You never asked."

She could kick herself now for not vetting her assistant more thoroughly. That another DJ had been using him for years wasn't an excuse. She realized that now. "And I didn't know about your criminal record either."

"The cops told you about that?" he asked, and he sucked in a breath.

Was he worried about her knowing? Or that the police knew? Probably the police, since he was hiding from them. What would he do to stay hidden?

She tightened her grasp on her pepper spray. She didn't want to use it, but she would if she felt threatened. "Yes, they were concerned with you taking off after that man was wounded at the club. You need to talk to them."

"I didn't see anything," Troy said, his voice rising with irritation. "I've got nothing to tell them!"

Fancy barked.

"Heel," Kiki told the puppy. She didn't want Troy doing to Fancy whatever he'd done that had made the dog yelp before Kiki had followed her into the houseboat cabin. "They still need to speak to you, Troy. To rule you out—"

"I'm a suspect?" he interjected and jumped up then.

And Fancy jumped too, her body bristling as she growled low in her throat. The puppy obviously didn't trust Troy any more than Fletcher did, and probably any more than Kiki should.

She needed to call the police.

Or Fletcher.

Troy raised his foot, as if to kick Fancy who'd jumped toward him.

"No!" Kiki screamed. "Don't hurt—"

Pounding cut off her protest. The sound of running footsteps against the dock. She whirled around and Troy shoved past her, knocking her back against the kitchen cabinets. Then his footsteps echoed that other pounding. And then a splash.

And the boat rocked, hitting against the dock.

Somebody had gone into the lake.

Troy?

Or whoever had been running down the dock?

To rescue her?

Or…

Chapter 13

Kiki's scream affected Fletcher the way it had at the club. His heart pounded with fear for her, for her safety. For her life.

She'd only let out the first note, and he'd started running down the dock, toward the slip number where her grandfather had said he would find the boat.

She had to be on it. Probably inside, because her scream had been a bit muffled. He'd heard the "Don't hurt—" and panicked. He'd drawn his weapon and started running.

He didn't need to check the slip numbers to find her boat because a man leaped off it, onto the dock, and started running toward the end of it. Toward the water.

In the moonlight, Fletcher could see the guy's long, straggly hair and the tattoos on his arms. Was this Troy?

The same Troy others had seen at the club tonight? And then he'd come back here?

Had he been hiding? Or had he suspected that Kiki would come out to the boat and he'd been lying in wait for her? She had to be okay. Through the glass window of the cabin, Fletcher could see her standing.

She didn't look to be injured.

And Fletcher couldn't let Troy escape from him again. So he chased after him. And when Troy jumped off the end of the dock into the water, Fletcher holstered his weapon and followed him into the lake.

Despite it being mid-June, the water was surprisingly cold. And it sucked at Fletcher's clothes and boots.

Those already heavy boots got heavier as the leather sopped up the water. And they began to drag him down, like cement blocks tied to his feet. He kicked and chopped at the water with his arms, trying to fight his way back to the surface as the breath he'd held burned in his lungs.

He had to get out of the lake now, or he might not be able to. He couldn't see anything in the water. Troy might have gotten out. Or Fletcher might have gone so deep that he couldn't see even the moonlight on the surface anymore.

He kicked harder, using his strength. Suddenly light shone on him, and he realized he was at the surface again. But the boots kept pulling at him, dragging him down. He reached out for the dock, grabbing one of the wood posts.

The light shining on him was from a cell phone held

in Kiki's hand. "Are you all right?" she asked. "Do I need to call 9-1-1?"

He panted for air, dragging in deep gulps of it while hanging on to that post. He had to pull himself up and out before his grasp on that post slipped. "I'll be fine…" he said between pants.

The light dimmed. And then Kiki reached down to grab his arms and try to pull him up. He worked with her until finally he lay on the dock, water dripping from his saturated clothes.

"Are you all right?" she asked again as she knelt beside him, leaning over him. She was so beautiful and held so much concern in her dark eyes.

And he remembered that kiss in the parking lot before everything had gone to hell.

"Want to give me mouth to mouth?" he asked, unable to resist teasing her.

She chuckled and leaned back. "I guess you are all right then."

He nodded then tensed. "Troy? Where is he?"

"He got out of the water before you did," she said, her breath hitching a little.

"Did he hurt you?" he asked, reaching up to grasp her arms.

She flinched and shook her head.

"But you're hurt."

"That's from that other guy on the dance floor."

He had hurt her, but despite that, he hadn't deserved what had happened to him.

"Did he make it?" she asked, her voice cracking slightly now.

"The last update I got, he was alive, but in a coma," Fletcher shared. And he'd just let one of the suspects in his attack get away. He used his elbows to push himself up so that he was sitting. "Where did Troy go?"

She shrugged. "He got out of the lake farther down the shore." She pointed in the distance. "And ran off into the woods."

Fletcher struggled to roll over onto his knees and then push himself up to his feet. But his legs were weak from all the kicking he'd had to do to keep from getting sucked to the bottom of the lake, and they nearly folded beneath him.

Kiki caught him around the waist. "You're not going to catch him even if you could run."

He could barely take a step; his boots were so heavy with water that it was hard to lift his foot. "These damn boots," he grumbled.

"Yeah, it's the boots," Kiki said. "Grandpa leaves some clothes on the boat. Let's get you something dry."

"But Troy…" He'd been so damn close to catching him. To maybe catching the Slasher. He had to stop that maniac, had to make sure that he didn't hurt anyone else.

"He's gone," she repeated. "And he got a hell of a head start on you. You're not going to find him."

He pulled his cell from his pocket, and water streamed out of the case. He cursed.

"Do you want to call 9-1-1?" she asked. "I have my phone."

Fletcher shook his head and spattered water around the dock and across her face.

"You're like a dog," she remarked.

And he glanced around. "Your grandpa said you had Fancy. Did something happen to her?" He hated to think of the sweet little pup being injured.

"I locked her in the bathroom on the boat," she said. "I didn't want her getting in the water. Or Troy hurting her."

"Troy hurt her?" he asked. A man who could hurt an animal could easily hurt people, too.

Her teeth lightly nipped her bottom lip and she shrugged. "I don't know. She got onto the houseboat before I did, and she made a yipping noise. She seems fine though."

"Want me to call Ruby?" he asked. "Have her check Fancy out?"

"No," she said. "Ruby's pregnant. She needs her rest, especially after what she went through and then losing your dad so soon after that. We can't wake her up."

Fletcher's heart warmed with a flood of appreciation for this woman. "You're a good friend to her." So good that he shouldn't have involved Kiki in his undercover operation. He'd put her in danger.

And Ruby would probably never forgive him if something happened to her friend because of him.

"This was a bad idea," he murmured.

"What?"

He glanced around, wondering who else he and Troy might have awakened when they'd run down the dock. There were quite a few other boats in the marina. And maybe Troy wasn't as far away as Kiki thought he was.

Maybe he had circled around and come back. Maybe he was out there somewhere, listening.

Waiting.

Fletcher couldn't talk to her here. And he had to make sure that his weapon worked after jumping in the lake with it, in case Troy came back.

"Where's that boat?" he asked. And he pulled his T-shirt away from his body.

"I'm sorry," she said. "You must be getting cold." But she was the one that shivered as a breeze blew across the lake, making all the boats rock. "It's this way."

Her arm was still around his waist, as if she thought he needed help walking. While his boots were still so heavy, his strength had returned along with his usual reaction to her nearness: attraction. So he pulled away from her.

She still wore his shirt—the one he'd given her at the club. And it was wet now, her red leather vest showing through it.

"You're probably cold," he remarked. But he sure wasn't, not when just looking at her had heat flashing through him. Along with that damn desire he had no business feeling, not in the middle of a dangerous investigation. Not when his cover was putting her in danger.

"I'm fine," she said as she led the way down the long dock. She stopped outside a houseboat. Whimpering emanated from somewhere inside it.

"Poor Fancy," he said. "Are you sure she's all right?" He jumped over to the boat deck. And glass crunched beneath his wet boots. "He broke in here."

"Yes."

"To do what?" he asked. "Wait for you?"

"I think he was just hiding out," Kiki said. "But he admitted to being at the club earlier."

Fletcher cursed. Had he been that close to the Slasher just to lose him in the water?

Fancy must have heard Fletcher's voice because her whimpering became yips again. But not yips of pain. Yips of excitement.

The puppy had fallen hard for Fletcher.

Kiki had to make sure the dog was the only one who fell for him. Not her.

She couldn't stop shaking, but it wasn't with cold. She'd been so scared when he hadn't surfaced from the water. She'd known it was him when she'd heard that splash. Him who'd come clomping so loudly down the dock in the boots that had probably nearly killed him.

But he was strong. He'd fought his way to the surface again. And now he rushed inside the houseboat.

Fancy's yips got louder when he opened the bathroom door. And when Kiki joined them inside, she found him running his hands over the little dog as if checking her for injuries like his sister, the vet, would have.

His genuine concern for the puppy got under Kiki's skin in the best possible way. As if he wasn't hard enough to resist with the way his wet clothes had molded against his muscular body.

With the way his slick hair highlighted all those chiseled features of his handsome face...

"I think she's okay," he said. "She's not flinching or pulling away from me."

That was because the dog was smart. She liked those big hands of his moving over her little furry body. And suddenly Kiki was very jealous of the puppy. She wanted those big hands of his moving over her body. But she wanted to be naked. And she wanted him naked, too.

"I'm glad she's okay," Kiki said.

"That's why you screamed," Fletcher said. "Because you were worried he was going to hurt her?"

She nodded. "But I don't want to talk about Troy right now," she said. She didn't want to talk at all. "You need to get out of those wet clothes."

Maybe he'd picked up on the huskiness in her voice as the desire she felt for him grew, because he tensed and met her gaze. His green eyes darkened as his pupils dilated. "Kiki…" he murmured, and his voice was even raspier than hers.

And Fancy wriggled down from him to go over to the couch and sniff at it before dropping down on it, her head on her paws as if exhausted.

Maybe she was.

Kiki should have been, too, but adrenaline still coursed through her body, making her tremble. "Is this what you think is a bad idea?" she asked, referring to that comment he'd made on the dock but hadn't expounded on.

He clenched his jaw so tightly that a muscle twitched in his cheek. Then he sighed. "I shouldn't have involved you in this investigation. I shouldn't have put you in danger."

"You didn't," she said.

"But Troy—"

"Is my assistant," she reminded him. "I know you think he's the Slasher, too, but I can't imagine…" She shook her head. "I don't want to talk about Troy. And everything else that happened would have happened whether you were there or not. You didn't put me in danger."

She had.

And she was probably the most at risk right now. But she didn't care. She stepped closer to him and told him, "Take off your clothes."

He sucked in a breath and murmured her name again almost as if he was warning her. He didn't have to say anything else.

"I know," she said. "This is a bad idea. But nobody needs to know about this but us."

"You're already distracting me," he said. "If we—"

She shrugged off the shirt she wore over her vest. His shirt which was wet from where she'd touched him. Then she reached for the zipper at the front of her vest. "Maybe if we do this, we'll be less distracted," she suggested.

He chuckled. "Somehow I don't think it'll work like that." But he leaned down to take off his boots. His holster followed. He took a few minutes to take his weapon apart, probably to let it dry out.

Before he could do anything else, Kiki took his hand in hers and tugged him toward her bedroom. She had her own on the boat just like her grandpa had his, although he rarely stayed there now. After pushing open the pocket door, she stepped into the room, which was so small that there wasn't much floor space around the queen-size bed. So she climbed onto it and reached again for the zipper on her vest, pulling it down so that the red leather fell away from her.

Fletcher groaned as if he was in pain.

"Did you get hurt when you jumped in the lake?" she asked, concerned now that she hadn't called 9-1-1.

He shook his head. "No. You're the one killing me. You're so damn beautiful." He leaned over then and pressed his mouth against hers, kissing her deeply, sliding his tongue between her open lips.

She groaned now. No. She moaned. Then she pulled back. "You need to take off your wet clothes," she reminded him. And she reached for the button on his jeans.

He shoved what looked like the ammo clip from his gun into his pocket. Then he pulled his wet T-shirt over his head as she lowered his zipper.

His breath hissed out as her fingers brushed over his boxers, over his straining erection. As she pushed his jeans down over his lean hips, he slid her open vest from her shoulders, freeing her breasts.

And his breath hissed out again. "You are so beautiful." He cupped her breasts in his hands, running his thumbs over her skin and then over her nipples.

She moaned again as pleasure coursed through her. Her breasts had always been sensitive, but never more so than now. In this moment.

He lowered his head then and closed his mouth around one breast and stroked his tongue across her tight nipple.

"Fletcher," she whispered. She wanted him so badly.

Then he was undoing the button and lowering her

zipper and pulling off her shorts and underwear. "Are you sure?" he asked, his voice gruff with the desire burning in his eyes.

Like it burned inside her.

She eagerly nodded. "Very sure and very impatient." She wanted to go fast and furiously, joining their bodies.

But he took his time. As he turned his attention to her other breast with his mouth, his hands moved over her body. He caressed her skin, traced her curves and then he touched her core.

And she whimpered like Fancy had.

And Fancy yipped with concern.

Fletcher got up and closed the door. Then he was back between her legs. And he made love to her with his mouth and his tongue, driving her out of her mind until pleasure coursed through her with an orgasm that left her quivering.

But it wasn't enough. She wanted more. So she pushed him back onto the bed and pulled off his boxers. Then she lowered her mouth to his shaft. She closed her lips around him, and he tensed. Then he was gently pushing her shoulders back.

"No. I want to be inside you," he said, his voice hoarse. "I need to be inside you." Then he cursed. "But I don't have any—"

She fumbled inside a small cupboard next to the bed, feeling around until she found a packet. She tore it open with her teeth and rolled the condom over him. He was so big. So hard.

She straddled him, easing him inside her until he

filled her. The sensation had her muscles tensing again, pressure building inside her. She leaned down, her breasts rubbing against his chest. The hair tickled her skin, teased her nipples. She moaned and moved.

And he grasped her hips and thrust up, driving deeper. Driving her out of her mind.

It was like they were dancing to the same music, the same beat inside them, their hearts pounding together. They moved in unison.

Then his hands moved from her hips to her breasts, and he stroked her nipples with his thumbs.

She came again, intensely, and a cry of pleasure slipped through her lips. Then he tensed beneath her and began to pulsate inside her as he found his release.

His pleasure.

Her name slipped through his gritted teeth.

She couldn't remember the last time she'd ever been so in sync with a lover. Maybe never.

Fletcher rolled her onto her back and kissed her, brushing his mouth lightly across hers, as he drew out of her body. Then he opened the pocket door and disappeared for a while.

She had just begun to wonder if he'd left when he came back, smelling like soap and midnight rain and sex. And she welcomed him back into her bed, into her arms.

They made love again, slowly, savoring every second. And after another soul-shattering orgasm, she fell asleep. She didn't know how long she'd been out when she felt Fletcher jump next to her.

He must have fallen asleep, too, only to jerk awake.

Then she heard it, the noise he must have heard. The sound of Fancy's low growl. Was she warning them of an intruder?

Had someone broken into the houseboat once again?

Chapter 14

Tension gripped Fletcher as he silently cursed himself. How the hell had he fallen asleep?

He knew how, though. He'd been completely satiated and exhausted and comfortable. And he hadn't wanted his time with Kiki to end.

But no matter what she'd said, he'd put her in danger once again. The way Fancy growled outside the bedroom door indicated that there was some kind of threat out there.

Had Troy come back? Was he going to finish whatever he'd intended to do to Kiki?

Because Fletcher wasn't as convinced as she was that the man had just been hiding out on the houseboat. What if he'd been waiting for her to come back here?

What had he intended to do to her?

And if he was the Slasher, and armed with that dangerously sharp weapon that had already wounded so many others, how the hell was Fletcher going to defend her and himself?

He'd left his gun in pieces, drying out on the counter in the main cabin area. The magazine of ammo was in his jeans. Jeans he quickly stepped into and pulled up.

But before he could reach for the door, Kiki grabbed his arm as if trying to hold him back. "What is it?" she whispered, her voice a little shaky. She was as wide awake as he was now.

"I don't know," he whispered back. But he was going to damn well find out.

"Take my pepper spray," she said, pressing a small canister in his hand.

He closed his hand around it. While it wasn't his gun, it was better than nothing. If the Slasher couldn't see, maybe he or she wouldn't be able to slice Fletcher up like they had their other victims.

He drew in a breath and then opened the pocket door. Morning had come, and sunshine poured through the windows in the houseboat cabin. In the middle of the living room area, Fancy did battle, growling and gnawing on one of the Fletcher's new boots.

Fletcher released the breath he'd been holding and chuckled.

Kiki leaned around him and peered out. Then she pushed past him and ran over to the puppy. Fortunately, for Fletcher's sake, she'd pulled on a terry cloth robe. "Drop it," she commanded the dog as she pointed at the floor.

The puppy whined and wagged her tail as she kept the boot tightly clamped in her mouth.

"I understand why she'd want to destroy those things," Fletcher said. "I'm not too fond of them myself."

"Drop it," Kiki repeated, pointing at the floor again.

Fancy whined one more time, as if pleading with Kiki before she finally dropped the mangled heap of damp leather.

"Impressive," Fletcher said. "You really know a lot about dog training."

Kiki shrugged. "I wanted to learn so that we can start getting her familiar with commands right away."

"Show me," he said. He wasn't really interested. He just didn't want to leave her. Not yet. Maybe not ever.

He pushed the thought aside and focused on the commands that she showed him.

"She doesn't know all of them yet," Kiki said. "We introduce them one at a time." She showed him Sit, which was holding out her hand in front of her, with her palm facing up, then raising it toward her shoulder. "Wait and Stay are almost the same." She held her hand out in front of her, her palm facing Fancy. "And probably the most important to keep her out of trouble."

She showed him a couple more. Lie Down and Up.

"She knows quite a few."

"She's a smart dog," Kiki said.

"And you're a good trainer. Maybe you've missed your calling."

"Music is my calling," she insisted. "I love it."

"I can tell that, too," he said.

"Do you love being a detective?" she asked.

He nodded. "It can be frustrating at times." Like now, trying to catch the Slasher.

"And dangerous," she added.

He shrugged. "Life is full of dangers."

And he'd faced one of the most perilous situations last night. Not when he'd jumped in the lake and nearly drowned. But when he'd drowned in her last night, in the emotions overwhelming him.

He wanted to be with her again. But he'd already dropped the ball on this investigation too many times. "I have to go," he said. The clock on the wall alarmed him. "I didn't realize it was so late already."

Her bedroom had been dark and so very comfortable with her soft bed and her softer body curled up in his arms.

"You were up late," she reminded him.

He wasn't sure if she was talking about the club or about what they'd done in the bed. But he nodded. "I need to go, to check on the victim from last night."

She tensed and nodded. "Yes, let me know how he's doing."

They both hesitated, staring at each other. He didn't want to leave her. He found an excuse for that. "You shouldn't stay here by yourself. Just in case Troy comes back."

"After you chased him off the dock, I doubt he's going to come back," she said. "But I should go back to Grandpa's, make sure he knows I'm okay, just in case he heard anything about last night. Did you tell him about it?"

He shook his head. "No. I didn't want to worry him."

"He already worries too much about me," Kiki said.

"He's going to hear about it," Fletcher said. "I'm trying to keep it all out of the press, but people are going to talk to the media eventually or post something somewhere."

"Like they did after the attack in Salt Lake City," she said. "I saw the reports about it right away."

"These last two attacks weren't discovered until after closing," Fletcher said. "That's why they were easier to keep quiet. And club employees don't want to talk about them and risk losing business for their bosses. Too much bad press could cost them their jobs."

She nodded. "That make sense."

"It's about the only thing about this that does."

She smiled. "Are you talking about the case or what we did last night?" she asked.

Thinking about what they did had him taking a step toward her, almost involuntarily.

But she held up her hand, palm facing him, like she'd done with the puppy.

"Wait or stay?" he asked her.

"You have to go," she reminded him. "And last night was to get rid of the distraction of whatever this is between us."

"Something-something," he said.

"What?"

"That's what your grandfather called it," he shared. "That's why he told me where to find you."

Her face flushed. "Oh, Grandpa…" she murmured.

"You're right," Fletcher said. "He is cooler than I am."

"Yes, he is," she agreed with a smile. "And I should go, too, back to the cottage to check on him."

"And I should go," Fletcher repeated. But he really didn't want to leave her and not just because he was worried about her safety.

But if he stayed, he was going to have to worry about *his* safety. He had to leave before he really started falling for her. Because her cool grandfather had already warned Fletcher that she wasn't going to settle down anytime soon.

Not that Fletcher wanted her to. He never wanted to settle down either. All he really wanted was to do his job and catch the Slasher.

He had a feeling that he'd been close to doing that last night, but the man had escaped. And Fletcher had nearly drowned. "I have to ask you something, Kiki," he said.

She tensed. "If it's about last night, you were probably right. It was a bad idea."

He sucked in a breath, feeling like she'd punched him. "That's not what I was going to ask you about," he said.

Her face flushed. "Then what?"

"Troy. Is he left-handed?"

Her forehead furrowed as if she was trying to remember and then she nodded. "Yes, I think he is. Why?"

"Because the Slasher is, too."

"She's fine," Ruby said as she lifted Fancy down from her exam table and placed her on the floor of the medical office area of Crosswinds Training Center.

Kiki released a shaky breath of relief. After the

puppy's run-in with Troy last night, she'd been worrying about her. She and Grandpa fostered puppies to help them, not hurt them. "That's good."

"How are you?" Ruby's green eyes narrowed slightly as she studied Kiki's face, but not with that same unnerving intensity that Fletcher did.

Fletcher.

Just thinking of him had a rush of heat flashing through her body. He was such an incredible lover. Last night, or this morning—whatever time it had been—had turned out to be more than a distraction. But like she'd told him earlier this morning, it had been a bad idea. Because, after how incredible it had been between them, she was afraid that she was going to want to do it again. And again.

"I'm—I'm fine," Kiki said.

Ruby's eyes narrowed. "I hate to say this because I was sick of hearing it myself, but you look kind of tired."

Kiki was well aware of the dark circles beneath her eyes. "It was a late night at the club," she said, which was the truth. But she knew that Fletcher wanted to keep the attack as quiet as he could, so she wouldn't share that with his sister. She also didn't want to worry Ruby. The pregnant woman had already been through enough.

"Is that all?" Ruby asked.

"Yes."

"Because I heard about those attacks outside some nightclubs," Ruby said. "And I've been worried about you."

"The victims have all been men," Kiki said. "So I'm

safe." She wasn't worried about her life. She was worried about her heart.

Not that she was going to give it to Fletcher. She was too busy, and he certainly was as well. Last night was not going to be repeated. A pang of disappointment hit her, but she ignored it.

Instead of looking relieved, Ruby's face tensed with concern. "Mom said Fletcher didn't come home last night."

"I'm sure he wasn't attacked," Kiki said, wanting to reassure her friend, who'd already been through too much, but also not reveal why she was so certain.

"I know," Ruby said. "He's probably fine. He's a really good detective. He's obsessed with work. Maybe too obsessed. The reason he didn't come home was undoubtedly because he was working all night. So there must be something criminal going on again in Owl Creek." She shuddered. "I was just hoping the danger was all behind us now."

"He's a detective," Kiki gently reminded her friend. "He's always going to be working some case or another."

"He wouldn't have stayed out all night unless it was something serious, though," Ruby said.

Kiki shrugged. "Or maybe he's seeing someone." He'd certainly seen a lot of her the night before. Or actually morning.

Ruby laughed and shook her head. "I doubt that. He's only been back a little while. And with the funeral and staying with Mom, he wouldn't have had time to meet anyone. Unless..." She looked at Kiki almost hopefully.

Kiki bit her tongue so that she wouldn't say any more. Fletcher didn't want anyone to know about the Slasher, so he probably wouldn't want his sister to know he'd gone undercover with Kiki to investigate. He'd also gone undercover with Kiki last night, but that had been for an entirely other reason, for pleasure. Heat rushed to her face and her body, just as it had last night.

"It's probably for the best if you two don't get involved," Ruby said.

Kiki fought hard to maintain a neutral expression, to give nothing away about how involved she'd gotten with Ruby's brother.

The veterinarian continued, "Fletcher has never had good luck with relationships."

"Why's that?" Kiki asked as if she was only mildly curious and not wildly so.

Ruby sighed. "He's too much like Dad maybe. Throws himself into his work and doesn't leave time for anything else."

"Seems like I remember another Colton doing the same thing," Kiki teased.

"Ditto, my friend," Ruby said. "You're so busy yourself, always going from city to city, living your dream."

"Chasing it," Kiki murmured. She needed to make a few more connections. Maybe this fall, once fishing season was done and she returned to LA. Maybe there she would find the connection to get a record label interested in her music.

Or maybe she needed to spend some time in Nashville or Detroit.

She could find the connections she needed there, too. Probably anywhere but Owl Creek. But the connections she had here were for her heart. Grandpa. And Ruby.

And Fancy.

"Thanks for checking her out for me," Kiki said.

"What did you think happened to her?" Ruby asked. "She seems fine, if just a little tired like you are." The puppy had passed out in a corner of the exam room.

"She was eating leather again," Kiki said, omitting the fact that Troy might have kicked her. Or done something else that had made her yip in pain like she had.

She definitely hadn't known her assistant very well at all. What if Fletcher's suspicions were right and he was the Slasher? Would she be able to forgive herself for not realizing sooner how dangerous the man was?

Maybe she would have saved some of the victims from disfigurements—or worse if the one she'd found last night hadn't made it.

Maybe that was why she'd wanted Fletcher so badly last night. Because she hadn't wanted to think about any of the horrible things that were going on.

She'd certainly forgotten for a while.

And she'd gone to the houseboat because she'd thought she wouldn't be able to sleep. But she'd slept in Fletcher's arms. She'd felt safe.

But that was kind of ironic given that she might have the most to fear from him if she did something stupid. Like fall for him.

Because his sister had made it very clear how badly Fletcher sucked at relationships. Not that her track record was any better.

She'd never found anyone who'd been supportive of her dreams and not critical. She'd never found anyone who was willing to work around her crazy schedule. She'd never found anyone who'd loved her besides her grandfather and her friends.

"Are you sure you're all right?" Ruby asked with concern.

Kiki nodded. "Yes, just tired. Like Fancy. Now that I know she's okay I'll be able to get some sleep." But she wondered if she would without Fletcher's arms around her, holding her close.

But that was just because of what had happened. She'd needed the distraction of sex with him and the comfort of his closeness so that she could forget about the Slasher for a little while.

But when she carried Fancy out to her SUV and opened the passenger's door, she noticed a piece of paper lying on the floor that she hadn't noticed before.

She opened it up and noticed, from the direction of the cursive, that a left-handed person had written the note: *I am not the Slasher.*

Troy.

He must have slipped it inside her vehicle last night or this morning. He'd realized he was a suspect. Or he was defensive because he was guilty.

And maybe Fletcher was right. Maybe she was in more danger than she thought from the Slasher. Because if she knew who he was, he might consider her a threat.

Chapter 15

The club closed for a week, under the guise of maintenance, after Kiki had found the latest victim. This had been a good thing for Fletcher because he hadn't had to worry about maintaining his cover. If he hadn't already been compromised…

One of the other officers or techs who'd shown up at the scene might have slipped up and revealed that he was not really a suspect. That he was actually running the investigation into the Slasher. He would know when the club reopened in a couple of days.

But his cover wasn't all he had to worry about losing, though. He'd lost his objectivity and his resolve, too. He needed to be focused on finding the Slasher, not on Kiki. But despite working hard to find out all he could about Troy Hoover, Bart Taylor and Dan Sullivan, he hadn't been able to stop thinking about her.

About what they'd done.

About how damn amazing it had been, and *she* was.

She'd dropped off the note Troy Hoover had left in her vehicle, probably when it had been parked at the marina. Hopefully not while she'd been at Crosswinds.

Hopefully Troy was not following her around, but if he was, at least he knew that she'd gone to the police with his note instead of blindly accepting his word that he wasn't the Slasher.

Fletcher hadn't been at the station when she'd brought the note by. After going home to change clothes, he'd made the drive to the hospital in Conners where Greg Stehouwer, the Slasher's latest victim, was still lying in a coma. Not wanting to blow his cover, Fletcher had avoided the waiting room where the victim's family was and had only spoken with the doctor who hadn't been able to tell Fletcher anything but that the prognosis wasn't good.

The Slasher's attacks might have escalated to murder, just as Fletcher had feared they would. And so, he'd spent the past few days trying to find out as much as he could about all his suspects.

But he couldn't help but think that he was missing something. Or maybe he was just missing *someone*. Kiki. Despite how tired he should have been, he wasn't sleeping well because he wanted to sleep with her.

To get some perspective on his case, and maybe on his life, he'd stopped by Book Mark It, his sister Frannie's bookstore café. The long three-story building on Main Street squeezed narrowly between other buildings. This one was all exposed brick and cement floors. Until the Slasher had struck in Conners, he'd been spending a lot of time there because there hadn't been much else to do.

Frannie bustled around, working the café and the book counter, serving drinks and suggesting book choices to her patrons.

His sister was in her element, like Kiki was in the club. Frannie didn't quite have the adoring fans that Kiki had, though. Nobody screamed her name and tried to grab her, except for an older lady customer who gave her a hug over the loss of their dad.

After she was released, Frannie blinked furiously, clearing a rush of tears from her hazel eyes. Fletcher flinched over the twinges of concern and guilt that struck him. He should have been checking in more with his family, making sure that they were all doing okay after Dad's death. The first week, he'd stopped by the bookstore often, but he and Frannie hadn't really talked about Dad. Just his boring cases.

He hadn't checked on his other siblings. And even though he lived with his mom, he hadn't been seeing much of her either with the long hours he'd been working. So much for staying there to be a comfort for her.

He hadn't been a comfort to anyone.

As Frannie walked to the door, Fletcher glanced around the shop. He wanted to talk to his sister, but he didn't want anyone else to overhear them. About their recent loss or about his case.

Fletcher had noticed a man sitting in the corner

when he'd first walked into the store. While he didn't know the guy's name, Fletcher recognized him from his other visits to Book Mark It. He'd been here before, planted in a corner, reading a book. Even sitting down, it was easy to see that the guy was tall, with his long legs stretched out in front of him. He had a book open, but it was almost as if he was using it to hide behind instead of to read. The guy was still there, and he seemed to be watching Frannie even more intently than Fletcher had been.

Maybe the stranger kept coming around because he was interested in the bookstore owner. Frannie was pretty, with golden highlights in her hair and hazel eyes that sparkled. But there was something about the way the stranger seemed to be watching, but not wanting to be seen, that unsettled Fletcher. And it wasn't just brotherly protectiveness gnawing at him, but police instincts.

He tried to get a better look at the guy's face. But the book blocked most of it. He only lowered it when Frannie walked back from the door, and the guy's dark eyes focused on her again. He had dark hair, too, cut very short, which seemed at odds with the scruff on his face. Some gray was mixed in that scruff, so he was probably older than Frannie's twenty-six. Maybe older than Fletcher, too.

"Looking for a book?" Frannie asked him as she nudged Fletcher's arm. "Or a tall coffee?"

"Looking for my favorite sister," he said.

She smiled and replied, "Ruby isn't here."

"I'm not looking for Ruby."

"Hannah isn't here either," she said, her smile widening as she teased him.

He chuckled. "You know you're my favorite." They'd grown up sharing their love of mysteries. While Frannie had looked for hers in books, though, Fletcher looked for them in real life.

"Shh," Frannie told him. "We're not supposed to have favorites. That's what Mom has told us."

"That's because there are so many of us, especially if you include our cousins." Which their mom always had after her flighty sister had taken off and abandoned her husband and her kids. "And we all know who her favorite is now."

"Lucy," Frannie said, her voice warm with affection for their niece. "Mom loves being a grandma, which is a good thing with Ruby and Sebastian going to have a baby."

"At least something good came of that whole ordeal," Fletcher murmured, thinking of the danger Ruby had been in, similar to the danger that he might be putting Kiki in.

Since she'd found that note from Troy, he had an officer making frequent drive-bys of Jim's cottage and the houseboat. If Troy saw that cop car, maybe he would keep his distance.

If Troy was the Slasher...

"How is Mom doing?" Frannie asked with concern.

Fletcher shrugged. "She seems fine when I see her, but I really don't see that much of her."

"Is that because you're too busy or because she is?"

Fletcher shrugged. "I don't know what she's been doing, honestly."

"So *you've* been busy," she said.

Fletcher nodded. "Still doesn't excuse my not being by more to check on you."

She raised her hands. "On me? Why?"

"We just lost our dad, Frannie."

"Yes, *we*," Frannie said. "We all did. And Mom lost a husband. And I should be checking up on her myself instead of asking you how she is."

"Stop being so hard on yourself," Fletcher said. "Looks like you're busy with your own business here."

Frannie gazed around her shop, and her chin lifted with obvious pride. "Yes. I love it."

"I can tell," he said. Just like Kiki loved what she did as well. But what Kiki did was going to keep leading her away from Owl Creek. If anything ever happened to Jim Shelton, she would probably stop coming back altogether.

"How about you?" Frannie asked. "Do you love your job, Fletcher? Solving mysteries for real?"

He glanced again to that man in the corner. Was he close enough to hear them? He leaned closer to his sister and whispered, "What's that guy's story? He seems a little stalkerish."

Frannie laughed. "No. He's a regular. He's harmless."

If she really believed that, Frannie hadn't given the guy much of her usual attention. Because there was something *off* about him, and usually she would have picked up on that.

"Stop," she said.

He tensed. "What?"

"Stop being so intense and suspicious of everyone, Fletcher."

"Occupational hazard," he reminded her.

She laughed. "You were always like that. Every date Ruby, Hannah or I brought home got the third degree from our big brothers. But you were the hardest on them."

"I wasn't hard enough on Owen," Fletcher said. Hannah's deadbeat husband had abandoned her and their daughter before Lucy's first birthday.

Frannie nodded and gave a fake shiver. "That's why we're smart, staying single and all."

Fletcher nodded. But staying single didn't sound as smart as it once had to Fletcher, not since that incredible experience he'd had with Kiki, and that hadn't been just what they'd done in her bedroom on the boat. He'd even had fun shopping with her. "I wish I was smarter," Fletcher said.

"Tough case?" Frannie asked. "I can make us some cappuccinos and help you figure it out."

He was tempted. He would love a sounding board about the case. But he was waiting for information back on Bart Taylor and Dan Sullivan, seeing if they had been present at the times and places of the Slasher's other attacks. Troy had been around for at least one other of them. Two, actually, for a total of three times.

He'd been in Salt Lake City and had found the victim. Then Conners. And he'd admitted to Kiki that he'd been at Club Ignition where Greg Stehouwer had been left for dead, not just disfigured.

Had that attack escalated because Troy knew he was a suspect and that the police were closing in on him?

Or was Fletcher's other instinct right and he was missing something? He glanced again to that man sitting in the corner, and he narrowed his eyes to glare at him. "Are you sure he's harmless?"

"Fletcher!" Frannie exclaimed, her face flushing with embarrassment. "Don't scare away my customers."

"Want me to make sure that's all he is?" he asked. "What's his name?"

Frannie shook her head. "No. I'm not giving it to you. Aren't you staying busy enough in Owl Creek? Already bored with a smaller police department?"

Fletcher thought of that other night, in Kiki's bed, in Kiki's arms. "I'm definitely not bored," he said. And that had nothing to do with his case.

Kiki was being followed. She wasn't a fool. She hadn't missed that vehicle driving by her house. Past her grandfather's charter business and the boathouse. Even slowing down in front of the club when she'd checked on her equipment.

And she knew who it was.

Or at least who was responsible for it.

Fletcher had undoubtedly asked an officer to keep an eye on her. Was it for her sake though? Or was he just trying to catch Troy?

He hadn't called or texted her since that morning on the boat, so he was probably just trying to catch Troy. The Slasher.

Were they one and the same?

Kiki shuddered to think that she might have been known someone so long and been working that closely with someone capable of such violence. Uneasy now, she glanced around her as she stood at Fletcher's front door. Had the officer followed her here?

The door opened, and she jumped, startled.

"Kiki," Mrs. Colton said with a smile. "What a lovely surprise."

"I'm sorry," Kiki said. "I should have called first." She hadn't wanted to call Fletcher since he hadn't reached out to her first. But she should have called Jenny before just dropping by.

"You are always welcome," Jenny assured her. "And it's always lovely to see you." She reached out and hugged Kiki.

And Kiki, who could barely remember her mother, felt a pang of jealousy for Fletcher. Then she remembered that he'd lost his father. Jenny had lost her husband.

"I'm stopping by for two reasons," Kiki admitted. "I know you have a ton of family, but if you'd like help with anything that might be hard for them to deal with, I'd be happy to step in."

Jenny's brow furrowed with confusion so Kiki explained, "Like cleaning out closets for instance. Grandpa still had so many of Grandma's clothes in his closet when I first moved in with him that I didn't realize she was dead for the longest time. I thought she was just gone on a trip."

Mrs. Colton smiled. "That's sweet, and I expect that

he might have wanted to think that, too. Maybe that's why he kept her things for so long."

Kiki held up her hands, indicating she would back off. The bag from a shoe store dangled from one of her hands, though, the box bumping against her arm. "I'm sorry. If you're not ready, I totally understand. It hasn't been that long."

Jenny shook her head. "No, it's not that. I've already taken care of Robert's things."

Kiki had no idea what that meant. Had she tossed everything out? Or maybe she'd given his things to their sons.

"I'm sorry. I didn't mean to overstep," Kiki said. God, if Jenny told Fletcher about this, he would think she was stalking him.

"Please stop apologizing, Kiki."

Heat flushed her face with embarrassment. She was acting like a fool. Like the mother of the boy she liked had caught them making out or something.

She was being ridiculous. But being here, after being with Fletcher, unnerved her. Her offer to help Jenny had been a sincere one. But she was beginning to wonder about her own motives now. Had she just hoped to run into Fletcher while she was here, at the house where he was staying?

Had she missed him, so she was being pathetic and hoping to catch a glimpse of him?

She had another gig at Club Ignition this weekend, just a couple of days away, so she would see him then. Unless he'd chosen to pursue his investigation a different way than going undercover.

"You're not overstepping, Kiki," Jenny assured her. "I appreciate the offer so very much. Come inside, and we can visit."

Kiki's stomach flipped with nerves at the thought. She would have had a reason to be inside if she'd been helping Jenny with something. But since she'd refused, Kiki needed to gracefully extradite herself before Fletcher came home. Not that he wouldn't realize she'd been here when his mom gave him what Kiki had bought for him.

Why hadn't she thought this out more thoroughly before she'd decided to do this? Why hadn't she considered how it might look to Fletcher and to his mother?

This was a bad idea. But she found herself going inside, because she couldn't come up with an excuse. While Jenny poured them iced teas in the kitchen, she glanced over at the bag Kiki had sat on the counter.

"Is that for me?" she asked.

Kiki was tempted to press the cold glass of tea against her face. "This is actually for Fletcher," she admitted.

Instead of being offended, Jenny let out a breath of relief. "Good. I received so many lovely flowers and cards and casseroles, but I would just like life to get back to normal now."

Maybe that was why she'd already gotten rid of her husband's things. Or dealt with them somehow.

"I'd like everyone to stop worrying about me," Jenny continued, then her face flushed. "I'm sorry. That sounds rude."

Kiki shook her head and assured her, "No. I totally

get it. You're used to taking care of other people." As a nurse and as a mom and doting aunt. She was more comfortable in the role of caregiver.

"And nobody needs to take care of me," Jenny said. "I'll be fine."

"You will," Kiki said. "I've always admired how strong you are."

Jenny reached across the counter and squeezed her hand. "You're the strong one, Kiki. You've already been through so much, but you put yourself out there, in those big clubs, pursuing your dream. That takes a lot of guts."

Pride suffused Kiki, but she shrugged off the praise. "That's not difficult for me. It would be harder giving it up than going on." That was true. Music was such a part of her life. She couldn't ever give it up. For anyone.

Jenny glanced at the shoe store bag with curiosity and confusion. "So you brought this for Fletcher?"

It didn't make very much sense to Kiki now either. But Fancy had chewed up his boots. And he'd hated them so much that she'd been determined to replace them.

"I didn't even realize you two knew each other very well," Jenny said.

"We don't," Kiki said. "Not really."

And he obviously hadn't told his mother about his investigation. "We just ran into each other, and the puppy I'm fostering damaged one of his boots. I just wanted to make sure it was replaced."

"I'm sure Fletcher wouldn't expect you to do that," Jenny said. "He doesn't care much about material things. Just his career." She uttered a soft sigh.

Maybe she'd compared him to his father.

Though she was close friends with Ruby, Kiki wasn't around Owl Creek enough to understand all the personal dynamics of the Colton family.

Jenny's forehead furrowed with concern for her son. "I'm worried about him. He works so hard that even though he lives here, I barely see him." She let out another sigh, this one a bit shakier than the last. "I hate to think that there is that much crime in Owl Creek to keep him as busy as he's been lately."

He'd been successful in keeping the Slasher's latest attacks out of the news. But it was only a matter of time before someone leaked the stories. Then Jenny was going to be even more worried about her detective son.

As worried as Kiki was. Because she'd seen first-hand how vicious the Slasher was.

What the hell was wrong with this town? Why was there no mention, anywhere, of the attacks? Social media in the area had commented some about a mugging in Conners and a bar fight in the parking lot of Club Ignition. The gossips in the local gathering spot, Hutch's Diner, had been spreading the same rumors. Of muggings and bar fights.

There had been no mention of the Slasher. Not that the Slasher could take credit for everything that had happened.

But wasn't copycatting the highest form of compliment? Or maybe someone else was wanting to get some attention.

Either way, it hadn't worked.

Was trying to hide the truth some new police strategy? Had someone profiled the Slasher and figured out how necessary attention had become to them?

And now they were trying to cut it off?

The Slasher would show what they thought of that. And whoever had put the gag order on the media was going to damn well regret what they'd done.

Chapter 16

Greg Stehouwer wasn't coming out of his coma. At least that was what his doctors believed. His head injury was so severe. The doctors had advised his family to pull the plug. The Slasher would be a killer.

Fletcher felt sick that he hadn't managed to stop whoever the hell it was before it had escalated to murder, just like he'd feared it would. When he showed up at the hospital to speak to the medical examiner who had agreed to inspect the wounds on Greg's face and chest, one of the family spotted him.

"It's you!" the man yelled. "You're the one who got in the fight with him. Why aren't you in jail?" The man looked a lot like his brother with fine blond hair, blue eyes and the same athletic build.

Fletcher pulled out his badge. "No. I'm the one in

charge of this investigation. And I am so sorry about your brother." Sorrier than this man would ever know.

The guy stammered, "But—but you're the one who fought with him—"

Fletcher shook his head. "I never went out to the parking lot. I didn't leave when your brother left. You did, though."

The man's face flushed with fury and he glanced around, as if making sure nobody had overheard them. An older couple sat together on a couch, hugging each other and crying. Probably his parents who had refused to give up hope despite the doctors' grim prognosis. They'd refused to pull the plug so far, believing he would come out of it.

"He's—he is my brother," the man said. "I wouldn't hurt him."

"Where did you go after you left?" Fletcher asked.

"We started driving back to Conners. We were going to hit the clubs there."

If the groom-to-be had acted like he had at Club Ignition, Greg probably would have gotten tossed out of them, too.

"But then Greg changed his mind. He wanted to go back to teach you a lesson."

"I never saw him again until after he'd been attacked. So you let him go back alone?"

"I have a wife and kids," the man replied. "I wasn't going to get into a fight in the club." He glanced at Fletcher's badge again. "What were you doing there that night?"

"The DJ is a friend of mine," Fletcher said.

The man's blue eyes narrowed. "You're investigating that Slasher thing, aren't you? Is that why you were there?"

Fletcher clenched his jaw. While he felt badly about what had happened to Greg Stehouwer, he didn't want to reveal too much of his investigation to this man or to the press or to the people he wanted to fool tonight in the club.

Tonight. He had to drive back to Owl Creek. Had to get dressed to play the part of Kiki's assistant. His pulse quickened at the thought of seeing her again.

He'd wanted to stop by so badly this past week or at least run into her around town. But he'd also had to work this case, had to try to follow up and find all the information he could about Troy Hoover and Bart Taylor and Dan Sullivan. His possible suspects. But he couldn't help but think he was missing someone.

The man nodded. "That's why you were there. You're trying to catch that Slasher. That's who did this, isn't it? That damn Slasher!"

"I don't know," Fletcher honestly replied.

A short while later, when he spoke with the medical examiner who had inspected the deep slashes on Greg's face and chest, he was even less certain.

"His wounds don't look the same as the other ones," the doctor said. The guy was older, with iron gray hair and a mustache. "I took photos of his injuries to compare to the injuries the other victims had sustained."

"You had no problem matching the wounds from the victim at the club in Conners to the wounds on the Slasher's other victims. But you have some doubts about this one?" The same uncertainties had been going through Fletcher's mind since Kiki had found Greg so far out in the club parking lot and with such a serious head wound. One that had essentially killed him, if the doctors were right and he was brain-dead.

The medical examiner lowered his voice to a whisper and told Fletcher, "My preliminary assessment is that blade seems to have been duller and maybe a little wider. Plus, the angle doesn't match the others."

"So a different weapon?" Or a different assailant?

The guy shrugged. "I don't know yet. To say conclusively, I'll need to compare these wounds more closely to the photos taken of the other victims. If you want to wait around…"

Fletcher glanced at his watch. If he didn't hurry, he was going to be late getting to the club. Most of Kiki's equipment was still there, so she wouldn't need his help loading and unloading it until later tonight. But he needed to see her.

Hell, he'd needed to see her all week, but he'd forced himself to stay away, in case Troy Hoover was watching. The officer checking on her hadn't noticed anyone suspicious hanging around, though.

So she'd been safe.

And she had to stay that way. But going back to the club was dangerous. So would telling her not to do the job she loved, though.

Fletcher didn't want to get between her and her music. He just wanted to get between her and the Slasher.

"Call me later with what you find out," he told the medical examiner. "I have somewhere I need to be."

And someone he desperately wanted to see again. She'd bought him boots.

His mother had thought the gesture was sweet on her part, but she didn't know how much he hated those boots. Kiki did. Was it a joke? Or revenge for his not calling or texting her all week?

God, he was a coward. He hadn't known what to say to her or how to act. And knowing she was as averse to relationships as he was, he hadn't wanted to act like they were a couple, even though…

No. He had no time for relationships. A man was essentially dead now. Fletcher had to focus all his energy on finding his killer and making sure that nobody else got hurt.

Hopefully tonight ended without another victim or casualty. But Fletcher had a bad feeling about it, especially when he walked into the club and found Dan Sullivan inside already, arguing with the bartender.

"You have to give this up—" the bartender cut himself off when he noticed Fletcher. "What the hell are you doing here?"

Fletcher pointed toward the DJ booth. "Checking to make sure all of Kiki's stuff is still in the right place, so she'll be all set when she gets here." He'd had to rush to beat her there. Thankfully Mom hadn't been home when he'd run in and changed into Kiki-approved club clothes and those new boots.

"Nobody touched her stuff," Bart said, defensively.

"Are you sure?" Fletcher asked. "The bag I left up there went missing that night." With the glass that had Bart Taylor's prints on it inside. He looked pointedly at

Dan Sullivan. "Seems like people can come and go here pretty freely."

"I guess so," Bart said. "Figured you would have been arrested for what happened to that guy in the parking lot."

Fletcher tensed, wondering if the bartender knew just how seriously Stehouwer had been wounded. He shook his head. "Kiki backed me up that I never went out to the parking lot."

The older man snorted. "Of course she would back you up."

"Some security footage did, too," Fletcher said. "Never showed me going out there."

"The camera at the front door doesn't reach that far out into the parking lot, and there aren't any farther out there," Bart said. "You kept going out to the alley that night."

Was that why Stehouwer had been attacked in the parking lot? Because the Slasher had noticed how frequently Fletcher had been checking their usual crime scene?

"You could have walked out through the alley to the parking lot," Bart said.

"Seems like you really want me to be guilty of this," Fletcher said, "and I thought we were going to be friends." He glanced from one to the other of them, wondering what they'd been arguing about. "Just like you two are friends." They hadn't acted like it the other night.

But Bart had known a lot about Sullivan. Maybe they were more than customer and bartender. Bart shook his head. "He's just asking me to help him find someone."

Dan's daughter.

But was she anywhere to be found?

Fletcher had turned up a couple of Jane Does that might have been matches for the girl. Deceased.

He wasn't going to say anything to the desperate father until he could confirm it, though. He really needed the guy's DNA. And Bart's.

If only the Slasher had ever left any behind. But they hadn't left anything that would have proved their guilt.

"There are no cameras in the parking lot," Fletcher repeated back to the man. "But there are some inside here." He pointed toward the ones hidden up among the lights in the tall ceiling that had been painted black like the brick and metal walls.

The bartender shrugged. "I gave all that footage to the police."

Liar.

But if Fletcher called him that, Bart and Dan would realize that the only way Fletcher could know what he'd turned over was because he'd seen what had been turned over to the police. They'd gotten the parking lot footage and some from maybe one camera inside, but there was more than one. So why hadn't the guy turned it over?

What was on it that he'd been trying to hide? And how the hell was Fletcher going to be able to get a look at it?

Kiki had no idea if Fletcher was even going to show up at the club. Maybe he'd decided to go another direction with his investigation. Maybe he was worried that his cover had been blown the other night.

Or maybe…

He just didn't want to see her again after what had happened. Not that she cared. Sure. It had been hot. Pretty incredible.

But that didn't mean they should do it again. Maybe it meant that they shouldn't. That they couldn't risk getting used to that level of passion and pleasure.

Kiki already had a playlist together in her head. Nobody had sent her any special requests this week. Not even her girls, Janie, Claire and Amy. They'd messaged her to make sure the club would be reopened, but that had been it, which was weird.

Usually Claire asked for a few slow ones. And Amy wanted the music without the lyrics. Janie was the one after Kiki's heart and usually requested all the ones about female empowerment. Beyoncé and Joan Jett and Aretha Franklin and even The Chicks. Janie was going to be happy tonight because Kiki had gone really old school and queued up some Nancy Sinatra. *These boots…*

That had been more for Fletcher, though, if he showed up in those boots she'd bought for him. Even though she didn't have much equipment to carry in, she arrived a little early. Just to make sure everything was set up how she liked it and to get her new playlist perfected. Not because of Fletcher.

But when she walked in and found him standing at the bar, her heart did a little flippy thing in her chest, like Fancy when Kiki tried to get the puppy to follow the Spin command. She tried to ignore it and him, like he'd ignored her this past week.

"Ah, Kiki's pissed at you, too," Bart remarked.

"Nobody has any reason to be pissed at me," Fletcher said, but he didn't sound very convincing, like he didn't quite believe it himself. "Kiki, tell them that you weren't lying when you gave me an alibi the other night."

"What?" she asked. "Why would I lie about that?"

"Because you two are a little closer than you and Troy ever were," Bart called back to her.

She shrugged. "Yeah, we're old friends. So there's no way he would have left that guy out there for me to find." She didn't have to fake the shudder that swept over. "And if he had, he wouldn't be here right now. He'd be in the hospital, too. I was mad when he interfered on the dance floor. You think I would condone him doing something like *that*?"

Bart and Dan Sullivan both shook their heads and laughed. "Sorry," Bart said.

And she didn't know if the bartender was apologizing to her or to Fletcher. Then he set up a mug of coffee on the bar in front of the undercover detective and made it clear.

"I didn't mean to give you such a hard time," Bart said. "With all this crazy Slasher business, everybody who works in clubs and all the owners have been on edge. I had to talk the manager into reopening Club Ignition tonight. She wasn't sure she wanted to."

"Is that why Troy hasn't been around?" Dan asked Kiki, walking across the floor toward her. "The Slasher scared him off?"

Or he *was* the Slasher.

That was what Fletcher believed.

She nodded. "Yeah, he was freaked out. He was at that club in Salt Lake City and the one in—"

"Hey, hon," Fletcher interjected as he rushed over to her with that coffee in his hand. Obviously he still needed his caffeine to stay up late. He set the mug on top of one the speakers and asked, "What do you want me to help you with?"

Kiki realized she'd probably been about to say too much. Did Fletcher consider Dan a suspect, too? Or Bart? Her?

As a detective, he probably automatically thought the worst of everyone he met. Maybe that was why he hadn't called or texted this week.

Maybe he hadn't known if he could trust her.

She narrowed her eyes at him in a bit of a glare. "I got this, *hon*."

He grinned. "Good thing the equipment is already here. I have another new pair of boots to break in..." He raised his foot, holding up one of the work boots she'd bought him. He'd laced them a little looser, maybe in case he went into a lake again and had to get them off fast.

She hoped he didn't go in the water again. But she felt a bit like she was drowning as she stared at him, desire overwhelming her. With the boots, he wore another pair of distressed jeans. A white tank top type of undershirt underneath a light flannel jacket. And his hair was still a little damp from what must have been a quick shower. He looked sexy as hell, like one of the rock stars whose posters she'd hung on her bedroom walls growing up.

She'd like Fletcher in her bedroom again but not on the wall. Maybe holding her up against it.

His green eyes dilated, as if he was feeling the same overwhelming attraction that she was. She'd really thought that making love with him would remove the distraction. They wouldn't have to wonder anymore how it would be because they would know.

But now that they knew…

She just wanted to do it again.

He jumped over the barricade to join her in the small confines of the overcrowded booth. And her pulse quickened with his nearness, with the heat and hardness of his body so close to hers.

"Thanks for the boots," he said, and he leaned down as if he was going to kiss her.

She pulled back slightly. "I just didn't want you to sue me, you know, over my dog destroying your boots."

"You're claiming Fancy as yours?"

She shrugged. "For the moment. Just fostering her." But she was getting more attached than she'd been to the other puppies she and her grandfather had fostered. Just as she was getting more attached to…

She tensed at the thought she didn't even dare let herself fully formulate. "And don't go reading anything into me dropping off those boots," she continued, lowering her voice to a whisper. "I know that the other night wasn't anything special. Just a one-off, a hookup, a release of all that—"

He closed the distance between them and pressed his mouth against hers, kissing her deeply, passionately. When he finally raised his head, she couldn't think at all.

She could only feel. How very badly she wanted him. But had it been real at all? Or just part of his cover?

"Why did you do that?" she whispered.

"Because I really, really wanted to," he said.

"I thought it was a bad idea," she reminded him of what he'd said last weekend and that had been even before they'd made love.

"It still is," he said, "because now I want you even more, and I know it's going to be even harder for me to stay away from you."

"Why do you want to stay away from me?" she asked. Was he worried about falling for her like she was beginning to worry about falling for him?

"Because I don't want you in danger," he said.

She wanted to argue that she wasn't in any danger. But it had been strange the way that Troy had showed up on the houseboat and then how he'd left that note in her vehicle. He must have shoved it through the window or something because she always locked it.

But even if Troy wasn't the Slasher and she wasn't in any physical danger, she was in danger of another kind. Because when Fletcher had kissed her, she hadn't wanted him to stop.

Chapter 17

The weekend had passed without incident, unless Fletcher considered what had happened after the club, later that night. How he'd gone home with Kiki to that houseboat again.

How they'd made love all night.

That night and the next and the next after that. Mom probably thought he'd moved out. He *had* been looking for a place of his own.

He was staying in Owl Creek, in his new position as lead detective, so he needed a house. He'd pulled up a couple that were listed online and had done the virtual tours. That was about all he had time for.

Around his investigation.

And Kiki.

She wasn't staying. She was working on music that

she'd played for him a couple of times when he'd awakened to find her working. She'd written songs to sell and songs to sing and produce on her own. She was going to be big someday soon. Bigger than Owl Creek.

So he had to protect his heart, just like he had to protect his life. Just because nothing had happened last weekend didn't mean that the Slasher had left Owl Creek. In fact, Fletcher was pretty damn certain they were still here.

Troy Hoover. Bart Taylor. Dan Sullivan. Troy had definitely had some means and opportunity to commit those crimes. Bart wasn't always tending bar here in Owl Creek. He worked other clubs, too. And Dan Sullivan had been looking everywhere for his daughter, hitting clubs all over the west coast and neighboring areas. He could have been in those other cities where the attacks had taken place.

Fletcher needed to step up his investigation even though nothing had happened last weekend.

At least nothing at the club. A lot had happened on that houseboat between him and Kiki.

But he was extra uneasy as they unloaded her equipment tonight. He had a feeling that the Slasher was going to act out again. If it was for attention, though, they had it now. Greg Stehouwer's brother, Gerard, had talked to the press, insisting that the Slasher had attacked Greg and that the police were doing nothing to find the psychopath.

Instead of being insulted over Gerard's complaint about the police, Fletcher was relieved that Gerard hadn't blown his cover. And that the man had no idea how Fletcher was working his brother's case. It hadn't become a murder yet. Though Greg was still in a coma, his parents were holding out hope that he would regain consciousness.

Fletcher wasn't as hopeful, even though the doctors had sounded a little less bleak the last time he'd checked with them. Apparently, the guy had started breathing without the ventilator.

While it was a sign of improvement, there was no guarantee that he would wake up. And even if he did, he probably wouldn't be able to help Fletcher identify the Slasher.

According to the medical examiner, the person who had attacked Greg Stehouwer wasn't the same person who had disfigured the other victims. The wounds had been too different. So, was the Slasher one person or two different people working together?

Once again, as he and Kiki carried equipment into the club, he found Bart Taylor and Dan Sullivan together at the bar, their heads bent close as they kept their voices so low nobody could overhear them. Fletcher tried. They seemed to be working on something together. When they noticed him, they jumped apart. They were definitely hiding something.

But what?

Had they figured out who and what he really was?

"Hey, Fletcher," Bart called out. "Want your usual?"

He chuckled because his usual wasn't an alcoholic drink like bartenders usually served but a cup of coffee. Strong. After how little sleep he'd gotten over the past week, he definitely needed it. He stopped at the bar to stick his finger through the handle of the steaming mug while he juggled the other equipment he carried. "Thanks."

"How about you, Kiki?" Bart asked.

"Got my usual tea and honey," Kiki said, raising her thermos.

Fletcher grimaced, remembering when he'd tried her concoction. Like a hot toddy without the whiskey and the heat, it had been lukewarm, overly sweet tea. No wonder she had so much energy all the time.

Fletcher yawned then. He really needed his caffeine. After rolling a speaker into place, he took a long sip from his mug.

"You still not used to the late nights, old man?" Kiki teased.

He chuckled and whispered, "I'm not the one who fell asleep on me last night."

Her face flushed, and her dark eyes glittered with desire. "I'm wide awake now, though. And you're not."

"Maybe because someone woke me up so early this morning," he said.

"Do you have any complaints about that?" she asked, and she ran her fingers down his chest.

Through his thin T-shirt, he could feel the heat of her touch, and his skin tingled while his heart pounded fast and hard with excitement.

"No complaints at all," he assured her. He didn't remember the last time he'd been so happy or satiated. That thought brought on a rush of guilt that swept away some of the happiness. His dad was dead. Greg Stehouwer was basically brain-dead and other men had been permanently disfigured. He had no right to feel happy, at least not until the Slasher was behind bars. Permanently.

While the last weekend had been quiet, Fletcher didn't believe that the Slasher had left Owl Creek. He or she was here. Or maybe there were two of them, like the medical examiner had speculated after ruling that Greg Stehouwer's wounds were different from the other victims.

Two people.

Like Dan Sullivan and the bartender.

Or two totally unrelated people. Maybe whoever had attacked Greg Stehouwer was hoping that the Slasher would be blamed for it. Greg was as rich and important as he'd claimed that night on the dance floor, and once he got married, he was going to get even richer with a payout of a trust from his deceased grandparents. Money was always a strong motive for murder. And whoever had attacked Greg Stehouwer hadn't been simply trying to disfigure him.

Was that what the Slasher had been doing to the other victims? Trying to ruin their lives for some reason like he or she believed theirs had been ruined?

Like Dan Sullivan.

He'd lost his daughter. Did he blame every guy he saw in a club for taking her away from him? Fletcher had sent out her picture everywhere, and he was waiting for a call back from a few coroners whose Jane Does had matched the description of Dan's missing daughter.

One was in LA. There was another in San Francisco and one in Salt Lake City.

After helping Kiki set up her equipment, Fletcher headed toward the bar where Sullivan was sitting. He set his empty mug on the granite bar for Bart to refill.

"You've been the first customer here the last couple of weekends," Fletcher remarked to Sullivan. And Bart had been letting him in before the club even opened. "Do you have a lead that your daughter is in Owl Creek?"

Dan shook his head. "No. No leads. But I think I'm starting to fall for this town. All the fishing and hiking."

"You been doing a lot of that during the week?" Fletcher asked.

The guy shrugged. "Some. It's a beautiful area. Did you grow up here?"

Fletcher tensed, wondering if his cover had been blown. Just as he'd been checking out Dan Sullivan and Bart Taylor, they might have been checking him out. Since he had grown up here, Dan and Bart could have run into a lot of people who knew him and knew what he really did for a living. And it wasn't acting as Kiki's assistant but as the lead detective for Owl Creek PD.

"I did grow up here," he admitted. There was no point in lying about that if Sullivan had already figured out the truth.

"Is that how you know Kiki?" A female voice asked the question.

And Fletcher turned, expecting to see a waitress behind him. But it was one of the women he called Kiki's superfans. He didn't know which one was which, but this one was the redhead with the frizzy hair and bright smile.

He smiled back. "Yes, it is."

"She's amazing!" one of the other ones gushed as the blonde and the brunette walked up to the bar, too.

"Doors open, huh?" Fletcher asked.

"The bouncer let us in a little early," the blonde said with a wink.

"He always lets the prettiest women in first," Fletcher said.

They giggled at his compliment. He had a soft spot for them because of their adulation of Kiki. He had become one of her superfans, too.

"Are you going to dance with us tonight?" the brunette said with a bit of a whine. And then Bart handed her a glass of wine across the bar.

"If I'm going to keep up with you ladies, I'm going to need more coffee," he said.

"I already refilled your cup," Bart said, pointing at it. "It's probably getting cold."

"Let's get this party started!" Kiki's voice echoed throughout the nearly empty club. More people were coming through the doors, but they obviously hadn't been lined up around the block like that first weekend Fletcher had gone undercover as her assistant.

Greg's brother going public about the Slasher attacking him here had definitely affected their business. The only reason anyone had probably showed up at all tonight was because of Kiki. She was amazing.

She wore the red leather vest and shorts, probably

because she'd left it on the boat that first time they'd
made love and she hadn't gone back to the cottage to
grab any of her other club wardrobe. This was Fletcher's
favorite, though, because it reminded him of that night,
though not everything that had happened then had been
good.

He could have drowned. And maybe he had in a way.

He'd drowned in the pleasure she gave him. In her.

To get the dancing started, she sang along with the
songs she played, mixing them between two of her four
turntables. He didn't know how she kept everything
straight, especially when she had to be as tired as he
was.

He reached for the mug of coffee. It was getting a
little lukewarm, so he drank it fast and had Bart fill it
again. He had a feeling he was going to have to stay
alert tonight. That something was going to happen.

Because that feeling was an uneasy one that had
goose bumps lifting on his skin. And he wore a flannel shirt over his undershirt, so he shouldn't have been
cold. He should have been too hot in the flannel, especially with the way Kiki looked.

Just the sight of her, her body moving to the music
she played, had him a little light-headed, a little dizzy
on her beauty and the sound of her husky voice singing along with that music.

He was in danger. And not just from the Slasher. He
was in danger of falling for Kiki.

Kiki was so pumped with excitement that she couldn't
stop dancing. The music flowed through her like her

blood. She'd written some great stuff over the past week. And she'd made some incredible love with an incredible man.

A very sweet man in the way that he played with Fancy and worked with her on her commands and the way that he listened to all Kiki's songs and acted so in awe of her. Sometimes just the way he looked at her with that strangely intense look of his...

He hadn't been looking at her that way tonight, though. It was as if he could barely hold his lids up over his eyes. At the moment, he was a very tired man.

She felt a pang of regret that she'd kept Fletcher up late and then woken him up early. He was obviously tired, so tired that he'd been nearly nodding off in the booth.

So it was probably good that her girls had cajoled him into joining them on the dance floor. But he wasn't moving with his usual rhythm. He seemed sluggish, and he stumbled and nearly fell. It was almost as if...

He was drunk.

But his coffee cup sat atop the speaker, vibrating with the beat. She leaned forward and sniffed it. She didn't smell alcohol in it, though she wouldn't have expected to since she'd never seen him drink anything but coffee. But the way he was acting...

He was more than tired. It was as if he'd been drugged.

Alarm shot through her. Was that what had happened to those other men? Why they hadn't managed to fight back harder against the Slasher? Because they'd been drugged first?

She gazed out into the crowd, looking for him. But now, later in the night, the dance floor was full. She couldn't even find her girls now.

Maybe they'd taken him back to the bar. Or outside for some air.

He definitely needed it. But if he went into the alley tonight as he usually did, to check for victims, he might become the next one.

The Slasher had figured out who Fletcher really was. A Colton. Rich and spoiled like all those other victims.

After the recent death of his father, he was probably even richer. It had been easy enough to figure out who he was after just following him around for a bit, like to that bookstore his sister owned.

There were a whole lot of Coltons in this town. So if one more died, like his father had, he wouldn't be missed. Would Kiki miss him?

The Slasher felt a pang of regret. But it couldn't be helped. Kiki would realize, in the long run, that the Slasher had done her a favor.

Had saved her from that inevitable speech rich guys like Colton gave to women like her.

It was fun while it lasted, but it wasn't going to work out in the long run. They were too different.

And what they really meant was that they were better.

And they wanted someone better.

The Slasher knew what Fletcher Colton wanted. Not just someone better.

Detective Colton wanted the Slasher and he'd just been using Kiki. So really, this was a favor to Kiki. Getting rid of Fletcher Colton for good.

Chapter 18

Fletcher's head pounded, and his vision blurred, the strobe lights blinding him with blue, red and purple flashes. He needed more coffee. Or maybe some fresh air.

He'd gotten away from the girls and off the dance floor with the excuse that he needed to use the restroom. And he had...

To splash cold water on his face. But that hadn't woken him up. And when he stepped back out into the club, those lights flashed at him, making his head pound harder than the music. The music.

Kiki. He needed to talk to Kiki. To tell her something...

But he couldn't think any clearer than he could see. He moved back into the bathroom, where the lights didn't flash, just buzzed overhead from the fluorescent bulbs. That light was harsh but shouldn't have made him feel as dizzy and light-headed as he felt.

Maybe he needed air.

His stomach roiled, too, though. And he stepped into a stall to use the toilet bowl as his stomach expelled everything he'd eaten and drank that day. Just coffee.

So why was he so tired? So light-headed?

Maybe his blood sugar was too low. Or…

He reached into his pocket for the handkerchief he'd shoved into it earlier, but paper crinkled in his fingers instead of cloth. A note.

He pulled it out and had to blink a couple of times to focus on it, to read the scrawled writing. *Looking for me? You know where to find me. If you're brave enough…*

The Slasher. He or she hadn't signed the note, but they hadn't had to. He knew who had given it to him even though he hadn't noticed when it had been shoved in his pocket. Who had passed it to him? And when?

On the dance floor?

Or when he'd been standing in the short line for the men's room? A couple of guys had pushed past him. And he'd also walked by Dan and Bart at the bar. When he'd stumbled, Dan had jumped up and helped him steady himself.

"Whoa, there, you must be burning the candle at both ends, Fletcher."

He had been. But the way he felt now was more than tired. He'd probably been drugged.

So he knew he shouldn't go out to that alley. Not

now. Not alone and definitely not in this condition. Whatever this was.

But maybe throwing up would help clear his head. And the fresh air…

Not that the air in the alley was fresh. And not that he should go out there alone.

His head had cleared enough from vomiting that he knew to call for help. He reached for his cell and sent a picture of the note to the officer who was always on standby in the area when Fletcher was working undercover at the club. His back-up would be here within minutes. Would meet him in the alley…

He left the stall, stopped to wash his hands and his face and to gulp mouthfuls of water from the faucet. Now, if he headed to the alley, the officer would certainly be almost there, too.

The alley was behind the kitchen, so that only employees were supposed to use it. Maybe that was why Fletcher hadn't found anyone out there yet when he'd worked undercover at Club Ignition.

Maybe that was why Greg Stehouwer had been attacked in the parking lot instead. But he hadn't received a note. Or if he had, it hadn't been on him when Kiki had found him.

Of course, the detail of the note hadn't been leaked to the press. And if the person who'd attacked Greg had been a copycat, they wouldn't have known that detail.

But this person, the one who'd slipped Fletcher the note, knew it. They had to be the Slasher.

He started down the hall toward the bar area and just as he neared it, he stumbled again. But Dan Sullivan wasn't there to catch him this time. He didn't see Bart either. One of the cocktail waitresses was behind the bar serving drinks.

Where had those two gone? Were they waiting in the alley for him?

And where was Kiki?

Even though music played, it wasn't with the energy and mix that she gave to the beat. He glanced across the dance floor to the booth. It was empty.

Where was she?

Hopefully in the restroom. But he had a horrible feeling she'd gone into the alley. Maybe looking for him. And she was going to find what was waiting for him.

The Slasher.

He couldn't wait for backup, not if Kiki was in danger. He had to go out there now and hope like hell that he wasn't too late.

Kiki hadn't found Fletcher. She had found someone else, though, hidden among the dancers on the floor. Troy. He'd caught her wrist when she'd tried to pass him. And she'd nearly used the pepper spray she had clasped in one hand.

"Kiki."

"Troy! What are you doing here?" Was he the one who'd drugged Fletcher? He'd had to be drugged to be as sluggish as he'd been. Because he'd been tired before but had never moved like that.

"I need your help."

She shook her head and tried to pull her wrist free of his grasp. But, like the groom from the bachelor party a couple of weekends ago, he tightened his grasp instead of releasing her. "Let me go!" she told him.

She didn't want to pepper spray him. Not there in the middle of a crowded dance floor.

Too many other people might get hurt. But she didn't want Fletcher getting hurt. Or was she already too late for that?

"You need to listen to me," Troy implored her. "I'm not the Slasher. But I think I know who is."

"That's why you need to talk to the police, Troy," she urged him. "You need to tell them what you know."

He shook his head. "They're not going to listen to me. And I don't really have any proof. You need to listen to me, Kiki. I want to tell you."

She shook her head. "I'm not the police, Troy. I can't help you with this."

"I thought you were my friend."

She shook her head again. "No. I don't even really know who you are."

He released her then, so abruptly that she stumbled back into some other dancers.

"Kiki! Kiki, play my song next."

She wasn't going to play any songs. She had to find Fletcher. She had to make sure that he was okay. She shoved her way through the other dancers, ignoring them as they tried to catch her attention, as they tried to stop her. She kept her grip tight on her can of pepper spray.

She had a feeling that she was going to need it. Either because of Troy or because of Fletcher.

He wasn't at the bar. She would have seen him, in his blue and pink flannel shirt, if he had been. He claimed to hate that shirt, just as he claimed to hate the boots that he kept so loosely laced now. But he'd worn that shirt a few times. Just to cover his holster, he claimed.

He had his gun.

The pressure on her chest eased a little with that realization. He was armed.

But if he'd been drugged, like she was worried he'd been, he might not be able to fire that weapon in time to save himself from the Slasher's attack. Because if he had been drugged, it had probably been the Slasher who'd done it.

Where would the Slasher be waiting for Fletcher? The parking lot where Greg Stehouwer had been attacked? Or the alley?

She chose to check the alley first. Because it was closer and because she could rush through it to the parking lot where she'd found Stehouwer bleeding in the weeds.

One of the waitresses who was tending the bar glanced at her as she ducked under the counter and passed through the doorway into the kitchen. A lot of employees went to the alley to smoke, but Kiki rarely went into the kitchen and definitely not into the alley unless she'd been carrying her equipment in or out through that door.

With the location of the parking lot and the front door, though, she could park by the entrance and bring her stuff in that way. But because those spots were designated for people with disabilities, she had to move it after she unloaded her equipment.

But even though she hadn't used the alley often here, she knew where it was. She rushed through the kitchen, past the enormous dishwashers that leaked steam into the room, to that steel door.

When she pushed it open, she saw Fletcher in the faint glow from the light at the top of the short stairwell that led down to the asphalt where he stood, his gun gripped in his hand. But she saw only him.

A dumpster was just below that stairwell, jammed between this old warehouse and the one next to it that was still abandoned. Nobody had renovated it yet like they had Club Ignition.

She'd thought once or twice about how it would make a great sound studio. It was all brick and metal and thick insulation. The acoustics in it were even better than in the club. But she didn't have the money for something like that—at least not yet. And right now she didn't have the interest.

All her focus was on a certain detective.

"Fletcher!" she called out to him.

He tensed, then turned slowly toward her, as if he was about to pass out. He had definitely been drugged. And as he turned, something jumped from the shadows on the other side of that big dumpster. It didn't look like a person to Kiki—who couldn't see anything but plastic, like some kind of synthetic suit with a hood and mask—but then a knife blade flashed.

And she knew who it was. The Slasher.

She screamed again. "Fletcher! Behind you!"

But the blade was already swinging toward him as he turned with the gun in his hand.

Kiki rushed down those steps as she raised her can of pepper spray. With the Slasher wearing a mask, it might not affect them at all. But Kiki had to try to protect Fletcher.

She had to make an effort to save him. Because he wasn't aiming or firing his weapon. Instead, when that blade came down across his arm, he dropped it onto the ground. And then he fell onto it, too, his blood sprayed across the asphalt beneath him.

Kiki screamed again as she rushed toward the Slasher. She pressed hard on the canister button, sending that pepper spray out toward the attacker who turned that knife on Kiki now.

Instead of saving Fletcher, Kiki might have become just another victim of the Slasher.

Chapter 19

Fletcher felt no pain from his wound being stitched, just the tug and pull of the needle moving through his skin. The cut across his forearm wasn't all that deep, but it had bled like hell, the torn sleeve of his flannel shirt saturated with blood. It continued to ooze through the stitches pulling the wound together.

At least they'd numbed the area on his arm.

His head still hurt from whatever drug had been in his coffee. A doctor at the hospital in Conners had taken a sample of his blood to test it. To see what had been slipped to him.

"This is going to take a lot of stitches," the ER doctor warned him as he continued pushing the needle through his skin like he was hemming some curtains.

Fletcher knew he was lucky that it was just his arm.

And not his face like the Slasher's other victims. Or his chest.

Or his heart.

Because he didn't think the Slasher had just intended to disfigure Fletcher. They had probably intended to kill him. If not for Kiki, they would have probably succeeded.

"Kiki Shelton. Is she here, too?" he asked, and his voice was raspy—probably from that drug. He knew he'd asked already, but his mind was still a little foggy from whatever he'd been slipped.

"Yes," the doctor replied. "She's fine."

"So she's in the waiting room?" he asked. That was the only way she would be fine. If she'd been in the ambulance with him, which was how he vaguely recalled things, then she wouldn't be fine.

He couldn't remember what all had happened in that alley. Between the drugs and then the blood loss.

And the pain.

He'd felt that then. Not just in his arm or his head. Even his eyes stung. They burned still, so much so that he lifted his free hand toward his face.

"Don't," the doctor warned him. "I'm not sure we got all the pepper spray off you. You might have some on your hand that you'll get in your eyes."

"Pepper spray?"

"Yeah, it probably saved your life," the doctor replied. "The woman who rode in with you—"

"Kiki Shelton." She had been with him. He could vaguely remember her hand on him, touching him, as if she'd wanted to make sure that he was still alive.

"She probably saved your life. She used it on the attacker, but with that alley being so narrow and the air conditioner condenser being right there, the pepper spray went all over the place."

"How is Kiki?" he asked with concern. "I'm a detective, Doctor, with Owl Creek PD. I was working undercover at that club as Kiki's assistant." And if she'd gotten hurt because of him...

"She got it the worst," the doctor admitted. "We had to flush out her eyes and then put bandages over them so that she doesn't strain them."

So she was essentially blind. Was that why she'd held onto him in the ambulance? Or had she been worried about him? She must have been, or why else would she have come out into the alley like she had?

"And the Slasher?" Fletcher asked, his voice raspy. Now he knew it was probably from the pepper spray.

"Slasher?" The doctor's hand stilled midstitch. "Is that who—of course. That's who."

"Who what? Did they come in, too?"

The doctor shook his head. "No. They got away."

Fletcher cursed.

And the doctor nodded now in agreement. "That psycho needs to be caught. I saw what they did to those last two victims."

"How is Greg Stehouwer?" Fletcher asked.

"A frickin' miracle," the doctor replied. "The neurologist said there's brain activity now. He'll probably wake up soon. But he'll still have a long road to recovery after he does."

At least he was alive. That was something.

"I see why you put yourself at risk like that to catch this sociopath," the doctor said. "You're lucky Ms. Shelton was there."

He was lucky. She wasn't. "You think she'll be all right?" he asked, his heart beating fast with fear for her. And with something else.

Something he couldn't let himself acknowledge.

The doctor nodded. "Pepper spray doesn't cause permanent blindness. Usually that lasts for up to forty-five minutes at the most. Ms. Shelton's case is a little different because I think she rubbed it in. She made it worse. But I'm sure she'll be fine."

"And she didn't get cut?" Fletcher's stomach lurched with the horror of her being harmed like those men had been.

Already the numbness in his arm was beginning to wear off and he could feel the nip of the needle, the strain of his skin, as the doctor finished closing his wound.

He didn't care about his pain, though. He just didn't want Kiki to be in pain.

"She didn't get cut," the doctor assured him.

"Where is she?" Fletcher asked. He had to see for himself that she was okay.

"We put her in an individual room in the ER area," the doctor said. "She needs to rest for a while, and then hopefully her vision will be fine and we can remove those bandages."

Hopefully.

But what if it wasn't?

If Kiki lost her vision because of him, because of

his involving her in this investigation, he would never forgive himself. And he doubted she would either.

Some rescuer Kiki was. She would stick to playing music from now on instead of playing detective. Rather than helping Fletcher, she'd probably distracted him. And he'd gotten wounded because of her instead of catching the Slasher like he'd been trying to do.

In addition to the laceration on his arm, the pepper spray had also affected him, making him cough and gag like she'd been doing.

And the burning.

It hurt so much. Even now, with the cold bandage wrapped over her eyes, her skin burned. And her throat ached from all that coughing. She needed her honey lemon tea right now more than she needed the sleep the doctor had advised her to get.

Like she could sleep at all with that image in her head. Of that person, bundled up in a hazmat suit, lunging at Fletcher with that huge knife.

It had been like a machete. So sharp.

It could have killed Fletcher easily. Or taken off his arm.

The wound had been bleeding so much. She needed to check on him more than she needed to rest her eyes. She couldn't rest without knowing how he was.

Hinges creaked as the door opened. And even through the bandage, Kiki could see a faint lightness. But then the hinges creaked again, as the door closed, shutting out the light.

"Hello?" she called out.

Had a doctor or nurse come back to check on her?

"Can you take these bandages off now?" she asked. "I'm fine. Really."

She waited a beat, but nobody responded. Had someone just opened the door and then closed it again?

But then she heard the squeak of a shoe sole against the linoleum flooring. And another sound...

Of someone breathing.

She was not alone.

"Hello?" she called out again. "Who's there?"

But only that eerie silence greeted her again. Who was it? And why wouldn't they identify themselves? Was it because they didn't want anyone to identify them?

Was it the Slasher?

The Slasher's eyes burned with nearly the same intensity as their rage. Why had Kiki Shelton messed everything up? She was supposed to stay up in her damn booth, playing her music like she always did.

Except for those rare instances when she came out into the crowd. But even then, she never made it farther than the dance floor.

She shouldn't have come out to that alley. Shouldn't have interfered like that.

Fletcher Colton should have been dead. Or at least hurt a hell of a lot worse than he'd been.

He had to be the one who'd stifled the story about the attack in Conners. He'd been working that case, too. The Slasher had found that out, too.

That the lead detective of Owl Creek Police Department had been helping out in Conners. Like he'd claimed to just be helping an old friend when he'd posed as Kiki's assistant.

But maybe they were old friends. Maybe that was why it seemed like there was something between them. Something that could have cost Kiki her life.

Something that still would if she was stupid enough to get in the Slasher's way again.

Chapter 20

The hospital rushed his blood work results. His coffee had definitely been tainted with rohypnol. As out of it as Fletcher had been, he wouldn't have survived that skirmish with the Slasher in the alley if it hadn't been for Kiki and her pepper spray. She had saved his life.

The backup officer hadn't gotten Fletcher's text right away. Since Fletcher had had no issue with the cell reception when he'd called to report finding Greg Stehouwer, there must have been a cell signal jammer inside the club. Or maybe the Slasher had brought one.

It seemed as if they'd thought of everything, like the hazmat-type suit they'd worn. No wonder they never left any DNA or fingerprints at the scene.

Eventually the text had gone through, though, and the

officer had arrived and then called the ambulance that had brought him and Kiki to the hospital in Conners.

So Kiki had been his backup instead of an officer. She'd saved his life. And he had to make sure she was really all right. So even though he knew she was supposed to be resting, he wanted to check on her and had wheedled her location out of the ER doctor.

But Kiki wasn't resting. As he approached her room, he heard her voice rise, demanding to know, "Who's there? Who are you?"

He could hear the fear in her voice, too. So he pushed open the door to the darkness of the room. Only the light from the hall spilled into the space, revealing a bed and a shadow looming over it.

That shadow lunged toward Fletcher, or maybe toward the door, but he blocked them and shoved the person to the floor. Then he fumbled against the wall and turned on the light.

It illuminated the man lying on the floor. He was thin with long, stringy hair that looked like it hadn't been washed in a while. And his eyes were wild and bloodshot, like an animal that was starving for food or…

The guy tried to scramble up from the floor, but Fletcher held him down with one of those heavy boots Kiki had bought him. "Sit back, Troy. You're not getting away from me this time." And he used his cell to call for the backup that had followed him and Kiki to the hospital.

Kiki.

She sat up in the bed now, pushing at the bandage

that had been wrapped around her head. The compress dropped onto the sheet that covered her. Her eyes and skin were red, but she blinked and focused on the two men.

"Why didn't you say something, Troy?" she asked, her voice sharp with anger. "Why'd you just stand there in the dark?"

Troy lay back on the floor as if resigned, but he didn't answer her.

Then she focused on Fletcher and said, "What are you doing! You shouldn't be out of bed! You're hurt."

Fletcher would rather have her angry than afraid, even if she was angry with him. "I'm fine," he said. Thanks to her. "How are you?"

"Pissed off," she said. She pointed toward his arm. "You're still bleeding."

The bandage covering his wound was turning red with fresh blood. He must have reopened the stitches when he shoved Troy to the floor. "No reason to be mad about my cut. It's been stitched up."

"I'm mad that you went into that alley alone."

"I couldn't find you," Fletcher said.

"I couldn't find *you*," Kiki said. "And I could tell from the way you were acting that somebody must have slipped you something."

"They did," Fletcher confirmed. He looked down at Troy. "What the hell are you doing here in her room? How did you even know she was here?" Unless he was the Slasher.

"He was at the club," Kiki answered for him.

Fletcher nodded. "Of course he was. You've been

everywhere the Slasher has attacked someone, Troy. Why is that?"

"It's not me," Troy said, his voice quavering with fear, and his body started shaking so badly it seemed like he was more than afraid. He could be having a seizure, or maybe going through withdrawal. Fletcher had seen people acting similarly in his years as a police officer.

Fletcher struggled to imagine this guy as the Slasher. How would someone like him have eluded the authorities for so long in so many different places?

The organizational skills it had taken to plan and execute the attacks didn't seem like something Troy was capable of doing. The Slasher had been so careful and had made certain to leave behind no clues.

No DNA. No fingerprints.

The note. Fletcher had the note. Maybe there would be something on it since the Slasher hadn't managed to take it back like they had from the other victims.

Was that why Troy was here? But then he would have been in Fletcher's room and not Kiki's.

"What the hell are you doing here?" Fletcher asked again.

"I had to talk to Kiki," Troy said. "She has to know the truth."

"You said that you know who the Slasher is," Kiki said. "You told me that on the dance floor. Who is it, Troy?"

The guy's skinny body shook harder, as if he was convulsing.

"What's wrong?" Kiki asked.

"I think he's going through withdrawal." Fletcher stepped away to call out, "We need help!"

But then Troy was up from the floor, trying to shove past Fletcher. Fletcher caught him again and dragged him down to the floor, holding him against the linoleum. Pain throbbed in his arm and in his head. He was in no condition to subdue a suspect. And no matter what Troy claimed, he was still a suspect.

Maybe he was even faking the shakes. He was doing it again, clicking his teeth together and trembling.

"What's wrong with you?" Fletcher asked.

A nurse appeared in the doorway and gasped. "What's going on?"

"Get security."

The officer Fletcher had called stepped around the nurse. "Detective Colton, I'm sorry—"

Fletcher shook his head, forestalling another apology. The guy had been apologizing since he'd found Fletcher and Kiki in the alley. "You're here now. We need to arrest this guy."

"Is this the Slasher?" Officer Blaine asked.

Fletcher shrugged. "I don't know." And he really wasn't certain. "But he has an outstanding warrant for drug possession and another for failure to pay child support."

"We need to assess his medical condition," the nurse said. "Before you take him out of here. He appears to be having a seizure." She stepped into the hall and shouted for a doctor.

Troy's shaking body pushed against Fletcher's wounded arm, loosening his grasp. Maybe he was faking, just trying to escape. But with the officer standing inside the room now, there was no escape.

"Wait," Kiki said. She swung her legs over the side of the bed, and she joined him and Troy on the floor. She wore a thin gown instead of her club clothes. "You wanted to talk to me, Troy," she reminded the guy. "You wanted to tell me who the Slasher is."

But the guy's eyes rolled back into his head, and he convulsed even harder. And Fletcher had a feeling that he wasn't faking now.

The doctor, the one who'd stitched up Fletcher, rushed into the room then with the nurse. Fletcher and Kiki and the officer stepped back into the hall to get out of the way. But then they had to flatten themselves against the wall as the doctor and nurse rolled out a gurney with Troy on it, his body still convulsing.

"Do you really think he knows who the Slasher is?" Officer Blaine asked Kiki the question.

She shrugged. "I don't know."

"Stay here," Fletcher told the officer. "Make sure he doesn't get away. We need to arrest him for those outstanding warrants and hold him for questioning."

The officer nodded and rushed off to catch up to that gurney, leaving Fletcher and Kiki alone. Even with the red and swollen eyes and skin, she was so beautiful. He wanted to close his arms around her and hold on and never let her go. But being close to him had already put her in danger.

"I'm sorry," he said. "I never should have gotten you involved in this investigation." Unable to stop himself, he reached out and touched her face, skimming his fingers along her cheek. "I'm so sorry you got hurt."

She shivered a bit, probably cold in her thin gown. "I'm fine," she said. "But you're not. You're bleeding more now. The wound must have reopened." She pointed at his arm where the bandage had gotten saturated, and blood trickled down over his hand to drop onto the floor.

"It could have been much worse," he said. The Slasher had lured him out to the alley to do more than maim him. "You saved my life."

But it killed him that she'd been so close to the Slasher that the Slasher could have done to her what they'd done to so many other people. And he had to make sure that she was never put in that kind of danger again.

At least not because of him.

Kiki wasn't usually squeamish, but all that blood on Fletcher's arm made her light-headed. Or maybe that was still the aftereffects of the pepper spray that had gone all over her and probably all over him, too, since his eyes were scarlet and swollen like hers.

She couldn't stand and watch as the doctor unbandaged and stitched his arm, so she slipped back into the room where she'd left her bandage lying on the bed, the bandage that had covered her eyes and made her feel so helpless. She hated that feeling, hated how it brought her back to the edge of a memory she never wanted to let into her mind again.

Of her parents' accident, of being in that car with them and not able to help them. And so, she'd shut it all out with music, singing to herself until help had arrived.

But it had been too late for her parents. Just as it had almost been too late for Fletcher and for her. The siren in the distance had probably scared off the Slasher more than her pepper spray had.

The pepper spray had covered her clothes, too, so the red leather outfit was sealed into a plastic bag. She had nothing to wear home but her gown. And she wanted to go home.

She couldn't call Grandpa, though. She didn't want him to see her with her eyes and the skin around them so red and puffy. She didn't want to worry him like she was worried. The Slasher was still out there.

She didn't think it was Troy, and she didn't think Fletcher did anymore either. But he still had Officer Blaine sticking close to him, making sure he didn't escape again.

She needed to escape. She could have called Ruby to bring her some clothes and give her a ride back to Owl Creek, but she didn't want to wake up the pregnant woman at this hour. And she didn't want to worry her either.

A knock sounded at the door, and it creaked open to Fletcher. He walked inside, a bag dangling from his hand. "I had Frannie bring you some clothes," he said.

"Frannie's here?" she asked. While she knew Ruby best, from Crosswinds, she liked all of Fletcher's sisters.

"I just had her drop some stuff at the desk that you could wear home. And I had your vehicle towed here, too. The doctor said you'll be able to go home. So you can get dressed and leave."

"Trying to get rid of me?" she asked.

"Trying to get you out of danger," he said. "You never should have been in that situation tonight. It's my fault."

"It's the Slasher's fault," she reminded him.

"But still, until the Slasher is caught, you should stay away from the clubs," he said.

"Now you're really pissing me off," she said. "You have no right to tell me how to live my life."

He stared at her with that strangely intense gaze of his. "I have no right?" he asked, and a muscle twitched along his tightly clenched jaw.

Was he mad at her?

Or just mad about what had happened?

Kiki got that; she was angry, too.

She was mad at the Slasher. At Fletcher for putting himself in danger. And mostly she was mad at herself for caring so damn much about him. This was his job—catching criminals. Of course, the work could put him in danger because of the treacherous people he was determined to catch.

But after losing her mom and dad, Kiki didn't want to lose anyone else she loved. Not that she loved Fletcher.

But she could fall for him. If she wasn't careful…

She was on the verge, feeling kind of like she was balanced on the edge of a cliff, and it wouldn't take much of a push for her to fall over it. To fall in love.

The past few weeks had been amazing. In the bedroom and out of it. Fletcher was fun and funny and sweet. And sometimes the way he looked at her…

She felt like she might not be the only one on the edge of that cliff. But he was looking at her differently right now. He seemed to want to push her away from the cliff and away from him.

"You have no right to tell me I can't do my job," she said. "Any more than I have a right to tell you that you can't do yours."

That muscle twitched along his jaw again.

"You were the one who was really in danger tonight," she pointed out. "You're the one the Slasher drugged and lured to the alley. Not me."

"But you put yourself in harm's way," he said. "Because of me. If I hadn't been there…"

"I might have gotten nervous about some other guy getting hurt and followed him into the alley," she said. "So don't take it so personally, Colton."

His lips twitched now along with that muscle, as if he was tempted to grin no matter how mad he was at her. "I will take it personally if you get hurt," he said. And then almost reluctantly he added, "I don't want you getting hurt because of me, Kiki. Because of this investigation."

"The club will close down for at least another week," she said. If not permanently since another attack had taken place. She hoped that didn't happen. She really enjoyed spinning at a venue in her hometown. "So you don't have to worry about anything happening to me there."

"I will worry until the Slasher is caught," he said.

"Maybe Troy really does know who the Slasher is," she suggested.

If so, she had no doubt that Fletcher would find out. He would get the truth out of him. And then maybe all of this would be over. But to her, right now, it felt like it was already over between the two of them.

And she wasn't sure if that was because Fletcher wanted to keep her safe or if he wanted to keep himself safe from falling for her.

She could relate to that. She didn't want to love anyone else and lose them like she had her folks. Maybe it was best if it ended now before anyone got hurt any worse.

Chapter 21

Troy Hoover had recovered remarkably fast, getting released from the hospital within just a couple of days. Maybe it was the methadone he was given, or maybe he'd just been faking all along. Fletcher didn't know. And he didn't care because now that the man had been released from the hospital, he was in police custody in Owl Creek. At the moment, he was in the interrogation room with Fletcher seated across from him.

"The Slasher wants to kill me," Troy insisted.

Fletcher furrowed his brow. "Why? The other victims were all rich and were usually at the clubs for bachelor parties." Troy was neither rich nor a bachelor.

He owed child support, but he'd never officially divorced his children's mother.

"I don't know," Troy said. "Maybe he thinks I saw him or something. That I know who he is."

"If you do know who he is, then he's right about you," Fletcher pointed out. "Who is it, Troy?"

"That old guy that hangs around the bar," Troy said, his voice cracking with fear. "He even paid Bart to try to get me to come into the club. That's why I kept going in because Bart kept calling me and telling me to show up."

That explained those quiet conversations that Fletcher had interrupted between Bart and Dan Sullivan. "Why?"

Troy shrugged. "I don't know why. The only thing I can think of is he's the Slasher."

"But you have no proof of that?"

"He's real rich and real smart. I'm sure he's covered his tracks."

"Then why would he think you're a threat?" Fletcher asked. "If there's no evidence to link him to those attacks?" Sullivan wouldn't worry about the testimony of a known drug user implicating him when there was no evidence that could back up Troy's wild claim.

"I don't know." Troy yawned. It was getting late. After his release from the hospital, he'd had to be driven to Owl Creek, processed and arraigned. "I don't know."

Because Troy was a drug user and, from his doctor's report, had done some significant damage to his body, it wasn't likely that he'd been able to execute those crimes like the Slasher had. But Dan Sullivan…

He was a distinct possibility. And even Bart.

Troy had only the bartender's word that Sullivan was the one trying to lure him into the club. What if

Bart was acting on his own? Why would either of them want Troy at the club? As Fletcher had pointed out, he wasn't the Slasher's usual victim. But maybe this had nothing to do with the Slasher.

Maybe there was another reason they'd wanted Troy at the club. Who knew? Maybe he owed Bart the bartender some money. Fletcher wasn't as concerned about Troy as he'd once been, so he stood up and stepped out of the interrogation room. "He can go back to his cell," Fletcher told an officer. He was still wanted on those other warrants and had to make whatever bail the judge had set for him.

Having shut off his phone while he was in the interrogation, Fletcher turned it back to the buzz of notifications of voice mails. His pulse quickened with hope that one was from Kiki. He hadn't seen her since that night at the hospital. But that had been for her sake as much as his.

He didn't want his investigation to put her in danger again. But the only way to make sure she was really safe was to close the case. To find the Slasher.

He checked his voice mail and found two messages. One from the hospital in Conners and another from the medical examiner in San Francisco. He played the one from the hospital first. The doctor thought that Greg would be regaining consciousness soon.

And if that happened, Fletcher wanted to take his statement. If he could talk, that was. If he remembered anything after that blow he'd taken to his head and if he'd avoided the potential brain damage it may have caused.

But if he could talk, Fletcher wanted to know if the man had seen his assailant. Though, given what he'd discovered about Greg's trust, Fletcher wasn't all that certain that the Slasher had attacked Greg or someone else had.

He rushed off to Conners, but it was late when he arrived. This late at night, the ICU was relatively dark and, except for the beep of the machines monitoring the patients, mostly quiet. Visiting hours had ended long ago. Only doctors and nurses walked around the floor, and patients were monitored through the glass walls separating their rooms from the nurses' station. It must have been a shift change or something because nobody sat at the station now.

And when Fletcher glanced through the glass wall to Greg Stehouwer's room, he noticed a shadow looming over the bed, reminding him of how, just a couple of nights ago, he had found Troy looming over Kiki's bed.

But Troy had just been standing there.

This person clutched a pillow in their hands, and they pressed that pillow over the face of the patient lying in the bed. Over Greg Stehouwer.

Fletcher rushed into the room, locked his arms around the person and pulled them back. The person thrashed in his grasp, trying to break free. But Fletcher dragged the attacker to the floor, like he had with Troy that night. This time, at least, his arm was healing and the stitches didn't reopen like last time.

Troy was skinny and not very strong. But this guy fought back, throwing elbows, trying desperately to break free and escape.

"I'm Detective Colton. You're under arrest," Fletcher told the guy. "Stop resisting!"

An elbow landed in his ribs, knocking the breath from his lungs, and the guy surged to his feet. But Fletcher drew his weapon then. "I will shoot you!"

The guy froze, and light suddenly flooded the room, illuminating Greg's attacker. His brother. Gerard stood over Fletcher, his face flushed, his hair disheveled. He glanced at the nurse who'd entered the room. Her face was flushed, too. And the glance they exchanged...

"I'm Detective Colton," Fletcher said again. "Call security." He didn't trust her to do that, though, because it looked like she might be part of this. Had Gerard paid her to make sure that the nurses' station was empty when he'd attempted to end his brother's life? "No," he said when she started moving toward the doorway. "Stay here with your coconspirator." And he called Conners' police department for backup instead.

For the past couple of days, the houseboat had felt so empty without Fletcher that it was difficult for Kiki to stay there. And even harder to sleep.

But she didn't want to put her grandpa in danger, just in case Fletcher was right to be so worried about her safety. Although, if he was worried, why hadn't he checked on her? Why hadn't he called?

Or better yet, why hadn't he come home?

No. Not home. This wasn't his home. It wasn't hers either. She was just staying there while she was in Owl Creek and that was just for the rest of the summer.

Fletcher had sent that patrol car past the place several times. She'd seen it earlier that evening when she and Fancy had started out for their walk. Maybe a long walk in the night air would clear her head and hopefully her heart, too, because it was too full of feelings right now. Feelings she didn't want to have.

Kiki had taken such a long walk that both she and Fancy were worn out. All she wanted to do was go back to the boat and crawl into bed. But then she remembered that the sheets and pillows would smell like Fletcher. And she knew she would just lie there, yearning for him.

To be with him. To have his arms wrapped around her, holding her close like he had every night for the last several nights.

Her footsteps slowed on the dock as she neared the slip where the houseboat was anchored. She didn't want to be there without Fletcher.

Was it already too late? Had she already fallen for him?

It didn't matter how she felt if he didn't return her feelings. And even if he did, how in the world could a relationship between them last?

His life was here in Owl Creek. His job. His family.

She only had her grandfather here and some friends. But her life, her career, was taking her other places and probably always would.

"Ah, Fancy…" she murmured with a weary sigh.

The puppy whined and pulled at her leash, tugging Kiki toward the boat. Then Kiki looked up and saw what the puppy must have spotted. A light was on inside the cabin. A light that Kiki hadn't left on since it hadn't been dark out yet when she and Fancy had left earlier.

Since she hadn't left that light on, who had? Fletcher?

Had he come back to the boat after all? Maybe she'd read him all wrong at the hospital the other night. Maybe he hadn't been trying to create distance between them the past couple of days; maybe he'd just been busy.

Eager to see him, she helped Fancy onto the boat deck and then jumped onto it herself. Fancy, her leash trailing behind her, rushed through the open door of the cabin. But instead of yipping with excitement, as she did every time she saw Fletcher, she growled instead.

And Kiki knew that it wasn't Fletcher who'd turned on that light but someone else. Someone Fancy instinctively didn't like or trust. And the little dog had very good instincts about people.

If Fancy didn't like or trust the person, Kiki shouldn't either. She should turn and run for help.

But she couldn't leave the little puppy alone on the boat with whoever was in the cabin making her growl like she was. Kiki couldn't let anything happen to the dog she was supposed to be fostering and protecting.

She just had to figure out, with her pepper spray gone, how she was going to protect them both.

Chapter 22

Fletcher was lead detective for a reason. He was good at breaking a suspect. And it had taken only a few minutes in the interrogation room for him to get the nurse to talk. She'd openly shared how Gerard had spent the past couple of weeks trying to charm her into doing what he wanted. Into killing his brother.

She'd refused to unplug his machine when he'd needed it to breathe. Or so she claimed.

But Fletcher intended to find out exactly how the doctors had realized Greg was able to breathe on his own. Maybe she *had* unplugged it. She was demanding immunity, though, to spill all on Gerard. So Fletcher encouraged her to talk some more.

And she'd admitted to making sure that he had a clear shot at his brother. That he'd intended to suffocate him and just make it look like he'd stopped breathing again.

Greg was still alive, though.

And Fletcher made sure his brother knew it when he walked into the interrogation room where he'd left him. He glanced around. "No lawyer? I thought you called your parents. Your wife…"

Nobody had retained a lawyer for him, probably not once they'd realized that he was going to be charged with the attempted murder of his own brother.

Gerard didn't say a word, just gritted his teeth as if it was a struggle to hold back what he really wanted to say. Maybe it wouldn't take Fletcher much longer to break him than it had the nurse.

"Your little friend had no problem talking to me," Fletcher shared. "She gave her statement about how you tried to hire her to kill your brother. You wanted her to finish the job you weren't able to do on your own."

The guy glared at him.

"So you're not what I expected the Slasher to be," he said. And he still wasn't. "But it's going to be good to charge you for all those crimes, too, in all those other states. Close all those cases. And you can pick what prison you'd like to spend the majority of your life in."

"I'm not the Slasher."

He wasn't. He had alibis for the other attacks. Fletcher had already checked that. "Those other precincts can't wait to close those cases—put the Slasher away for good."

"I'm not the Slasher," Gerard repeated.

"No, but you borrowed the Slasher's MO when you

tried to kill your brother in the parking lot of Club Ignition. And I know you're the one who did that, Gerard. The warehouse next to the club, the one nearest the parking lot, is in the process of being renovated, too. In order to protect the materials being delivered, they installed a security system."

Gerard shook his head. "That's not true."

No. It wasn't, but Fletcher needed his suspect to think it was.

"You would have said something sooner if you saw..." Gerard trailed off and swallowed deeply, nervously.

"If I saw you trying to kill your brother on camera," Fletcher finished for him. "We didn't know about that security footage until the other night, when there was another attack outside the club." He gestured at his bandaged arm. "It's all over now, Gerard."

Tears rolled down Gerard's face. "He doesn't deserve it. He doesn't deserve it," he murmured.

"No. He didn't deserve to be attacked like that," Fletcher agreed.

"No. Greg doesn't deserve the trust. He's only marrying Melanie so he can get his hands on our grandparents' money. He never visited them. He was never nice to them. Not like I was. He doesn't deserve it."

So, as Fletcher had suspected, it was all about money. "And if Greg is gone, the rest of that trust will go to you?"

Gerard nodded. "I deserve it. He doesn't. He doesn't deserve it."

Fletcher sighed and stood up, leaving the man to

cry alone in the interrogation room. He'd closed that case, but the Slasher's identity was still up in the air.

And that was the person Fletcher wanted to catch the most, especially since his arm was throbbing again. That dull ache kept reminding him of why he was staying away from Kiki—that it was to keep her safe.

But he missed her so damn much.

After stepping out of the interrogation room, he checked his phone again like he had earlier. But there were no new voice mails. Kiki hadn't called him.

He hadn't returned the medical examiner's call yet. But since it was earlier in San Francisco than it was in Owl Creek, he hit the button to call the ME back.

"Detective Colton returning your call," he said.

"Detective Colton," the doctor greeted him. "I'm glad you called back. I have some interesting information about Caitlin Sullivan."

"You found her?"

"I did, and her father knows it. He identified her body but refused to take it."

"What?"

"She had overdosed on drugs," the doctor said. "And he was furious about it. Said she got what she deserved and her dealer would be next."

Was that why the Slasher attacked those men? Did he think the men he'd targeted had been drug dealers? Was that the motivation for all those attacks?

Kiki rushed into the cabin after Fancy, trying to catch her leash, trying to pull her away from the man kicking out at her as the puppy tugged on the already frayed legs of Troy's tattered jeans. "Come!" she commanded the dog. She just managed to catch her leash as she moved to make the hand gesture. She didn't want Fancy anywhere near Troy.

She didn't want Troy anywhere near her. Wasn't he supposed to be in the hospital? Or jail? Fletcher had been determined to arrest him.

"What are you doing here?" she asked as she held tightly to the leash. Fancy struggled to get to Troy who sat on the couch where she'd found him the last time he'd broken in.

There was no broken glass this time. Not since she'd fixed the door. But she must have left it unlocked. Maybe she'd done that in the hopes that Fletcher would show up.

She wished he was here now.

"I wanted to talk to you, Kiki," he said. "To say I'm sorry…"

She was, too. So sorry that she hadn't checked him out more thoroughly before she'd asked him to help her. "No. I mean… Why are you here? And not in the hospital or…"

"Jail?" he asked. "Your old friend arrested and interrogated me."

"And let you go?" Fletcher wouldn't have done that if he still suspected Troy was the Slasher.

His usually pale face flushed in the glow of the lamp that he'd turned on next to the couch. "He didn't let me go. But I got bail."

"And you had the money for that?" But not to pay his child support?

"I—I thought you paid it," he said.

She stared at him in disbelief. "Really? Why?"

"I—I thought we were friends, Kiki," he said. "We've known each other so long."

"I don't know if I ever really knew you," she said. And she didn't want to get to know him. "I had no idea about the drugs, Troy."

"I'm going to get clean," he said. "I'm going to go to rehab."

"And your kids?" she asked. "How could you just abandon them? Stop supporting them?"

"I-it's more complicated than that, Kiki," he said. "There's more to the story. I'm no good for them. Not now. But maybe after rehab…"

"I hope you go," she said.

"I already signed up at the hospital," Troy said. "A doctor got me a room at a place. I can go now that I got out of jail. That's why I thought you paid the bail. I thought…"

She shook her head. "It wasn't me, Troy. I want you to go to rehab. But I really just want you to leave. And please, don't come back again."

She didn't think he would have been given bail if he'd actually been charged with the attacks the Slasher had committed. But it didn't matter to her. She didn't want to deal with Troy anymore.

"Kiki, I'm really sorry," he said.

"I'm sorry, too," a deep voice said from behind Kiki. And she whirled around as Fancy snapped and snarled at the man who'd snuck up on them both.

"Mr. Sullivan?" she asked, staring at him in shock.

"What—what are you doing here?" And why had he apologized to her?

Troy's face paled again until he looked like death, and he stared at Mr. Sullivan in shock. "It was you," he murmured. "It was you."

"What was him?" Kiki asked. The Slasher? Was Mr. Sullivan the Slasher? He stood between her and the door, and she didn't know how she would get away from him, especially if he had that knife she'd seen in the alley. That long, sharp machete that had cut through the air and slashed Fletcher's arm.

She should have checked on him and made sure that he was okay. That his wound had healed.

Regret weighed heavily on her for so many things. Fletcher. And not replacing her empty canister of pepper spray. She had a feeling that she was going to need it now.

"I bailed Troy out," Mr. Sullivan said.

"Why—why would you do that?" Kiki asked. "I didn't even know you knew each other."

"We don't," Troy said. "I've just seen him around the clubs when he's been looking for his daughter."

Mr. Sullivan shook his head. "I know where she is. Thanks to you, Troy. You're the one I've been looking for. I didn't know it was you until Bart told me, but now I know you're the one who got my little girl hooked on drugs."

Troy shook his head. "No, no. Not me."

"You don't deal drugs out of the clubs?" Dan Sullivan snorted. "Don't lie to me."

Troy's pale face flushed again. "I—I might have

from time to time when I needed money. And people needed something to feel good."

Dan's face flushed now. "Caitlin didn't need to feel good. She needed to grow up. To deal with life like an adult instead of running away and hiding from her problems like a child. Like you've been running away and hiding, Troy. It's time to face the consequences of your bad choices now, just like Caitlin faced her consequences."

Kiki tensed. He'd always acted like such a distraught father. "You knew where she's been all this time?" she asked with surprise. "You knew she was dead."

"Caitlin paid for her mistakes," Dan said. "Now it's time for Troy to pay for his."

"What about me?" Kiki asked. "I didn't know what he was doing."

Dan snorted. "Really? You worked with him for how long and had no idea what he was doing?"

She shook her head. "I really, really didn't know." But she doubted that was going to matter to Dan Sullivan. Because she saw now what he'd been holding behind his back...

It wasn't a knife like the one the Slasher had used in the alley. This was a gun, which was even more dangerous. He wouldn't even have to get close to them to kill them. And she had no doubt that was what he intended to do, or he wouldn't have brought the weapon with him.

"Then I really, really am sorry," Dan said.

Troy shook his head. "C'mon, man, she's not part of this," he said. "Let her go."

"What? So she can get help for you? Like that rehab you think you're getting into?" Dan shook his head. "I can't have that. I can't have you getting better, getting your life back when you took mine."

"I didn't have anything to do with this," Kiki said. "So if you kill me, that's going to make you as bad as you think Troy is. Actually, worse. He didn't know that your daughter was going to die." And Dan had every intention of killing her.

And Kiki had every intention of making sure that didn't happen. She wasn't going to die like this. But she wasn't sure how to stop Dan from shooting her and Troy.

Chapter 23

Fletcher had intended to talk to Troy again about Dan Sullivan. But when he went to see him in the cells, he found that he'd been bailed out. And when he found out who had bailed him out...

"Dan Sullivan," Fletcher murmured. "Why in the hell would he have bailed out a drug user like Troy?" But then he knew why.

For revenge.

Troy could be more than a drug user. He could be a dealer as well. He'd mentioned something about rehab during their interview earlier. But a call to his doctor confirmed he hadn't checked in yet. So where would he have gone?

Security footage from the jail showed him walking out on his own. Nobody had picked him up. He'd just walked off. The marina wasn't far from the police department. Every other time he'd come around town, Troy had sought out Kiki. Fletcher figured the man was in love with her. He understood all too well how easy it would be to fall for her, especially after watching her DJ, after hearing her sing and seeing her dance and how the music flowed through her like joy.

And how that joy flowed over onto everyone around her.

Troy might not have been the only one who fell for Kiki. Fletcher didn't think Dan Sullivan had, though, so he probably wouldn't care if Kiki wound up as collateral damage in his quest for revenge.

Fletcher jumped in his Owl Creek PD vehicle, but he didn't engage the lights and sirens. He didn't want to alert anyone that he was coming. Except Kiki.

He hoped she knew if she was in danger that he would rush to her rescue like she'd rushed to his. But he had to make sure that he could actually rescue her and that he wasn't already too late.

Once he parked his SUV, he hurried along the dock, but this time he was careful to keep his footsteps as quiet as he could. He didn't want anyone to hear him coming and he kept to the shadows the boats cast on the dock despite the brightness of the full moon. But as he neared the boat, he knew someone had noticed him.

Kiki and Troy stood on the rear deck, near the railing, with Dan in front of them, his back toward the dock, toward Fletcher. Fancy stood next to Kiki, quivering and snarling with fear and anger.

She knew the man was a threat even if she didn't understand that he was holding a gun. The barrel pointed directly at Kiki's big heart. Fancy was the one who saw him, and she started yipping until he held up a hand the way that Kiki had taught him. The hold command.

Stay.

Don't Move.

Don't React.

He silently told her all those things, and somehow the puppy must have understood his commands because she stayed next to Kiki and she stayed quiet, barely betraying any interest in him. So he was able to creep closer.

But if he jumped on the boat, it might shift beneath his weight and reveal his presence. He hadn't ever seen anyone on the boat docked next to hers when he'd stayed with Kiki. He could probably get on it without bothering whoever the owner was. But if he stepped onto it, would it shift enough in the water to move her boat, too?

From where he was, he couldn't get a clear shot at Sullivan. The cabin blocked most of his body, leaving just his hand and that gun most visible to Fletcher. Fletcher was a good shot, but hitting a hand wasn't easy.

And if the man pulled the trigger convulsively, he was going to put a bullet right into Kiki's heart. And that was like putting a bullet in Fletcher's, too. He couldn't lose her. Not like this...

Fletcher was there. Kiki knew it from the way that Fancy's tail had wagged and the way that she'd whined. Kiki couldn't see him, but it was enough that Fancy had, enough that she'd minded the command he'd given her.

Wait.

Stay.

Kiki had to tell herself to do the same thing. She had to stall for more time, like she had earlier, when she'd convinced Dan not to shoot them within the cabin but to come up to the deck.

To make them jump into the water with the anchor tied around their feet.

"People will hear the gunshot," she'd told him. "I'm not the only one living on their boat. Other people will see you, will stop you. You won't get away."

She wasn't sure that he'd wanted to, though. Maybe, because his daughter was dead, he intended to kill himself once he'd killed her dealer.

And Kiki.

But clearly, he wasn't done yet. "I have to kill Bart, too," he told them as he pushed them closer to the railing behind them. "I know he's part of this." He pointed the gun at Troy. "He works with you, with the drugs."

Troy let out a shaky breath. "He didn't have anything to do with your daughter, sir. I don't think I did either. I didn't recognize her picture when you showed me. I don't think I knew her."

"You sold to her," Dan insisted, waving his gun in a hand that shook with his fury.

As upset as he was, he might accidentally pull that trigger. She tried to ease between him and Troy. He might be less likely to pull the trigger and kill her since he knew for certain that she had nothing to do with his daughter's death.

"There are a lot of dealers in the clubs," Troy insisted. "Customers. Bouncers."

"Bartenders and you," Dan said. "I know you and Bart work together. That's why I paid him to get you into the club. I was going to kill you by cutting you up like that maniac cuts up his victims in the alley." He focused on Kiki again. "But you brought that cop into the place."

So much for Fletcher's cover.

She didn't want to lie to Sullivan and set him off any more than he already was. Because she'd felt that faint motion as the boat moved in the water. Either someone had stepped onto it or onto the boat next to it, causing a ripple along the surface of the water. "He is a cop," she admitted. "He was going undercover to catch the Slasher. How did you know that?"

Dan pointed his gun at Troy again. "He told Bart. He saw you both outside his van that first night, saw that he drove a police vehicle."

And so, Troy had given him up, maybe warning Bart to lie low with the drug dealing while Fletcher was there.

"Not all clubgoers are that bad," Kiki said in defense of her job. "Some people are just there to dance, to enjoy the music, to meet other people."

Dan snorted. "You're naive, Kiki."

"No, I see the good in people. I don't think the worst of everyone I meet."

"That's why you're here," he said. "With an anchor tied around your ankles."

She'd done the tying. It was about as tight as Fletcher

laced his boots now. She would be able to get it off, and so would Troy if he didn't panic. He was panicking now, his body shaking, his breath coming in pants that were getting higher and shallower, like he was about to hyperventilate.

If he went into the water like that, he was going to drown before they ever got the rope and anchor off. She had to keep stalling to give Fletcher time to rescue them. But would he rescue them or put himself in more danger, like he had the night he'd gone into that alley looking for her?

"It's time now," Sullivan said. "Enough stalling. Time for the two of you to jump over the railing. Time to end this."

Troy started crying now. Soft, gasping sobs. And tears rolled down his face.

Instead of being moved, Dan Sullivan laughed. "You're not making me feel sorry for you. Not at all." He looked at Kiki and his mouth slid into a frown. "You, I feel sorry for—having to die with a scumbag like him. It would be better for you to die alone."

Even if Dan and Troy weren't there, she wouldn't have died alone. Fletcher was there. She could see him now inside the cabin of her boat, moving toward them. Fancy saw him, too, and whined deep in her throat, as if anxious to rush toward him, to leap and lick all over him like she usually did.

Kiki wanted to do the same, but she was too scared. For her and Troy and for Fletcher, too.

Dan had to think he was in charge. He seemed like a man who was always in control. Could that be why his daughter had rebelled with the clubbing and the drugs? Maybe he'd been too controlling.

Instead of crying, Kiki shook her head as if she pitied him. "This is sad."

"What do you mean?" he asked.

"That you're not strong enough to deal with your grief and your regrets about your daughter," she said.

He bristled and tightened his grasp on the gun. "You don't know what you're talking about!"

"I lost my parents," she said. "In a traffic accident. I didn't blame the other driver even though he left the scene. I didn't have to chase him down and avenge my parents."

"You must have been a kid when that happened," Dan guessed. Correctly. "And you would have felt better if you had."

"I felt better letting them go with grace and with honoring their memories by being the best person I could be," she said. "I didn't become bitter and crazy. I didn't lose control so badly that I turned into a monster."

"Shut up!" Dan yelled at her. "You don't know what you're talking about! Shut up!" And he swung that barrel back from Troy to her, focusing it on her heart. And his finger moved toward the trigger.

Troy stopped crying to gasp and he even pointed at Fletcher, tipping Dan off to him sneaking onto the boat. Kiki reached out, trying to lower his arm, trying to get him to stop. And Troy toppled back, falling over the railing. The rope wound through the anchor and lashed around both of their ankles. If Troy was heavy enough, he might pull that anchor over with him, and then Kiki would go into the water, too.

But she cared less about that than about Fletcher as Dan spun around toward the cabin, his gun raised and his finger moving toward the trigger, squeezing and firing off a bullet in Fletcher's direction.

Fletcher's gun was out, too, but he might not fire back, might worry about hitting her and Troy with the way they were behind Dan. But then they weren't there as Troy fell into the water, taking a piece of the deck railing with him as the anchor struck it, breaking it.

And that rope tightened around Kiki's ankles, pulling her off the boat and into the water, too. And then down into the depths of the lake.

She was worried about herself and Troy, but she was the most worried about Fletcher. She had a chance to loosen that rope again, to free herself and Troy from the anchor.

But if Fletcher had been shot...

Chapter 24

The first bullet missed Fletcher. The second was never fired because Fletcher didn't miss. He dropped Dan Sullivan to the deck. And then he went over the railing after Kiki and Troy. She broke through the water, coming up as he sank down into the lake.

She tossed her head, sending water spraying, and then she started slipping under again. And Fletcher could see Troy pulling her down as he flailed and panicked.

Fletcher swam to him, trying to break his grasp on Kiki. But he kept pulling at her, pinching her skin, pulling her under the water. So Fletcher swung his fist, knocking the guy out. And then he carried him up as Kiki shot back to the surface.

Sirens whined in the distance. Fletcher had sent out a text to dispatch. They'd been on their way with the order to come in stealthily. Maybe a report of shots fired had had them turning on the sirens and lights.

Backup arrived too late to save Dan Sullivan. But it had probably been too late to save him long before Fletcher shot him. He didn't know if the same was true about Troy, but instead of going to the hospital, he'd wanted to go to that rehab program. So after giving his statement for the police report, he was given a ride to the facility. Officer Blaine was to make sure that he really checked in, because Fletcher still had his doubts about the man.

Fletcher still had a lot of doubts about a lot of parts of this case. And even about Kiki.

Fletcher had wanted Kiki to go to the hospital, too, but she'd insisted she was fine. He wasn't so sure that she was because she kept trembling even though the water hadn't been cold. And thanks to how loosely she'd tied the anchor rope to her and to Troy, neither of them had been under water for very long.

Fletcher wasn't fine. Physically there wasn't anything wrong with him. He hadn't reopened the stitches on his arm. But emotionally…

He was as on edge as he'd been when he'd seen Sullivan pointing that gun barrel at Kiki's heart. Even after they finished giving their statements to police and everyone had left, he was still jumpy. Maybe more so because it was just the two of them. And Fancy, who'd curled up at his feet as he sat on the deck, watching the sun come up.

Kiki had gone inside to change out of her wet shorts and shirt. And clearly when she walked back out, drying her hair on a towel, she hadn't expected to see him still there. Her dark eyes widened in surprise. And he couldn't tell if she was happy or upset that he hadn't left.

Then those eyes suddenly welled with tears that sparkled in the light. And Fletcher jumped up and rushed to her, closing his arms around her.

Kiki, being Kiki, didn't cry. She didn't give in to tears, but she closed her arms around him and clutched him close. And they just held each other.

He was alive. When she'd gone over the side, she hadn't known what she would find when she resurfaced. Fletcher dead? The thought had horrified her, making her move even faster to ease out of the rope and fight her way out of the water. She'd helped Troy, too, but in his panic, he might have drowned them both. If not for Fletcher jumping in after them...

Kiki and Troy were probably alive because of Fletcher. So maybe it was just gratitude that had her clinging to him like she was.

Or relief that they were all alive.

Well, not all of them.

Dan Sullivan hadn't made it. But she suspected he'd been gone a long time ago—lost to his hatred and bitterness and madness.

She was just glad she hadn't lost Fletcher. Yet.

She knew he was slipping away from her though. That their time together was coming to an end. They had no future. His life, his career, his family, were all here in Owl Creek.

He released a shaky breath that stirred her hair and

made her shiver. "I'm so glad you're all right." But then he pulled back and cupped her face in his hands, and he stared into her eyes with that intense stare that unnerved and excited her so damn much. "Are you really all right?"

She nodded and released a shaky breath of her own. For the moment, with him here, holding her, she was all right.

"I'm not," he said.

She could feel his body shaking against hers now. "Fletcher…"

"I was so scared when I saw him pointing that gun at you, so worried that it might accidentally go off and hurt you or…" He shuddered again.

And she closed her arms around him, then tugged him inside with her, through the open door to the cabin and then through the cabin to her bedroom.

Fancy was on their heels. But Kiki shut the little puppy out. Instead of whining, the exhausted dog just leaned against the door. She wanted to know that they were close.

That was what Kiki wanted, too. Just to have Fletcher close even if it was only for a little while longer.

"Kiki…" he murmured, and then he lowered his head to hers. At first his lips just brushed across hers in a gentle, almost reverent kiss.

Then she reached up and tangled her fingers in his damp hair, and she held his head against hers as she deepened the kiss. She teased him with her tongue.

His breath caught and then he kissed her back just

as passionately, just as desperately as she was kissing him. "Kiki…"

"We need to get you out of these wet clothes," she said, as she tugged his damp T-shirt over his head.

He shucked off his jeans and boxers and stood before her, gloriously naked. He was so perfect. His chest and thighs so muscular. His stomach so lean.

She lifted the T-shirt dress she'd pulled on to replace her wet clothes. And his breath shuddered out in a ragged groan.

"You are so beautiful," he said. His fingers, shaking slightly, traced her every curve with the reverence that had been in his first kiss. Then his lips replaced his fingers.

He kissed her everywhere, and passion overwhelmed her, making her legs shake. She tumbled back onto the bed, pulling him with her. She loved the weight of him, the heat of him, on top of her. His heart beat in time with hers, fast and furiously.

"Fletcher, I need you," she admitted. She felt a flicker of unease as she said it, concerned that she wasn't talking about just now, but forever.

But she'd never needed anyone like that.

Instead of joining their bodies like she needed him to do, he moved down hers. He kissed her breasts, flicking his tongue across each nipple, and then he moved lower, making love to her with his mouth.

She clutched the sheets as the pressure built inside her and then released in an orgasm that left her shuddering and gasping for breath. She closed her eyes, riding the peak of pleasure. And she heard a cupboard open, a packet tear and then he eased inside her, stretching her, filling her completing her.

He began to move, building that tension again. She clutched at him, locking her legs around him, grabbing his shoulders. She met his thrusts, arching up, holding him close, pulling him deeper.

He groaned. And his mouth covered hers, kissing her, imitating with his tongue what he was doing with his body. And that pressure inside her burst again, filling her with pleasure.

Then his body tensed. A deep groan slipped between his lips as he found his release. He flopped onto his back, carrying her with him so that she was on top and their bodies were still joined. And he stared up into her face with such an expression...

Of awe and wonder.

It probably mirrored the expression on her face.

"You are amazing," he whispered. Then he arched up and kissed her, and it was that soft tender kiss that had her heart swelling and warming.

And...

No. She could not fall for Fletcher, but she had a feeling that it was already too late.

They made love again. More slowly, more reverently, before finally settling onto the bed to rest sometime later. But Kiki couldn't sleep. And his body was tense beside hers despite all the orgasms they'd had.

"Why did you come here?" she asked. She hoped it was because he'd missed her like she'd missed him.

"I found out that Dan Sullivan's daughter was dead

and that he refused to claim her body. It also sounded like he was going after her drug dealer."

"Troy."

"And when he bailed him out, I figured he was going to go after him, wherever he was."

So he hadn't come to see her. He hadn't missed her the past couple of days like she'd missed him.

"And I figured, knowing how he kept turning up wherever you were, that Troy might be here, putting you in danger and…" His gruff voice trailed off and he shuddered and pulled her closer. "I was so worried that I would be too late."

"You were right on time," she said with a slight smile. Then she asked, "Is it over?" And she wasn't really asking about the case. She wondered about the two of them…

"I don't think Dan Sullivan or Gerard Stehouwer are the Slasher," he said.

"Gerard Stehouwer?"

"Greg's brother is the one who tried to kill him. Twice, actually. Once in the parking lot and once in the ICU."

She had a feeling that Fletcher had stopped that from happening, just as he'd stopped Dan Sullivan from killing Troy. "Then who is the Slasher?" she asked. "Do you still suspect Troy?"

"I don't know. I have the note the Slasher slipped me. There is some DNA on it. We'll see if it matches Troy's or Gerard's or Dan's."

"And if it doesn't?"

"Then the Slasher is still out there." He tightened his arms around her. "But I will catch whoever it is, Kiki."

At what cost, she wondered. His life? Her heart? She had a feeling they were both in danger.

According to the latest media reports, the stupid people of Owl Creek believed that the Slasher was either dead or in jail. That the grief-stricken old man or the rich frat boy was the Slasher. The Slasher hated this, hated how other people hadn't just copycatted but tried to pretend to be the Slasher.

That wasn't admiration. That was disrespect.

And the Slasher had already been disrespected enough. It was time to end this once and for all.

Chapter 25

Fletcher knew it was a risk coming back to Club Ignition with Kiki. It was a risk to him because the more time he spent with her, the more he was falling for her. And she wasn't going to stay. As she played and sang and danced, he could see the star that she was, burning much too bright for Owl Creek.

He didn't want to hold her back. But he was so damn tempted to try. But that would have been selfish. And he cared about her too much to be that way with her.

"You know your cover is blown," Bart told him as he poured a cup of coffee for Fletcher and pushed it across the bar.

Fletcher had brought his own thermos, like Kiki brought her tea. He wasn't taking any chances anymore. At least not with his life.

With his heart.

He took a chance every time he was around Kiki.

Fletcher chuckled. "I really am an old friend of Kiki's," he said. "And I really am her assistant." But he wanted to be so much more.

Bart snorted and shook his head. "Okay, sure, but you're still a cop, too."

"Lead detective," Fletcher said with pride in the title. Now if only he could live up to it...

His new boss was happy with him for closing a couple of big cases. Greg Stehouwer's attack. And Dan Sullivan's attempted crimes.

His boss thought Fletcher had closed the Slasher case, too. But Fletcher didn't think so.

The Slasher was still out there. Maybe even here tonight now that Club Ignition had reopened.

"Did you get promoted after closing the Slasher case?" Bart asked.

"It's not closed," Fletcher said. At least not as far as he was concerned.

"So that's why you're back here."

"I'm just helping out Kiki until she can find a new assistant."

"I thought Troy was getting clean," Bart said. "That he went into rehab."

"That doesn't mean Kiki will work with him again." Fletcher studied Bart's face. "Sullivan said you worked with Troy selling drugs. He was coming for you next."

"I guess I owe you a thank you then," Bart said. "You made sure that bitter old man won't hurt anyone else.

And he was wrong about me. I'm not selling anything but drinks."

Fletcher pushed the coffee mug across the bar toward Bart. "I was drugged that night that Kiki and I were attacked in the alley."

"Then I guess you should have kept a better eye on your cup," Bart said. "Because I didn't put anything in it."

"The other victims had been drugged, too," Fletcher said.

"It wasn't me," Bart said. "I'm not a drug user. And I am damn well not that violent Slasher. Anybody can get close enough to drop something in someone else's glass."

And a note in their pocket?

Fletcher might have believed that Bart had drugged the drinks, but he wouldn't have been able to slip him a note, not when he rarely left his place behind the bar.

"You're the detective," Bart said. "So you must have thought about how a lot of these were at bachelor parties. They usually do shots, line them up at the bar, but a lot of people buy the groom drinks, too. A lot of women."

"Women…" The DNA on that note had recently come back as not a match to Dan Sullivan or Gerard Stehouwer because it had belonged to a woman. An unidentified woman.

Fletcher's boss hadn't considered it that much of a lead. And Fletcher had agreed because the Slasher had never left any DNA behind at any other scene, so he would have made certain not to leave any on the note either. They'd assumed that the woman must have just touched the paper at some point.

Bart's head bobbed in a nod. "Yeah, it's not just guys buying girls drinks anymore. You know, women's lib. A lot of women buy drinks for men, too."

The Slasher was a woman. It made total sense. It was how she was able to get so close to shove a note in the guy's pocket. And how, even though that knife was sharp, the wound on Fletcher's arm hadn't been deeper.

The Slasher was a woman, but which woman? Was she here tonight?

The club was packed. Probably because the news had all made it sound like the Slasher had either been arrested or killed. But Kiki knew that wasn't the case. The DNA results on that note shoved in Fletcher's pocket hadn't matched Dan Sullivan or Gerard Ste-houwer's. It had belonged to a woman.

Fletcher hadn't been as quick to accept that, though, pointing out how the Slasher had never left any DNA behind before and probably would have made certain to leave none on the note.

Sure, no DNA had been left at the scene of the crimes because the Slasher wore that hazmat-type suit. Ones that had been all too available during the pandemic. But the Slasher wouldn't have been able to wear that suit inside the club without being noticed, especially when slipping a note into the pocket of their chosen victim.

The Slasher had chosen Fletcher once. Had slipped Fletcher that note.

It had to be a woman. And Kiki remembered who'd

been dancing so closely to him when he'd started acting so out of it.

Her girls. Amy, Claire and Janie.

She hadn't seen any of them when she'd gone looking for him. Of course, she hadn't looked for him in the ladies' room, so they'd probably been in there.

Or...

Maybe one of them had been in the alley, waiting for him to come out that door. Waiting to attack him.

She shuddered as she remembered that night, how close she'd come to losing him. And the turntable skipped a beat. She steadied her hand and kept spinning while her thoughts spun as well.

She and Fletcher had both been scared about coming back to the club, but they'd each been frightened for the other. She'd promised she would stay inside her booth, and he'd promised he wouldn't drink anything but the coffee that was in the thermos next to hers. And he wouldn't go out into the alley without backup.

An officer from Conners was here tonight, blending in with the crowd. There was another bachelor party here; maybe they thought it was safe, though.

That the Slasher was gone.

But Kiki saw her girls jumping up and down in the crowd. They weren't all dancing together; they'd joined that group from the bachelor party. Some of the guys were grinding up on them. Some of the women were returning the favor.

And then she noticed the slip of paper in Janie's hand, how the strobe light flashed against the white material and bounced back at her.

How had Kiki never noticed that before?

Because she hadn't been looking for it.

Then the paper disappeared. And then Janie did as well, disappearing into the crowd. Had she slipped that paper into a man's pocket?

And which man?

Kiki called out, "Where's my assistant at?" Then making her voice sound like Lucille Ball's, she said, "Fletcher, I need you."

The crowd laughed at her impression. But she didn't see Fletcher among them. Where had he gone? Was he already in the alley? If he was, he was in danger.

Because Kiki was pretty sure the Slasher was heading out there now.

The machete was sharper than it had ever been, the blade honed so that it would slice through skin and maybe even bone now. If Janie could swing it hard enough...

And she was damn sure that she would.

She wasn't just going to maim this idiot. She was going to kill him.

Maybe that was what it was going to take for her to finally get the respect she deserved. The respect her ex-fiancé hadn't given her.

He'd called her stupid and ugly and so far beneath him that he'd been a fool to ever propose to her. He hadn't been a fool when Janie had paid his way through med school.

No. She had been his everything then. He'd showered

her with compliments and gratitude even as he'd kept putting off their wedding day.

And even though he hadn't been home much, she'd believed it was just because of his long hours. Especially during his residency.

Residents didn't make any real money, he told her, so they would get married after he became an attending physician. Then he would be making so much money that they could have the wedding of their dreams. The wedding she deserved to have for everything she'd done for him.

But once he'd gotten his job offer and his six-figure salary, he'd asked for his ring back. He'd never intended to marry someone like her. As a rich doctor, he could do so much better than her.

Once Janie had taken care of his face, his new fiancée had thought she could do better, too, and she'd dumped him just like he had dumped Janie.

But that hadn't been enough for her. Because when she'd gone out to the club, she'd seen all those other grooms-to-be flirting with women, eager to cheat on their fiancées. Janie had decided that they didn't deserve their brides. They didn't deserve their happiness, and she'd taken it away from them.

She wanted to take away more than someone's happiness tonight. She intended to take away his life. And Kiki wasn't going to stop her this time.

Chapter 26

Fletcher had the note. *Meet me in the alley and I will show you a good time...*

It wasn't his. He'd taken it off the man who'd stumbled through the kitchen, intent on going out to the alley to meet the woman who had slipped him the note on the dance floor.

The Slasher wasn't going to get the hapless groom-to-be that she'd tried to lure outside. She was going to get Fletcher. He drew his weapon from his holster and pushed open the door to the alley. The metal hinges creaked, announcing his arrival. But nothing moved in the shadows.

Was the Slasher out there?

Or had this been a distraction? An attempt to get Fletcher's attention somewhere else while she attacked...

Kiki?

No. Kiki was safe. Someone had actually helped him out with that, jamming the door to the DJ booth so that Kiki hadn't been able to get it open. She could have jumped over, like he regularly did. But he'd planted an officer in plainclothes next to it to keep Kiki safe.

What about him?

Was he safe?

He started down the wooden steps that led from the door to the asphalt of the alley. And he made sure to clomp his boots and shuffle, so he sounded like he was drunk.

Or drugged.

Fletcher would have him tested to determine what exactly was wrong with the man besides poor judgement. Fletcher's judgement might have been a little poor to walk out here on his own, especially after he made that promise to Kiki that he wouldn't.

But he wasn't alone. As he hit the bottom step and made certain to bang his shoulder, loudly, against the dumpster, the Slasher jumped out from the other side, brandishing that sharp weapon.

But he had his gun trained on her, and then lights flooded the alley and other officers jumped from their hiding place inside the abandoned warehouse on the other side of the alley.

The Slasher held tight to the hilt of the knife, though, as if tempted to swing it. To try to kill him.

"Drop it, Janie," he said. The groom-to-be had told him that the redhead must have given him the note, that she'd been dancing closest to him. "Or I will kill you."

Finally, the knife dropped, clattering against the asphalt. And Janie dragged off the hood and mask and gasped for breath. "I hate you! I hate you! You can't stop me. You can't stop me now."

"It's over, Janie," he said. "You're under arrest."

"But it's not my fault," she said. "They don't have to cheat. They want to. And I want to make sure nobody ever wants them again."

He could imagine what her motivation was. "Jilted bride?" he asked.

"I hate you!" she screamed, and she bent down to grab the knife. But the other officers were there, grabbing her arms, pulling them behind her back to cuff her. "I hate you!"

He didn't doubt it. She was obviously full of hate right now. Just like Dan Sullivan had been.

And he thought of what Kiki had said to the man, about how she'd chosen forgiveness. How she hadn't wanted the bitterness and hatred to consume her. She'd chosen to live with happiness instead.

Just thinking of her, how incredible she was, made him smile.

"I hate you!" Janie raged as the officer struggled to lead her from the alley to where a patrol car waited to bring her to jail. She wouldn't get bail. Maybe a psychiatric evaluation, but not bail.

"I'll meet you at the station," he called out to his officers. He had to collect that groom-to-be and make sure his blood got tested and his official statement taken. But when he opened the door to step back into the kitchen, it wasn't him he found.

Kiki stood near the dishwasher with the officer at her

side, and she was shaking. "You promised!" she yelled at him. "You said you wouldn't go out there!"

"I wasn't alone," he said. "I had officers hiding out in the other building. We got her."

"Janie?" she asked.

He shouldn't have been surprised that she'd figured it out. She was as smart as she was beautiful. He nodded. "We got her. It's all over now."

She nodded now. "Yes, it is." Then she turned and walked away.

And he couldn't help but think she was talking about more than his case. About more than the Slasher, that she was talking about them as well.

And he was more scared than he'd been when he'd walked into that alley, uncertain of when and where the Slasher would come at him. At the moment, Kiki scared him more than he'd ever been scared because he didn't want them to be over. Now or ever.

Fletcher had scared her again, like that night he'd gone into the alley in place of the Slasher's chosen victim. The thought of losing him like she'd lost her parents had devastated her. She'd come so close so many times.

Thank goodness the Slasher had finally been caught. Janie.

There would be other dangerous cases for him. Other chances for her to lose him. And she'd thought that would be unbearable—more than she could survive because she'd also realized, during all those moments when she could have lost him, how much she wanted and loved him. Too much.

He'd stayed away from her the past week. Maybe he'd been busy wrapping up all the cases he'd closed. Or maybe he'd taken what she'd said in the heat of the moment at face value and believed she didn't want anything to do with him anymore, as her undercover assistant or as her lover.

But because he'd stayed away from her, Kiki had felt like she lost him already. During that week she'd slept very little, missing him too much, but she'd written and, in her songs, she'd found clarity. That there were no guarantees, but that love was worth the risk of loss. And that if it was meant to be, if they were meant to be, that they would figure out a way to be together and to be happy.

But she knew she wouldn't be happy, truly happy, if they weren't together. "Okay, Fancy," she told the puppy, who'd been moping as much as she'd been with missing Fletcher. "We're going to go get him back." This time she had a shirt in a gift bag. A pink and blue flannel one to replace the one that he'd claimed to hate. The Slasher had ruined it that first time she'd gone after Fletcher.

Janie.

Kiki still struggled to understand why, even though she'd talked to Claire and Amy and found out more about Janie. They hadn't been as close to her as she'd made it seem, but they'd known about her broken engagement. They swore they hadn't known that she was the Slasher. She believed them.

Jenny Colton was probably going to believe she was a stalker when Kiki showed up with another gift for her son. But before she could leave the boat, it shifted beneath the weight of someone jumping onto it.

She turned toward the door and saw Fletcher coming across the front deck toward her.

Fancy jumped up and yipped her happiness. While Kiki was excited, too, she contained herself. He'd stayed away for a week. Maybe he'd figured they were over, too. Whatever they were.

She wasn't even sure. They'd never put a label on what they had. What had her grandpa called it? Something-something...

It burned between them now as he stared at her. She wore a dress today—just a simple sleeveless, button-down denim one. He wore jeans and a T-shirt, like he was dressed to go undercover with her again.

But of course, it was Saturday, so he probably wasn't working today. He also carried a bag in his hand. One from a pet store.

"Hi," he said.

"Hi."

He pointed toward the bag that dangled from her fingers. "Were you going somewhere?" he asked.

She nodded. "Your house."

"My mom's?"

She nodded again.

"I don't live there anymore."

"You don't?" she asked, and nerves gripped her. "Are you leaving Owl Creek?"

He shook his head. "No. I bought a house of my own. Close to the police department and Frannie's bookstore. It has a nice, fenced yard that would be perfect for Fancy."

"You bought a house for Fancy?"

"I'm going to see if Sebastian and Ruby will let me adopt her," he said. "They can still train her and use her as a scent dog. But when she's not working, she can stay with me."

She narrowed her eyes and studied his face. That look was in his vivid green eyes, that intense look that always unsettled her. But this time it had the opposite effect. Her nerves settled and she smiled. "So that gift bag you brought is for her?"

He nodded and pulled out a chew toy. "Figured she might leave my boots and shoes alone if she had this instead." The puppy took the toy from him and dropped onto the floor to gnaw away at it.

"What about you?" he asked. "What's in your bag?"

She pulled out the flannel shirt. "I felt like I needed to replace this. I know how much you love it."

"I really do love it," he said. But he was staring at her, not the shirt. Then he stepped closer to her, until his body just about brushed up against hers.

"You must be relieved this case is over," she said. "You can go to bed early, sleep late… No more loud music or crowds."

"I actually miss it," he said.

"Liar."

"I miss you. And you know you can come to my house and visit Fancy anytime you're in town," he said.

She smiled. "That's generous of you. To let me visit the dog I've been fostering…"

"In addition to that fenced yard, it also has this special sound room in the basement. Former owner was a musician. You might like that."

"I might," she said.

"You can use that whenever you want," he said. "And you can stay however long you want, between gigs, you know…like…forever…"

Kiki's smile widened as joy filled her heart. "Sounds good to me."

"What part? The sound room? The fenced yard?" he asked.

"The forever." And she pulled his head down to hers, kissing him with all the love she felt for him. And all the passion.

The passion swept her up as Fletcher lifted and carried her into her bedroom. He kept his mouth on hers, kissing her deeply as he lowered her onto the bed. Then his fingers were on the buttons on her dress, undoing them all until the material fell away from her body, revealing her lacy bra and underwear. He unclasped the bra and hooked a finger in her underwear, pulling it down until she was completely bare.

And that look was in his eyes still. That intensity that burned for her. And she felt like she was burning up with the desire coursing through her. "Fletcher…"

She reached for him, but he gently pushed her back on the bed. Then he covered her in kisses, from her lips, over her throat and collarbone. He kissed both breasts and flicked his tongue across the nipples.

And she writhed against the bed as the pressure built

inside her. She pulled at his clothes, dragging off his T-shirt, undoing his button and lowering his zipper.

He eased back then, pulled off the last of his clothes and pulled out a condom packet. She took it from him, tore it open with her teeth, then eased the latex over his shaft, running her hand up and down the length of it.

He groaned. "Kiki…"

She pushed him onto his bed and straddled him, easing him inside her. She wanted him so badly. Needed him so badly.

They moved together like they were dancing, in perfect sync, and they even came together, screaming each other's names. She collapsed onto his chest, panting for breath, her heart hammering against his.

He held her close, his arms wrapped tightly around her like he never intended to let her go.

She lifted her face to stare into his, which was tense and serious despite the pleasure they'd just given each other. "What's wrong?" she asked him.

"Nothing," he told her. "I just hope you didn't misunderstand me."

She tensed now and eased away from him. "What do you mean?" Had she read the situation wrong?

"I don't want you to give up your career, Kiki," he said. "You're too talented and you bring people so much happiness and joy. I can't be selfish. I know I have to share you with the world—that you're going to be a star."

Only Grandpa had ever believed and supported her that much. Tears stung her eyes and she blinked furiously.

He touched her face. "Kiki, what's wrong?"

She shook her head. "Nothing. I just love you so much."

"I love you," he said.

She had no doubt. Not about his love or about their future. They would figure out how to make forever work.

* * * * *

Don't miss the stories in this mini series!

THE COLTONS OF OWL CREEK

MILLS & BOON

Peril In The Shallows
Addison Fox

MILLS & BOON

Addison Fox is a lifelong romance reader, addicted to happily-ever-afters. After discovering she found as much joy writing about romance as she did reading it, she's never looked back. Addison lives in New York with an apartment full of books, a laptop that's rarely out of sight and a wily beagle who keeps her running. You can find her at her home on the web at addisonfox.com or on Facebook (Facebook.com/addisonfoxauthor) and Twitter (@addisonfox).

Visit the Author Profile page at
millsandboon.com.au.

Dear Reader,

Welcome back to the 86th precinct in Brooklyn and the second book in my **New York Harbour Patrol** series. I'm having so much fun with these books, imagining all that lies beneath the waters surrounding the city I love and call home.

In this book we meet Detective Arlo Prescott, a hotshot at the 86th and one of the precinct's brightest talents. He's coming off a big case and is pulled into an investigation when Officer Kerrigan Doyle finds bodies in a shipwreck.

Kerrigan has recently joined the police diving team that works out of the 86th. She transferred in from Queens and loves the people she's working with. She's especially intrigued by the case and wants answers.

Arlo and Kerrigan are paired up to uncover the mystery of the bodies on the boat, and his seniority and experience do much to help season her youth and ambition. But along the way, they're fighting a building attraction for one another as well as the growing danger around them.

Because a threat *is* growing. And the person behind it is power hungry and very, very determined to run the city's drug trade at all costs.

I hope you enjoy this new book in the series about those who make their living protecting the waters in and around New York City. Their courage and drive to defend the home they love run as deep as the waters that surround it.

Best,

Addison Fox

DEDICATION

For my new editor, Emma. I know this is the start
of a beautiful partnership.

Chapter 1

Kerrigan Doyle loved the water. To this day, her mother still told the story of Kerrigan's first trip to Coney Island and her squeals of delight as her father dipped her toes, over and over, into the lapping waves of the Atlantic one late-August afternoon.

It had been a solid quarter century since that first dip, but she'd never lost her soul-deep, unceasing desire for her first love.

Too bad she hadn't figured out a way to find any other loves, Kerrigan thought, before chastising herself for the mawkishness.

It wasn't like she'd put that much time into the dating scene. A fact that her best friend, Laverne, had berated her for this past summer.

"Get out and live a little," her friend had told her. "You spend all day with those hot divers, Kerr. Can't you spend a few evenings with one, too?"

While Laverne only had her best interests at heart, her friend's work at one of the large accounting firms in Manhattan insulated her from some of the more challenging aspects of the modern dating scene. Laverne was a working city girl, out most nights of the week with an ever-rotating crew of fellow twentysomethings who all had a steady paycheck, a love of martinis and an expectation of "work hard, play hard" as the foundation of their lives.

For all her progressive thoughts and go-get-'em excitement for her friend, Kerrigan was well aware she couldn't enjoy the same lifestyle. She believed it was essential to maintain a reputation as a damn good cop instead of as a man-hunting twentysomething.

She'd seen it happen before. It might not be fair, but the woman ended up on the short end of the stick when things went sideways.

And while she hadn't been one of New York's finest all that long, she'd seen enough crash-and-burn relationships to recognize that was a potential minefield she wasn't interested in navigating.

Chicken.

That inward voice whispered the word, even if it wasn't the most apt moniker for herself. She'd completed the police training course *and* the diving course for the special division of the NYPD with flying colors. And she'd had the best times for a female recruit in department history. *And* in the nearly two years since she'd joined the special arm of the NYPD that specialized in underwater work, she'd built a rock-solid reputation for herself.

One that had paid professional dividends, such as the dive she was part of today.

The waters around New York City held their own challenges, as the hard-flowing currents and the confluence of freshwater and saltwater ensured her dives were always interesting. That she was considered one of the experts who not only knew how to navigate those waters, but also work within them, was a source of deep pride.

Her work challenged her and constantly kept her on her toes. It might be all-consuming but working under the water required her full focus. She'd explained this to Laverne repeatedly, to little effect.

Shaking off her rambling thoughts, she keyed into the quieting chatter as their lead detective, Wyatt Trumball, stood on the deck of the small boat. They were currently bobbing in the water between Governors Island and the solemn face of the Statue of Liberty, rising up in all her green splendor from the grounds of Liberty Island. Ellis Island was a bit farther in the distance and Kerrigan felt a small shot of gratitude for her intrepid ancestors, who'd been processed through that small spit of land after arriving from Ireland more than a century and a half before.

Driving, cold rain beat down on the exterior of the boat and Kerrigan sunk a bit deeper into her sweatshirt. October in New York was a tough month—the weather could be damn near perfect, or it could be a dire example of all Mother Nature could toss, including hurricanes.

They'd been close to the latter all week, as the residual effects of a storm that had hit farther south had made a total mess of the entire coastal region. She could already imagine the conditions for the day's dives.

Wyatt was clearly aware of the dangers as he began their briefing.

"A suspected drug boat went down here around four a.m. Our good friends in the Coast Guard gave solid chase, but ultimately lost them to a couple of hard waves the perpetrators didn't know how to navigate."

"Coast Guard didn't try to engage?" Gavin Hayes asked, concern on his face.

"They did and called for NYPD backup. But the overnight storm and the tail end of the hurricane that hit Florida three days ago didn't do anyone any favors."

She heard the grumbles and even a bold curse that their water-based comrades could have done more when Wyatt held up a hand. "The fact the drug runners set the boat on fire to avoid detection sealed the decision to call off the op. Especially once it sunk and the Coast Guard already had the coordinates of its location in hand. They've also kept a team in place all night, despite this lovely weather we're having, so let's cut them some slack." Wyatt's grin was more grim than humorous.

The grumbles quieted, and Kerrigan didn't miss the downward cast of a few gazes as Wyatt finished up.

"When it became clear there weren't survivors, the focus shifted to our work today. We're on recovery duty."

More muttered curses went up around her and Kerrigan already knew why. Recovery was a nasty business under the best of circumstances, but a deliberately torched boat left a serious mess behind. In addition to mutilated bodies, the accelerants used needed to be handled with extra care and caution.

She let out a small sigh of her own as she imagined her descent into the water and the approach to the boat.

She braced for what they'd likely find. Already brackish water would be thick with the accelerant and the evidence was likely in multiple pieces, or heavily decomposing from the fire and then time in the water.

And the bodies…

It was part of the job, and she would willingly complete it, but dragging the dead off the floor of the ocean never made for an enjoyable aspect of her work.

But it *was* the job. Along with evidence recovery, bomb checks, standard patrol and any number of routine duties that were required when living in a city surrounded by water.

Wyatt continued his briefing. "You're going out in pairs, four to a Zodiac boat. The goal here is to get in and get out as safely and as quickly as we can. The harbor's a bitch today and she's not looking too happy to give up her secrets. Soon as we get the bodies and a recovery area set up around the boat, we're pulling out."

"You don't want us to secure evidence?" Gavin asked.

"If it's in easy reach and you can safely secure proof, you're cleared to do so, but the entire boat's coming into impound and will be scoured top to bottom once retrieved."

Kerrigan considered the orders before returning her attention to the full briefing on her tablet. Wyatt was thorough, as always, but there were some additional details on expected dive conditions, the specs and size of the boat, theories on who was navigating the cache of drugs through the waters and the ultimate destination of said drugs.

Endless, Kerrigan thought. The battle against the criminals who sought to ply their trade in New York never stopped. Or even slowed, really. There was an element of hopelessness to it, and she worked hard not to let it creep in too often. But something about the deeply gloomy day and the useless loss of life dragged at her.

It was an invisible weight they all bore and most days she handled it just fine.

So why was today any different?

Shaking it off, she scanned the high points of the briefing once more, pictured the area she'd go out on the Zodiac boat and how she and her dive partner— it looked like she was working with Jayden Houston today—would split up the search-and-rescue.

And then it was time to go.

"We're partners today, Kerr."

She smiled at Jayden, his dark brown eyes crinkling at the corners in return. "We are, on an absolutely glorious day for a dive."

"Come on now, you mean you don't love diving in dark soup with a side of rip current?"

"We're living the dream, Officer Houston."

Jayden slung an arm around her neck as they walked onto the soaked deck of the police boat, the light rain that had accompanied them from their headquarters at the 86th Precinct now coming down in torrents. "That we are, Officer Doyle. A fact I tell my husband, who is currently ensconced in his very comfortable and, might I add, warm office uptown. And I still wouldn't have it any other way."

She patted a hand on his impressive chest before slipping from beneath Jayden's arm and crossing to her equipment. She efficiently loaded it all into the waiting Zodiac boat, mimicking the work of her fellow officers as they all got ready to face the mission. And as she nestled her gear into the inflatable that would lead them to the dive site, she had to admit Jayden had a point. With a smile she couldn't hold back, Kerrigan stared through the rain that poured in near sheets over New York Harbor, the city skyline barely visible in the distance.

She really was living the dream.

An absolute nightmare stared back at her from the harbor floor. She and Jayden were the second team down, following Wyatt and Gavin by about four minutes. The detective had radioed up the condition of the boat and the suspected location of the bodies, so Kerrigan and Jayden had made that quadrant their focus.

Only to find a tangle of nets, discarded boxes and a clear effort to ruin the crime scene before the boat had inevitably gone down.

They limited voice communication whenever possible because of their breathing apparatuses, but Kerrigan didn't miss Jayden's sharp intake of breath. "This is bad."

"Nightmare."

Their words were garbled but she'd done this work long enough—and had more than enough contextual clues—to understand and be understood.

And this was monumentally bad.

The realization that the boat was going down in the storm had obviously driven the drug runners in their last moments. A significant portion of the boat had been doused with fuel, then set on fire. The water was thick with gas, and she could catch light whiffs of it, even with her breathing apparatus.

With steady, deliberate movements, she swam closer to the boat. The always restless water was churning even more than usual with the continued aftereffects of the hurricane. The harbor was never particularly clear, but the agitated waters ensured her headlamp barely made a dent in the dense, murky depths.

Jayden voiced his location and what was in his view, and she responded with what she could see. Although they weren't more than ten feet apart, the most she could make out of her partner in that short expanse was an outline of his body in his thick diving suit.

All the more reason to find what they'd come for and get out.

Wyatt had warned them the dive would be difficult. The continued agitation of the water, pressing on her body as she fought to keep her position, and the general condition of the torched boat only added to the overall challenge of making the recovery.

"Got something, Kerr." A hard curse followed, very unlike her normally jovial dive partner.

Kerrigan voiced a quick reply and worked her way through the thick muck toward Jayden.

Only to come face-to-face with two charred bodies, lashed haphazardly to the still-intact railing of the boat.

Detective Arlo Prescott watched the sheets of water run off the edge of the police boat and burrowed more deeply into his NYPD-issued jacket. The weather had been a mess the past three days, with puddles the size of small lakes springing up at every intersection in Brooklyn. He'd done his level best to keep his head buried in work, but he had to go home sometime, and the late October nor'easter had given the city a solid dousing.

The only plus side, he mused as they drew alongside a couple of Zodiac boats, stopping to allow their occupants onto the larger NYPD vessel, was the decided lack of street crime, since the lingering storm had driven most people inside.

Unless the bastards were dumb enough to try a water escape. Arlo sighed to himself as he saw his closest friend in the NYPD, Wyatt Trumball, climb out of the Zodiac and into the police boat.

Which, based on today's outing, those idiots most certainly had. Proof once again that crime happened on the water just as it did on the streets.

"You look like a drowned rat, Trumball." Arlo offered the man a hand, pulling him into a close, one-armed hug. "A freezing-cold drowned rat."

"You should see the other guy." Wyatt stepped back, his gaze already scanning the rest of his crew disembarking from the now-tethered Zodiacs. "Or guys, I should say."

There was a second police boat in the water, dispatched to manage the evidence recovery of the drug runners' fishing vessel. And then there were the smaller speedboats that would keep lookie-loos out of the surrounding water as they dealt with the bodies.

Arlo had already been warned these bodies were more gruesome than the Halloween decorations beginning to line the houses in his Red Hook neighborhood.

It never failed to amaze him that even in the worst weather conditions nature could throw at them, there'd still be some dumb jerk who wanted to watch the show. The grislier, the better.

"Hell of a way to go," Arlo said as he considered his friend.

The past few months had been a challenge for Wyatt. A series of safes strapped to bodies he and his dive partners had recovered from the waters had ultimately led to an even bigger mystery. One that had blown the 86th wide open, shaking the precinct to its core.

As Wyatt's investigation had progressed, it had become clear the bodies and the safes were a diversion for the cops, one meant to keep eyes focused on the water and off the drug smuggling running through Sunset Bay. The plan was also designed to shake faith and trust, when it had been revealed the masterminds had a long-standing vendetta against the retired chief of detectives, Anderson McCoy.

A vendetta that had started nearly thirty years ago with McCoy's willingness to look the other way so his own son could avoid prosecution.

They were all dealing with it, Arlo admitted, in what had come to be known as the Nightwatch case. Working through that betrayal was something they were all struggling with, but no one more than Wyatt. He'd not only found the bodies that kicked off the case, but he'd also fallen in love with Anderson's granddaughter, Marlowe, in the midst of the explosive revelations.

Proof, Arlo thought as he watched his friend help the rest of the dive team onto the boat, that responsibility might carry weight, but love did, too.

It was a stark reminder of why he avoided it himself. Love might work for some, but he wasn't interested in the responsibility. His job and his commitment to the city of New York were the only unassailable commitments he wanted in his life. He'd learned the lesson young that people might be loyal to their job or their ideals or their friends, but not necessarily to their family.

Not one single bit, he thought as a ready reel of images flipped through his mind on a loop. Family was easy to walk away from.

Too easy.

Because when something was taken for granted, it was always easy to walk away.

The last diver came up from the Zodiac boat and Arlo mentally counted off how many individuals had been needed for this mission before he stopped, every last thought fleeing his head. A tall, statuesque, neoprene-clad form hovered at the entrance to the boat, long dark hair spilling out of a swim cap. The goddess/diver pulled off the cap, crushing it in one hand. Long, slender fingers ran through her crown of hair in a one-handed shove out of her face, and what was left behind were high cheekbones, lush lips and dark brown eyes that were nearly black in the overcast mist on the boat deck.

Damn, but she had a heartbreaker of a face.

Heartbreaker everything, he amended.

He'd never considered dive suits particularly attractive, especially the ones the NYPD used for their missions. Thick, and designed to withstand both the cold and the often disgusting and unhealthy mess beneath the local waters, the woman wore it well.

Better than well, Arlo thought.

She wore it like a second skin and he felt his breath catch as she started to strip out of it.

"Yo, Prescott!"

Wyatt's bellow had him shifting his stare and Arlo caught the woman's gaze, then he quickly ducked his head. As attractive as she was, he'd be damned if he wanted to stand there like he was ogling her.

But, wow, she was a knockout.

A fascinating one, if the dark look that came into her eyes at his perusal was any indication.

Arlo gave Wyatt his full attention, tamping down the rush of interest at the goddess on deck. The team had wired in the news they'd recovered bodies, so he'd already braced for what was coming off the floor of the harbor. But even the advance warning couldn't quite prepare him for what they'd discovered, now laid out on tarps beside the entrance to the boathouse.

No time like the present, Arlo mused as he dropped into a crouch to assess what the dive team had pulled up. The effects of the saltwater and the active marine life near the wreck had already done even more damage than the deliberately set fire, but he could make out the solid strength of the bodies. There was a visible neck tattoo on one that the medical examiner's office would capture and document, as well as the basic quality of clothing and shoes.

These guys had been prepared for the trip into the water, as their feet were clad in waterproof boots. Both men also wore thick, wind-breaking jackets that would have kept them relatively dry as they went about their work on the boat.

The stench of gasoline filled the air, rising off the bodies along with the distinct scent of death. But it was the quiet voice behind him that had Arlo looking up, right into those fathomless brown eyes.

"If you turn the bodies over, Detective, you'll see the cause of death."

Arlo was a cop who favored humor to manage the job, and he couldn't quite hold back the sarcasm. "Drowning, wasn't it?"

"I'd say the bullets to the back of the head were far quicker."

Chapter 2

Since joining the academy and making the commitment to police work, Kerrigan had spent a lot of time managing her personal judgments as well as her assumptions that she knew why or how people got mixed up in crime.

Part necessity and part personal attitude, she'd joined the NYPD to make a difference. She wanted to believe in the good in people, despite the continued evidence to the contrary.

And she'd come to accept that for those who made bad choices, there was a system in place so they could atone for those decisions and—hopefully—make a better life in the future.

Naive? Maybe, she often admitted to herself. But it was a belief she *needed* to do the job and do it well.

Yet none of it could prepare her for days like this one.

Whatever these two men had involved themselves

in, their choices were inexorably tied to the brutal, terrible acts human beings could perpetrate on each other.

"Bullets?" the new arrival asked. "You recover any casings under the water?"

"No, but I saw the condition of the bodies as my partner and I removed them from where they were tied to the boat railing. Both men were tied up with haphazard knots obviously done in a hurry."

"Would you help me? I want to see those wounds."

Kerrigan realized her mistake as she crouched down beside Detective Arlo Prescott.

She knew who he was, of course. Most everyone in the 86th knew of the hotshot detective who'd developed a reputation as one of the NYPD's best detectives. He also did a considerable amount of work with the harbor team, so it was inevitable she'd come into contact with him from time to time. Up to now, though, she'd only seen him from a distance.

Although she'd helped out on dives throughout the city since joining the team, her home base had been her precinct in Queens. She'd only become a full-time member of the harbor team out of Sunset Bay, Brooklyn, about six weeks before.

Which meant she'd better get her heart out of her throat and get used to seeing the very able-bodied, dark blond, blue-eyed detective.

Not that his eye color mattered one whit to her.

Even when the full heat of those baby blues had been focused on her, snapping her to attention as she'd stripped off her dive suit.

It was something she did several times a day, but never before had the action seemed fraught with meaning, or the remotest trace of sexiness. Yet, somehow, getting caught up in one look from Arlo Prescott meant that routine had become so much more.

Since Laverne's voice and her friend's steady admonishments "to find herself a hot cop and enjoy herself" had grown a bit too loud in her head, Kerrigan kept her attention focused on the grisly forms in front of her.

They were in a covered area of the boat, designed for privacy in handling recovery work, but the thick rain outside the space had left the deck wet and slick. The atmosphere was cold enough to have them both breathing out puffs of air as they spoke.

"Help me roll him to his side."

Arlo did as requested, the waterlogged body even heavier than the two-hundred-pound-plus frame would suggest.

And just as she'd promised, the work of a single bullet was evident at the lower base of the skull.

"Damn." Arlo let out a low whistle. "No honor among thieves."

"Apparently not." Her voice was dry, a side effect of her breathing apparatus and the stress of the dive. She resolutely would *not* believe any hints of breathiness could be attributed to the sexy man currently holding a dead body with her and giving off glorious heat where his body crouched close to hers. "Other guy's the same. I think he was the second shot because his bullet wound isn't quite as clean."

Arlo laid the body back, wiping his hands on his slacks as he turned to her, still in his crouch. "What's that?"

Once again, that attention was laser-focused on her,

but this time she didn't see any traces of interest. Instead, all she saw was cop.

And that, she knew what to do with.

Pointing toward the other guy, she expanded on the theory she'd puzzled through as she and Jayden had worked to free the bodies and bring them up to the surface.

"The second one." She pointed to the other man, who was still lying face up, untouched. "If you look at his wound, it's low on the back of the head, too, but it's clear he moved in some way. The shot isn't nearly as clean or even. I'd guess he figured out what happened to his buddy and braced to fight."

"With a third crew member. One who left no traces in the boat."

And there it was. That nagging, mental toothache that suggested the case had grown even more complex than they'd first thought.

"That's what I thought when we brought them up. There had to be a third person."

"One you didn't find?"

"No," Kerrigan replied. "No trace of anyone else."

Arlo nodded, obviously working through the problem as he spoke. "These two might have doused the boat, but neither of them thought they wouldn't get out."

She exhaled hard, affirming Arlo's hypothesis. "It appears that way, and while I'll leave it to the medical examiners to make the final assessment, I'm sure they'll find traces of the accelerant on the victims' hands that suggest the same. These two were destroying evidence, but in full expectation they'd get off the boat."

"Looks like."

He pointed toward the other body. "Help me turn him. I'd like to take a look at that gunshot and then we turn them over to the ME to see if we get an agreement there, too."

Kerrigan moved with Arlo, resettling into a crouch beside the second body. This man was a bit smaller than the first in heft, but roughly the same height. And just as she'd assessed on the recovery, the bullet wound wasn't as clean—the shot had shifted at the base of the skull with the man's movement.

"Hell of a way to go." Arlo shook his head before gesturing to let the body back down. "And you've done a proper assessment, Officer...?"

He let the question hang there, obviously waiting for her name.

"Officer Doyle, Detective Prescott."

"You got a first name, Officer Doyle?"

It wasn't protocol, per se, to ask her first name, but she'd addressed him by his rank and he'd technically done the same.

"Kerrigan. Kerrigan Doyle."

He nodded and then surprised her when he reverted back to her rank. "This is good work, Officer Doyle. I'm more than happy to have you on this case if you want to see it through."

"I'd—" She broke off, the small bubble of happiness at having his professional attention popping at the remembrance of the way his gaze had settled on her when she'd stripped off her suit. "Thank you, sir. I'd appreciate the opportunity."

Something dimmed in his gaze, but it fell away after that quick flicker. And then he nodded, tilting his head toward Wyatt. "I'll clear it with Detective Trumball. This is very good work."

He got to his feet, stepping back as he spoke. And before she could say another word, he turned on his heel and left.

She wouldn't feel bad for that flash of frustration that he might have only asked her out of some misplaced sense of attraction, but she could honestly acknowledge that she was a bit disappointed as he walked away. She wanted to progress in the NYPD and working with a celebrated detective was one of the pathways to do that.

But what if he'd only asked for her help because he liked how she looked wet?

It was a harsh assessment—and possibly an unfair one—even as she still shivered from the memory of that intense stare. It hadn't been lascivious, but rather, she'd seen real, tangible interest in his eyes.

A two-second glance, Doyle? Get it together.

She'd have to, she realized as she stared down at the two vics. Because working with one of the lead detectives in the 86th would be a huge boon to her career.

Kerrigan consoled herself with that as she crouched down beside the bodies once more, her gaze roaming over the charred clothes and the premortem wounds. And as she pictured those gunshots—one clean, one not so much—she couldn't help but feel there was one more thing she was overlooking.

But what?

There was a third person on that boat, and that meant they had a lead. A lead she'd been given the opportunity to see clear through to its inevitable end.

It wasn't much, but it was something.

Something, Kerrigan knew, that she was determined to make into everything.

Arlo knocked on the door of the ME's office, a large box of doughnuts in hand. He knew the rules of order and waiting in line—and was well aware his harbor bodies weren't the only priority in the medical examiner's office—so he'd come bearing a gift.

He'd given the ME more than a day, after all.

Thirty-six hours, to be exact, to give proper time to examine the bodies and allow that team to do their essential work when the bodies still had fresh tales to tell.

He'd still brought breakfast.

For those who were smart and paid attention, a truism could be learned very early in a law-enforcement career: copious amounts of sugar could, and often did, work miracles in a cop shop.

A fact his new "partner" on the harbor case must have known, because Kerrigan Doyle was gesturing with a heavily glazed cruller toward their chief medical examiner, Lorelei Mayes, who at this very moment had a jelly bear claw in hand.

"Officer Doyle? Dr. Mayes?"

Both women glanced over at him, their irritation at being interrupted smoothing away as their gazes landed in unison on the box in his hands.

But it was Lorelei who smiled first, a gleam in her eyes.

"I see the bakeries in Brooklyn have been busy this morning."

Arlo shot her a wry grin. "Or as I prefer to say, great minds thinking alike."

He didn't miss the slightly guilty flush that added color to Kerrigan's cheeks, and he kept his smile in place even as a shot of annoyance skated over his skin.

She'd done nothing wrong, yet the sexual politics at the precinct likely made her feel as if she had. And he knew why. Some people—hell, more than some—would have been frustrated with Kerrigan's early arrival, effectively beating him to the punch with the doughnuts, but he was far more pragmatic than that.

Whatever got the job done.

And it was also one more notch in the column that the woman had a real future as a detective. A rank she could still make on the harbor team, just as Wyatt had. Career progression was readily available to all cops in the NYPD, but they made adjustments by pairing the experts in the harbor team with the "landlubber cops," as Wyatt had often called him.

The fact that Kerrigan Doyle had taken on the work with him for this case in addition to her dives was a sure sign she wanted that career. Her ideas and careful consideration of the victims pulled off the harbor floor were more indicators she was smart and focused. But that she'd arrived early this morning told him all he needed to know.

The woman was as bright as she was ambitious. But more than that, she was determined. He'd take a partner or a trainee any day of the week who showed that level of commitment to the work.

"Well, the bribery was unnecessary this morning, despite the sweet, delicious flakiness of this bear claw." Lorelei's gaze still twinkled with some amusement. "My team and I worked late to finish up your water rescue last night."

"Thank you."

Lorelei waved a hand. "It was our pleasure. The storm's been nasty, and this crime had an extra layer that bugged all of us."

"And we were waiting for you to discuss the specifics," Kerrigan quickly added. "I only just got here."

He didn't miss the quick answer or her eagerness for him to know she hadn't usurped the chain of command.

"As Dr. Mayes knows, I'm not particular on how the news gets shared. The more good minds working on this problem, the faster we catch our killer."

"I did finally figure out what was bugging me," Kerrigan said, seemingly more at ease with his acceptance. He was pleased to see that momentary concern over jumping rank had settled, and her natural eagerness was rising back to the surface.

"What's that?"

"The third person. They had to be quite a bit shorter than the two victims. The angle of the gunshots coming so low at the base of the skull."

Once more, she'd impressed the hell out of him. Her quick, thoughtful assessment on the boat and now this. She was observant, a necessity for police work. But she was tenacious, too.

Which shouldn't have been a surprise. It was a key trait of any good cop and Arlo had observed long ago that it was beyond essential for the men and women who worked the harbor. His own knowledge was limited more by what he knew of Wyatt's work than his own experience, but the harbor team was top-notch. They worked in unceasingly harsh conditions, in a city so large that crime in and around the water was a forgone conclusion.

Yes, the NYPD had made impressive strides over the last several decades to ensure New York was one of the safest large cities in the world, but it still held millions of people within its border. Not all of them were content to skip to work and turn in early for a good night's sleep.

An image of the dead drug smugglers rose in his mind, something that had happened regularly for the past thirty-six hours.

"That's good, Officer Doyle. It'll add to the profile of the killer and it's one more piece of the puzzle."

"I'd also agree with the officer's assessment," Lorelei added. "The angle of the gunshot is consistent with someone of lower stature. Especially since we found no gun residue on either victim, it wasn't a situation where one vic turned on the other, then was turned on by a third. Assessment indicates it was the same gun, same general angle."

"And what about Officer Doyle's other hypothesis?"

"Other?" Lorelei turned to look at Kerrigan. "We hadn't gotten that far."

Arlo nodded, encouraging Kerrigan to continue. "Please, Officer. Give Dr. Mayes your full assessment."

Kerrigan reached for a napkin, then set down her half-eaten cruller on top of it on one of Lorelei's pristine counters. She grabbed a second napkin and wiped her hands as she spoke, all purpose and efficiency.

"I believe the victim with the neck tattoo was shot second. His wound was consistent with the other one, but the hole is irregular, as if the victim became aware of the perpetrator and moved to fight him off."

Lorelei's attention never wavered as she moved toward a small laptop. She set down her own doughnut—

right on top of the surface—but did wipe her hands before tapping on the keys. After reviewing a few files, she stepped back.

"That's a strong deduction, Officer. I'd agree with that assessment as well. We'd noted the difference in wounds in the file but hadn't added that level of insight. It's a good one. And I'd say it means you're looking for one cold-blooded son of a bitch. Shots to the back of the head at point-blank range show determination and a certain sort of willingness to quickly end a life."

Arlo had already moved into the case with the same assumption—he'd even briefed his captain the day before with a similar description—but the affirmation still sent a shudder down his spine.

What were they dealing with?

He never assumed a criminal wasn't capable of humanity's worst sins, but that didn't mean there wasn't a hierarchy to what they dealt with. While there was considerable premeditation in the crimes he and his fellow officers worked, there were a lot of crimes of opportunity as well.

But this one?

This one had greed, avarice and a determined willingness to do evil at all costs.

Shaking off the second shudder, he gestured toward the files still up on the laptop screen. "You get an ID?"

"We got a hit on one of them. Jordan Bilks, age thirty-four," Lorelei recited, using the computer's track pad to scroll through the report. "Spent time upstate and got out on good behavior about fourteen months ago."

"I guess *good* was the operative word there." Arlo said. "Which one was he?"

"The first fired on, if we work under Officer Doyle's theory."

"For now, we do." Arlo didn't miss the slight creasing of Kerrigan's lips that she fought back into a straight line.

"We'll keep working on the second."

"Even with the neck tattoo, there's no hit in the database?" he asked.

"No, which was a surprise. I expected we'd get something off that tat," Lorelei said, working through a few more screens. "But nothing's popping on the ink."

One more mystery for them to puzzle through, Arlo acknowledged. While the bodies had decomposed considerably prior to coming to the surface, there was a harshness to both men that suggested career criminals to him. It was a snap judgment, but one he trusted all the same.

Yet, no hit on the second vic.

"You have a sense of age on the second one?"

"Estimates put him between thirty and thirty-two. His overall health and muscle tone are consistent with that age range, but he was a smoker and that had begun to take a toll. I'd put his initial tobacco use as early as eleven or twelve."

Lorelei never ceased to amaze him, the smallest details part of her evaluation and assessment.

"Looks like Officer Doyle and I have our work cut out for us."

"My team does, too." Lorelei turned her attention away from the computer and picked up her doughnut once more. "I want to run some of the details on their clothes and that tattoo has some specific markings to it.

The skull in the lower left corner of it has some meaning."

"Gang?" Kerrigan asked.

"Possibly, or some sort of badge of honor. I want to see if we can match any aspects of it to other known criminals."

"It's appreciated." Arlo tapped the lid on the box he'd brought in. "Please give the team my best and tell them to enjoy."

"Will do." Lorelei nodded.

Arlo glanced at Kerrigan once more. "Officer Doyle, let's go update the captain on what we've got."

"Of course."

She followed him quickly, waiting until they were nearly to the elevators before turning toward him. "I am sorry if it looks like I jumped the gun. I just wanted to see what they had."

He stopped short of the elevator bank, turning to face her and the anxious expression that put small crinkles around those dark eyes.

Pretty eyes, he realized as he stood there. It was an observation that shouldn't happen with a fellow cop he'd taken on to offer a bit of in-the-field training. But he couldn't deny the thought, either.

Vowing to think about it later, he keyed back into her underlying concern. "Are you under the impression I'm upset?"

"This is your case. And I'm thrilled to be a part of it."

"Officer Doyle. Part of police work is having the sheer tenacity to keep at something. I'd hardly discourage anyone from wanting to solve a crime as quickly as possible."

"No, I didn't mean you would. It's just that—" She broke off, letting out a small sigh. "I just know there's protocol and earned rank, and I don't want to give any impression that I don't appreciate your experience or your seniority."

"Tell you what." He hit the button for the elevator. "You focus on learning what you can and if I have a problem with anything I'll be sure to let you know."

"Oh. Okay."

"We're square." He gestured to the elevator door as it opened. "Now let's go talk to the captain."

Kerrigan wasn't a shy recluse, and she didn't back down from going after what she wanted. So what was it about Arlo Prescott that had her twisted up?

The late-afternoon recovery and the wait on the ME's office had kept their communication to nothing beyond email for the past thirty-six hours. It had been a buffer, she realized now, giving her some space to ratchet down that initial rush of heat when she noticed how attractive he was.

Moreover, she'd diligently avoided thinking of how he looked at all. She'd worked several dives the day before and had only checked her emails as time permitted between her duties. The opportunity to investigate the case wouldn't interfere with her work, which was something she'd assured Wyatt of when he'd let her know he'd approved the pairing with Arlo.

Everything was fine *and* she had the support of her boss to expand her skills.

So what was it with all these weird, mixed emotions?

Maybe because the man's damned attractive.

A thought that had slammed into her as he'd strolled into the ME's space with that box of doughnuts.

Especially since she'd immediately flashed back to the heat in his gaze when he'd watched her after she'd come out of the Zodiac boat.

She didn't need this. A crush on a coworker wasn't in her best interests. One on the superior who was offering her career growth only doubled down on the bad idea.

Which meant she had to bury it.

Crushes were nothing more than flights of fancy, anyway.

She'd nearly convinced herself of that fact when he followed her into the elevator, the doors closing them into the small space.

She wasn't a small woman—her tall frame usually put her at eye level with most men. But with Arlo, she had to look up slightly. She'd have to settle her arms on his shoulders if they kissed.

Not helpful, she mentally admonished herself. And since the bad-idea train was dangerously close to stopping, she searched for something innocuous to focus on. "You like the doughnuts at Sunset Bakery?"

"They're my favorite. Nobody makes a Boston cream like they do."

"I haven't been in Brooklyn very long but I'm partial to Cake Brothers."

He shook his head, a grave look covering his face. "The Rosetti boys have nowhere near the light touch Josie and Cora Callahan do."

"Come on, you heard Dr. Mayes. That was a delicious and flaky jelly bear claw."

He extended a hand as the elevator door opened,

keeping the conversation going as they walked to the captain's office. "You've got a lot to learn, Doyle."

"Duly noted, sir."

She heard the note of sass under her own words and was pleased and more than a little surprised when he turned back to her, a broad grin splitting his face.

"But I think you'll do."

Chapter 3

Arlo was still trying to figure out those peculiar moments discussing doughnuts in the elevator fifteen minutes later as he and Kerrigan brought Captain Dwayne Reed up to speed on the case. He hadn't found his footing yet with her, so the shots of wry humor underlined with just the right bit of cheeky wit felt like a start.

He was the elder statesman here and he'd taken her on for training. She'd earned it, but he was the lead, all the same.

Even so, the responsibility for her sat heavier than he'd anticipated.

Because she was a woman?

Or because, no matter how hard he wanted to push aside that fact or ignore it, he *was* aware of her. And, even more to the point, attracted to her.

Which had made jokes over doughnuts a strange yet comforting way past all of it.

He'd always been known for his sense of humor. It came easy and often, and he'd always believed that the ability to laugh was a necessity in life. Especially in a job where staring at murdered and burned bodies was all part of a day's work.

How refreshing—and unexpected—to find it in Kerrigan.

Like I have the corner on the market? he wondered to himself, even as he glanced at his trainee, standing straight and tall, respect for their captain stamped in every inch of her body.

It was novel, Arlo admitted to himself. And a reminder that while he respected his fellow female officers, he had never partnered with one. Where he'd exchanged jokes, often bordering on ribald, with his male colleagues, he would never dream of doing the same with a female officer. Yet, she had a solid streak of good humor all the same, one that didn't need the gross or the sexual to make her point.

Humor she had the maturity to keep in check. Here she was now, pivoting quickly to demonstrate proper deference to their captain, the job and all that lay before them in the case.

Captain Reed asked several questions and each time, Arlo had nodded his head, suggesting Kerrigan provide the response.

Dwayne focused on Kerrigan. "Your instincts are solid, Officer. And that was excellent work, evaluating the body before ascending to the surface. That couldn't have been easy."

"Thank you, Captain."

Dwayne smiled, the deep grooves around his dark brown eyes creasing. "I've told Trumball over and over

I don't know how he goes down in that water, day in and day out. But I can't deny the miracles you all work when you're down there."

"It's an honor, sir. I love my work."

Dwayne's eyebrows shot up. "And you still want to be partnered with this one?"

It was the first time Kerrigan gave Arlo more than glancing attention, her focus now fully on him as she responded to their captain. "I'm wholly committed to my work for the harbor team. But I'm also a cop and I'd like to continue the progression of that aspect of my career as well. Working with Detective Prescott is a huge benefit to learning that part of the job."

"So noted."

"Wyatt cleared it as well," Arlo added for no other reason than to assure Kerrigan. He well knew their captain missed nothing when it came to his team at the 86th.

"Trumball already let me know." And then without a pause, Dwayne was on to the next topic. "You have any sense yet what group this might be associated with?"

"No." Arlo shook his head. "I've run all the usual suspects and no one's popping as having a boat with those specs. Or the sheer stupidity to try manning it in waters churned up by an October hurricane."

Which, in and of itself, was strange. Boats cost money and effort and had pesky little things like serial numbers on them. Simply torching one—with cargo *and* men—meant there was someone operating in the harbor with a lot of cash to burn. Literally.

"Talk to Vice and see if anything's hit for them. Any new turf wars they're aware of or anything suspicious," Dwayne said.

"Of course. Initial efforts are already underway to run down the boat's owner. The team at Impound has instructions to send over any noticeable markings or serial numbers as soon as they find them."

Dwayne nodded but had already returned his attention to Kerrigan. "You've only been at the 86th for a few weeks. How are you finding it?"

"I'm very happy with the move. Detective Trumball leads a good team."

Which explained her earlier comment over doughnuts that she hadn't been in Brooklyn long, Arlo noted. *Interesting.*

Ambitious, hardworking cop.

Most people found comfort in their home precinct, yet she'd put in for a transfer. It wasn't completely out of the ordinary, but it was another notch in the ambition column. Especially if she felt she wasn't getting enough opportunities a few years into the job.

He vowed to ask her later before Dwayne's words registered. "Thank you for the dedication to seeing this through, Officer. Detective?" Dwayne's dark gaze was laser-focused on him. "I'd like a few more words, please."

"Of course."

Kerrigan stepped out and Dwayne waited a beat before speaking. "You think it's wise to bring in someone who is, essentially, a rookie?"

Arlo respected Dwayne in every way, aware their captain carried the burden of leadership in a way that only ever reflected positively on his team. He fought the hard fights and protected his people from the more political aspects of the work.

Which made his question something of a surprise.

There was no one at the 86th—and Arlo would even go so far as to say the entire NYPD—who wanted to see their team progress and succeed more than Dwayne.

"You have a problem with my partnering with Officer Doyle?"

"No problem. But she's new and all the evidence suggests some dark stuff is going on. Shot and burned bodies?" Dwayne's mouth firmed into a hard line. "That's personal and final."

"Especially to henchmen who were seemingly loyal."

"Exactly," Reed agreed. "To go out in a storm like that? The payoff might be good but there's an undertone of loyalty, too. And to be done like that? Cold-blooded shots to the back of the head, execution-style? This one doesn't sit well, Arlo."

It didn't sit well at all, especially with Dwayne's perceptive additions.

"All I'm asking is if you're sure you want to bring her into this. Her first big case."

Arlo considered the calm, collected woman who'd stood on the boat two days ago, helping him roll dead men in the rain. "She pulled up the bodies. Had the wherewithal to assess the gunshots and formulate theories, all while swimming in the morass of a storm and the leftover mess that was a doused and torched boat. She's earned it, sir."

"No doubt about that. But I want you to proceed carefully. Whatever we're dealing with, it's not going to be an easy case."

"No, it won't be."

"Officer Doyle's got incredible promise. I never want to see any of my brethren harmed in the line of duty. But the bright, eager ones? The ones with a future?"

"Yes?"

"I always worry it's that brightness that puts them at most risk."

The joke was nearly out of his mouth, a glib response that he was one of the brightest and he'd survived, when he caught Dwayne's serious gaze.

He *was* one of the brightest. And he'd proven himself to the 86th, over and over.

None of it could stop the nightmares that still came like clockwork over his first big case. He'd been bright and eager once, too.

And it had nearly killed him.

Kerrigan took the captain's dismissal in stride, but she couldn't deny the raging case of curiosity at whatever he and Arlo were talking about in his office.

The captain seemed pleased with her contributions but that didn't necessarily mean anything. The harbor team was small in size, and he might not want her stretching her time like this, no matter how complimentary he was with her work so far.

Which was just like her, she admonished herself, and forced calming thoughts through her mind.

Other people knew how to do their jobs, too. And no matter how determined she was to prove herself, the captain could talk to any member of his team however he wanted. The man's rank gave him that privilege, but so did reputation. If he hadn't wanted her working this one, she'd have heard about it by now, not a few days into the case.

Dwayne Reed held the responsibility of leadership comfortably on his shoulders and she'd do well to keep her eyes on her own paper and not worry about his.

Metaphorically.

A point that she'd do well to remember against her earlier flights of fancy, too. There was nothing to gain by looking at Arlo's deep blue eyes or slim waist or appealing height as he stood beside her in the elevator.

This was her shot and the reminder to keep her eyes on her own paper applied to attraction, too. Even more so than worrying about the captain.

The discussion with Reed filled her thoughts once more and gave her focus. Once Arlo came back, she'd offer to keep up the grunt work running down the boat's ownership and free him up for whatever else he needed to do.

She wasn't afraid of hard work. And while she had no expectation they'd find out the owner was one of the murdered men, they'd at least have a trail to follow.

Arlo left the office, closing the door behind him, and headed her way.

That lingering shot of awareness floated through her. *Damn it, how was the man's walk even sexy?* But with force of will, Kerrigan tamped it down and focused on the tasks that lay ahead.

"I hope you don't mind I waited. I can head down to the squad room and start on the boat research."

"Yeah, about that."

"You'd rather I did something else?"

"Actually, I was thinking your expertise on the water meant you had to have some familiarity with boats."

Once again, he'd caught her off guard. She hadn't come into this assignment thinking she'd be dismissed, but she also hadn't expected to be taken on as such a partner. Yet here they were, and Arlo seemed genuinely interested in tapping into her knowledge.

"Well, yeah. I mean, we train on all types of watercraft and I also grew up near the water. My dad has a boat. My uncles have boats." She smiled as she thought of her big family and weekends throughout the summers of her life spent on the water. "I have a pretty decent working knowledge."

"Know any boat sellers we can go talk to? I want to get a sense of how someone could essentially make a major asset with serial numbers, ownership and documented provenance disappear out of any and all databases. Because I've been running that boat for a few days and nothing's coming up."

Her mind was already whirling with the possibilities, but there really was only one choice. "Let's go see Big Will at Brooklyn Yacht."

"*Big* Will?"

"Yep. Big Will Gentry. The man's six-nine and about three hundred and fifty pounds." At Arlo's widened gaze, she rushed on. "He's a gentle giant. He's owned the business for about forty years. His father owned it at least thirty more before him. Rumor has it his sons will be taking over but Will's not too excited to retire."

"Let's go."

The rain that had blanketed the city for a week like a thick, soupy mess had given way to a perfect fall day as they headed out of the precinct and toward Arlo's car.

"Did the rest of the meeting go okay with the captain?"

At the sound of the locks unclicking, she pulled open the passenger-side door, cursing herself for diving straight in. His meeting with Captain Reed was none of her business.

And just because it happened after their debriefing didn't mean it had anything to do with her.

Arlo didn't respond right away, as he buckled in and then navigated out of the 86th's parking lot. It wasn't until he'd reached the entrance to the highway, heading onto the expressway, that he spoke. "The captain's good with you working this case, if that's what you're worried about."

"I'm not usually so—" She sighed, letting the words fade away.

She wasn't so what?

Wishy-washy?

Afraid of going after what she wanted?

Attracted to her coworkers? A small voice whispered that at the end.

"Not so what?" Arlo asked, his gaze, blessedly, on the late-morning traffic.

"I know my value and I know what I want, Detective. I'm a hard worker and I've wanted to be a cop since I was a kid. I'm just afraid it'll be taken away and that's on me to figure out how to navigate."

"Taken away how?"

"You've got a reputation for being the best. And I'm thrilled and terrified to be partnered with you. I want to do my best."

There.

It was out. All the way out. Or most of it, anyway. The failing-him part did terrify her.

And the rest?

Well, she'd manage the attraction. She had no choice.

It had been a long time since he'd trained someone so new, but Arlo still remembered his own feelings at that stage of his life. The ones that had pushed him to be the best and terrified him, both at the same time.

It wasn't a comfortable place to be. Arlo recalled the push-pull of emotions vividly, but it was necessary to progress in the job.

To keep moving forward.

Which was why he wasn't going to BS her or dismiss her questions. "Captain Reed is good with you on this."

"Why do I sense a *but* in there?"

"Because he's worried about the really dark, violent overtones of this case."

Dwayne's words had haunted him since he'd walked out of the man's office. He hadn't quite gotten his equilibrium back yet.

And to be done like that? Cold-blooded shots to the back of the head, execution-style?

Arlo had tried to shake it off, but even the bright, sunny day couldn't chase away the darkness on this one.

"He doesn't think I can handle it?"

"Not at all. But it's his job to carry the burden of leadership over his squad. And I can tell you straight, he's worried."

Traffic was heavy, but moving, and Arlo risked a quick glance over at her. Her mouth was set in a grim line, the good-natured smiles of earlier vanished.

"I can understand that. The weight of responsibility on him must be enormous."

He heard the hesitation beneath her words and opted to keep quiet, giving her time to puzzle through the details.

"I just have to ask if he'd be as worried if it were Jayden on the team. Or any other male colleague, for that matter."

"I get why you have to ask, but I've known Dwayne Reed a long time. He's fair and he plays it straight without consideration of gender. What I haven't seen much of in all that time is this level of concern over a case."

Or he hadn't, Arlo admitted to himself, if he didn't count the Damson job.

"Any murder would raise questions. What was on that boat?" Kerrigan let out a long, low sigh. "It's brutality on a whole different scale."

"Which is the cap's point."

In another ten minutes they'd cleared the traffic and were exiting for Sheepshead Bay. Kerrigan navigated him through the streets toward the water and in the distance he saw the sign for Brooklyn Yacht.

"This is a bit late to ask, but I'm assuming Big Will sells more than yachts."

"Most definitely. He's probably sold a quarter of all the pleasure boats in the area."

Arlo pulled into a spot in front of the entrance and glanced around as he got out of the car. He'd always been an observer, a skill that had set him up well as a cop, but he'd honed the practice over nearly fifteen years on the force.

Sunlight glinted off several boats visible in the docks behind the building. They shimmered in the distance, floating on the water.

"What did they do during the storms?" Arlo nodded his head toward the docks as Kerrigan met him around the back of the car.

"Same thing anyone else with a boat does. Tie down what they can and pray for the best."

"Sounds like a tough way to make a living."

"Big Will has a good business. He's got volume on

his side, which also helps. But the small mom-and-pops? It's definitely a challenge but they put up with it." Kerrigan grinned then, that smile lighting up her face before settling deep in her eyes. "People who love the water really love the water."

"A fact you, Trumball and the rest of you harbor nuts prove every single day."

The heavy moments in the car seemed to have faded as she tilted her head toward the building. "Come on. Let's go find Will."

Arlo followed her into the cavernous showroom and was amused to realize it had a similar look and feel as a car dealership. Which only reinforced that, regardless of a person's reason for buying a boat, it was still a vehicle that got you from point A to point B.

"Kerrigan!" The bellow emanated from the back of the showroom mere seconds before a large man who could be no one other than "Big Will" emerged from an office.

Arlo's first thought was that the man was aptly named. His second was the clear and obvious affection between Big Will and his newest partner.

After a quick round of introductions and a confirmation from Kerrigan that they were there on official police business, Will waved them both into his office and shut the door.

"That was some bad business that went down in the harbor." Will shook his head. "And your team found the bodies."

"We were assigned to the recovery, yes."

"You know about the downed boat, sir?" Arlo pressed. It wasn't a surprise, exactly, but it did mean news of the drug smugglers' demise had moved into the community quickly.

"Word travels." Will shrugged. "And a boat like that going down? There's interest."

"Will, if you know anything that can help us, we'd appreciate it." Kerrigan's respect for the man was obvious, but so was her tenacity to do the job right. "We'll do our best to keep your name out of it, but if you know something, we need to know."

The man was at least seventy and he'd clearly spent many of those years out on the water. Time, sun and water had weathered his face into craggy lines, but knowledge was a bright beacon in his blue eyes.

"I'll help however I can but let me guess. No serial numbers?"

Kerrigan remained silent, leaving a confirmation to Arlo. Even more impressive, she didn't turn toward him for verification. Instead, she was all cop, handling official business with her partner. It was a reminder of why she'd gotten this opportunity in the first place. And whether she stayed on the water or eventually moved inside the precinct, Arlo had no doubt the woman would make a damn fine detective.

She was cool where it mattered, and her instincts were rock-solid.

Taking advantage of the runway she'd already created, Arlo nodded his head. "No, sir. All provenance was removed. We have reason to believe that was handled by the current owner before going out on the water."

Will's inhale was sharp, his expression grim. "We don't keep track of everything we sell after it leaves here. I'd expect other sellers are the same, but the rumors in the business are strong. Word has it a drug-smuggling ring has been trying to get its hooks into the local trade. My sons and I have been careful. We do all the standard credit checks, but we've been keeping a close eye on new buyers."

"You think smugglers are working with boats from around here?"

Even as he asked the question, Arlo recognized the situation carried the potential for even bigger problems than they already faced.

A local smuggling ring?

He had no reason to doubt Will, but he was going to have a few words with his colleagues in Vice. How the hell was it possible an entirely new node on the drug trade was operating and no one had caught wind of it? All too often, it felt like they were just trying to keep up. But this? How could this level of crime go so completely unnoticed?

"No." Will shook his head. "The boats are likely coming up from farther south. Somewhere along the way they're going through the standard chop-shop process, retrofitting amped-up engine parts and erasing serial numbers and key markings."

Once again, the sheer ingenuity of criminals never failed to both impress and dismay. And proved, as always, there were people who *wanted* to live in the shadows.

"I really do appreciate your taking the time to talk to us."

"For you?" Will beamed at Kerrigan. "Anytime. And I will keep an eye out. I can promise you my sons will, too. There's too much crime in our city as it is. Polluting the water with this sort of bad goings-on?" Will let out a low whistle. "It's immoral."

"I wish there were more who felt just like you, sir."

Will took the acknowledgment in stride and promised to share anything else he might think of. With a quick light returning to his gaze, he offered to show Kerrigan a new addition to his fleet and Arlo waved them on.

Although he knew next to nothing about boats, Arlo took his time strolling around the showroom. Their proximity to lunchtime meant the place was pretty empty, but he saw a well-dressed woman on the far side of the room talking to an older couple.

Keeping his head down, he made a show of casually looking at a few of the speeders they had positioned around the large show floor. Beyond identifying the ship's wheel and the throttle, he had very little understanding of what he was looking at.

Which gave him that much more time to surveil the rest of the building.

Additional offices ran along the back wall, adjacent to Will's office. A small kitchen was visible in the back corner, and he saw someone puttering around at the sink, clearly occupied with their task.

Everything appeared in order. A prosperous business managing through a quiet part of their day.

He went back to perusing the boats, feigning interest as he waited for Kerrigan. Despite recognizing very little, he nearly missed the movement in the back of the showroom. Would have missed it, Arlo suddenly realized, if he'd stared any longer at the list of manufacturer upgrades posted on the side of the boat.

But whatever it was that grabbed his attention,

once caught, he listened to his instincts that something was off.

A younger man, not nearly as tall as Will but still a
familial match, stepped out of the office beside his father's. He glanced at Will's open door, obviously hes-
itating, then ducked into the office on the other side.

Arlo didn't like jumping to conclusions, but he
couldn't deny his interest when the man not only shut
the office door behind him, but also snapped the floor-
to-ceiling shades covering the office window closed.

A closed office meeting wasn't a crime.

Far from it.

But he'd already been curious when Big Will shared
that he knew about the sunk boat and the bodies in
the harbor *and* rumors of a new drug-smuggling ring.

Now his son was holding closed-door meetings the
moment their father stepped out of sight.

With the other son Kerrigan mentioned?

Was it a coincidence?

Kerrigan's smile was bright as she walked back into
the showroom from the dock area. She hadn't seen the
man slip into that other office and he considered asking her about it.

"You ready to go?" she asked.

"Where's Will?"

"He got into a discussion with one of his mechanics.
I let him know I could see myself out."

Arlo glanced once more at that closed office door
and considered saying something right there, but then
thought better of it.

He had no concerns about Kerrigan's honesty, but
maybe it was time to do some digging on Big Will and
his sons.

Not every hunch paid off.

But one that carried dark insinuations about her friends? Well, he'd handle that alone, come what may.

Arlo shook off the small stabs of guilt as he and Kerrigan walked out of the showroom.

His decision was made, and he'd do what he had to do.

Chapter 4

Kerrigan walked the perimeter of the boat debris spread out with numbered markers noting various pieces of evidence. She had several afternoon dives, but opted to start her day looking at what the salvage team had hauled up from the harbor floor.

She had her memories and what she'd observed on the dive, but it was time to look at the drug runners' boat in the light.

The evidence-management team worked around her, and she was careful to keep her distance to avoid any risk of contamination, but what they'd managed in only a few days was impressive. The sheer volume of items and boat debris laid out in a cavernous room of the evidence warehouse was stunning.

The port side of the hull was mostly intact, and it had been placed at the far end of the warehouse. She'd spoken briefly with an arson investigator brought in from the fire department who was consulting on the work as they'd walked it together. The woman's congenial approach and willingness to share what she knew had been a good start to the morning. It had given Kerrigan a few things to consider as she now navigated the pieces that had already been separated from the boat.

Namely, that the majority of the damage was isolated on the starboard side, along with the bodies. More to hide? Kerrigan wondered. Or had they just run out of time?

It was the starboard-side pieces where she was standing now.

Recovery photos had already been sent to her and Arlo, the first step by the evidence team before any aspect of the boat was touched or pulled apart. Although they would continue to photograph and record as the boat was reviewed and, in places, disassembled, those initial photos were the best record of what actually came off the harbor floor.

She'd studied them late into the night, now trying to associate the pieces before her with what she remembered in the images.

"It's a massive job."

The low voice over her shoulder was friendly, congenial even, so why did that husky timbre manage to send a wave of shivers low down on her spine?

Kerrigan whirled to face Arlo, determined to shrug off the ridiculous reaction. "Detective." She nodded. "Good morning."

"Good morning, Officer Doyle. Looks like we're both getting an early start."

"I spent a lot of time with the photos last night, trying to associate them with what I saw on the dive. But

we were also so focused on the body recovery that I
didn't get a good look at much."

"Recovery in the midst of a hurricane's lingering
effects, I'll add."

She didn't miss the clear note of approval in his gaze,
and she found herself looking a few beats too long in
those dark blue eyes before coming back to her senses.

"It's not the easiest to see in the depths of New
York's waterways on a good day, so that's a fair point."

Even now, she could conjure the feel in her mind of
being down in the dark on that dive. The water had been
flowing hard, pushing on her and Jayden as they did
the work. Every dive required her full focus, but that
was one of the ones where she'd truly earned her keep.

"What do you see now as you look at this?" Arlo
asked. She had to admit just how excited she was to
share her theories.

And if it led to more of that approval she saw in
his eyes...

"The deliberate setting of the fire obviously impacted
the whole boat, but there's more significant damage on
the starboard side." Kerrigan gestured to the pieces of
the boat railing, where even now she could remember
the way the bodies had been lashed to it. "Jayden and I
had to remove the bodies from that railing."

"That's where they were tied down?" Arlo kept his
fair distance, just as she had, but he did move to examine where the evidence team had laid out the boat
railing.

"Yes." She pulled the image from the dive fully to
her mind. "More than six hours under the water had already done a lot of damage but their hands were bound
to the railings, and both were sort of slumped over it."

"That takes some work on the part of the killer. Especially if the gunshots had already taken care of them."

Kerrigan weighed that remark. "You're right. That's a lot of unnecessary work. Why go to the trouble to lash them to the railings?"

"One more question we have to figure out."

They moved in and around the debris but Kerrigan kept coming back to the railing, Arlo's observations racing through her mind. Why did the killer attach the bodies? It wasn't like a man was a threat with a bullet in his head?

Theater?

"Arlo." He glanced up from where he was standing among various pieces of decking and walked over. "Come look at this."

Although she knew the starboard side had sustained more damage, upon closer review it looked like the boat had burned in layers.

"Look at this here." She pointed toward a large piece of decking. "See that arc of charred wood? It looks like the flames followed the pour of the fuel as the deck was doused."

"It makes sense. The boat went down pretty quickly so while the fire would consume if given the time, the rain, as well as the harbor water, likely put it out."

"But then look here." She gestured toward a piece of decking that was still attached to the base of a seating banquette. "This looks like fuel was poured straight on it. Like it had a wider mouth from the fuel container."

She was already glancing toward the entrance, ready to flag down the fire commissioner, when Arlo spoke.

"Seems like a funny coincidence. Two bodies and more fuel."

"It's possible it's just because this was the last area where the victims were. Like maybe they had emptied the last of their fuel?"

"But you don't buy it?" he asked, his voice neutral as he pressed her to work it through.

"It just seems as if it could be more deliberate. Like the area was doused with more fuel."

"The ME didn't note any additional fuel on the clothing. I think we'd have seen more burn damage on the vics if that had been the case."

Kerrigan considered his statement. "Maybe just more fuel on the ground, beneath them. This had to have happened fast, and methodical behavior starts to go out the window."

"I suppose it does."

"I'm going to go get the arson investigator. I'd like her take on this."

"Calhoun. She's good. I spoke with her on my way in." He moved into a crouch beside the piece of decking. "Let's see what she says."

He got back to his feet. "And then let's go get some breakfast. Despite the grisly subject, I'd like to talk this one through."

She could hardly deny the suggestion when her stomach chose that moment to let out a large growl. Arlo hadn't missed it, either, his wry grin at the ready. "I guess you agree?"

"Sure. I could definitely go for some breakfast."

It was only as she headed off to the other side of the warehouse that Kerrigan recognized the challenge now before her.

Having breakfast with her partner wasn't a crime. Nor should it be a problem. She and Jayden had eaten any number of meals together, just as she had with the rest of the harbor crew.

But this was different, Kerrigan knew.

Whether she wanted it to be or not.

Because no matter how she wanted to slice it, dice it or try to wish it away, she didn't get a funny little flutter low in the belly when she thought about sitting opposite her other male colleagues sharing a meal.

Arlo had learned his first week on the job that coffee was damn near sacred to a cop. Drinking coffee and eating doughnuts might be an age-old police cliché, but it was for a reason.

He'd played a game with himself from that first week, often trying to guess how a fellow officer might fix their cup.

Coffee regular? It was a New York standard for a reason, with milk and two sugars dropped neatly into a steaming mug of joe.

Just black? Some of his best friends consumed it that way, including his first chief of detectives, who'd drunk roughly a gallon a day.

And then there were the rare few, heaven forbid, who drank decaf. An awful waste, in his opinion, in any possible combination.

But Kerrigan?

The heavy cream, dumped in until the coffee resembled the color of oatmeal, along with four sugar packets, was a surprise.

"What?" She glanced up as she finished off the last swirl of her mug with a spoon. Sunlight filtered in behind her, haloing the crown of her head, and he was just fanciful enough to admit he was a bit dazzled.

Which was why his tone likely came out a bit drier than he intended. "How can you possibly drink that?"

She glanced down at her mug. "My coffee?"

"More like sugar and cream with a splash of coffee. Is it even hot?"

"First you pick on my doughnut choices and now you piss and moan about my coffee?"

"Consider it more a surprising observation."

"Over my coffee?" Her dark eyes sparkled but he could also see the genuine curiosity there.

"I guess I took you for a black coffee type?"

"Oh?"

"You divers are tough. Seems you'd take your coffee the same way."

"Obviously not."

She looked about to say something, then seemed to think better of it, so Arlo pressed the point.

"What is it?"

She hesitated by taking another sip of her coffee before sharing her thoughts. "The harbor team seems to have a special reputation."

"A well-deserved one, I'd say."

"But it's like we're held separate somehow. The words are always complimentary, but we're still seen as something other from the department. I noticed it with the captain earlier. And, truth be told, it comes up often."

"What you do is special."

"Sure, I get it. But it's also cop work in a city surrounded by water. Somebody's got to do it."

"But not many people do. Diving work is special under any circumstances. But in the waters around

New York? Which, and I realize we're about to eat, and you live it on the daily, but they're horrifically nasty. Wyatt's told more than a few stories."

She sniffed, her affront at an assessment held by oh, basically *everyone*, oddly sweet. "They're not as bad as they used to be."

"That's like saying toxic waste only has a half-life of a century."

"Well, it's not the Caribbean, but what is?"

"Not much." Arlo settled his scarred menu in the small wire holder against the window.

Why was he pushing this?

He'd spent the better part of the past day feeling ill at ease for his decision to run Big Will and his family. It had seemed like the right decision inside the showroom, but once he'd begun running queries and checking files in the database, it didn't feel quite so cut-and-dried.

Kerrigan was his partner on this.

Yet he'd kept her out of a line he was tugging because of what? Concern her feelings could get hurt?

Or, worse, that she couldn't handle it?

He wasn't one to run from his mistakes and he nearly said something right there, anxious to clear the air, but he didn't want to lose the momentum of their conversation.

Nor did he want that lone choice—made in the moment—to negatively color an opportunity to help her get past whatever it was that was gnawing at her.

So he'd save it for another time.

"My point's still valid. The job's impressive, just like the cops who choose to do it, day in and day out."

"But it's the job. It doesn't deserve special attention. Or not to the degree everyone seems to put on it."

Arlo did understand the special attention. While it was an ego boost, it could be a bit much at times. He'd been fortunate to have a strong run of closed cases, and while he more than appreciated the attention for it, closing cases was his job.

Police diving was hers.

And too much attention could mess with your head if you let it.

Which made her overall reticence interesting. Because the anxiety he kept sensing in her didn't seem at all tied to cocky behavior or an overabundance of attitude. Instead, there was an obvious processing on her part as she tried to find her place in the department.

"It's important to you, isn't it? To know where you fit."

The sparkle vanished from her gaze, even as she held her voice steady. "Isn't that important to everyone?"

"Yes, but I can see you working through it. It's okay, to be part of the team and still have a specialized role. You can have both. Be both."

"I'm not trying to sound ungrateful."

There it was again. That subtle insinuation that having an opinion or ambition or thoughts about what she was doing was somehow ill-advised.

Which meant he had to tread carefully.

Someone had made her feel that way.

She had far too much competence and inner drive for it to have simply surfaced without provocation.

"You don't sound ungrateful. You sound like you're trying to figure it out."

Although she was toying with the handle on her

coffee mug, she kept her attention focused on him. Direct. Solid. A willingness to stick to it, even if it was difficult.

"Not everybody thinks a woman belongs on the force. That goes double for specialized services."

"Has someone said anything to you? You have problems with other officers?"

"I know how to take care of myself. But it doesn't mean there isn't pressure. It also doesn't mean there aren't men concerned about going down on a dive with a female partner. Or other cops, male or female, worried about going out on an op with a female partner. It's real, Arlo."

"You were trained, same as me. Same as the other divers. What does the rest matter?"

She shrugged at that, but he saw the slightest smile return to her gaze. "You're a detective. A damn smart one best as I can tell. Don't suddenly develop a case of ignorance as if you think it doesn't happen."

"Doesn't mean it's right."

His comment hung there as their waitress brought over their breakfast orders. His stack of pancakes along with eggs and bacon and an omelet and wheat toast for her.

She prepared to dig into her breakfast when he pressed the point again.

"I meant that. You belong on the team."

She took another sip of her coffee, obviously marshaling her thoughts. "I'm not trying to dismiss your question, or dance around it. I suppose I am a bit tetchy about my role. I'm here because I want to learn. I want harbor, yes, but I want more. I want the detective's badge."

"Why's that? The tetchy part, not the badge."

"I joined the NYPD to make a difference. I have a love of the water, so Harbor Patrol was a natural choice, but I'm a cop to the core. I love this city and I want to see it shine."

"Then why worry what others think?" When she looked about to argue, he held up a hand. "Hear me out."

She nodded but didn't say anything.

"You work hard. You do the job. Expertly, I'll add. No one who partners with you can argue you don't pull your own weight, especially when I saw you drag a body out of the harbor and then saw you use your mind to work through the puzzle of that same body's gunshot wounds.

"Lean into that. Lean hard, because from where I'm sitting, you're doing the job and then some."

"Thank you."

"You're welcome." He nodded, aware he'd veered dangerously close to elder-statesman, speech-giving territory. "Now let me eat my lumberjack breakfast in peace."

"You got it."

Arlo's words were still occupying Kerrigan's thoughts that afternoon as she and Gavin prepared to descend into the spiky waters of the Harlem River around the Macombs Dam Bridge.

"Some moron tosses a gun over the bridge and we have to go hunt for it." Gavin was one of her sunnier colleagues, so the fact he was complaining was out of the ordinary.

"It's the job, Gav."

"I know." He shook his head as he did a final check

of the gauges on his oxygen tank. "I know it is. But life would be a hell of a lot better if people'd quit shooting one another."

"I won't argue with you there."

"Fifteen." Gavin sighed. "It's the young ones that get me. Fifteen damn years old and he gets in a fight after the Yankees game. He's too young to just be a moron. He's a kid."

Only the child who tossed a gun used to kill another wasn't a kid anymore, Kerrigan thought as she did the final check of her own equipment. And wasn't that nearly as sad as the loss of life the fifteen-year-old's gun had inflicted? Two lives ruined, with one simply left to exist above ground.

She shook off the dark thoughts—there'd be time for them later—and focused on the dive. The water ran a bit easier here than farther south, but it was still a tough dive. All the waters around New York were, Kerrigan thought as she dropped her mask over her face and fitted in her breather. With no more preparation left, she sunk into the water, reorienting herself to the immediate shifts in sound and physical weight.

They had a limited field for the search. The likelihood the gun was within a ten-yard radius around the perimeter of the bridge was in their favor. Witnesses hadn't been plentiful and the kid who did the shooting still hadn't talked, but video from the bridge's shelter house had indicated the gun fell straight down versus being tossed.

Gavin took the north side of the bridge and she'd taken the south. She used her thickly gloved hands to sift the silt at the bottom of the river, working in slow, progressive movements. Visibility was limited, as usual, but the sun was bright and filtered in a bit from above. She settled into a rhythm, communicating with a quick confirmation of "negative" to Gavin every ten feet or so. Other than his *negatives* in return, the work was quiet.

Steady.

Which gave her far too much time to think about breakfast with Arlo.

Lean hard, because from where I'm sitting, you're doing the job and then some.

She *was* leaning hard, damn it.

So why was she so far in her head?

She was devoted to her job and she'd willingly taken on the additional work with Arlo. She had confidence in herself—she wouldn't do the job if she didn't—so why was she second-guessing herself over everything?

Those last few months in Queens had been bad but she'd survived. The Internal Affairs investigation had been unfortunate but necessary, and she'd simply done her job.

But it had left scars.

And despite getting the rep as the team snitch, she was the one who'd been left feeling betrayed.

None of it had anything to do with her work now.

Hell, it hadn't had anything to do with her work then, either. She'd just been made to feel as if it did.

With that fire lit in her belly, she focused on the task at hand and off the voices that kept racing through her mind. Arlo was perceptive and he'd hadn't taken long to notice her concerns and that lingering sense of injustice she hadn't fully shaken.

Which meant it was time to shake it.

High time, she thought.

This wasn't her precinct in Queens any longer. She'd only been here a matter of weeks and she'd already had more opportunity to progress than the entire two years before. She might not have liked the reason she chose to leave, but she was damn glad she had.

Silt filtered through her left hand as her right hit something.

Immediately keying back in, she recognized the distinct shape and, as she picked it up, weight of a gun.

Gavin's "negative" filtered in through her comm unit and she replied a garbled "I've got it" around her breathing apparatus.

A "great job" filtered through her comm unit from Jake Sewell, the officer manning the Zodiac, and Kerrigan began her ascent. Sunlight greeted her as she broke the surface, even as she felt the cold swirling in the air.

Fall was definitely here, the weather taking a real turn after the rain the week prior. Before even getting out of the water, she dropped the gun into an evidence bag Jake already had out. Once she'd ensured the transfer, she climbed into the Zodiac and got to work stripping out of her gear. Traffic rumbled above them over the bridge, those passengers unaware of anything that had transpired in that very spot the night before.

It was a strange counterpoint to her memories of her time in Queens, yet oddly comforting.

The information she'd given to Internal Affairs was confidential. Her new colleagues had no reason to know what had happened. They had no reason to judge her. Just like the passengers up above on the bridge, they were oblivious, too.

She'd be sure to keep it that way.

"Kerr." Gavin caught her attention as Jake navigated

them toward the waiting NYPD boat about a quarter mile downriver. "Great work."

"Thanks."

"Come out with us tonight once shift's over. We're all heading to that new bar in Sunset Bay."

"Bulldog's?"

"That's the one."

She'd avoided any fraternizing up to now beyond a couple of beers at a retirement party last month, but she recognized the offer for what it was.

Camaraderie.

Partnership.

And a big step in the right direction to firmly put the past behind her.

Chapter 5

Arlo pulled up in front of Wyatt's house in Park Slope and his friend walked out with his new love as Arlo came to a stop. Although he'd seen Wyatt briefly in their chief-of-detectives weekly meeting, they hadn't spoken much since the harbor recovery on the boat.

He'd known Marlowe was coming out for the evening and while he was looking forward to seeing her, he'd already considered how much he was willing to discuss the case. Since she was the granddaughter of a cop and now the girlfriend of one, she understood the requirements of the job. The fact she was a civilian who did a lot of work for the NYPD as a locksmith added more weight.

And still, he struggled with how much to say to someone outside the department.

Like you've got the time to quibble, Prescott. Or a hell of a lot to say.

He was stuck. Or *they* were stuck, he corrected himself, since Kerrigan was certainly a part of this.

Despite digging, questioning and making calls up and down the eastern seaboard to every boat expert he could find, he had nothing. Kerrigan had been pulling her weight as well, reviewing a number of case files from the past decade that had any resemblance to their current situation, no matter how tenuous.

It was tedious work, yet she'd done it willingly, balancing it with her dive work and writing some of the most thorough reports he'd ever read.

And still, they had nothing.

Their lack of leads was an increasing frustration, one that had begun to eat at him. Even the quiet digging he'd done into Big Will's business had proved fruitless. Not finding the man engaged in criminal behavior was a positive outcome, even if it meant Arlo was also now trying to figure out how to discuss that one with his new partner.

His decision to run the boat salesman had seemed rather straightforward in the moment. Now it felt like he'd held out on Kerrigan, and he didn't like the way it had settled low in his gut. It didn't help that he still had to write up his report on his findings, so the clock was ticking to handle this one.

Not the best headspace to have on a free Friday evening.

Wyatt pulled open the door, gesturing Marlowe to take the front seat, but she pressed back. "You sit with Arlo. I'm sure the two of you have a lot to discuss."

Wyatt looked about to argue when Arlo heard the lightest whisper of Marlowe's voice float in the open car window. "Take the time to talk to him."

They settled into their seats and Arlo navigated through the neighborhood toward the main thorough-fare between Park Slope and Sunset Bay. As miles went, it was just over two to the bar, but with Friday-night traffic, they practically crawled, light after light.

"Brooklyn sure looks different from when I was a kid." Arlo loved the renaissance the borough had en-joyed over the past decade—it was now an epicenter of young professionals, trendy hot spots and activity.

He might love it, but navigating it was an entirely different matter.

"It's amazing, isn't it?" Marlowe added. "I grew up here and there are days I wonder when I got so *un*cool."

"You'll always be the coolest to me." Wyatt shot her a grin over his shoulder, to where she was sitting in the back, behind Arlo's seat.

"You sweet talker." Marlowe blew him a kiss.

"You're both googly-eyed," Arlo said, but he couldn't deny how good it was to see his friend happy.

"And you're both cops," Marlowe added. "Talk shop while I check a few emails."

"How's the case going?" Wyatt asked.

Whatever reticence Arlo had evaporated, as Mar-lowe's understanding went a long way toward settling him. He did need the thoughts of a fellow cop and Wyatt was one of the best. Plus, their friendship gave them a sort of short-handed communication style and Arlo unloaded.

"No leads. No provenance on the boat. No chat-ter, at all, despite having two drug runners torched in the middle of a freaking storm." Arlo shook his head. "Nothing about it makes sense. People talk, Wyatt. And no one's saying a word about this one."

"Somebody should have blabbed by now," Wyatt agreed. "Or at least gossiped in a way that indicated someone knows something."

"And yet there's nothing." Arlo fought a sigh as he turned onto Fourth Avenue.

"How's Kerrigan working out?"

It was nearly out of his mouth, that decision he'd made on Big Will's business, when Arlo pulled it back. He'd dug that hole and he'd dig himself out of it. Especially because sharing that small detail would likely put Wyatt's antennae up.

"She's fantastic. Eager and smart and she's got a good eye."

"She does. I've kept a watch since she came into the team a few years ago. She's smart and incredibly prepared and has been a huge asset to the harbor team. I'm glad we've got her at the 86th."

Wyatt inadvertently gave him the entry he needed, and Arlo took his shot. "I read her file. She's quickly making a name for herself. Her assessment of the bodies, especially the ballistics, was smart."

"I believe it."

"Why'd she transfer in?"

For the first time, Arlo saw his friend clam up and Arlo knew he'd hit on something.

"Had a bit of trouble at her old precinct. She handled it and that's about all I know." Wyatt only paused a beat, then added, "You said you read her file."

"Broad personnel overview. Her experience and her résumé's about all. Key cases she's worked."

"That's too bad, Arlo," Marlowe said from the back seat as Arlo saw the sign for the bar come into view on the next block.

"What's too bad, sweetie?" Wyatt asked, turning to face the back seat.

An unmistakable note of humor laced Marlowe's words. "Looks like Arlo's going to have to pump his new partner if he wants to know her backstory."

Kerrigan took a sip of her beer and considered her surroundings. While she'd hardly call Bulldog's a cop bar, there were a heck of a lot of off-duty cops from the 86th there tonight.

It made sense, she admitted to herself. Bulldog's was a new hot spot and it was a Friday night. For all their pride in being an elite group of people who had their own watering holes and eateries, she'd yet to find a single cop who didn't enjoy a fun night out.

Sunset Bay's newest bar definitely qualified. Especially after word had spread that a group was heading out this evening to check it out.

"Fancy seeing you out tonight." Jayden sidled up to her, his smile broad as he extended his longneck in a gesture of cheers against her glass of chardonnay.

"Right back at you. I thought you and hubs had date night tonight."

Jayden frowned, even as it didn't fully reach his eyes. "He had a client come into town who decided they wanted to enjoy a Friday night in New York and he's on deck to help entertain. We moved date night to tomorrow."

"That stinks."

"Since it's a client Darius brought in *and* that win was responsible for his rather lovely holiday bonus, I'm hardly in a position to complain."

"And I bet you upgraded your reservations to an even swankier place for tomorrow night, too."

"You know me so well." Jayden's grin went positively Cheshire. "Speaking of knowing, how's working with Detective Prescott?"

"It's good. The case is an endless series of dead ends, but the work's good and challenging. I'm learning a lot."

"Hmm." Jayden took another sip, his warm brown eyes anything but innocent as he looked over his beer.

"What's that supposed to mean?"

"Nothing at all except the man's attractive and reportedly single. As are you."

"Jayden!" Kerrigan fought the rush of heat that flushed her face and worried that her voice had gone a bit too loud.

As in get-the-neighborhood-dogs-barking loud.

"You know that doesn't matter," she said in a quieter voice.

Her friend shrugged, even as all traces of teasing dried up. "It does matter, even when we don't want it to. But why does it have you so bothered?"

"I'm not bothered. I'm trying to do my job and make a name for myself. Not a reputation."

"Your rep and good standing is unassailable. You have to know that."

While she appreciated his support and suspected Jayden knew more about her Internal Affairs dealings at her old precinct than he let on, she couldn't see her way to his optimism. "It can all go away with one bad decision. I'm not interested in making one with my boss."

"Partner and elder statesman, maybe, but not boss. There's not even a whiff of boss in there and you know it."

Perhaps it was because of his support of her and

their strong friendship that Kerrigan was a bit surprised Jayden continued to press the point.

"He's my new partner, nothing more."

"Well then, let's put that to the test."

Jayden's knowing grin was back as his gaze settled somewhere over her shoulder. She turned to see what he was looking at, only to find Arlo already weaving his way through the bar toward them. Wyatt and the woman Kerrigan knew to be his girlfriend, Marlowe McCoy, followed close behind.

Kerrigan wanted to curse Jayden for his perceptiveness, but even she couldn't quite deny the pure shot of heat that lasered through her as she took in that tall form, blondish-brown hair and firm jaw.

What struck her even more than how he looked was the way his eyes roved around the bar, assessing as he moved.

He was all cop and she found something about all that protective focus deeply compelling.

About as compelling as Jayden's words, which hadn't stopped rattling around in her mind.

There's not even a whiff of boss in there and you know it.

She did know it and it didn't help.

Arlo reached them first, his smile broad. "Kerrigan. Jayden."

She'd begun to get a sense of him over the past week and while the smile was genuine, there was a distinct sense of tension hovering beneath the surface. She didn't get the feeling it was because of her and Jayden, but she sensed it all the same.

"Arlo." She nodded before turning her focus to Wyatt and Marlowe. She'd met Marlowe shortly after the Nightwatch case closed and the woman had lived up to her reputation. She had a cool look about her, the sleek blond hair and slim figure accentuated by the habitual black she wore. Her kick-ass job of safecracker added to her intriguing persona. If asked directly, Marlowe would have introduced herself as a lock-and-vault technician, but safecracker was way cooler.

Not to mention, a description that fit.

What also fit were Marlowe and Wyatt, Kerrigan thought. They were a matched pair and as someone who'd known Wyatt since joining the harbor team, she'd never seen him happier.

"This place is hopping," Wyatt said after he and Marlowe had both leaned in for a quick hello kiss. "They've gotten a reputation as Sunset Bay's hottest nightclub in a very short time, and I can see why."

"It took us ten minutes just to wait for the valet," Arlo added.

That lingering sense that something was bothering Arlo continued to nag at her, but he kept his conversation as light as his tone and she finally resolved to ask him about it at work. It was Friday and if he was working through something, she couldn't expect him to spill it during an evening out.

"Why don't we go get some drinks at the bar?" Wyatt deliberately glanced at her and Jayden's drinks. "We'll get refills for you both. You want to stick with what you've got or change it up?"

After confirming the same drinks would be fine, Jayden followed Wyatt and Arlo to the bar and Kerrigan was left alone with Marlowe.

"It's good to see you again." Marlowe started in immediately, her warm words at odds with the cool look.

"Wyatt's been singing your praises. I know you all had a tough dive with that horrific storm."

"It had its moments."

"Burned boats and people?" Marlowe shook her head. "It's moments like that when I admit to myself that my life is boring and I'm okay with that."

"It's a tough way to die."

"Which means it was a tough way to live." The other woman appeared to hesitate for a moment before she pasted on a wry smile. "Don't mind me. I'm still working through the reality of losing a loved one to bad choices."

Although it was the Nightwatch case that had brought Marlowe and Wyatt together, the case had also led to her father's murder while in prison upstate.

She might not have anticipated being the person Marlowe would share such personal information with, yet she also understood the impulse.

In a lot of ways, Kerrigan and the rest of Wyatt's team were a safe space. All of them were aware of the case and its outcomes. There wasn't any need for explaining or providing backstory, since the cops at the 86th already knew all the details.

Marlowe had been open with her. Kind, too. And Kerrigan was determined to give the same in return.

She put a hand on Marlowe's arm, hoping the compassion she felt for the woman's situation—and the resulting heat on her grandfather's decisions to hide his son's sins—was clear. "It takes time. Grief doesn't just evaporate."

"Wyatt keeps telling me that. He's always saying it comes in waves." Marlowe let out a small laugh as she brushed the tips of her fingers beneath her eyes to wipe away a few stray tears. "And that's not diver-speak."

"He's right. And while it's not intentional diver-speak, it is pretty accurate. Some things just have to be felt. And they don't come on a set timetable or, sadly, often with any warning."

"I know you're right. You're both right." She took a deep breath, straightening her spine. "Which is why I'm going to enjoy my evening out and not be a wet blanket."

"You're not being—"

Marlowe stopped her with a raised hand. "Yeah, I am. But that's okay since I'm hoping to play on your sympathies and ask how things are going with Arlo."

"Arlo?"

"He's impressed with your work. You can consider that the highest compliment."

"I take it that way. His reputation as one of the department's best detectives is why I feel so lucky to be working with him."

For someone who'd been so forthcoming up to now, it was interesting to see how Marlowe quieted, obviously weighing her words. The timing coincided with a shift in the energy in the room as a song ended, and her words came in louder as she spoke.

"He's definitely good at the job. And I know you all are. It's an aspect of being a cop that's sort of embedded in what makes you who you are. But there's a lot of weight on him. On Wyatt, too. I saw it after Nightwatch. And I guess what I'm saying is that no matter how dedicated or driven, you're human, too."

While it was an incredibly astute observation, Kerrigan wasn't quite sure what to say in response. They *all* were focused on the job. And if she was honest with herself, she liked it that way.

She wanted to go under the water with others who were as committed as she was. Same went for going out with a partner or facing down a possible perp.

If you weren't fully, wholly committed to it, how did you ever get up the courage to go through the door? To make the dive? To do the work that carried inevitable risk?

But the job carried weight. A heavy one, that had to be figured out along with the rest of their lives.

"It is the job, Marlowe. It carries weight because we are talking life and death on both sides. As well as that in-between limbo where we're chasing people who are lucky to be alive, but they're ruining the life they have."

"Doesn't it get tiring?"

"Some days."

"And others?"

"It's the others I live for. Those are the ones when I know exactly why I was called to this job. Yes, it carries weight, but it's a privilege, too."

"I told you she was great."

Arlo's voice filtered in behind her, loud enough to make it through the pulsing, throbbing background of the club, but still low enough that it sent a few shivers skittering down her spine.

When had they come back with the drinks?

And how much had he heard?

Since he'd obviously heard some of what she'd said, Kerrigan opted to hit it head-on as she set her empty wineglass on their small, high-top table and took the fresh glass Arlo extended. "Don't mind me. I'm just waxing poetic on police work."

"Wax away," Arlo said, and for the first time since he'd arrived, she saw an easing in him. In the set of his shoulders and the small light that now danced in the deep blue depths of his eyes. "It's what makes you a good cop."

Kerrigan reached for her glass of wine and took a sip. It was already more than she'd planned, promising herself on the way over she'd only have one drink.

But, damn it, she didn't want to leave.

Didn't want to walk away from that appreciation in his gaze or his support of her chosen profession.

His support of her.

"Kerrigan was just telling me about how she gets through the hard days," Marlowe added, leaning into Wyatt before looking up into his eyes. "Seems like devotion to the job runs rampant in this crew."

"You know going in that it's not easy work." Wyatt wrapped his free arm around Marlowe's shoulders. "But it's meaningful work. In the end, I've come to realize that's all that matters."

Wyatt's words lingered in his mind as Arlo took a pull on his beer. It wasn't easy work. They all knew that going in and even as far back as the academy, when everyone was shiny and eager, their instructors made sure everyone understood what they were signing up for.

Yet he'd still made the choice.

So had Wyatt and every other cop on the force.

And so had Kerrigan.

He'd been caught off guard to see her already inside Bulldog's and the walk to the bar had given him a few moments to settle himself. To cover up the instant hit of attraction he'd felt at seeing her long dark hair waving around her face before falling like a dream down her back.

Why was it easier to see her as a partner when they were on the job? Now all that professional distance had seemingly vanished.

He'd had female partners before. Not many, especially since he'd worked with his first partner, John, for more than six years of his career. But he had worked with women and none of them had gotten under his skin. They'd been valued colleagues, nothing more.

And now he had someone under him, training with him, and he was having a hard time keeping any sense of distance.

Was it that first moment, when their eyes had met across the boat?

Before he knew who she was or recognized her profound desire for the work?

Because no matter how he sliced it, he kept coming back to that single instant in his mind. That moment of sharp awareness that went soul-deep.

Since he was at risk of looking like he'd zoned out of the conversation, Arlo lifted his beer toward their small circle. "To doing the hard and the meaningful work."

"Hear! Hear!"

The light clinking of drinks echoed up from their group and in short order several more cops joined their circle, the conversation turning more casual with the excitement and enjoyment of a night off.

The new additions were welcome, shifting his focus off Kerrigan and onto various friends and acquaintances.

"You must be riding high after taking down that big drug ring." David Remus, a fellow detective at a nearby precinct in Brooklyn Heights, was quick with the compliment as he moved in next to Arlo and Wyatt. "That was a big catch, Prescott, and outstanding work."

"It felt good to get that much product off the streets."

"Heard you got a lot of the low-level dealers out of circulation, too."

"We did."

"That must feel pretty great, too."

It did, and Arlo wouldn't say otherwise, but for all the hype and excitement others had about the big bust, he still felt oddly ambivalent about it.

Yes, they'd removed a lot of product. Thousands of kilos of heroin and cocaine as well as a sizable bust of fentanyl off the streets meant huge benefits for the community. And those lower-level dealers often led to bigger busts when they turned on higher-ups.

But beyond removing the product, not much else had transpired in the past two months. The lower levels had been strangely reticent to squeal for a deal.

"Admittedly, I'd have liked a better hit rate on the upper echelon. The worker bees are satisfying, of course."

"But they're not the real prize," Remus affirmed before taking a sip of his drink.

"You've still got the year's big bust," Arlo said, curious if David had felt that same lingering sense of dissatisfaction. "How'd it feel after?"

"It felt pretty good. But we also got lucky and took down one of the big dogs."

"That's right," Wyatt said, his eyes lighting up. "You got the Papa."

David's takedown had included the head of a drug cartel nicknamed "Papa" by both his rank and file, and the media. He'd been a seriously big fish and Wyatt's quick thinking added another piece to the puzzle. The same one that had eluded him and Kerrigan for more than a week.

Because getting the Papa had been a big deal. But with such a powerful leader off the market, the drug corridor was open to new players.

Was that what he was dealing with? People who'd switched loyalties and were still trying to figure out where they fit into their new organization?

It was a new line to tug and he was suddenly anxious to discuss it with Kerrigan.

"Arlo, do you have a quick minute?"

He turned to find her standing there and the moment was strangely sweet, almost as if he'd conjured her up.

"Sure."

"I won't be long but let me get you a refill on that beer while we're at it."

He didn't doubt the generosity, but it was curious that Kerrigan obviously wanted to pull him out of the conversational circle. He followed her in the direction of the bar. It was only after he was in line that she leaned in, her voice urgent.

"I'm sorry to seem like I was eavesdropping, but I was standing right behind him, and I keyed into David's comments. His takedown last year? What if it's tied to our boat? And maybe to your bust a few months ago, too?"

Since it played so closely to his own thoughts, he ran her quickly through his theory as they waited their turn at the bar.

"It makes a lot of sense, Arlo. Not one single lower-level drone has turned on the higher-ups from your bust. That has to mean something."

"It's definitely an angle."

"What if it *is* the angle?"

"How so?"

"The two dead guys on our boat. They were awfully loyal to end up done that way and no one's talked for over a week? It goes back to the lack of chatter. Just like none of your lower-level guys turned witness after that last bust."

It made sense. Hell, it made a lot of sense, Arlo admitted. "We need to find a leak."

"There's a new leader in town and whoever they are, they've got everyone running scared."

Chapter 6

Kerrigan felt the adrenaline spike in her system as clearly as she felt the thumping bass emanating from the DJ's booth. She and Arlo finally had a lead to chase.

Even if it had come at the expense of a personal evening out.

They'd opted to abandon the wait at the bar and head back to the precinct, both anxious to review his last case and bump it up against the boat murders. Wyatt and Marlowe had been quick to wave them on, confirming they'd take a ride service back home later.

And here they were, Kerrigan inwardly sighed, an hour later and still looking for any semblance of a clue, a lead or even a criminal with a suspicious hangnail.

They had nothing.

"There has to be something there," Kerrigan said, shocked at the level of disappointment that coursed in her veins. "There's no way there's not a link. Even if it's something small, or a midlevel dealer jumping to a new organization."

"Whoever's replaced the Papa, they've buried their tracks well. You and I've been running that boat down all week."

"And we don't have a damn thing to show for it." She fought the curse that tinged the tip of her tongue and kept on with her depressing list of proof. "The boat. The dead victims. And maybe worst of all, the complete inability to follow where the product is moving."

She would own the fact that it had been a busy week, and a long one, but there had been a real shot of hope as they talked it over waiting in line for their turn at the bar.

And now for there to be nothing?

She might not have the level of experience Arlo did, but she was a trained cop. There was no way they were circling around the same thoughts and coming up this empty.

"Hey there." His eyes were a dark, fathomless blue as he stared at her across his desk. "We'll find something."

"We should *have* something. Anything. This is just maddening."

"Maybe the fact we're here on a Friday night, giving up a free evening, is influencing our attitudes."

"Bulldog's really was something." Kerrigan thought about the bar they'd left, one more example of how Sunset Bay had been changing. Now there were young people thronging to businesses and restaurants and snatching up every available apartment a matter of hours after it went on the market.

As she thought about the crowd of people six deep at the bar, filling every interior table and spilling out to the heated decks at the back that overlooked the water, Kerrigan recalled something else she had seen in the files.

"Wasn't there a bar at the center of your last takedown?"

"Yeah, McNulty's."

"That's only two blocks from Bulldog's, right?"

"It is." Arlo's gaze had sharpened. "You think there's something there?"

"I realize downtown continues to expand and grow and hot spots are a part of that, but nightclubs and bars? They're places that deal in cash. They all become real easy places to clean money."

Arlo shot her a smile. "You sure you haven't been working Vice?"

"Nothing beyond my academy training and a deep devotion to police procedurals in book or TV form."

Arlo placed a hand over his heart. "Which means you no doubt see me as your grizzled partner, while you're the young ingenue determined to solve the case."

She couldn't help laughing at that, especially because it was a definite trope in the detective shows she loved so much.

"I wouldn't quite say *grizzled*."

Once again, that dark gaze captured her, drawing her in, as he asked, "What would you call me?"

"Why don't we go with *seasoned* and leave it at that?"

"I guess I can live with that."

Their locked eyes added too much weight to the air between them. Kerrigan glanced down at the notes she'd scribbled on a notepad as they'd reviewed his prior case.

"It's still early." She tapped the notepad. "Why don't we pop over to McNulty's? See how they're handling taking second place to Sunset Bay's newest hot spot."

"You think something's there?"

"Yes. No." She shrugged, not quite sure why she was suddenly curious about the other bar.

Or why it suddenly felt so important to *move*.

To push back against the desire that gripped her when she looked at him for too long.

"I'm not sure, but something seems…unfinished about your last case."

"I won't argue with you there."

"You want to go check it out?"

He was already standing before she had the words out. "Let's go."

Arlo drove back in the direction they had come from earlier, the traffic just as busy as the start of the evening. He was still processing his thoughts on those quiet moments with Kerrigan in his office, but even he couldn't deny there had been a few moments that were…fraught.

If it was simply a matter of his own awareness, he'd feel better. Or so he consoled himself.

But there was something in the deep brown of her stare that made him think he wasn't alone in how he felt.

And *that* was another matter entirely.

He was training her. He'd taken on the professional responsibility for her growth. To turn it around or, worse, come off like he was taking advantage of the situation and hit on her?

Technically, it wasn't against the rules for them to date. He wasn't her boss and they'd done nothing inappropriate.

And yet, he couldn't quite get a handle on how he'd gotten himself into this situation.

Or maybe a better question, why he couldn't separate this swirling attraction for her from the work?

"This traffic is something else. I know it's Friday night, but we've barely inched these last few blocks."

It was just the inane sort of small talk he needed, and Arlo grabbed at it like a lifeline.

"I know they say the city never sleeps, but I still remember the day Brooklyn had a little bit of lazy in her."

Kerrigan's laugh was quick. "Not anymore. This is now a young professional's paradise. 'Work hard, play hard' seems to be everyone's motto."

"That it is."

"Does it bother you?"

He came to a stop at a red light and used the physical pause as a chance to turn and look at her. "Bother me how?"

"Progress is great, but it does come with change. And not all change is welcome."

Did she speak from experience?

He nearly pressed her on it right then and there, but held back, somehow recognizing he'd have better luck letting their conversation play out instead of immediately seeking answers.

"I'd say it's more good than bad and it is fun to be a part of. If my grandparents could see Brooklyn now..." He let the thought hang there, even as he imagined his sweet grandmother who used to hang wash out the back of her side of a double house in Red Hook.

"Have they passed away?"

"Sadly, yes. Both my grandfathers when I was young, one of my grandmothers when I was in high school and then my last remaining grandmother a couple years ago."

"I'm sorry to hear that. I know it's the natural order, but I also know I'll be devastated when I lose mine."

"You have all of your grandparents?"

"I do. My mom's parents are out in Suffolk County on Long Island and my dad's parents retired to Florida."

It was interesting, he realized, but this was the first somewhat personal conversation they'd really had. They had talked quite a bit about her diving, which obviously veered into the personal, but nothing that spoke of family.

"Are you close with them?"

Kerrigan let out a wry chuckle at his question. "Are we close? Let's just say we're the Sunday-dinner, family-text-string, all-the-way-up-in-each-other's-business sort of close."

"That's nice."

"Most of the time. But sort of like change, it's not always welcome."

"By you?"

She hesitated briefly and even though he wasn't looking at her, since the light had turned green, he sensed she would have preferred to pull back the observation.

"By outsiders. People see my commitment to my family and either don't understand it or get disillusioned about it really quickly."

"Others? Boyfriend others?"

"Just…others. People outside of that close-knit family structure."

He turned onto the block to McNulty's and realized once again that he had an opportunity to keep pressing or let the conversation ride and see what she shared.

Or, more to the point, what she was comfortable sharing.

"What about you? Is your family local? Do you have brothers and sisters?"

He fought the punch of disappointment that her willingness to share details about herself had wisped away like smoke, even as he understood self-preservation as much as the next person.

"Two brothers. Two half brothers. My father and stepmom live in Virginia and my mother is divorced and living her best life, as I understand it, in Sedona."

"Do your brothers live around here?"

"My half brothers still live with my dad. My older brother is in Boston and my younger brother followed him a few years ago. Said there wasn't anything left in New York for him."

"You're here."

"I guess I am."

As answers went, it was as vague as her earlier comment about "others" and Arlo realized he wasn't interested in sharing any more.

Funny how much more interesting it was to ask the questions than to be on the receiving end.

"We're here." Arlo effectively put an end to their conversation as he scanned the crowd milling around on the street and in front of the bar as they waited for the valet. "They're not pulling a crowd the size of Bulldog's, but it's not empty, either."

"This bar was central to your takedown, yet they're open and still doing a steady business." Her attention was focused through her window as she shared her observations. "A competitor might have dealt them a financial blow, but being at the center of a bust didn't?"

"The bar owner wasn't involved. In fact, he was shocked by what was running out his back alley."

"And you bought that?"

It had been a long time since he would have called himself offended but the sensation was strong before he caught her eye.

She side-eyed him back, her expression more than a little satisfied. "That one was too easy." And then her grin turned into a saucy laugh as she turned her full attention toward him and off the scene outside the car. "I'm messing with you, Arlo. I read the files and I know you did thorough work. The bar owner was clean and you more than proved that."

The arrival of the valet prevented him from saying anything else and he judged the interruption to be a good thing as they both climbed out of the car.

He'd observed several times now Kerrigan's uncanny ability to focus on the work and still maintain a broader awareness of the moment. She could be as serious as needed or equally as light-hearted.

She had proven herself unique and unexpected from the start and clearly Kerrigan-on-a-Friday-night was another level of fascinating.

And you like it, Prescott. A whole damn lot.

The truth was, he did like it. He'd more than enjoyed his hard-won reputation at the 86th, but over the past few years, as his case record had grown bigger and gotten better, people had begun treating him with kid gloves. What had felt good at first had begun to feel forced, like he was somehow unattached from the team.

Elevated in a way that felt separate instead of honored.

Which could easily be a big layer of self-delusion, but he'd felt it all the same.

Kerrigan's subtle poking and seeming willingness to tease him and keep him on his toes was…

Well, hell, it was welcome.

"For the record, we did run the bar owner," he began once he was out of earshot of the valet.

Kerrigan had gotten out of her side of the car as he'd handed off his keys and was now walking beside him toward the entrance to McNulty's.

"Extensively. I read the case file."

Arlo nodded at that as they closed the last few yards to the bar's entrance. "He was just a local guy who made good. Got sick of his big-city job and opened a bar that catered to the after-work crowd."

He'd thought it curious at the time and had pressed the owner angle repeatedly in his investigation of the leadership of the gang. Yet, no matter how he looked at it, the guy was clean.

It had been Captain Reed who'd finally suggested Arlo ease off.

Sometimes people are exactly who they show you they are, Arlo. I know the job works hard to beat that out of us, but don't let the work take that away from you.

Sort of like Kerrigan?

Because up to now she'd shown herself to be rather straightforward. Even those few insecurities she'd carried at first had been real and shared outright instead of hidden away.

While cops were driven and called to the profession, he had worked with those who'd let a natural and normal amount of fear override their common sense. It wasn't incurable behavior, but it did bear attention.

And addressing it head-on was one more feather in the captain's hat that Arlo had always admired.

Dwayne trusted his team, but he also made sure they were armed with the proper tools. Both the physical pieces they carried as well as the often more important tools. Their minds and their ability to think through a problem.

"You do that well."

"I do what well?" Kerrigan looked up after edging around a couple obviously into each other and oblivious to the crowd navigating around them on the sidewalk.

"Your balance. The good-natured teasing with the need to be serious. Your quick assessments and your ability to remain level-headed. It's a skill that often takes time to develop, yet you seem to innately manage through each situation."

"Thank you." Kerrigan's expression had gone slightly hazy, those always expressive eyes clouding a bit. "Really. Thank you. Any compliment from you is welcome but that's an incredibly nice thing to say."

"I mean it. I suspect a lot of it's your natural intuition, but I have to imagine your dive training also serves you well. You have to stay calm and in control at all times, yet you have to move fast and make decisions quickly."

"Well. Yeah. I guess I do."

He could see the flustered satisfaction in her face as pink heightened her cheeks. It made him glad he'd said something even as he couldn't deny it was also fun to stymie her as the tiniest bit of payback for her teasing in the car.

"It's a trait I see in Wyatt as well. That ability to stay

calm, even when things are going to bits around you, is an incredible skill. Lean into that."

"I'll do that."

He nodded as he pulled the bar door open for her. "Good."

Dyson Gentry avoided glancing over at his brother, Decker, even as fingernails of ice scraped up and down his back. He'd known this was a bad idea from the start.

Damn it, he'd *known* it.

But he'd gone ahead with it all, anyway.

The family business was a good one, but it never changed. Hell, they already sold a ton of boats every year. There was nowhere else to go. No new revenue streams to make them feel like they were moving forward. And no amount of pleading with his old man had convinced Big Will Gentry to expand the business beyond their very large dock in Brooklyn.

Only Dyson's dreams were bigger than that.

But it was Decker who had the ambition and the balls and just enough frustration with their father's unwillingness to expand to put it all into motion.

Now that they were sitting here, beneath that unrelenting stare, he had to admit his brother had been the one to take the initiative and he'd been grateful for it at the time.

Only now…

Now the partnership that had seemed so promising was balancing on the thinnest of wires.

"Can you please explain to me how the police have managed to identify your business establishment as the purchase location of my boat?"

Dead eyes.

It was all Dyson could think as he stared across that desk. He wasn't sure he'd noticed it before, yet as he looked now it was all he could see.

Flat, dead and as cold as the Atlantic in February.

"The cops have no idea your boat came through us. They had a casual conversation with my father and asked a few basic questions about boats. There wasn't any hint they thought of us as the supplier at all—"

"We weren't made," Decker added, cutting Dyson off. "Our father doesn't know about our side work. Because of it he came off like the always congenial, good guy he is."

Dyson's shred of hope that his brother had finessed things fled on swift wings, even as those icy fingers skimmed his back once more.

Was that really Decker's voice?

They weren't twins but close enough in age that most people figured them for it. He'd always believed he knew his brother, but ever since going in on this deal he'd had those strange moments of awareness when he realized his brother had thoughts he didn't share.

Even more, he had *knowledge* of things he didn't share.

It had been a bit awe-inspiring at first, but Dyson had quickly come to the conclusion that there was an edgy layer there in Decker he wasn't comfortable with.

Nor did he fully recognize his sibling because of it.

We weren't made.

Who said things like that? Thought like that? Or, maybe more troubling, when had his brother begun to talk like that?

"There were cops inside your establishment asking about my boat. I don't care if your father's the damn mayor, you promised me anonymity. Not one single thread, invisible or otherwise, tying me to Brooklyn Yacht."

Decker leaned forward and there was just enough menace in the physical position that the two goons who'd stood sentinel, flanking the wall, moved forward. "You're not tied to anything."

"See that it stays that way."

Dyson took a moment to glance at Decker, not entirely sure if they'd been dismissed or if they needed to stay put.

He didn't need to wait long for the answer.

"Now. There is one final matter I'd like to clear up."

"And what would that be?" Decker asked, even as he shot Dyson a sharp glance to hold his tongue.

Although his own curiosity was running high, Dyson couldn't deny that once again he questioned how much he really knew about his brother.

It had increasingly nagged at him since they'd gone in on this deal, working with a chop shop down in Maryland that specialized in this sort of boat work. They'd supplied the pieces and the parts, and Decker's contact had put it all together.

Rather easily, Dyson thought.

And more proof that the man sitting next to him had become someone else. Someone he'd never even known existed.

How had he missed this side of his own brother?

"You will replace my boat."

"We procured it. You destroyed it. Find someone else." For the first time, Dyson heard the quiver of concern beneath his brother's attempt at a casual response.

Those dead eyes remained unwavering, seeming to both take them in and stare them down all at once.

"No, I really don't think so. You're in this now and you're going to see my boat is replaced. I will, of course, pay for your services. But I want it in New York by next Friday."

"That's impossible!" The words were out of his mouth before Dyson could stop them and in his outburst he realized his mistake.

A mistake that had opened a door he'd never have thought existed when he started down this path.

"Nothing's impossible, Mr. Gentry. Not with the right motivation."

Although a strong streak of self-preservation welled up inside, he still pressed on. There was no damn way they could get an unregistered, hot boat up here in a week. "As my brother said. We helped you. We secured the merchandise you needed. It's not our fault you torched it to get out of a tough situation."

"Funny, but I see it different. You told me that boat could handle the waves."

"You took her out in a hurricane," Dyson pointed out.

"Hardly. We took her out in a storm I was assured she could handle. She didn't, so now you'll work to secure me a replacement."

"It can't be done that fast." Dyson shook his head. "We need a month, minimum."

The lightest sigh drifted across the desk. In it, he should have recognized the absolute lack of sympathy or understanding.

It was only when that small utterance was followed

by the scariest of truths that Dyson recognized they had made yet another misstep.

"Big Will's been talking to all and sundry about the cruise he and your mother are taking for their anniversary. I find it a bit silly, actually. A boat seller taking a vacation on a boat but—" shoulders lifted in a delicate shrug "—to each his own. They leave in two weeks, I believe?"

The cold ice that had merely skated down his back up to now wrapped a tight, unyielding fist around his spine. "He's not in this."

"But his sons are. It would be such a shame for their parents to meet a dreadful end as they headed out on the start of a loving adventure."

For the first time, Decker moved, his hand covering over Dyson's forearm.

"You'll have the boat by next Friday."

"An eminently reasonable response."

With the flick of a hand, Dyson knew they'd been dismissed. He stood, surprised to find his knees were wobbly.

One of the goons standing guard duty against the wall gestured them to exit the office and follow him down the hall. Dyson did, his brother's footfalls solid and heavy behind him as they exited the same way they entered, through a door into an alley behind the bar.

It was only as the door slammed behind them that Decker let out a hard breath.

Dyson turned to his brother. "What the hell are we doing?"

"We made a deal. We're now seeing it through."

"Threats against Mom and Dad? And where the hell are we going to get an unregistered boat in a week?"

"I got us into this mess and I'll handle it. I knew what I was getting us into."

"What do you mean 'you knew?'"

He still had enough sense to keep his voice low, but Dyson wasn't willing to let Decker off so easily. His brother might have been the brains behind what they were doing, but he'd questioned the job and the partnership.

"I knew going in that we'd have to see this through."

"See what through?" Dyson asked.

"The deal we made with a stone-cold bitch."

"Nice place." Kerrigan let her gaze roam casually around the bar as she took the glass of wine Arlo extended her way and tried to infuse a happy-go-lucky vibe into her demeanor.

"Upscale. Trendy. Nice thick wood bar, well-polished brass and welcoming barstools." Arlo took a sip of his beer, his own gaze returning to her from where it had settled over each item on his list. "It's solid."

"Is it what you remembered?"

"They've cleared out some of the tables to make way for another pool table in the back but otherwise it's the same."

"We keep staring like we are and the whole bar's going to make us as cops."

"Cops get nights off, too."

"You don't want to stay further under the radar?"

"At this point, if there is something suspicious going on I'd like to draw out an attack. It's been damn near a week and nothing's turning up. Maybe it's time some of the low-level rank and file know we're looking."

Kerrigan knew it bothered him—that distinct lack

of chatter about the boat and the dead dealers—and she suddenly had a sense of what he was after.

"Are we putting ourselves out here as bait, Arlo?"

"Bait's too subtle. I want the whole damn neighborhood to know the cops are out looking for the perp who did that boat. Someone needs to trip up and if we can force them to fall sooner, I'm all for it."

They hadn't come in here with a well-baked plan, more a hunch that they wanted to take a look at the same place the last drug bust went down and see what they could find. But his reasoning made a certain sort of sense.

Whether there was anything to see at McNulty's wasn't really the point.

What was the point was the idea that the cops were out in full force, turning over stones and hunting for answers. The more people who lurked in the shadows recognized that, the bigger the chance someone would get scared and start talking.

She saw a small standing table open on the far side of the room and gestured him toward it. They'd have a good view, yet still be able to keep their backs to the exposed brick wall that made up the eastern end of the building.

They settled their drinks on the table and Kerrigan was surprised to look down at her watch and see it was still just shy of ten o'clock. They'd covered a lot of ground and still had most of the evening ahead of them. Which somehow shot Jayden's earlier wisdom right back to the forefront of her thoughts.

Partner and elder statesman, maybe, but not boss. There's not even a whiff of boss in there and you know it.

There wasn't a boss relationship here and she'd do well to remember that. Both for the romantic aspects Jayden was overtly pressing for as well as how the two of them managed the case. She was his partner on this and her thoughts and ideas were welcome.

Necessary, even, to a successful outcome.

She could appreciate his tutelage and his willingness to guide her, but ultimately solving this case was about the two of them working it together. What she hadn't banked on was the level of personal involvement that would permeate that partnership.

A fact that seemed even sharper with Arlo's own admission on the drive.

My older brother is in Boston and my younger brother followed him a few years ago. Said there wasn't anything left in New York for him.

You're here.

I guess I am.

It sounded lonely.

He sounded lonely.

As someone who was so close to their family, she recognized she had a bit of a biased view on how much families could support and stand behind each other. Especially when life reinforced the point over and over that many weren't nearly as fortunate.

But she hadn't expected Arlo was living that reality.

Was it his reputation? Or his obvious ease and ability to build relationships, which she'd seen clearly with Wyatt and even with Captain Reed?

Either way, it was unexpected and—

Her train of thought skittered away as Kerrigan keyed in on the sensation of being watched. It was a subtle wisp of awareness that shifted rapidly, as her gaze met a dark one on the opposite side of the room.

Was he security? Another bar patron?

Whatever it was, she felt the threat as clearly as she knew her own name. Determined to remain casual, she leaned into Arlo, her lips brushing the edge of his ear before she caught herself and pulled back slightly.

"Keep it casual but my eight o'clock. Against the wall."

He caught on quick, his voice low as he turned his head slightly, his lips brushing the edge of her brow. "What am I looking at?"

She fought the instant awareness of him, the subtle tick of his breath against her skin shooting sparks.

Damn it, Doyle. You've got a bigger problem at the moment than your partner's sexy lips grazing your skin.

"I'm getting really bad vibes off the dude, over near the entrance. About six-three with the leather vest, arms crossed."

He held his part, playing her doting date, but she sensed the tension in him and the shift of his attention across the room.

"I can't get a solid look at this angle."

Scenarios flashed through her mind, one rapid frame after another, even as one kept flickering as the right choice.

"Remember that compliment you gave me earlier? About how good I am at staying calm?"

"Yeah."

"Stay calm, Arlo. And try to keep up."

Without giving him another opportunity to respond,

she wrapped her arms around his shoulders, shifting them just enough so he had a view across the room.

Then she pulled down his head, their lips a fraction of a breath apart, and gave herself up to the moment.

Chapter 7

Need.

Sharp, sweet, all-consuming need swamped him as Kerrigan's mouth met his.

He knew his role. Knew the part he was playing and why she was even kissing him in the first place, but damn it, he wanted a taste of this.

He wanted it as badly as he wanted his next breath.

It was the only reason he could think of that he kissed her back, his eyes closing instead of focusing sharply on his quarry.

Soft, plump lips pressed against his, a veritable feast for the taking. Lost in the moment, he pushed for more, his tongue pressing past her lips to tangle with hers.

It was madness. Utterly. Totally.

And he was a drowning man who simply wanted *more*.

"What have we here?"

The interruption, the high-pitched voice, and the

sudden acknowledgment that he had completely abandoned his responsibility to support his partner had Arlo pulling back.

"Look at you two lovebirds on a date!"

The voice was cloyingly sweet, nearly as much as the bottle blonde who stood beside their table.

"Wendy?" Kerrigan spoke first, that calm he'd complimented her on settling the moment she put on a smile for their interloper. "Wendy Parker?"

"Yes! I can't believe it's you. I'd heard you'd moved to Brooklyn from the old neighborhood."

"Word travels fast. I only moved a couple months ago."

Wendy waved a hand. "You know how it is. Forest Hills only thinks it's a big place but it's as small-town as anywhere else."

"I suppose it is," Kerrigan agreed.

Wendy eyed him, her stare just barely proper, before she extended her hand. "I'm Wendy."

"Arlo," he said, taking her hand. Cool, slim fingers remained in his grip just a fraction longer than they should. "It's nice to meet you. Do you live here in the neighborhood?"

"Nearby. But there's so much action in Sunset Bay, it's hard to stay away. Especially on a Friday night."

"We were just saying that very thing on the drive over," Kerrigan said, neatly picking up the conversational ball. "Brooklyn feels like another world sometimes."

"About time, too. We spent so many years playing second fiddle to Manhattan. It's nice that the boroughs are finally getting some attention."

It was a familiar lament among his parents' generation, but Arlo found it funny coming from someone so young. Although the changes he and Kerrigan had discussed about Brooklyn were true, they'd been in progress for a while. Real estate and neighborhood growth didn't happen overnight. And it certainly had been happening longer than the time this woman had been an adult.

New York City was made up of five boroughs. From Manhattan, which so many thought of as "the city," to Queens, Brooklyn, the Bronx and Staten Island, it was a vast, vibrant place. That was only truer when you looked at the distinct and often individual neighborhoods within.

So, yeah, maybe he was getting old, but he hadn't heard a lot of young people frustrated about their counterparts over the bridges and tunnels to Manhattan.

Since he was veering dangerously close to bad-conversation territory—admittedly brought on by the interruption of that kiss—he plastered on a smile and tried to engage with their new visitor.

"What brought you to Brooklyn from Queens?"

Wendy's gaze dipped slightly, her smile taking on a distinct edge. "I guess I'm not a big fan of second fiddles anywhere in my life. I wasn't interested in going into the family business, so I struck out on my own. I have two clothing boutiques and am about to open a third."

"That's great!" Kerrigan's eyes widened. "Are you Wendy's Closet?"

"Yep."

"Speaking of keeping up with the old neighborhood, I did hear some good news about you. My mom was talking about your stores recently. Said she'd heard you were starting your own clothing line, too."

"I am. Fast fashion trend is all the rage, and it felt like the right next step for me, you know."

Although he had zero knowledge of the fashion industry, even Arlo was well aware that the "fast fashion" industry hadn't made friends with anyone. With its heavy toll on the environment and its labor practices in foreign countries, it was a difficult business.

Yet this woman had obviously seen it as part of building her empire and pushing even farther away from her hometown roots.

"Listen, I didn't mean to interrupt your date, but since I saw you over here, I couldn't resist coming to say hi." Wendy was already pressing a kiss to Kerrigan's cheek in farewell when it dawned on Arlo he hadn't seen the woman with anyone.

It was nearly out of his mouth to ask where her friends were when she laid a hand over his forearm. "It was lovely to meet you. Enjoy your evening."

And then she was gone.

"That was a blast from the past." Kerrigan picked up her wine, shaking her head. "And it's funny, but my mom *had* just mentioned her a few weeks ago. Sounds like she's making quite a name for herself."

"She certainly seems determined."

Kerrigan glanced up at that, her gaze sharp. "That's a bad thing?"

"No."

"Then?"

She left her question hanging there and Arlo wasn't exactly sure how to respond.

"Then good for her?"

"Somehow I don't get the sense you mean that."

"Nah, I mean it." When she only continued to stare at him, he added, "Really, I do."

To be fair, he had no real reason to be so immediately sharp or suspicious about the woman. It was his rotten luck Wendy had interrupted the kiss, but beyond that, she hadn't said much or stayed nearly long enough to have pulled this sort of reaction from him.

"I haven't known you very long, but I can tell you I'm not buying this attempt at Zen."

"Zen nothing. I think I just have too much on my mind."

Her eyes widened as her gaze darted to the door. "I totally forgot about the bouncer from before."

Since he'd forgotten, too, he scanned the area near the bar's entrance, subtlety be damned. "He was standing over there?"

"Yep, by the door. Maybe he's one of the bouncers and was just checking the room to make sure no one was getting out of hand."

"You believe that?"

"I—" She stopped, shook her head. "I want to believe it, but, no, not really. His attention felt way too personal."

That admission shot a hard spike into his chest and Arlo heard the flat notes in his own voice. "Then where did he go?"

"I got a bit too involved in my little hometown reunion to say."

Since he'd gotten far too involved in their kiss, Arlo could hardly chastise, but he still couldn't quite remove those hard edges from his tone. "Which reinforces that it's been a long evening for both of us, following a long day and an even longer week. Let's call it a night?"

"Alright."

She collected her purse, and it was only after they'd crossed the bar and gotten outside to wait for the valet to take his ticket that Arlo noted they were both scanning for the mystery bouncer.

"There's no sign of him. The guy I saw."

There were any number of reasons why the guy had disappeared, including everything from a shift break, if he was employed by the bar, to a patron opting to go home for the evening.

But possible reasons aside, it didn't sit well that Kerrigan had felt such a strong response to his presence.

"Maybe it really was nothing." Kerrigan slipped into the passenger side before he could open the door for her, so Arlo waited to respond until he was back inside the closed car.

"I never bet against a cop's intuition."

"Which takes me right back to Wendy. I know she's a lot and a little hard to take. She was a few years ahead of me in school and I remember that aspect of her personality even back then. To be honest, I don't think I even realized she knew me."

"She seemed to know you *and* have kept up with you."

Kerrigan shrugged. "We're from the same neighborhood. That's all it is."

"That small-town feel you're both insisting is alive and well here in New York City?"

"Remember I mentioned how close I was to my family?" When he only nodded, she continued, "My mother has her fingers, her toes and both her eyes on the pulse of Forest Hills. There's nothing that happens, and that includes someone sneezing in the park, that my mother doesn't manage to hear about."

"You do realize it's sort of funny that you both referred to Forest Hills as small-town. Especially when the population of Queens is over two million people."

"It's a neighborhood, Arlo. As long as people make walls and gardens and territories, it doesn't matter how big it gets, it'll always feel small."

Although he couldn't quite agree, as he drove away from the bar he had to admit the evening had taken more than a few odd turns. "So our evening was a serious bust in terms of cracking our case, but we did get a few unique moments out of it."

"Oh?"

"We now have one mysteriously threatening bouncer and one irritatingly perky high-school alumnus to show for our trip this evening."

"I guess we do."

She'd given him directions to her apartment building earlier and he headed that way after turning off the main thoroughfare of Sunset Bay.

And recognized how diligently both of them had avoided mentioning that kiss that, to his mind, was the most interesting moment of all.

Kerrigan laced up her sneakers and snagged her gym bag from the hallway on her way out. She'd already stowed her Murphy bed against the wall and tidied up her sleeping arrangements to maximize the space.

Her apartment was small, but it was hers, and not for the first time she was happy to have it all to herself. Both the physical aspects of living alone as well as the emotional ones.

She lived in her head and when she was deep in a case or working through a personal problem, she didn't want anyone around.

Because of that fact, she'd prioritized independent living at the expense of other amenities and took extra shifts when she could to help pay for it *and* add to her savings.

So, yeah, her oversized studio was small, but it was hers and that was all that mattered.

What it also meant was that she had a full Saturday stretching out before her with no plans beyond her workout and spending time with herself.

Not the best way to stop thinking about kissing Arlo Prescott.

It had been a foolish move on her part, dragging him close as a way to get a better look at that strange man by the front door of the bar. And yet…

What other choices did they have?

Whatever had been directed at her from that goon by the door had carried some seriously dark overtones.

Not that dark if one touch of Arlo's lips made me forget all about those bad vibes.

And hadn't that been the rub? The lone fact she kept coming back to, over and over. She might have felt threatened by that man at the door, but one kiss from Arlo and she'd been distracted.

More, she'd let her guard down.

And if those criminals Arlo was so determined to lure *were* out there, she'd put herself in a position of weakness by forgetting about the threat.

He'd complimented her levelheadedness and her ability to remain calm, but she didn't feel either this morning.

Which meant there was nothing to be done but to diligently focus all her attention and effort on getting it back.

Her move to the 86th Precinct had brought with it access to a new gym and she loved the facility. In addition to the indoor Olympic-size pool she and her fellow harbor-team members used regularly, there was a full suite of cardio machines and an impressive weight room. Several officers taught classes as additional options and she'd already enjoyed a regular Zumba session that was so popular they needed to manage the class size via a sign-up sheet.

The pool was pretty empty when she got there, and after changing into her suit, she easily found a lane and began her laps. Water sluiced over her in calming waves as she swam, one end to the other, her timed breaths coming in easy rhythm with her movements.

It should have relaxed her. That mix of movement, the comfort she always found in the water and the good, steady rhythm found in using her body were usually a balm for whatever she was dealing with.

But a half hour later all she'd managed to do was count off a solid fifty laps all while images of kissing Arlo swam in her head.

"Damn it."

She ripped off her swim cap as she headed for the locker room, irritated with herself and even more irritated with her racing thoughts, which were a solid match for racing hormones.

And that was going to be her excuse to herself later when she thought back on how she plowed into Arlo as he walked down the hall toward the men's locker room.

"Whoa! Where's the fire?"

"Oh! I'm sorry. I—" She glanced up, something discordant settling in her chest as the man who'd dominated her mental musings was suddenly standing before her and looking even better in person.

"You're here early."

"I wanted to get my laps in and I'm so sorry I barreled into you like that." She reached out, trying to wipe away the moisture that was already forming on the leather of his jacket. "And I got you wet, too."

"I'll dry."

"Sure. Of course. Well, I—"

"Look, I just got here but I can always come back later. I got a late workout in yesterday afternoon so I'm still feeling ready to tackle pancakes if you're up for breakfast."

Realistically she should say no.

It was the smart thing to do. And with the power of that kiss still humming through her body with more effect than her steady laps, it would be wise to just make an excuse and walk away.

Especially since something tickled hard against the back of her throat at the idea that she now knew something about him. Something more than the way he kissed.

He'd had pancakes at breakfast a few days ago and now he was offering them again. And something about that small fact tugged at her much harder than it probably should.

"I don't want to interrupt your workout plans."

"Since pancakes and breakfast with you sounds a lot more interesting than running a treadmill and doing bench presses, save me." When she hadn't yet answered, he added, "Please."

"Pancakes do sound good."

His smile was broad and it was silly to think about his personal situation. And yet...

Kerrigan couldn't stop thinking of his comments yesterday about his family. How all had left the area, claiming there was nothing left for them.

It was sad.

More, it seemed terribly lonely.

While she wasn't exactly in the same situation based on the strong bonds she had with her family, she did understand what it was to be alone.

Hadn't that dismal thought accompanied her as she'd headed over this morning?

Now she wouldn't be alone for part of her day.

And Arlo wouldn't be, either.

"Let me go get dried off and changed, and I'll meet you in the lobby."

Twenty minutes later they walked into a restaurant about two blocks from the precinct. Like the bars they'd visited the night before, this place was going for a bit more upscale and instead of the scarred Formica tables with booths of the local diner, they got aged wood and cane chairs. Within moments they were squeezed into a two-top in the midst of the brunch crowd.

A waiter got them coffee and took their orders for pancakes, then headed off back into the throng. "Thanks for joining me. I didn't realize I was quite this hungry until I caught a whiff of this place."

She'd already eyed several plates set down on tables around the restaurant and knew he'd selected well. "It's a great suggestion. And I'm going to enjoy every single bite of those pancakes."

His easy smile faded, and she caught the sense of

seriousness a heartbeat before he spoke. "I'm glad you came here with me for another reason. I owe you an apology."

An apology?

"Last night, you were dealing with whoever that goon was at the door and I got a bit carried away by that kiss. It was unprofessional and I'm sorry for it."

Since she'd spent the better part of twelve hours restless and upset with herself for initiating their kiss, there was no earthly reason she should be upset by his apology.

And yet...

"You're sorry for that? It was a ridiculous thing I initiated in a moment of panic. Don't give it another thought."

"It didn't feel ridiculous."

"Well, it was. You're my partner and it was a dumb impulse to make a scene at the bar instead of owning what was happening and just getting up myself and dealing with that jerk."

"That's not what I meant." Arlo shook his head, nearly sloshing the coffee in his mug as he set it down on the table with a hard thunk. "Why would you even think about instigating something with a man who gave you the creeps like that?"

"I'm a trained officer. I can handle a man who's acting like a problem."

"Unarmed in a bar where he could be carrying a weapon? Or possibly high on any number of things? No way."

"Are you suggesting I can't?"

"I'm suggesting you found a way to handle the situation without jumping into something rash. They're not the same."

"Yet here you are, apologizing for kissing me back."

"I'm not—"

"No, Arlo, what do you mean? Because you're suddenly offended at the idea I can take care of myself, yet you're equally offended at kissing me. You can't have it both ways."

That sense of calm he'd credited her for was nowhere in evidence, but she at least recognized the need to pull back.

Or, more to the point, to shut up and not make it worse.

"I wasn't offended. I was the opposite of offended." He toyed with the handle of his coffee mug before looking back up at her. "I enjoyed it."

Whatever impulse had him inviting Kerrigan to breakfast had then given way to some misbegotten need to discuss that kiss.

He should have let it lie.

Just like last night, when they'd both, by unspoken agreement, avoided discussing what had happened, he should have left things that way.

And instead, here he was apologizing? And, apparently, insulting her about her abilities to defend herself, which hadn't been in the cards, either.

Because no matter how well-trained and competent she was, the thought of her confronting the man who'd put such fear in her eyes had him seeing through a dark miasma of anger.

"I enjoyed it, too."

Her admission floated toward him across their small

table, kindling a level of satisfaction he had no business feeling yet was helpless to deny.

"So let's put it behind us. It's out in the open now and we can move on."

"Absolutely."

"Good." He took a sip of his coffee, trying to regain his equilibrium, but it had taken a serious vacation since the night before.

Hell, it had pretty much vanished the moment he'd seen her standing at the edge of the boat, stripping out of her wet suit.

"Can I ask you something?" Kerrigan's voice was quiet, her back arrow-straight as she sat opposite him. It was a jarring change from when they'd walked over to the restaurant, the two of them comfortable and relaxed.

He'd ruined that with his harebrained attempts to apologize. Or maybe, more to the point, to assuage his guilt?

"Of course."

"Is this going to change things between us?"

Until that moment, he hadn't considered his apology as anything more than something she deserved, but now that he considered it from her perspective, he got a sense of her worry. "If you mean will it change my respect for you and my belief you can do the work? Absolutely not."

"Okay."

"If you mean that it's going to be something we both have to live with? There's not much I can do about that."

Wow, Prescott, is this your first day talking to a woman?

He'd never considered himself clumsy with women,

but something about this exchange had put him on his back foot. First, his ill-advised apology for kissing her wasn't the best choice. But now he was rubbing salt in the wound?

Her jaw set into a hard line. "We're going to have to do something about it because it can't get in the way."

"I'm attracted to you, Kerrigan. It's already in the way. A kiss only cemented that fact even more."

Their waiter arrived with their pancakes, and Arlo used the break to simply look at her across the table.

The truth was out.

She was a beautiful, *interesting* woman and at least he'd finally admitted to his attraction for her. Which meant now was also the time to tell her about his dive into Big Will's background and his business because he had to get that report written up and added to the file.

"Kerrigan, I need to—"

"So what you're really saying is that things *will* change. Look, Arlo, I don't make it a habit to go around kissing my coworkers. In the line of duty or outside of it. I can't afford gossip or questions about my competence."

"There it is again. Why are you so convinced someone's going to question your abilities?" He gave her a beat, then two, before he pressed on. Because unlike last night in the car, he wasn't willing to wait and see if she might say something.

It was time to push.

"It's been the pervasive thread between us for the past week and I can't help but feel it all hinges on whatever happened at your first precinct. Get over it. Deal with it however you need to and then get it out of your head."

"Or what?"

"Or you're going to fall victim to it."

As pep talks went it was as poor as the bad apology for the kiss, but he was getting desperate. There were some very real ghosts in her past and it was long past time she exorcised them.

"I'm a professional. I'm past it."

"I don't think you are."

"So now you're playing armchair psychologist on top of telling me all the ways I can't go off and defend myself?"

"It's not armchair psychology to acknowledge that whatever happened at your last precinct is still affecting you."

"I'm fine."

"You say that, but no matter how good a cop you are, below *and* above the water, letting those demons in and allowing them to feed never ends well."

"Then how about this, Detective Prescott. I'm more than capable of handling this case and seeing it through to the end. Not only am I capable, I'm going to do that. And when it's over? When we have whoever these bastards are in custody? I'm going to remind you of this moment and all the reasons you thought I couldn't handle it."

"That's not what I said, Kerrigan."

"Save it."

She fumbled in her coat pocket for something and it took him a split second to realize it was a handful of cash. "This should cover my portion of breakfast. I have a dive Monday morning, but I'll be in the precinct after lunch. I'll see you then."

More than a few eyes followed her as she stood and

stalked from the restaurant and Arlo left them all to stare.

All he could focus on was the uneaten stack of pancakes on the opposite side of the table.

And the unmistakable lines of hurt he'd put on the face of the woman he wouldn't be sharing them with.

Chapter 8

Kerrigan finished checking the gauges on her oxygen tank and fought the roiling waves of exhaustion and sadness she'd managed for nearly forty-eight hours. She'd even feigned work overload to get out of Sunday dinner with her family.

If her mother had suspected something more was up, she didn't say, but Kerrigan knew she needed to get herself together. Because if she canceled for next week, her mother would be at her doorstep with a meat loaf, a vat of chicken soup and a box of tissues to talk it out.

And what, exactly, would she say?

I have the hots for my new partner, and he thinks I'm damaged goods from my first job.

Oh, but he's attracted to me, too, so there is that.

A lot of *that*, actually. Because no matter how upsetting their conversation had been, she was attracted too.

And wasn't that the rub?

She wasn't damaged but she did carry a hell of a lot of baggage with her from that Internal Affairs investigation. She'd believed it behind her. She'd kept her head down and had focused on her dive work, but here she was, with her first shot at working a high-profile case, and she was letting her past intrude.

Was Arlo right to question her?

Since every partner deserved to know they were heading straight into the fire with someone capable of handling the heat, yeah, she admitted to herself.

He did have a right to question.

Especially when that very baggage had driven every insecurity she had on this case.

"Yo, Kerr. You ready?"

Jayden had given her a wide berth this morning when she'd remained quiet through his chatter about his dinner date on Saturday night. Her automaton-like responses of "that's nice" and "sounds delicious" hadn't carried any heart and their friendship was solid enough that Jayden recognized she needed some space.

Even if she did owe him an apology for being a bad friend who couldn't even make a bit of Monday-morning small talk.

"You sure you're good to dive?"

"I'm fine. The quiet underwater will do me good." She stood up from where she'd crouched beside her equipment and put a hand on his arm. "And hopefully break my crappy mood this morning. I'm sorry."

"Save it." He grinned and she saw the partner she knew and loved behind that smile. "And since I'm going to be singing happy songs about that crème brûlée for at least another week you'll get my dinner story a few more times. You can ooh and aah later."

"It's a deal."

Jayden drifted toward the front of the cabin of the small police boat they were using today, and she took a seat on the deck with her tablet. She wanted to review the details one more time on their evidence recovery.

She scanned the report and figured this would be a quick drop down into the water. They had a lot of data since a beat team had chased a group of thugs across the Brooklyn Bridge the night before. The team had a good description of the weapons. Kerrigan already knew she was on the hunt for a sawed-off shotgun and two semi-automatic rifles that were a lot better off at the bottom of East River than in the hands of criminals.

Gavin gave the morning briefing and since the recovery was pretty straightforward, he was only sending her and Jayden down on the bridge dive. Once they had the evidence, their team would move on to whatever other duties awaited.

It was easy. Routine, even. And it was something she innately understood.

Since she had very little to prep for, her errant thoughts went straight back to the same place they'd been all weekend.

Is this going to change things between us?

If you mean will it change my respect for you and my belief you can do the work? Absolutely not.

If you mean that it's going to be something we both have to live with? There's not much I can do about that.

She'd played that exchange over and over and kept coming back to the sheer audacity of Arlo's words.

Live with it?

They'd have to live with kissing each other?

It infuriated her, both for his matter-of-fact attitude about the whole thing and—even more, she had to admit—because she couldn't let it go.

Live with it.

She'd kissed him in the line of duty and while she'd stand by that, there would have been other ways of handling the situation. Heck, she could have dropped something on the floor or just told him flat out to look at the thug by the bar door.

But no.

She'd used a kiss as an excuse to get him into the proper sight line.

It was selfishly motivated, and she could direct as much heat and anger in Arlo's direction as she wanted, but she needed to own her actions.

And maybe that was the root of the problem. She was angry at herself. For letting this attraction she had developed color her judgment, certainly in the moment, but overall, too.

Was she still raw over her exit from her last precinct? Yes, of course. That damage wasn't going away anytime soon and maybe it shouldn't. Experiences like that left a mark but they also prepared you for things to come.

She was tougher now and she no longer wore rose-colored glasses. Which also meant if feelings were getting in the way, then she wasn't doing her job well.

And since feelings *were* getting in the way it was time to get her head in the game.

She flipped over to her email while she waited for the boat operator to get them in position and scanned what had come in that morning.

Only to find an email from ten o'clock the night before.

The subject carried the case number and a very clear description of what was inside.

Report: Background check | Will Gentry, Dyson Gentry, Decker Gentry

She'd already written up the interview notes with Big Will after they'd gotten back to the precinct. Nowhere in that write-up was there a discussion of running a background check on Big Will or his family.

Which meant Arlo had taken it upon himself to do it.

She clicked into the report attached to the email, something dark and ugly greasing her stomach.

He hadn't told her.

And unless he'd gotten a wild hair yesterday to run the family—something he'd most certainly *not* discussed with her—it wasn't just something he'd been thinking about.

It was something he'd done.

Kerrigan read the date stamp on the report and had her answer.

Arlo had run the family the same day they'd visited Brooklyn Yacht.

He hadn't mentioned it then. Or in any of the numerous days or conversations they'd shared since.

As projects went, it wasn't completely out of the ordinary. It made sense to get a full picture of suspects or anyone who might have knowledge of a crime.

She'd believed Big Will was innocent, but she'd never suggest a cop's instincts weren't fair or valid or not worth pursuing.

Yet he'd deliberately kept her out.

And she had the date stamp to prove it.

* * *

"Arlo?" Captain Reed moved up beside Arlo's desk. "You have a minute?"

"Of course."

Arlo had been running through old case files all morning, trying to see if there was anything he'd missed on the drug-bust case he'd closed a few months ago.

So far nothing.

Just like he hadn't had anything from Kerrigan, either.

He'd left the restaurant shortly after she did, the pancakes he'd ordered like dust in his mouth. The minimal amount of food had made it easier to get through his workout without feeling weighted down and he'd processed, over and over, with each *thwap* of the treadmill belt how badly he'd messed up.

"I saw the report that you put in on the smuggling-boat case."

"The Gentry family?"

"That's the one. I know you've been busy, but it's not like you to be so late in your reports. Everything okay with that one?"

It was an example, yet again, that Dwayne Reed knew his team.

"I struggled with that one a bit."

"With reviewing potential suspects?" Dwayne's dark gaze sharpened. "They gave you a problem during your initial interview?"

"No, not at all. Kerrigan and the owner know each other, and he spoke easily with us about what he knew and how the boat business works."

"So he was more of a source than a potential perp?"

"More or less." Arlo felt the heat creep up his neck.

"Nonetheless, I felt it important to run him, but I did it without telling her."

He hated the way this one made him feel, that sense that he'd betrayed his partner, even though he knew full well he was doing his job.

"Why'd you keep it from her?"

"I was concerned her friendship with the owner would make it difficult to be objective."

"Did you tell her that?"

"No, sir."

"That sounds like a real problem here." Dwayne paused, obviously weighing his words, before continuing. "You know you have my full support on this. Kerrigan does, too. You brought her in, Arlo. She deserves to be all-in."

"I know that. And it's why it took me so long to write up the report."

Dwayne just nodded at that before he leaned forward, bracing his forearms on his knees. "Partnerships aren't easy. You've been doing this long enough to know that. But we support working in a partnered environment for a reason, Arlo."

"Yes, sir."

"Since I can see your face, I recognize you've been through this over and over in your mind. I suggest you start with your partner and apologize."

"I'm not exactly her favorite person right now."

"Oh?" There was a shocking depth of meaning in that lone word and Arlo quickly retrenched.

"She's eager. She wants to solve this case. I want to support that in her. That drive. That ambition. But I can't help feeling, just like you said last week, that there are some really dark overtones in this one."

"You get any new leads?"

"No, and that's part of the problem. We've been turning over every rock we can find. That look into the Gentry family was an example. I don't want them to be guilty, but nothing is popping. No one is talking. And when you add in two grisly murders on the boat, it makes you wonder."

"What lines are you tugging?"

Arlo filled in the captain on the theory they had been working, that somebody had stepped in and replaced the Papa. Dwayne keyed in on that, his attention sharp and reinforcing Arlo's gut that they had something with that. "It's a good angle and it makes a lot of sense. Switching leaders always causes havoc. Taking the Papa out of circulation? That's a lot of upheaval and a lot of room for new ambitious leaders to move in."

Not for the first time, Arlo acknowledged how much of human nature was wrapped into criminal activity. The hierarchies. The loyalties. Even the strange use of "family" as a way to bring people into the work together.

Although most of his friends were cops, he had some that worked in the corporate world. Hell, his brother was one of them. And the way they talked about their companies, referring to them as families and as teams. There was an odd match there.

Did it get people to fall in line? Make them feel more loyal? Or was it the simple human need to belong to something?

"I know it's frustrating when you don't have a lead, but you and Kerrigan are working some good angles. Keep at it. Keep pulling those lines." Dwayne stood. "And apologize to your partner."

"Yes, sir."

"Now I really know you're remorseful."

"What do you mean?"

"I haven't gotten a single 'Dwayne' out of you. It's all been 'yes, sir,' 'no, sir.'" A broad grin split Dwayne's face, his teeth flashing bright white. "It's your tell, Prescott."

At the idea he even had a tell, Arlo mentally bristled, but he still couldn't resist asking… "Respect is a problem?"

"It is when you hide behind it."

Dwayne left on that note, his ability to read his people and to know when to give them space on full display.

Which meant Arlo was left with all the thoughts racing through his head, his lingering guilt and the very real need to figure out his apology to Kerrigan.

He decided figuring out that apology was a good place to start.

Kerrigan moved through the dark, murky water, her gloved hands removing pile after pile of silt, and cursed her inability to come up with a weapon. Jayden had found the sawed-off shotgun quickly, but neither of them had had any luck finding the semi-automatics.

Gavin's voice echoed through her comm unit. "You guys have about twelve more minutes of air. Start wrapping it up down there and get going on your ascent. We'll do a second dive for the other pieces."

The water around the bridge was some of the deepest in the harbor and they had to manage their ascent slowly or risk adding in decompression stops. She knew the logistics, but damn, she'd worked out a rhythm for combing the harbor floor and she really wanted to find those guns.

Couldn't one thing go right?

Even as she thought it, she disregarded it. The specifics of her training were absolute. You followed protocol and you followed the instructions of your lead. Gavin was lead and he said to come up, so they'd get fresh tanks and start again.

Jayden sent back his affirmation, and Kerrigan was about to do the same when she heard a shout through her comm unit.

"Kerrigan. Jayden. Start that ascent now." Gavin's voice brooked no argument through the headset. "We got a jumper on the bridge."

The instructions were clear, delivered as an order, but her reaction was in immediate violation of her training.

Her single biggest goal under water was to remain calm.

To control her breathing.

And at those four words—*we've got a jumper*—it all shot to hell.

Desperate, Kerrigan focused on her breathing first. She *had* to get this under control.

Breath stuttered in her lungs, and she put a hand over her breathing apparatus, struggling to find a calmer way to handle the news of the jumper, to no avail. Especially when Gavin's voice came through their now-open comm line, apprising her and Jayden of the situation, confirming the jumper was getting closer to the edge of the bridge.

Additional cops on scene.

Second police boat en route.

Coast Guard notified and moving in as well.

She listened to it all, her breath still coming in sharp, spiky gasps as Gavin relayed what was happening. The waters that had felt calm and welcoming even a few moments before as she'd worked now felt cloying and thick.

A distinct sensation of being trapped filled her, a match for the deep despair triggered by the thought of the jumper.

Kerrigan fought through the natural reactions of her body, cataloging her way through the mental checklist that was as much protocol as her lifeline.

Manage your air.

Control your ascent.

Slow and steady on both.

She made it another few feet, her gaze focused on her depth gauge, even as she fought her adrenaline for every single foot.

Breathe, damn it. You know the way. Slow and steady.

Slow.

Steady.

Her training was expansive, and the harbor team was fully prepared to support bridge suicides. The unpredictability of it was a challenge, but the goal was always to minimize loss of life. She'd been fortunate to have a high rate of success so far, but she'd also never been involved in one while working another dive.

Nor had she been involved in one since the events at her last precinct.

The chatter continued through her comm unit, Gavin doing his best to keep her and Jayden aware of what was happening. His voice helped settle her, even as she felt the hitch in her breathing as the memories of what had come before continued to swamp her.

"Patrol's on the bridge. They're keeping their distance, but they made contact with the jumper."

It's a civilian, Kerrigan reminded herself as she stared diligently at her depth gauge, carefully moving steadily upward. *It's not the same*.

But it was the same.

Somewhere deep inside she knew that. Taking one's life, no matter the reason, was the same.

"Kerrigan! What's your depth?"

Gavin's voice echoed through her comm unit, and she held tight to it, using it as a lodestone to keep her moving steadily upward. "Forty-two."

"Keep it steady."

Steady.

She upbraided herself for letting the past into her head and tried to clear her mind of everything else. Under the water, her problems at the surface had to take a back seat. Her breath, her equipment and her work could be her only focus down here.

Yet she'd let all she was dealing with up above color her judgment.

Breathe.

She kicked slowly, keeping her ascent properly paced to avoid decompression issues, and finally felt her breathing slow.

Finally felt her world right itself.

The hull of the police boat became visible above her and she kicked the last few feet to the surface. Breaking through the water, she swam the remaining distance to the police boat, Jayden visible at the top of the deck, waiting for her.

The quiet beneath the water, with only her comm unit for sound, had vanished. In its place was the cacophony of the boat engine, the whipping of the wind and the shouts coming from the bridge.

She looked up to see the commotion surrounding the jumper and was surprised to realize the situation was happening almost directly above their boat.

"Finally!" Jayden hollered from the edge of the ladder, his hand extended to pull her up.

She grabbed the bottom rung, carefully navigating the steps, when the shouting got louder, echoing off the comm unit in her ear. Jayden twisted to look up at the bridge and Kerrigan's gaze followed his. The already loud shouts exploded as a large form fell over the edge, flailing as it headed for the water.

Without conscious thought, she pushed off the ladder, falling back into the water. Her only goal was to get to the fallen man.

"Kerrigan! No!" Jayden's scream from above her faded out as soon as she sunk beneath the water. She moved on blind instinct, pushing herself as fast as she could in the direction she saw the man fall.

Gavin's voice echoed in her ear, loud and firm. "Kerrigan. Stop your dive immediately. We've got a crew ready."

She ignored the summons, focused on the churned-up water in front of her.

She was close. So, so close. And she could *save* him.

It wasn't like last time. She wasn't responsible for this, but she could help him. She could make sure that he got help.

That was her only thought as she swam closer.

Not the steady shouts in her ear, ordering her back.

Not the roiling water as she swam ever closer to the body she could see sinking in the murky darkness.

Not the underlying knowledge that she had no more than three minutes of air in her tank.

Still, the man fell, and she reached out, trying to grab the hands that were, even now, raised above the body as he sunk. Kicking out, she pushed herself downward to try and get to him. Pressure exploded in her ears as her fingertips caught the edge of his jacket sleeve and she gripped as hard as she could, grasping that thick material and pulling hard to stop his descent.

It wasn't much, but she held on tight, using her other hand to grip the man's fingers.

Kerrigan had no idea if he was alive, but she'd stopped his descent and now she had to get him to the surface. Keeping tight hold on her prize, her forearms strained at the minimal grip she had, centered in the flex of her fingers and wrists.

And still, she refused to let go.

Vaguely, she keyed back into the shouts in her ear. The steady orders to surface had given way to new shouts from Gavin.

"Wyatt's on his way. You are ordered to ascend, Kerrigan. Now! You don't have any air."

That reality—one she'd known but had deliberately ignored in favor of action—became clear as her tank gauge read one percent. She had her bailout cylinder, and she could use that, but the only way she could get to it was to let go of her tenuous hold on the jumper.

But he'd need it, too.

So she tightened her grip, her wrists straining as her fingers cramped. But there was no way she was letting go.

No way she'd fail now.

Kicking upward, she pushed her body to its limits, dragging the man and working her fingers, small movements that gave way inch by inch, to get a better grip. She had to get a hand free to get him air from her bailout cylinder. He'd been under too long at this point and he needed air.

Stopping the ascent to focus on her grip, she managed to secure his wrist in one tight grip, then used her free hand to reach for her cylinder.

She just had it in her hand when the man's eyes popped open, his movements suddenly jerky. She saw a world of hurt in those eyes a split second before he began waving his free hand, knocking the bailout bottle from her grip.

She scrambled for the cylinder, but it fell beyond her reach, the tip of her gloves just brushing the edge of it as it descended into the murky depths of the river.

Her gaze darted back to her oxygen gauge and she was determined to do something to help him, even if it was to share her breathing apparatus, when she registered the readout.

Her oxygen was gone.

Chapter 9

"Kerr!"

Wyatt's voice echoed in her ear a moment before she registered his form descending above her. She still had a grip on the fallen man, but his continued flailing was straining her wrist to the point of breaking.

Did she let go?

She *had* to surface for air.

Wyatt took in the situation immediately and she used her free hand to make the signal for "no air." In moments, he had his own bailout cylinder off his belt and in her hand while his dive partner secured the jumper.

Kerrigan took a steady pull on the bailout tube, the air welcome as she fought to calm herself and her breathing for the second time in five minutes.

In.

Out.

Slow and steady.

Satisfied she was taken care of, Wyatt gestured her to start to the surface as he and his dive partner secured the jumper. His partner, Connor, was holding his own bailout cylinder to the man's lips to get him oxygen.

Whether it was the innate self-preservation humans were hardwired for, or an unwillingness to fight three of them, Kerrigan saw the man take the breather between his lips, nodding as Wyatt's partner gestured him to take breaths.

They had no idea what injuries the man might have sustained, but he seemed to have the wherewithal to hold the cylinder and keep breathing.

With a small push against her shoulder, Wyatt pointed up in their understood gesture for the surface. "Go."

She knew she'd already broken several regulations and put herself in serious danger by going after the jumper, so she just nodded and started her ascent.

And surfaced to find a boat full of concerned faces.

Jayden was already at the base of the boat ladder, his hand extended toward her. She took it and felt the hard strength of him as he half pulled, half dragged her into his chest.

"God, you took five years off my life." He whispered it against her ear the moment he had his arms around her. "What were you thinking?"

"I—"

Adrenaline had emotion cratering her stomach and she suddenly feared she'd start crying if she answered him.

It was only his knowing stare as he pulled back that

kept her in the moment. There'd be time for tears and admonishment later.

But she'd be a fool to think she'd escape, either.

Arlo glanced at his watch for what had to be the tenth time in as many minutes and wondered where Kerrigan was. She'd said she had a morning dive but would be in after lunch. It was nearly two and he still hadn't seen any sign of her.

She'd said those words in anger before leaving him to two plates of pancakes. Before he'd sent the report on the Gentry family. Had she reconsidered and wasn't coming in at all?

Could he blame her?

Wyatt waved at him from the entrance to the squad room. Arlo lifted a hand in greeting, curious to see his friend at this time of day. Although Wyatt was a fixture around the 86th, he was out on dives on most weekdays.

"To what do I owe the visit?" Arlo eyed the white paper bag his friend set down on the desk, the garlicky scent of a meatball sub wafting from it. "With lunch, too?"

"I need to talk to you. Mind if we go snag a conference room?"

For the first time, he registered the weariness in Wyatt's gaze and the haggard lines that creased his forehead.

"Sure."

He followed his friend to a small room off the main corridor and found his curiosity spiking even higher when Wyatt closed the door.

"What's going on?"

"Kerrigan had a bad dive today. I wanted you to hear it from me."

"Is she okay?"

"She's fine. Shaken up and taking a few days off from her dive work, but she's alright."

Whatever else he was expecting, the news that Kerrigan had almost been hurt had him reeling.

"I need to go see her."

"I need you to talk to me first. Let me tell you what's going on."

He didn't just consider Wyatt a colleague, but he was also a valued friend, so the serious tone shot something damn near frigid straight through Arlo's midsection.

"What is going on, Wyatt?"

"Kerrigan ran out of air today on her dive."

It felt like his stomach curdled at that news. "She what? But that's not possible. You dive in pairs. And don't you have extra air? That backup you carry?"

"We have all those things, and she still ran out of air. I found her in time and was able to give her my backup."

"It doesn't make sense. She's a good diver. An experienced one, too."

"She's all those things."

He heard the pause in Wyatt's voice as clearly as a gunshot.

"But what?"

His friend's eyebrows narrowed over blue eyes that missed nothing. "But I'm worried she's taken on a bit too much."

"She's assured me repeatedly she can handle it. That she could juggle the case, and her dive work. And from what I've seen that's true."

"I thought so, too. Even as late as Friday, talking

with her, it seemed she was handling it all. But the woman I saw today on that dive? She is not handling things."

His heated discussion with Kerrigan on Saturday morning filled his mind once again. It hadn't been far from his thoughts, but standing here, facing Wyatt, Arlo had to admit there was something there.

"She and I had a tough discussion the other day. Maybe it's on her mind."

"Tough discussion? Something so tough she wouldn't know how to manage a dive?"

"You keep saying that. What actually happened?"

Wyatt filled him in on the recovery work that Kerrigan and Jayden were responsible for this morning. It all sounded straightforward until Wyatt explained how she'd gone after a man who had jumped from the bridge.

"Kerrigan saved that man?"

"Yes, she did. People can survive a jump from the Brooklyn Bridge, but it's tenuous at best. She saved him because she was right there, and she acted quickly."

"And that's what you think is a problem? She acted with compassion and saved somebody?"

"She broke protocol, Arlo. She knows better. She put herself in direct danger."

The rules and regulations they all lived with were a part of the job. Necessary ones, yes, and they were drilled into everyone from the first day at the academy.

It didn't change the fact that sometimes gut instinct overrode the most specific training.

"She saved someone, Wyatt. And at obvious personal risk to herself. That's pretty amazing."

Even as he complimented her, pride swelling in his

chest, Arlo wasn't fully immune to Wyatt's accusations. Whether it was the cause or just an underlying symptom, his fight with Kerrigan on Saturday likely hadn't helped. But he also wasn't ready to write her off for doing something so heroic.

"Amazing, my ass. She nearly killed herself in the process."

"Look. I'm not disregarding your concerns. But tell me honestly. Would she have gone after him, anyway? Regardless of working a case alongside her dive work?"

Wyatt ran a frustrated hand through his hair. "I don't know."

"Would you?"

"Hell." Wyatt let out a few more curses before dropping into a seat at the small round conference-room table. "That's what's killing me about this. She had her bailout cylinder, and she was right there."

"What do you mean *right there*?"

"The jumper was nearly on top of her boat when he jumped. I'd have gone after him, too. Especially if I thought I could reach him."

"She did reach him."

"Yeah, I know. And she'd have been okay if the guy hadn't accidentally knocked the cylinder out of her hand."

That wash of ice was back—had he ever felt this cold?—as Arlo pictured all that had happened on the dive.

But she was alive. And so was the poor soul who'd believed jumping to his death was a preferable alternative. Now the man could get help. Now he had a chance.

It was minimal solace as he thought about all the

ways this could have gone very wrong, yet at the same time, Arlo couldn't shake that solid burst of pride.

Kerrigan had saved someone.

And she was okay.

Captain Reed's admonishment earlier to apologize still rang in his ears. He was going to do just that.

Kerrigan filled her teakettle with water and considered all the possible outcomes of telling her parents about her dive. There was no question she'd tell them—it was a solid promise she'd made when she'd entered the harbor program—but it was the "how" she was struggling with.

They deserved to know. Just as she'd expect to know about them and their safety, for any reason, in return. But letting them know she'd gone after a potential suicide victim with three minutes of air left in her tank wasn't going to sit well.

Hell, it hadn't sat well with her, either.

But what was she supposed to do? She was the closest to him. And she had a duty to help.

You have a duty to yourself, too.

That lone thought had remained steady each time she considered how to explain what had happened.

She set the kettle on the stovetop but didn't turn on the burner, instead grabbing her phone off the counter to call her parents. She'd nearly pressed the call button when she heard a heavy knock on her door.

"Saved by the bell," she whispered as she laid the phone back down and headed for her front door. A look through the peephole showed Arlo on the other side.

A quick glance down at her ratty old NYPD gym

shorts and torn navy blue sweatshirt had her cringing, but there wasn't anything to be done for it now.

Besides, if he was here, it meant Wyatt had already gotten to him and he knew about the dive.

And she might be mad at him, but after the danger in the water this morning, all that anger seemed inconsequential. It *was* valid—she reassured herself—but it didn't seem quite as important as it initially had.

She pulled open the door and drank her fill of him, standing on the other side. He had on dark slacks and a blue button-down shirt that should have looked staid and somehow just appeared solid stretched across his broad chest.

Reassuring.

And the place she'd like to bury herself for a few hours.

"Arlo."

"Kerrigan."

And then there were no words as her vision came to life in a near-perfect rush. One minute he was standing there and the next he had her in his arms, his cheek pressed to the top of her head while that strong chest cradled her close.

"I heard what happened."

"Arlo, I—" She tried to lift her head, but he simply lifted one hand and pressed it against her neck, keeping her flush against him.

"Please." He let out a hard exhale and she felt the tremors slide through his body. "Please just give me this for one minute."

So she did.

And they stood there like that in her doorway for a lot longer. She knew she should pull away—it wouldn't do to get so much warmth and comfort and physical support from this man—but she couldn't do it.

When his arms finally loosened, he still held on to her but took a small step back. "Can I come in?"

"Sure."

She gestured him into the large room that served as her living and sleeping area and was glad she'd cleaned up that morning before leaving. He moved to the love seat and armchair that dominated the corner of the room and she remained standing where she was.

"Can I, ah, get you anything? I was about to put on some water for tea."

"Don't go to any trouble, but if you're having some, I'll join you."

"Okay."

The kettle was already on the stove, so it was a quick task to turn on the burner. And then she slipped back into the room and took the seat beside the love seat.

"Wyatt told you what happened?"

"He did. He's pretty upset about it."

She laughed at that, but the sound came out harsher and more brittle than she'd intended. "I'm a bit upset about it, too."

"He thinks you've taken on too much."

Although she should have been prepared for that, the words still felt like a blow. One that cut her off at the knees, all while knocking her breath fully from her lungs.

Arlo must have seen it all brewing on her face because he quickly held up a hand.

"I think we do need to talk about the workload, but I told him I didn't agree with his assessment."

"You don't?"

"Not about today. You saved that man, at great personal expense to yourself. But you did the job, and I don't think you should be castigated for that."

The sweetest relief flooded her veins and Kerrigan had the oddest sensation of floating.

Not the feeling she had in the water, but something far lighter and airier than mere buoyancy in the water.

For the first time in a lot longer than she could remember, she felt free.

"You told him that?"

"I did."

"Is it truly how you feel? And why are you suddenly protecting me for this job?"

He shook his head, an odd mix of humor and something deeply serious filling his gaze.

"There you go again. First you were convinced I was hunting for some reason to get rid of you or believed your performance was flawed. Now you think I'm protecting you."

"I'm sorry." She waved a hand. She was aware her reactions were tied to her own concerns that her competency would be questioned.

Not that it actually *was* being questioned.

"Why do I keep getting the feeling that I'm being judged? Or worse, that I'm judging you for whatever came before."

"I—" She stopped, his words making a certain sort of sense.

And then the kettle went off, the loud whistle interrupting them. She realized it was her chance to not only get her thoughts together, but also to stand and take a few deep breaths and tell him the truth.

To stand tall and tell him *her* truth.

"Let me get our tea. Then I have something I need to tell you. About my last precinct. About the man I testified against to Internal Affairs. The one who committed suicide."

Arlo waited for her to make the tea, a mix of dread and relief flooding his veins.

She was okay.

He hadn't realized just how important it was to look at her with his own eyes until she'd opened the door.

But to hold her? To feel the press of her body against his and know that she was alright?

It had meant everything.

How had she come to mean so much to him in such a short time?

Yes, it was attraction—the lure and that deep tug of desire—but it was so much more. He knew he should fight his feelings, but it was hard to argue against something so real.

Kerrigan came back into the room with two steaming mugs and settled them on the end table that cornered the love seat and chair. Her apartment was small but cozy, and he could see her here. Could picture her deep in the oversized chair reading a book or sitting on the love seat as she watched TV.

What caught him off guard was how easily he pictured himself here, too.

Whoa, Prescott. A hug at the door is one thing. Something more permanent…

He let the thought taper off, unwilling to go too far down that rabbit hole.

They were still colleagues and partners. To assume anything more was a fool's game.

"So Wyatt told you all about what happened this morning on my dive?"

"He did. Although I'd like to hear your version."

"It was stupid and against protocol and—"

"*And* incredibly brave and heroic." He stressed those points again. Somewhere in Wyatt's recounting and the obvious self-recrimination she'd spent the past few hours marinating in, the message had gotten lost.

"I hope you don't do it again. Or maybe do it again but not in quite that way. You know. With air in your tank."

"Trust me, that's not an experience I ever want to repeat. It's a diver's worst nightmare and one my parents regularly have. Your arrival just helped me delay the inevitable phone call to tell them about it."

"I can be here for moral support if you'd like."

Exhaustion rimmed the delicate skin around her eyes, but he didn't miss how they softened at his offer. "I appreciate that. But I can tell them later. What I really need to do is tell you about what happened before."

"At your old precinct?"

She nodded, then reached for her mug of tea, wrapping her hands tight around the ceramic.

"I joined my precinct in Queens right out of the academy. I'm from Forest Hills and I wanted to go back to the community. I hadn't made the harbor team yet and while I was already working toward it, I had to put in my time on street patrol, too."

"And you wanted to go back to your neighborhood and be the face of the NYPD to the community."

He remembered those days. When all of your training and ambition were finally let loose and you had to learn the job from the ground up, step by step on the streets of New York.

"I did. And for the first year I was so busy I couldn't see beyond it all. I was working my shifts, and on top of that I was swimming several days a week, pushing myself to meet the requirements of the test. One morning, early, I headed in for a swim at the precinct's gym facility."

"So your Saturday pool visits have a history?"

A vague smile ghosted her lips. "Something like that."

Although he'd intended to lighten the mood a bit, he knew he needed to give her time to tell the story. He picked up his own mug and leveled his full attention on her.

"As I was changing into my suit, I heard this muffled crying from the far side of the lockers. I went to see what was going on and found a woman from my academy class. She'd been beaten pretty bad, and one eye was nearly swollen shut."

"Was she responsive to you?"

"Not at first. She told me she had trouble with an arrest the night before and was still dealing with the adrenaline rush. I would have believed her, but she slipped up on a few details."

"Enough that you realized she wasn't telling the truth. Or not the whole truth."

Kerrigan shook her head. "In the end, there was barely any truth at all. She was partnered with an older cop who'd just lost custody of his kids. He was already on the decline, dealing with the twin demons of gambling and drugs, and he was pretty out of control. He dragged her into a scam he was running on the side for extra money. The thugs he was meeting with didn't like the look of the new young partner and they took quite a few shots at her to gauge his loyalty."

"And he let them?"

She nodded her head, almost in slow motion, her gaze on a time and place only she could see. But it was obvious how it still affected her.

And how determined she'd been to stop such an awful wrong.

Her gaze cleared as she looked his way. "It's such a sad story it's almost cliché."

"They exist for a reason."

"I guess they do."

"How'd you get her to tell you what really happened?"

"She didn't tell me much, but I followed them a few days later. The whole situation didn't sit well with me. Especially because here I was, a recent academy graduate, all bright and shiny and excited about being a cop. And maybe she was, too, or maybe the job ultimately wouldn't have been for her, but no one would ever know because of how she started out."

"Media and entertainment love to make a big deal about cops going bad or rogue. It makes for good storytelling."

"But it's a heartbreaking reality in every way."

He'd been fortunate not to see a whole lot of it in his career, but Arlo had heard the stories. The cops who burned out or who were lured to criminal pursuits for the right payout.

Hell, wasn't that a bit of what they were all still reeling with from the news of Anderson McCoy's betrayal? Marlowe's grandfather had been protecting his son, but it was still a betrayal of the badge to look the other way at a crime so his son could stay safe.

"How'd it end?"

"I saw enough to take it to Internal Affairs. They already had a dossier on him and were keeping notes. His decline was evident to a lot of people, and he'd had a few cases that had some suspicious details to them. Add on the fact they paired a rookie with him and IA was quick to get as many details from me as they could."

"I believe I used the words *brave* and *heroic* before. Clearly, it's a pattern with you, Doyle."

"There's nothing heroic about tattling."

He could acknowledge that it was a bad experience in every way, but to stand up to a bad cop to ensure he couldn't continue his destructive ways was the very opposite of *tattling*.

It was necessary.

"There's everything heroic about it when it means standing up for what's right. This isn't the second-grade playground or a kids' pool party. He had a responsibility to his new partner and he sure as hell had one to the job. He failed on all aspects of that."

"He then deliberately waited until I was on shift one night. He followed me close enough to know where I was patrolling. Even now, I suspect he had someone help him goose my schedule so he could plan it all."

"You were there when he jumped?"

"He made sure of it."

Once again, her gaze had drifted to a memory only she could see. And as he watched her, Arlo understood a bit better why she was so determined to make a good impression on their case. Why she wanted to learn and grow and earn everything on her own merits.

And why she was so afraid of messing something up.

"I'm sorry this was your experience. And I can't change what came before, but I can feel regret that was a side of the job you had to experience. And there's something else I'm truly sorry for that I want to own up to. I kept you out of my review of Big Will and his boys."

"You did it deliberately?"

"At first, yes. When we left Brooklyn Yacht, I wanted to do a bit more nosing around about the family and I didn't want to alarm you. That was wrong. In every way."

"And then you sat on the report."

"Because I knew you'd see it and I wasn't ready to face the inevitable."

Her gaze never wavered as she looked at him across the small expanse between the chair and the love seat. The dark brown depths of her eyes were sharp, reading him as she seemed to weigh her words.

"I don't like it and I'm going to reserve the right to be mad about it later, but not today, Arlo."

"No?"

"No. Today's a day for focusing on the good, and what is good is being your partner and learning from you." She stared into her tea before continuing. "I was holding back from you, too. My last job and how it was coloring my reactions to things. Our relationship has changed since we went to see Big Will, and you've had a chance to see me work. But…"

She shook her head, seeming to shift gears. He was still curious what she was about to say, but as he stared at her, a picture of strength and vulnerability as she sat in that chair, Arlo had to admit the truth.

It didn't matter anymore in the face of almost losing her.

"It's time to move forward, Kerrigan."

"Water under the bridge." She grinned at her own words, the cliché not lost on either of them. "You know me now, and I'm going to move forward and trust that there aren't any more secrets between me and my partner."

Chapter 10

No more secrets.

The idea settled deep in her core, spreading outward. It was a satisfying thought, and with respect to their partnership, Kerrigan had every confidence they were over the hump.

Arlo had willingly addressed the background check he'd done on Big Will and his sons and she'd shared her past. Their partnership was back on solid ground.

But what else was between the two of them?

That was another matter entirely.

She had feelings for him. She'd been hard-pressed to deny them from the first, but the way he'd pulled her into his arms?

It had meant everything.

And that was something she needed to play close to the vest.

Which meant—as always—it was much easier to focus on work.

"Why did you run Big Will and his family?"

"I can't fully say. Something about our visit struck me as worth digging into. But part of why I didn't say anything was I couldn't put my finger on why."

"You can work a hunch without any reason other than it's an angle. I wouldn't have been upset."

"I know that now. But at the time the captain's words were still ringing in my ears about the dark, violent overtones of this case and then seeing you with someone you knew so well." Arlo tapped his fingers on the arm of the love seat. "I let it cloud my judgment. I didn't want to cast aspersions on your friend if I could help it."

"The captain's worried?"

"He's trying not to be, but, yeah, he is. The sheer viciousness of those kills on the boat has him engaged on this case. A bit of that rubbed off in my approach, I'm afraid."

"Because I'm a woman."

"Because you're new and eager and learning, and I overrotated a bit too much on the protection angle." Something distinctly mischievous lit his blue gaze. "I won't do it again."

She was helpless against that hint of mischief. "See that you don't."

"Besides. Not every hunch pays off and I'm glad this one didn't."

Although she had a fondness for Big Will and certainly didn't want to think anything problematic was running through his business, she didn't think Arlo was off base, either.

"Let's play this out. The Gentry family has a lot of

history in the boat business and a lot of access to a variety of stakeholders in that industry."

"You think something's there?"

"I'm saying let's not be too hasty and write it all the way off. Part of why we visited Brooklyn Yacht in the first place was because Big Will knows everyone. He knows the business forward and backward, and it stands to reason he'd have some knowledge of that unregistered boat that went down."

Kerrigan almost laughed at the look of pure, unmitigated relief on Arlo's face.

"You're really into this line of questioning."

"It makes sense. And while I'm not saying Will lied to us, he's running a big business with a lot of tentacles. Wholesalers. Mechanics. Parts. It's equally as likely he knows something as it's happening underneath his radar. But it's worth poking there a bit more."

"I think you're on to something with the associated aspects of the business. The search I ran focused specifically on Will's company, but I never thought about the other people who work with them. Especially other people who make a living with an adjacent business."

"The mechanic and parts aspect is definitely something we should run down. The boat that went down had no serial numbers on anything the evidence team has recovered." Kerrigan paused, thinking about the last report she'd read that detailed every recovered part, with photos. Not a single one had traceable provenance. "Someone who can do that?"

"They're running quite a racket."

"Which means we have a place to start." She was out of her chair before Arlo grabbed her hand, gently holding her in place.

"Tomorrow, Kerrigan. We can look into it tomorrow. You need to rest today."

"I'm good. I can do this."

He shook his head. "Nope. We'll start tomorrow and I promise not to start without you. But you've got a phone call to make and then get some rest."

"I'm fine."

"Then you'll enjoy an afternoon off and to yourself."

He got up so they were standing side by side. Once again, that same delicious sensation of his height advantage over her kicked in and she stared up at him. "Clever."

"Necessary."

His focus on her was absolute, the vivid blue of his eyes drawing her in.

Those eyes that were so mesmerizing.

Enticing.

And once again, she was reminded of the emotional secrets between them. Of what she wanted deep down but knew she couldn't have.

They stood there for more than a few extra heartbeats before Arlo seemed to come to some conclusion. With it, he stepped back and away, putting space between them.

"I'll see you in the morning."

Before she could say anything else, he bent down, pressing his lips to her cheek. He cheated the kiss a little, the edge of his lips pressing to the edge of hers. If it had been anyone else, she'd have said they missed the mark, but she knew full well Arlo Prescott didn't miss anything.

Which was likely why she still felt the brand of his lips—just there, at the edge of hers—long after he'd left.

* * *

Arlo scanned the digital board he'd created on his laptop and considered the information on the case. They'd been focused on how few leads they had and, as he looked at all the details they'd assembled so far, he had to admit perhaps they'd been too focused on the obvious.

Yeah, it would be great to close this quickly. Find the bastard responsible for such a nasty deed and get them off the streets.

But his gut, as well as Kerrigan's and the captain's, recognized something more was going on here.

What was beneath the surface?

It wasn't until he'd written those words on the legal pad beside his computer that he had to stop and laugh.

Clearly, he'd been spending too much time in the company of a diver.

"I'm not so sure what's funny about a murder board, but I'm sure you'll tell me."

Arlo glanced up to see Kerrigan, looking bright and fresh with four boxes of doughnuts piled high in her hands.

"You brought doughnuts?"

"I brought doughnuts *and* a challenge."

When he looked again, he could see the boxes were two different colors. Two from Sunset Bakery and two from Cake Brothers.

"Taste test?"

"Of sorts. I figure we can lure whoever's not heavily focused on something into the conference room I reserved for the taste test, sugar them up and then get their creative juices flowing by looking at the murder board we'll already have projected. There's something in those files we keep overlooking. It's time to bring in some other experienced eyes and ask what they see."

"Great minds."

"You brought doughnuts, too?"

"I didn't think that far ahead. But I was thinking we needed to look at everything all together again and see what we've got."

Kerrigan tapped the edge of his computer screen. "Something's in there. We just need to find it."

Twenty minutes later, ideas were flying as fast as the doughnuts. The four boxes Kerrigan had brought in had been rapidly emptied, leaving nothing but a conference room full of coffee and doughnut-fueled souls anxious to take down a killer.

"The gunshots bother me." Andrea Wainwright, a twenty-year detective sitting near the screen, spoke up as she studied the evidence Arlo and Kerrigan had laid out.

"Bother you how?" Kerrigan was sitting next to the woman and turned to face her.

"I agree with the assessment of the order of the shootings. They were a surprise and the first victim had no idea, while the second victim at least moved in some attempt at defending himself."

"The ME's office concurs on that as well," Arlo added.

"What I don't get is the killings at all. They were henchmen, so why take them down? The evidence suggests they were there to support and that is further proven by the fact they were dousing the boat with gasoline to make the escape. If there was going to be this big effort to make them take the fall, find another way to kill them. One that isn't so obviously murder."

Andrea's observations got a lot of chatter going and one of their newly minted detectives, Devante Johnson, spoke up. "There's something to that. I'm not saying the ME's office wouldn't have found it if they were poisoned, but the vics also spent time under the water and were already in decomp. But gunshots to the head? That's a bad, bad end they couldn't have done themselves. It's, I don't know—"

"It's vindictive," Andrea said, with a firm nod of her head. "You failed me and I'm taking you down. Which shows anger and impulse and a lack of self-control."

"Torching a boat that had to cost a fortune reinforces that, too," Kerrigan added, tapping the side of her coffee cup. "That boat's not cheap on the regular market. But to get it unmarked like that? Someone paid premium dollars to just set it on fire and sink it."

Arlo took in all the good feedback, pleased they'd pulled in the broader team. The ideas were good, but even more, coming together was a sign of their camaraderie and work as a unit at the 86th.

With Kerrigan's story from the day before it was even more important to him that she see what a good unit looked like. Dwayne Reed's leadership was important, and the training of his people was an obvious reflection of him. But their hard work and devotion to the work and to each other was on them, too.

And the 86th was someplace special.

With that pride at the forefront of his mind, he tossed out one more theory. "We have another angle we've been playing.

"With the takedown of the Papa, room's opened up for a new kingpin. What if this was either a loyalty test or a way to set the tone from the beginning? It's cruel and impulsive, but there could be more calculation there than we're giving credit to."

"Hell of a way to assert power," Dwayne said from where he was standing in the doorway.

Arlo welcomed in their captain, and everyone sat up a bit straighter as he moved into the room.

Dwayne's dark brown face creased into a broad smile. "I heard a rumor there were doughnuts in here."

"It was a taste test, sir," Kerrigan said. "Between Cake Brothers and Sunset Bakery. We figured it would be a bit easier to talk gruesome murder on a full stomach."

"A wise choice, Officer Doyle." Dwayne snagged the last cruller from Cake Brothers left in the box. "And on a personal note, I'm not picky on where my doughnut comes from, just that the sugar and dough ratio is correct." He took a large bite to punctuate his point, nodding his head as he swallowed. "And this one fits the bill."

"Would you like us to take you through what we've been working on, Cap?" Arlo asked.

Dwayne nodded, reaching for a napkin. "I heard the ideas about the Papa as I walked in. Take me through the others."

Since Dwayne's warm manner and open mind immediately put his team at ease, everyone was more than willing to share their theories. Their captain listened and nodded, giving everyone the runway to puzzle through the problem.

He waited until everyone had shared before offering his own theory. "I think there's something with the boat and the new-management-in-town angle you're playing with. Find the boat and you get a sense of who that might be. Alternatively, get a lead on the new king of the hill and you get some clues on what lines to tug about the boat. Who provided it and what they might be running."

"The boat has a lot of possibilities. Sellers, mechanics, even someone who gives out bank loans could know contacts," Kerrigan said, ticking off a list. "There are a lot of associated businesses wrapped up in the boat business."

"That's good, Doyle. And all those facets?" Dwayne added. "Somebody somewhere's going to talk."

Arlo considered the board one more time, recognizing Dwayne's words as truth. What thread could they pull that would finally give them that one person who gossiped about what went down in the harbor?

"We just need to find them."

"That you do, Detective. Based on what I've seen and heard this morning," Dwayne said, "I think you're close."

"The captain really supports us." Kerrigan followed Arlo out of the precinct as they headed for his car. "His leadership drives the whole team."

"Dwayne's special. He's one of the best cops I've ever known and one of the best men as well. He believes in the work, and he believes in the people who do it."

"Yet one more reason I'm glad I'm at the 86th."

One of many reasons.

Kerrigan pulled up the locations of the businesses she and Arlo had discussed after the meeting broke up. She was anxious to look into the mechanic angle. The boat itself could have been scrubbed clean in a chop shop that was anywhere along the eastern seaboard, but the owner would need someone local for maintenance.

The longstanding joke that the two best days of a boat owner's life were the day they bought their boat and the day they sold it rang with a specific sort of truth. Boat ownership required a willingness to do maintenance, either on your own or because you paid someone.

That would be even more important for a boat that had to be in fighting shape, able to move quickly at a moment's notice.

"Let's go to Waverly's first." Kerrigan read off the address in Brooklyn Heights.

"Why pick them first?"

"I met Buck Waverly a few times—he supports our mechanics on the NYPD boats. He's a good guy and I think he can give us a sense of the market and what we might be looking for."

"You think whoever owned the boat was working with a mechanic?"

"They had to have someone. I guess you could keep someone directly on the payroll who only works for you, but it's probably easier to just give the work to someone with a business front who's willing to take a cut of the action."

"And you're not worried Buck could be that person?"

"I hope not. And feel free to call me naive, but I also think a mechanic supporting chop-shopped boats wouldn't also try to work contracts for the NYPD." She shrugged. "But people are an endless surprise."

"That they are."

Sunlight glinted on his hair, the blond strands glowing gold. He slipped a pair of sunglasses out of his pocket and Kerrigan had the briefest thought that he looked like an honest-to-God movie star. She was almost tempted to look around, expecting to see a film camera capturing the shot.

"What's that look for?"

Arlo caught her staring and Kerrigan nearly shrugged it off, that lingering need to hide her feelings for him rising. But then she thought better of it.

They were partners and instead of dancing around every personal thing, maybe it would be easier to give in to some of it, make it feel less all-consuming.

"You pulled out those sunglasses and all I could think was how much you looked like someone who just stepped off a Hollywood soundstage. The quintessential cop, moving out on a big case."

"All flash, no substance?"

"Hardly." She considered, once again, the spirit of partnership she felt in that conference room this morning and knew that he was so much more to him than flash. "It was just an impression as you slipped on those shades."

"I'm not complaining." His grin was irresistibly sweet, and her heart did a hard double thump in her chest.

And again, she had to admit how compelling he was. Yes, he was handsome, in a way that was overwhelmingly the first thing you noticed when you looked at him. But with time, what came through even more clearly—and with even greater impact—was what a good man he was.

It was something so innate and he showed it, over and over.

The way he spoke with his colleagues. The way he'd mentored her and willingly listened to her ideas. And today, the way he'd led the meeting yet was able to support a wide variety of ideas and opinions.

It mattered.

And it was an example…

"Arlo."

She came to a hard stop about ten feet from the car.

"What is it?" he asked as recognition dawned in his eyes. "Light bulb?"

"I think so. This angle about the killings on the boat. Whoever did this took out two obviously trusted henchmen."

He nodded, waving a hand in a come-on gesture. "You've got something. Keep on."

"It's like I said about this morning. There's real support and camaraderie at the 86th. And here's a situation, moving those drugs on the boat, where you have, by nature, a small circle of trusted individuals. It might be criminal pursuits, but there should be a fair amount of camaraderie in that circle, too. Like us, they're dependent on each other.

"Plus," she added as the idea whirled faster and faster in her mind, "if they were high enough in the organization to be on the boat, they were likely part of the inner circle."

When he only waited, she continued. "Why kill people who'd obviously moved up the ranks? That sends a message, not necessarily a good one, that you can be removed, even if you're loyal."

"And what else do these organizations have besides loyalty?"

"Exactly. So maybe it *was* a test. Someone's trying to replace the Papa and they're marking their territory as they go."

"I'm following, but what if it was another hench-man? Someone at the same level or maybe a lieutenant in the organization?"

"To what outcome? If you kill the others on the boat and still let it and all the drugs sink, you've got noth-ing. And you took out a few operatives when it wasn't your purview to do so."

"Good." His smile grew. "This is good."

"Whoever it is, they're trying to break those bonds. Whether it's a tactic to break down what the Papa had before or a way of testing loyalties, there's so much here that's about breaking down to the bone. Culling people and making them feel alone, forcing them to act aggressively to keep their place or, even more, to stay alive."

Arlo gestured them to the car. "This makes a violent, sort of vicious, sense. But it's an angle and it works. And it explains why we're not hearing any gossip. No chatter or anyone running their mouths. They're all afraid and no one knows who to trust."

"It's standard manipulative behavior. I saw it with that cop at my old precinct. In a matter of weeks, he'd taken that rookie and methodically separated her from the team. He cut her off and made her feel alone. And once you achieve that, you leave people thinking they have nowhere to go and no one to turn to."

As upsetting as her experience had been at her for-mer precinct, it was fascinating, Kerrigan realized, to see how practically she could use that knowledge.

Especially because the theory fit. Almost too well.

Isolation did terrible things to people and in a world where the stakes were already high, it would be an es-pecially torturous tactic.

Yet a highly effective one.

Arlo pulled out of the precinct lot after she'd set Buck Waverly's address in the GPS. She was still musing on the possibilities of the case when she noticed Arlo's demeanor.

"What is it?"

"Behind us. I think we've got a tail."

"You think?"

Arlo pulled hard on the wheel, quickly turning off the main thoroughfare through Sunset Bay. When he let out a long, low curse, Kerrigan recognized the truth.

"We do have a tail."

"Yep." He gritted his teeth as he navigated the lighter, late-morning traffic, instructing her to call it in. "Let's get some marked patrol cars to bring up the rear. We'll see what they're made of and how serious they are."

She called in the ask of all available patrols and responses rapidly came in, affirming positions and engagement of the vehicle.

"Officers Kohler and Peachtree responding," a voice said through the dash radio system. "In pursuit, but keeping our distance. Officer Peachtree is running the plates."

A second car responded, giving similar coordinates, and Kerrigan waited for further direction from Arlo.

"He's not bugging out," Arlo muttered as he kept watch on the rearview mirror.

"Can you see who's in the car?"

"No, visor's low and there's something else on the dash limiting visibility. All the other windows are tinted."

Arlo continued through the neighborhood, moving them deftly toward the warehouse district on the edge of town. Although the neighborhood had been slowly reviving a few of the places as clubs or entertainment areas, most were still used for the needed warehousing of goods for retail.

"What's the endgame here, Arlo?"

He shook his head as they moved along, block after block. "No idea, but it feels like a taunt of some sort."

"More tests?"

"Of the cops? Or the rank and file pursuing the criminal arts?"

As jokes went it was a poor one, yet it had an odd sort of truth, too.

Especially if half of Brooklyn's criminals were currently trying out for a new puppet master. Kerrigan swirled that around in her mind, her eyes going wide just as she caught sight of a shooter perched on the roof of a warehouse on the next corner.

Arlo had already pulled through the intersection and all she could do was scream.

"Shooter with a gun!"

Chapter 11

Arlo slammed on the gas, rushing past the warehouse as fast as he could, helpless to do anything in the moment but hope they escaped any gunfire. He'd already mentally braced for the sound of shattering glass, when nothing appeared at all.

But then he heard a barrage of shooting a few moments later.

"Kerrigan! Down!"

He fought to understand where the noise was coming from, even as his senses processed there was no damage to the car, no shattering glass and no blown-out tires.

They were still moving forward.

But one glance in the rearview mirror and he could see all hell had broken lose.

Kerrigan was bent low, as he'd instructed, but remained on the car radio, communicating with the other patrol cars behind them. It was their collective shouts coming back through the radio that brought everything into clarity.

"Shooter on the roof! Shots fired into the car we're pursuing."

"In pursuit of car now out of control. Driver appears shot as car is veering wildly."

Arlo did a quick check of traffic and did a U-turn back in the direction of his colleagues and the out-of-control car.

"What in the ever-loving hell is going on?"

"They were shot, Arlo." Kerrigan remained calm. Level. Yet he heard the quaver under her words. "The car following us was shot."

"Why? What the hell is going on here? Why were they following cops only to get shot sniper-style? And how were they the target?"

The questions were rhetorical because he was already piecing together an answer. One that had a surprising amount in common with Kerrigan's theories in the precinct parking lot.

Not only was someone pulling the strings, but they'd also created a scenario where no one knew if they were safe.

Which only added a deeper dimension of darkness to this case.

She wasted no time, calling for emergency services even as shouts of "Officers in pursuit" echoed from the car radio as the second squad car to join them had already taken off after the shooter.

"We need to get to that car."

Just as their fellow officers had relayed, after the gunshots, the car that had been following them ran straight into a business storefront. Smoke streamed from the front of the hood as Arlo came to a hard stop beside the other squad car. The two officers who'd stayed on scene were already approaching the smoking vehicle slowly, weapons drawn.

Arlo and Kerrigan jumped out as soon as he put the car in Park, their weapons at the ready. They started in on their approach when Arlo realized the risks.

"We need protection behind, too. Someone has to keep watch for the shooter while we investigate the damage here."

"On it, Detective." Officer Peachtree was already moving into position at the back of the car, sweeping the perimeter.

Arlo was torn between following the other team headed after the shooter and dealing with the victims. But even at risk of losing the shooter, this was their most immediate need.

"Arlo." Kerrigan's tone was urgent. "This is bad."

"Yeah, it's bad." He took in the two men in the car, blood spreading across their chests and smeared on what was left of the windows.

Peachtree's partner raced back to the squad car for a field kit and returned with a box of rubber gloves.

"Officer Doyle's already called for emergency services, but we need to check for signs of life."

Arlo and Kerrigan slipped on gloves while the other officers kept watch on the car and checked for an external shooter, then they quickly changed places as the other two officers slipped on gloves.

By unspoken agreement, Kohler took the driver side while Arlo and Kerrigan took the passenger. Kohler reported back almost immediately that the driver was dead. And it was Kerrigan who leaped toward the passenger-side door when they heard a dark groan through the window.

"He's alive!"

She was already working on the door, pulling hard on it around the damage it had sustained from the crash. Arlo kept his sights on the victim, covering her from behind.

The door came open with one final creak of metal and Kerrigan moved up beside the man.

Peachtree came around the back of the car. "Officers in pursuit radioed back the warehouse is clear."

Even as he asked it, Arlo knew what the answer would be. "Any luck on the shooter?"

"Nope. None. But I'll back you up here. You help Officer Doyle."

Arlo stepped up beside her to help, the two of them working to disengage the man from his seat belt, then pulling him from the car. Although the EMTs would likely have handled it differently, using a board to brace the guy, he and Kerrigan didn't have the time. They needed to assess his injuries as quickly as they could.

And as they got him flat, Arlo recognized one more stark truth. This guy wasn't going to make it long enough for the EMTs to get there.

As pain-filled gray eyes stared up at him and Kerrigan, it was obvious the guy knew it, too.

"Fight for power," the guy hissed out before reaching up to grab Kerrigan's hand. She held tight to it, her innate compassion evident as she crouched beside the man.

"What's a fight for power?" Her voice was gentle as she tried to coax something more from him.

"The streets... Brook... Brooklyn... The drugs."

"Who?"

"Hidden." The man licked his lips, his breathing labored. "Rumors. New empire." He gasped, hard, before his head lolled to the side. "The street's saying she—"

The man took one last hard breath and then there was nothing.

Kerrigan settled the man's hand back by his side and sat back on her haunches. "She?"

Arlo was still processing it all, but the vic's words went a long way toward reinforcing their developing theory that everything was tied to the new turf war in Brooklyn.

But *she*?

They'd run it as soon as they got back to the precinct, but he couldn't immediately summon up any high-level women in any of the local crime organizations. That didn't mean they were absent, he acknowledged.

But it was still a development he hadn't expected.

"Arlo. The gunshots."

His gaze traveled over the man's chest before Kerrigan interrupted him. "On the boat. The gunshots. We theorized they were done by someone a lot shorter. A woman would likely be shorter."

"Of course." He nodded, her assessment spot-on. "That fits."

The screaming cry of the ambulance filled the air as it got closer. Two more patrol cars had already arrived to manage the scene, as well as the small crowd that had formed on the block.

The fact they were in a less-populated area worked in their favor, but the noise of gunshots and the crash had pulled people who were close by out of various businesses and into the street in curiosity.

He and Kerrigan made room for the EMTs and then moved to stand with Officers Kohler and Peachtree. It was Kohler who spoke first.

"They didn't get the shooter. There were shell casings on the roof of the warehouse they've taken into evidence, but the shooter's long gone."

Arlo knew it had been a longshot, too much time elapsing from the gunshots to the pursuit, but he was still frustrated. Even as the dying victim's words filled his mind once more.

Fight for power.

New empire.

The street's saying she—

Captain Reed had pegged it from the first. That they were dealing with something dark and vicious.

And it was escalating.

Wendy Parker reviewed the footage of the rooftop shooter and assessed his technique as she wondered if she had time for a quick manicure. They'd opened a new place on Sixth she wanted to try, and her tips desperately needed a touch-up.

Thoughts of her nails vanished as she watched the shooter run from the roof and she let out a harsh, quick curse.

"Don't tell me you were that big an idiot," she muttered even as she rewound the video.

The camera she'd placed on the warehouse rooftop opposite had caught everything clearly and she fixated once more on the casings dropping from the bottom of his gun.

Casings he never picked up before he ran.

Incompetent ass.

Did anyone know how to do their job?

That had been the biggest frustration she'd had since starting this project. The ability to think quickly, on their feet and with strategic focus, was sorely absent from the thugs she was stuck working with.

Crime, like any other matter in life, was a business.

Her mother had taught her that young and she'd used it as a mantra. Loyalty was an illusion and power without control was meaningless.

It was why she was so determined to do this right. The Papa had his day, but he'd been weak.

He'd gotten caught, hadn't he?

And all because his lower-level drones had big mouths and his higher-level lieutenants didn't know how to keep them in line.

It was how she'd been able to make her move in the first place. She was the one who'd drip-fed the clues to the cops about the Papa's organization. Her mother had been one of Queens' wealthiest madams for a long time and there were few secrets she wasn't privy to. Wendy had used that cache of information to put the pieces together.

And then she'd triangulated all the weak spots in the Papa's organization.

It had been a simple matter of strategy, and once all the elements were in place, she'd made her move.

Incompetent criminals aside, today's exercise was a risk. It was one she'd put into motion when she'd realized Kerrigan Doyle was assigned to the boat case.

For all her attempts to build the right connections and loyalties, layered over a base of fear, she hadn't spent much time trying to ingratiate herself with the cops. Her mother had always had a few on the take who were willing to look the other way with respect to her business, but Wendy needed bigger allies.

Could Kerrigan be one?

They were a few years apart in school and she'd always gotten a sense of the kid as well-liked but not part of the in crowd. Kerrigan had managed to stay off the radar of high-school politics, which was a feat in and of itself.

It also suggested a high likelihood that she'd be a problem.

There was no way of knowing, so it was time to play the angles. They'd gotten reacquainted again, so she had a good excuse to reach out. She'd make up some crap about news traveling fast in the old neighborhood and ask how was Kerrigan doing. Was she surviving such a difficult time on the force?

Wendy pictured the cop she'd met along with Kerrigan in the bar Friday night. *The hot cop*, she amended to herself. Hot or not, *that* one was a straight arrow. He'd led the big bust at McNulty's, and he had a reputation for getting the job done.

Various approaches flashed through her mind as she closed the video from the rooftop. She'd already killed the uplink connection so no one could trace the camera back to her.

It was necessary, but her expenses had been mounting and her mother was getting a bit pissed about continuing to front her. The drugs dropped in the Hudson hadn't helped. That supply was going to fund her enterprise for a few more months until she pulled in a really big score, but there was nothing to be done for it now.

Jordan and Dallas had been good partners, setting up the pickup down in Baltimore and working with her to bring it all up the coast. Dallas had made the connection with the Gentry boys, too. But he was itching for a promotion and thought her approach to the takeover of the Papa's territory unnecessary.

And then the arrival of the Coast Guard was serious bad luck. Dallas had argued with her as the Coast Guard was closing in that they needed to open the throttle and make a run for it on the boat.

Men.

She admired limitless thinking as much as the next person but hauling ass through a near hurricane wasn't the answer. Thinking a bigger gun or a faster car would do the trick wasn't the answer.

Brains.

Strategy.

Focus and vision.

Those were the pathways to the top.

So, yeah, she missed Dallas, and she missed sleeping with him even more, but it was a split-second decision on the boat and she'd made it.

This was *her* job. She wanted complete loyalty and if someone couldn't give it to her then they were of no use to her.

Focus and vision.

They were her stock in trade.

Kerrigan took a sip of coffee as she entered notes on the digital murder book they were keeping on the boat case. She closed her eyes and tried to remember all the things the victim had said as he lay dying in front of her.

The power struggle she and Arlo had theorized was spot-on. So was the fear factor that seemed to have spread through Brooklyn's criminal class.

And then that part at the end.

The street's saying she—

She.

A woman was behind this brutality?

As a woman who performed in a challenging profession, she'd never gone in for the gender distinctions often thrown around. People chose who they wanted to be and the life they wanted to live.

But in this case, it was worth considering.

The boat victims had been shot at close range, from behind. It was brutal, yet as they'd surmised in the assessment in the conference room this morning, there was an impulsiveness to it, too.

And then the shootings today.

Another hardcore, brutal act, to set up your own people for a job and then take them out.

It wasn't the first time she'd seen someone die on the job, but today was one of the most unexpected. The moment she'd seen that shooter on the roof, she'd fully expected the guy was aiming for her and Arlo.

A series of horrifying thoughts had raced through her mind, including not getting to say goodbye to her family and how sad it would be to never know who was behind the boat murders.

But there had been that other, lone thought that had threaded through all those deeply important ones, and it had felt extra weighted somehow.

Was it because she and Arlo were together, both their lives at risk?

Or because it was simply the way she felt?

But pounding in time with the thud of her pulse had been the insistent reality that she'd never get to kiss Arlo again.

Their kiss in the bar had been designed to manage the moment and the need to get a bead on the guy at the door. It had morphed quickly into something more, but it was still the sheer work of a moment.

But what would it be like to kiss Arlo because she wanted to? Or to be on the receiving end of a kiss simply because *he* wanted to?

It was heady, yet it left her feeling oddly bereft, too.

Regardless of how she felt about him—and his visit to her home yesterday had reinforced that he wasn't immune to the attraction that sparked between them—Kerrigan knew there was nowhere for it all to go.

They were working together.

When this case wrapped, she'd go back to her focus on the harbor team.

So why did she keep coming back to how much she wanted to try for something with him, anyway?

A light knock on the conference-room door pulled her from her errant thoughts and she looked up to find the subject of her musings and their captain. She immediately stood, placing her hands behind her back. "Captain."

"No need to stand, Officer. Arlo was just filling me in on today's events and I wanted to get your take on things as well." Captain Reed took a seat as Kerrigan projected the digital board onto a screen.

"I've added the events of today. The car that followed Detective Prescott and myself. The as-yet-captured shooter on the roof and the details we have so far on the victims."

"Anything strike you as you wrote it up?"

"The shooting overall. What was the enticement to

follow cops? And then to be shot at like that. I'd say turf war, but it doesn't feel like it's escalating like that."

"Like what?" Captain Reed asked.

"There's no sense of a gang war going on. This feels far more calculated. It has me circling back to the working theory Arlo and I have about someone replacing the Papa. And it's further reinforced by our victim's dying words."

"Which was a lucky break for us." Arlo pushed himself off the doorjamb and walked into the room. "I'm trying not to be a cynic and think we're too lucky. Or that we're not being deliberately pushed in a new direction by a dying man's words."

It wasn't an approach she'd thought about yet, but it was one worth considering. "You think him telling us those things was a setup?"

"I'm not ready to say that, either. Especially since the guy *was* dying. But what I keep coming back to, with whomever is behind this, is why take out your team? What's the possible endgame?"

"There's an endless supply of criminals waiting to step up and take their place," Dwayne pointed out.

"Maybe yes, maybe no. There's still time, training, dependability and some degree of trust built over time. That doesn't happen overnight."

"There's also the woman angle." Kerrigan returned to where she'd been before Arlo and Dwayne walked in. "There's an innate desire to push back on that and believe it's not possible. That a woman wouldn't commit such dark acts of malice. And yet—"

"And yet, it fits." Arlo moved closer to the screen, pointing to a few of the notes she'd added to the file.

"The angle of the gunshots on the boat victims provides a strong reinforcement to a dying man's reference of a woman trying to take the reins."

Kerrigan tapped lightly on the table as a new dimension opened in her evaluation. "If it is a woman as well, working in a man's world, she's likely sweetening the conversation and playing these men up."

The captain's attention was caught with that one. "Give me a sense of what you mean with that?"

How did she articulate it?

Yet, with the captain's kind gaze on her, she realized she had to try.

"While there are certainly women who commit crimes, if we move forward with the theory this is a woman looking to ascend to the top, she's battling a glass ceiling. I know it was coined for boardrooms, but the principles are the same. You're pushing to take over the leadership of a large number of people, most of whom are male."

"And there are men who don't want to work for a woman."

Kerrigan shrugged at Captain Reed's statement. "It's a sad fact. And I don't say it to paint every man with that brush."

Arlo held up a hand. "We're playing a theory and you're the woman in the room who has experience. Keep going."

"Take feminine wiles, for instance. It's an outward play. Fawning and flirting and smiling and laughing. It's sending cues beneath that fawning and flirting."

"Like what sort of cues?"

"Like 'I hear you.' 'You're important.' 'Tell me more.'

It's a way to captivate but it's got a layer of manipulation in it, too."

"And it would be a powerful way to motivate a group that's predominantly men," Dwayne said.

"Even more, though, it's second nature to all of us. Sort of how babies smile to get attention or dogs put on big eyes to get treats. These nonverbal patterns we fall into aren't always manipulation in a cold-blooded way."

Arlo picked up the thread. Easily. "But if you honed it and perfected it and found a way to use it—"

"No, to *wield* it," Kerrigan argued.

"There you go. To wield it. It could be a deeply powerful approach."

"Of course, it still doesn't explain why a woman would go to all that trouble to build herself up in the organization only to kill the men she was using to gain support."

"Loyalty test?" Arlo asked.

"Possibly. And I might have agreed up until today. But why send that pair out to tail us in an obvious way and then kill them?"

Dwayne looked at them both as they came to a halt in their theories, today's events still stumping them all.

"You need to get out there. Something's going on under the surface and you need to put yourself in a place to find out what's going on. Ask questions. Talk about how shocking it is that this happened at all."

Kerrigan thought about the thug at McNulty's who'd bothered her on such a visceral level. She had no idea why, but something in his attention had seemed too sharp. Too focused.

Too specific.

"Should we head back to McNulty's?"

"It's where my last case centered. It's as good a place to start as any."

Captain Reed stood at that. "The overtime's approved. Get out there and see what you can find."

Chapter 12

Arlo pulled up in front of Kerrigan's building at exactly eight o'clock. They'd batted a few ideas back and forth as to how they wanted to approach the evening, including inviting Wyatt and Marlowe out with them, but ended up deciding it was better to go alone. They were playing the affectionate couple tonight and he already knew they risked discovery as cops.

Bringing yet another cop into the mix might tip off someone and shut down any opportunity they'd have to get answers.

And if going it alone meant he needed to ignore the strange knot that had settled beneath his breastbone, then so be it.

Yeah, he was attracted to her. But he'd been attracted to other women in the past, none of whom managed to stay a part of his life for any length of time.

He wasn't cut out for relationships.

It would be easy to blame his family but, in the end, he'd realized that *he* was a part of that family, too. He did well with surface relationships, his DNA ensuring he was a congenial and fun date. The where-are-you-from? and what-do-you-do-for-a-living? stage of dating was where he shined.

Only the deeper it went, the more uncomfortable he got, as he ultimately checked out before things got too serious.

Whatever reasons he gave himself up to now about Kerrigan and the case—he was functioning as her mentor, they needed to keep their focus, even the fact that he didn't want to do anything to make others question her reputation—were all excuses.

What he really didn't want was to ruin the genuine relationship and camaraderie they had with his inevitable departure if he pursued something romantic with her.

Even if he hadn't gotten that kiss in the bar out of his mind for more than a few hours at a stretch.

Or the way she'd felt in his arms after her bad dive.

Or the desperate need he had to protect her earlier today as they realized there was a shooter potentially aiming for them.

None of it could matter.

Even as a very large part of him wished that it did.

He was just about to turn off the car when there was a knock on the passenger window. Hitting the button for the locks, he smiled as Kerrigan got into the car.

"I could have come up to get you."

She waved a hand, a couple of gold bangles sparkling and clanking at her wrist. "No need. This isn't a real date."

Although the comment had a breezy quality to it, so

much so that she probably thought nothing of it, something about it needled him.

This isn't a real date.

No, it wasn't. Hadn't he just been giving himself all the reasons why it wasn't?

So why had her words crawled under his skin?

"You still want to go to McNulty's first?" Kerrigan asked.

"I think it's a good place to start."

"Good. That will give me a chance to see if that guy's in there again. See if we might be able to figure out who he is, or if we can get him to react a little."

"Are we back to that?"

"Back to what?"

Even with the subtle hints of confusion, her light, easy tone was really poking at him. She was already in cop mode—undercover-cop mode—and he...*wasn't.*

She looked good.

She smelled good.

Here she was casually talking about wanting to draw thugs seemingly out of the ether.

And his brain had short-circuited the moment he took in the long length of her legs, where they stretched out in tanned glory from beneath her skirt.

What was she thinking?

What was *he* thinking?

"Arlo? Is something wrong?"

"No."

"Why don't you reel it back and try again?"

He glanced over as he put the car into Drive and put it right back into Park to turn and face her.

"I thought we'd settled the matter of the thug in McNulty's. No approaching him or trying to draw him out."

Makeup artfully highlighted the contours of her face, from the delicate bones around her eyes—a rich chocolate tonight beneath mocha-colored eyelids—to the sweeping arch of high cheekbones.

None of it could hide the brewing storm or the way that gorgeous mouth dropped down into a frown.

"Funny, that's not how I remembered it."

"We talked about the risks."

"It's all a risk. The only reason we're going out tonight is to figure out what is going on and why every criminal in Brooklyn is running scared. And there's something about that guy. The way that he looked at me the other night wasn't right. There was a sharpness and a sort of knowledge to it I can't shake, and I know in my gut something is off."

"Sharp how?"

"Sharp like he was focused on me."

"You're a beautiful woman. He was probably thinking of any number of nefarious things to do with you."

This isn't a real date.

"Arlo. What is going on here? I'm a cop. I need to do my job. Figuring out who that guy is and why he was so focused on me is something we need to try and determine."

"You *are* doing the job." He stretched a hand out between them. "Undercover clothes and all."

She looked momentarily stymied by his reference to her outfit but regrouped quickly.

"No, I need to do the job the captain approved overtime for. Scouting the bars and nightclubs in Brooklyn to figure out what is seething under the surface. People know things and we need to find someone willing to talk to us. That person knows something. I feel it."

"Which further reinforces my point. If that guy means you harm, baiting him and having him make you as a cop the moment you pull your gun doesn't make sense." He focused on the small bag in her lap. "You do have your gun?"

"Yes, I do. I have a rather wicked blade strapped to my thigh, too. I'm prepared. And I can handle myself.

"But I'm starting to question if *you* can. What is going on with you tonight? And if you need time to get your head in the game, we'll go tomorrow night instead. We had a big day today."

This isn't a real date.

"I don't need time." The words came out through gritted teeth, harsh enough to have her eyes widening as she stared at him across the small expanse of the front seat.

"Then what do you need?"

"*You*, damn it." He reached out even as everything inside was screaming at him to stop.

To not just ignore this path but to actively avoid it.

But for reasons he couldn't figure out, he'd lost the ability to focus.

To reason.

To say no.

Her eyes widened a bit more as his mouth closed the distance to hers, his arms going around her shoulders as he pulled her close.

And then he feasted.

Kerrigan had feared earlier that she'd never kiss Arlo again. That there'd never be another moment between them to know those lips, to explore that mouth.

Oh, how gloriously shortsighted she'd been.

That thought filled her mind, over and over, as Arlo's lips plundered hers.

She *should* stop him. Not because she wanted him to stop, but because she wanted him to continue far too much.

Yet each time she thought she had gathered enough willpower to break the kiss, he tilted his head just so, or artfully stroked his tongue against hers, or moved his thumb in a glorious stroking motion across her collarbone.

She might've told him this wasn't a date, but she had dressed like she was going on one.

Partly because it was a necessity, the two of them playing a couple this evening. And partly because she'd wanted to.

He'd told her she was beautiful.

A sigh slipped from the back of her throat as he nibbled lightly on her bottom lip, like an escape valve for the heat that continued to ratchet up between them, degree by exciting degree.

And then it all came to an abrupt end as Arlo pulled back.

The enticing blue of his gaze had gone dark, his pupils wide in the darkened interior of the car.

"I'm sorry."

She struggled to regroup at the quick change of pace. And while her words might have held a breathy tone she couldn't fully erase, she felt quite confident her meaning was clear.

"If you're apologizing for kissing me, please stop right now. If you're apologizing for underestimating my ability to take care if I have a potential problem in the bar, lean right on into that."

"Why do I have to apologize for worrying about you?"

"Why do you *have* to worry about me doing my job?"

And why did they continue to circle around the same argument? She understood why her family carried concern for her safety and well-being. Civilians didn't understand the job and, often, all they could see were those risks to their loved ones.

But a partner?

They understood those risks because they took them, too.

Which meant he had no right to question her decision. Nor did he have any right to try and alter their op out of some misguided sense of protection for a well-trained, damn fine cop.

"I can see the fight brewing. It's in your eyes loud and clear."

"Damn straight, it's in my eyes. I'm an NYPD officer. I work in one of the finest, if not *the* finest, police departments in all the world. I'm a good cop and I know how to do my job. And you questioning that undermines me in every way. It isn't just a waste of time, it's destructive. Are you trying to shake my confidence in my work?"

It felt like repetitive territory and whatever Kerrigan had expected for this night, this wasn't it. So why were they here?

Again?

"You took me on for this job. You worked with my captain and my shift lead to bring me on the case. You've encouraged me. You keep telling me I can do this, and I should be focused on growing and learning and—"

"I want you."

The head of steam she had going tapered off at his interruption.

"You what?"

"I want you. Against my better judgment. Against my own horrible history with dating. Against every feckless, unreliable trait likely passed to me by my family when it comes to interpersonal relationships."

His words were weighted in the darkened interior of the car, heavy with promise and potential and a layer of sadness she'd never expected.

When he'd told her about his family, she'd innately understood his experiences hadn't been the same, idyllic childhood as her own.

What she hadn't understood was how those experiences influenced what he believed about himself.

"You aren't your family, Arlo."

"Of course I am. Just like you are your family. They're the people who made us. Who influence us. To suggest we can turn those aspects on or off is silly."

He'd already started driving, heading off her street in the direction of McNulty's. Kerrigan wanted to argue, but she also recognized the no-trespassing signals.

And maybe they were warranted.

Hadn't she also questioned the viability of a relationship? Perhaps for different reasons, but the fact was they both kept turning away, despite the interest and attraction between them.

If she added on that incendiary kiss, the answer became even more clear.

Desire arced between the two of them on a damn-near visceral level.

Was it possible all that heat and need was causing her to lose perspective?

She could still feel the way her heart had slammed in her chest. Could easily conjure the memory of the touch of his fingers against the exposed skin of her collarbone. And even now, she could still sense the hard press of his lips like a brand against hers.

There *was* something between them. It was a point she came back to, over and over. But there was also a shocking amount keeping them apart.

She wanted to lean into the first but would be doing herself a disservice to dismiss the latter one.

Relationships—even the really good ones—took a tremendous amount of work. One like theirs, that was fraught with so much baggage before it even got off the ground?

Well, it would be damn near impossible to make work.

She might not have a lot of experience with her own romantic entanglements, but she understood the basics of relationships. And she also understood that the feelings she'd developed for Arlo Prescott had a depth to them she'd never felt before.

Was she really willing to put her whole self into something that had *disaster* written all over it?

She'd never considered herself a woman of half measure, but the situations she went all-in on were ones she could control. Because she only had to depend on herself.

A relationship with Arlo was the very definition of something she couldn't control.

Arlo pulled up to the valet stand at McNulty's and she allowed one of the attendants to open her door for her. As she slipped out, she saw Arlo coming around the front.

With a deep breath, she pasted on a smile she didn't feel and prepared to spend the evening playing the enamored girlfriend to his besotted boyfriend.

If it struck too close to home, she'd have to live with it.

The only sort of romantic relationship she could have with him was one where they both acted like they could have a happily-ever-after.

Because real life wasn't going to give them one.

Wendy knew the moment Kerrigan Doyle walked into McNulty's. She saw it on the bar cameras in her office and she briefly considered putting her plan into motion early.

And then opted to hold back.

It wouldn't do for Kerrigan to see her so quickly. She knew the woman went to her parents' home every weekend for dinner. She'd have to come up with a way to accidentally run into her next time she headed to the old neighborhood.

Which meant this evening, she'd watch and refine her strategy instead.

The warehouse shooter had finally reported in, apologizing profusely for the left-behind shell casings, but promising her they were untraceable. He bought them from a supplier in the Midwest and there was no way the cops would make him here.

Wendy doubted that, but she'd allow him his illusions for now. Plus, it was hard to find someone with his skills.

So she'd overlook the evidence he left behind and focus instead on what she wanted out of him next.

Her new boat would be ready on Friday, and she

was already lining up a quick score that wouldn't fully make up for what went down in the harbor, but it would ease some of the financial pressure in the short term. She needed to get product on the streets or risk losing ground to local mafia and a particularly ambitious supplier out of Philadelphia.

She'd come way too far to let that happen.

His sharpshooter skills would come in handy as extra eyes and gun power on the op.

The knock on her door was brisk as Mark "the Tank" Holman walked in.

The dude fit the role of bouncer to a *T* with broad shoulders and thickly muscled arms, ink up and down the length of them. He also sported an IQ of 180 and an ability to read people that was impressive.

"That woman from the other night. She's back."

"Did she see you yet?"

"Nah. I saw her at the valet stand and moved out of her line of sight until she got inside."

"She with that guy again?"

"Oh, yeah. Rumor has it they're partners."

"Which explains why they were together today when we had them followed out of the precinct. Do you think they're together, too, or casing us tonight?"

"I'm getting vibes on both."

Hmm. That was interesting. And if she was being fair, she definitely felt the relationship vibes the other night herself. She'd put down a bet they hadn't had sex yet, but working together was getting them both hot and bothered.

"You told me you thought you scared her the other night."

"She didn't like me looking at her."

"Then do it again. Let's see if we can get him riled up enough to act."

Arlo handed over his credit card to their waitress after she laid down a beer for him and a glass of wine for Kerrigan. The bar had a rollicking crowd, those who'd come in after work still here a few hours later.

Their decibel level had increased with their alcohol consumption and he and Kerrigan had to sit close to talk to each other.

A feat he wasn't sure was possible after their fight in the car, yet she'd kept up her side of the bargain with steady conversation and the physical cues of someone happily out on a date.

Even if she was still seething inside.

It was scorched earth, so why he kept marching back over it, he had no idea.

Which was a bold-faced lie to the one person he never lied to.

Himself.

He knew damn well why.

Kerrigan Doyle tripped his protector switch, a wildly unsubtle reaction to the bone-deep desire that kept catching him off guard.

He hadn't once questioned Officer Doyle's ability to deal with whatever was tossed her way.

But what was happening *to* Kerrigan?

Hell, *those* fears clouded his words with unhelpful sentiments and admonitions that she step back from the risks.

"I haven't seen him yet."

Her comment had been spoken in a low tone, even

though anyone's ability to hear her from even five feet away was unlikely given the noise level.

"I haven't, either, but we'll keep watch for him. In the meantime, who do we think looks like they have information to share? The waitress didn't even blink when you asked her about how business had been since the drug bust in here."

"Which was odd, don't you think? She didn't even try to shut it down. She just ignored the question outright."

"I'd say she couldn't hear you," he said with a wry smile and a glance at the happy revelers around them, "but I saw it, too. She checked out and she glanced back over here when she got to the bar."

"She knows something."

"That's my guess."

Even with the fraught moments in the car, they really had rebounded well into their respective roles once inside the bar. It was a trait he admired in her—that ability to keep focus on the work, even if she was dealing with other things.

It was professional and showed a seasoning well beyond her years. It also had him wondering more about the organization now being built from the ground up. What would it take to assess talent? To harness it and grow it and—

"You look like you have an idea."

"Talent and professionalism. They're the two biggest things we keep circling around."

Kerrigan ran her finger around the edge of her glass, stopping a small drop from running down the side. "Crime as a job."

"For lack of a better description, yes, that exactly."

"And how's it relevant here?"

"We keep looking at what's going on as a talent assessment. Someone's being groomed and evaluated for their abilities."

"You have another angle?" She was clearly intrigued, her hand falling away from her glass.

"What if it's actually a matter of cutting down?"

"Removing the poor performers?"

"Exactly. If you can't keep up, you're out. If you don't follow my rules, you're out."

Kerrigan picked up on his point, that seamless give-and-take they had keeping the idea moving. "If you can't run a successful op in the harbor, you're out."

"Exactly."

"You know, it makes sense. Especially if you think about it from a woman's perspective. If you're trying to build loyalty and keep yourself safe, you're going to test those around you.

"Can I trust you? Are you going to support me? Are you here for me?"

"It's another dimension."

They exchanged theories, their conversation moving back and forth, the time passing easily and quickly. Although they were technically on duty, they needed to make a show of doing the social things a couple did for an evening out. With that, Arlo eyed their half-empty glasses. "Should I ask our waitress to bring us a new round?"

"Sounds good. I've flagged the guy refilling water glasses so many times I need to excuse myself. But we don't want to draw attention by not drinking, either."

"Then I'll order some potato skins while I'm at it."

She slapped a hand over her breasts. "A man after my own heart."

Since the move did nothing to hide the attractive curves currently resting beneath her fingers, Arlo counted himself the toughest of men when he managed to pull his gaze away and just nod his affirmation on the food.

And then watched her wend a path all the way across the bar, the beautiful shape of her ass drawing more than a few glances as she walked.

He wanted to be mad.

Hell, he was irate and feeling rather vengeful that any man would dare look at her, even as he understood that beautiful women drew attention.

And goodness, she was gorgeous.

It wasn't just her body, even though the physicality of her work and her athletic grace were evident. Nor was it just that stunning face.

No, it really was the entire picture.

She was the most determined woman he'd ever met. She wanted to be the best and she pushed herself and competed every single day to do that.

But what he also hadn't been able to get out of his mind was how she'd helped their victim today. The man later identified as Christos Jenkins had been a full person to her. One whose hand she'd held as he passed from this world. It had showcased a level of compassion that had left him in absolute awe of her.

"Can I get you another round?"

Their waitress had returned, her smile bright, if perfunctory. Arlo quickly ordered them another round as well as the potato skins, then he opted to try once more.

"I know I said it before, but this bar really is something. When I'd heard about the cops shutting this place down for a while, I was sure I wouldn't get to come back here anymore."

Her gaze was sharp—overly so—as she made a show of picking up his empty glass and placing it on her tray. It was only as she stepped to the side and reached for Kerrigan's water glass, that she spoke.

Low.

Insistent.

And with a quaver in the voice that didn't just happen.

"I'd stop making those sorts of comments if I were you."

Arlo didn't make any move at all to suggest he'd heard her, but he did slip a card out of his pocket in a smooth move that was likely hidden from view by her body.

He tucked it beneath the napkin where his beer was sitting. "I'll just leave this here for you to pick up later, then."

She made no move to touch the card, or to even acknowledge it was there. "Wise up, pal, and do what I said. Stop. Asking. Questions."

He watched her go, her attention on weaving her way back through the crowd that had only gotten louder and more packed, a sea of bodies enjoying the evening.

It was only as his gaze shifted away from her that he caught sight of the man by the door.

Big. Burly. And while Arlo would ensure Kerrigan made the final ID, the man's attention was far too sharp to make him think it was anyone else but the thug who was watching her the other night.

Chapter 13

Kerrigan dried her hands and stared at herself in the mirror. Despite their dismal start to the evening, she and Arlo had managed to settle into a rhythm over the past hour sitting there at the table. She mentally congratulated herself on keeping her cool, even as a very large part of her felt like she was overheating every time she looked at the man.

Because, wow, could he kiss.

It hadn't been like the other night, when they'd spontaneously come together out of a place of distraction and subterfuge.

Those tender moments had been wild enough.

But tonight?

That kiss was all electricity and wild combustion, not to mention basically every single fantasy she'd ever had.

A fantasy she'd spent her life dreaming about and waiting for.

And, yeah, she admitted to herself as she leaned forward, lightly wiping away a small bit of mascara that had stuck on her lower eyelash, it could be as much about the lack of exciting kisses in her life as it was about the sexy guy she'd shared it with.

But...

She stepped back and assessed herself frankly in the mirror. It would be an easy brush-off to say she didn't know any better because she didn't have an extensive history of boyfriends. But a small, still-rational part of her brain didn't think so.

No man she'd dated before had made her feel quite like Arlo.

And no one had drawn such an immediate and all-consuming response to a simple kiss.

I want you.

Against my better judgment.

Against my own horrible history with dating.

Against every feckless, unreliable trait likely passed to me by my family when it comes to interpersonal relationships.

The mere idea of him wanting her was heady, but it was all the disqualifications that came after that had had her wondering.

Did he really believe those things about himself?

Or was it more of a defense mechanism to warn her off?

She wasn't a woman who'd ever bought in to the idea she could "save" the other person in a relationship. People came to their relationships with—hopefully—every intention of wanting to be in them. It would hardly do to think about Arlo's words as something she could

conquer or overcome with her will and sheer determination.

That way lay folly and, frankly, it showed disrespect
for the other person's words and feelings.

Yet even with that deep-seated belief, she couldn't
fully dismiss the feeling that he was trying to convince
himself as much as he was convincing her.

Kerrigan was so lost in thought she nearly missed
their waitress step out of a stall. The bathroom had
been loud when she'd walked in, but the large crowd
dissipated as she waited her turn for the sink, and it
was quiet and empty for the moment.

"Hello." She smiled and nodded at their waitress
and made a show of pulling out her lipstick to reapply.

The young woman beside her mumbled a hello and
focused on washing her hands.

She took in the skinny frame nearly gaunt beside
her in the mirror and considered various conversation
starters. The brush-off earlier hadn't been a simple act
of not hearing Àrlo's question and Kerrigan wanted to
find out why.

Which made it that much more surprising when the
woman reached over and turned on Kerrigan's sink
tap at full blast, a match for her own, which was still
running. She leaned in, her voice urgent beneath the
noise of the sink.

"I told your boyfriend this but figure you've probably got more brains than he does. Stop asking questions."

The woman made a show of washing her hands, her
gaze on the soap filling her palms.

Kerrigan got the sense the woman believed in the

warning she was giving, but what really bothered her was the clear shake in those soapy hands. "Why?"

"No one around here likes it."

The tart, edgy response reinforced all the reasons she and Arlo were here tonight. Their undercover efforts weren't misplaced.

But she kept her tone even, the slightest edge of her own winging back at the woman. "It was a simple question. A big bust went down in this bar. People are curious."

"Curiosity helps no one. And the people who are still here are just trying to keep their heads down, live their lives and make enough to get by. You get it?"

The waitress finished rinsing her hands, and in addition to that light shaking, Kerrigan could see the haggard lines of her face in the light of the overheads. Wide, scared eyes further reinforced all she was trying to warn Kerrigan away from.

"Yeah, I get it. Even if I don't agree."

"People who don't agree in here don't last very long." The woman reached over and turned off the taps in quick, harsh motions, her agitation clear.

"Then let me help you."

She snagged a handful of paper towels, quickly drying her hands. "There's no such thing as help."

With that she turned on her heel and marched out of the bathroom. A few women tumbled drunkenly through the door, blocking any attempt Kerrigan might make to quickly go after the waitress and pull her back.

Remorse permeated the space where the woman had stood. In that moment, Kerrigan finally understood exactly what she and Arlo were up against.

Whoever was running things and working toward

making a name for themselves had effectively scared everyone in their orbit. The turf war they'd imagined might still be a possibility, but Kerrigan would lay odds their discussion earlier was more on point.

Whoever was trying to take over was thinning the herd, paring away anyone they thought wasn't up to snuff.

In a world where there was minimal security, anyway, that sort of unrelenting "justice" would be hard to escape.

And what could people really do?

Go to the cops? Not with a rap sheet and a reputation.

Try to go up against someone amassing power? Not when you needed a fair amount of your own personal power to make the play.

She didn't think their waitress was a power player, but the woman was a reflection of the bigger problem. The criminals in Brooklyn were running scared, along with everyone in their orbit.

And if the fear she just saw reflected in the mirror was any indication, she and Arlo didn't have a lot of time left to figure out who was the cause of it all.

Arlo moved into the alley behind the bar, the large, fenced parking lot where the valets parked cars stretching out before him. He'd sent Kerrigan a quick text that he was heading outside and that he wouldn't be long.

But you didn't tell her why.

The thought taunted him, and he almost pulled out his phone and texted her again, but he didn't have time.

He needed to get a bead on the thug who was at the center of this.

If it meant he kept Kerrigan far away from the guy, then, yeah, that worked, too.

He'd pay for it later. By rights, he understood that. They were partners out on the job. She not only deserved to know where he was, but department protocol also insisted they work together.

And still, he wasn't turning back.

He kept his back to the wall and moved closer to the valet stand. The various young men who were responsible for parking cars were in a variety of places and by Arlo's quick count he thought there were four on duty tonight.

One had just come around with a car, another was running back across the parking lot, having just parked one, and one was on his phone at the valet station. The guy who'd taken Arlo's keys was nowhere in sight so he must be on point out in front of the bar.

It was a tough job but one that could pay well if you were working a hot spot and could pull in decent tips.

It was also a job rife with information about the community.

The guy with his cell phone had just lit a cigarette and Arlo walked over, his intention to bum one as his cover. A quick glance at the ground offered him the additional boon of an empty cigarette pack and he grabbed it and shoved it into his breast pocket.

Patting his pocket as he walked up to the guy, he pasted on a congenial smile. "I'm fresh out. You got an extra?"

The guy glanced up, his eyes narrowed, even as he took in the empty pack Arlo crunched in his hand.

"There's a machine in the back of the bar near the johns."

"I know but my girlfriend hates it when I smoke. I figured I'd just get one more and avoid the riot act. I've got a fresh pack at home."

The lie did the trick, and the valet extended his pack, tapping the box so Arlo could take a dislodged cigarette.

He realized his additional mistake when he had no lighter on him but played it off by snagging the small blue plastic one sitting on the edge of the valet stand. He made quick work of lighting up and cupping his hands around the flame.

The valet seemed uninterested in conversation, so Arlo took over.

"Big crowd tonight."

The guy shrugged. "Big crowds most nights."

Arlo let it go, keeping his gaze on the parking lot, when the guy inadvertently gave him the perfect opening.

"You'd better get out of here. Boss hates it when people come back here."

"Hates it why?"

"They don't like it." The guy turned to face Arlo. "Look, I gave you a smoke. You want me to lose my job?"

Arlo held up his hands and took a few steps back. "No, man. No way. I'll leave." He shook his head, putting on a solemn air. "This place sure has changed since the cops came down on it a few months ago."

The valet removed his cigarette from his mouth and spit to the side, disgust lining his face. "You're not kidding about that. I'd've quit if the money wasn't so good."

"I thought they caught the thugs running the drugs. You'd think it would make things better."

"It hasn't." The valet side-eyed him as he lifted his cigarette back to his mouth. "So get out of here."

"Yeah." Arlo lifted his hands once more. "I got it."

He considered pushing the situation once more but figured a hasty retreat was better. They might be in a rush to solve this case but blowing their cover a few hours in wasn't the best course of action, either.

With one last glance around the parking lot, Arlo turned to head back into the bar, only to find the thug they'd been after blocking the entrance.

Despite the snap of cold weather fall had brought, the man's broad frame was set off by the tats visible up and down his exposed arms.

It was a cultivated look, Arlo realized, designed to instill fear and obedience.

Fortunate for him, he wasn't impressed.

When something that looked a lot like anticipation filled the man's face, Arlo felt his own spiking in response and considered his next move.

The guy recognized him, that was obvious. Had he made him as a cop? Or was it tied to the fact he'd been escorting Kerrigan around?

Was she a target somehow?

But why?

Arlo made a show of leaning against the wall, bringing the pilfered cigarette to his lips. He had an excuse to be out there, whether the man liked it or not. His instincts told him to wait the guy out and see how he handled things.

He didn't have to wait long.

"You've been asking questions around my bar."

"Your bar?" Arlo took another drag on the cigarette but made a point not to exhale a stream of smoke directly at the guy. "You own it?"

"I'm responsible for it."

"Still not the same."

"You and your very pretty cop girlfriend need to stop asking questions."

Ice coated his stomach at the dual reference—to Kerrigan's looks *and* her status as a cop—and pushed himself up off the wall.

"My girlfriend and I came in to have a good time."

"Yet you both look like you're waiting for root canals." The guy stood where he was, still as a statue, but his entire demeanor grew harsher. Meaner. "It's interesting to watch. And your half-finished drinks only reinforce the fact."

Even without the guy moving an inch, Arlo felt him loom closer.

His attention was laser-sharp and it had obviously been focused on them.

He quickly cycled through the past few hours, trying to assess where they'd gone wrong. They'd laughed and talked at the table, but the guy had made them on the drinks, which was a bad move on their part.

But the questions?

Arlo knew the guy hadn't been anywhere near him when he'd questioned the waitress.

So how had he known?

"Seems to me you'd like questions. It's good for business when people get a cheap thrill knowing something big went down here."

"People have short memories and thirsty mouths. No one cares anymore. Except the cops."

There it was again. That direct challenge that the guy knew they weren't casual daters out for the evening.

But it was the distinct click of the switchblade he pulled out of his pocket—one that suddenly pressed firmly between two ribs—that had Arlo going still.

Killing a cop took gang warfare and criminal politics to a whole new level. There wasn't a cop in New York who wouldn't be out for revenge if the guy slipped that knife a few inches deeper into Arlo's skin.

But as he felt the sharp press of that knife, he recognized the truth.

If he didn't act quickly, that scenario was a frightening possibility.

Tia Lutz walked the three blocks to her car, cursing herself all the way. She'd had the lunch shift and agreed to help through happy hour and on into the early evening to help with the after-work crowd. She had nearly completed her shift, willing to take on one more table, and she'd gone and gotten *them*.

The happy couple with sharp eyes and pointed questions. Why the *hell* were they asking questions?

And why did she always get the shaft?

She knew some bad crap went on in the back office. She'd known it before, when the drugs were flowing out the back door. She knew now, despite the we're-good-neighbors-and-the-heart-of-Brooklyn routine the owners were peddling, bad crap was still going on.

But, damn it, she needed this job.

Getting into the hot spots around town wasn't easy and she needed the tips. Needed *something* to make the long shifts worthwhile, with her aching legs and the roaming hands and the suggestive come-ons.

And she knew she had a good thing. She kept her head down and her eyes on the prize. A growing bank account, which was her pathway out of this hellhole. She wanted a new life, maybe in the Carolinas or down in the Gulf Coast. Somewhere warm and nice, and a place where she could start over.

She'd been running on fumes too long and this was her meal ticket out of New York.

It might be the city of dreams for some, but it had been her nightmare with the expensive rents, neighbors who lived on top of you and the ever-increasing cost of just getting by.

She was getting out.

Tia fumbled for her keys, her hand brushing over the business card she'd swiped out of the guy's napkin. She didn't want to get caught with it but she also didn't want it left anywhere near her station.

She glanced down at it and just like she'd figured, the dude was a cop.

Truth be told, she was actually surprised he'd left the card. Not a great way to go undercover, was it? Handing off your business card to whoever was handy?

Did he think she was an easy mark?

Did it really matter?

She wasn't ratting him out and she wasn't ratting out her bosses, either. And all she really wanted to do was keep her head down, get another few thousand saved and get out.

Even now, she could picture the warm Carolina breezes waving over her face. She'd find a small apartment and a good, solid waitressing job and she'd have a new life.

A nice life.

Pretty blue skies filled her thoughts as she walked up to her car, unlocked the door and slipped in. She quickly locked the doors once she was seated and put her key in the ignition.

"Damn it!" She cursed as the car sputtered, trying to turn over.

Tears welled up, an image of whatever repair was needed taking a chunk out of her moving fund and firmly replacing her thoughts of blue skies.

Wasn't it always the way? Two steps forward and ten freaking ones back?

Taking in a heavy breath, she tried again, turning the key and willing the engine to catch.

That heavy grinding sound of the engine whirling filled the car, the lightest whiff of gasoline accompanying it. One lone tear fell just as the engine caught, turning over.

"Yes!"

Swiping at her tears, she reached for the gearshift as she depressed the clutch, a strange creaking noise filling the car.

That was a new one.

And as visions of heading to the auto-body shop consumed her once more, a loud popping noise filled the air as the car exploded around her.

Kerrigan fought the waves of anger as she stalked out the back of the bar toward the rear entrance. She ignored all the signs saying Employees Only and stayed her course as she knew exactly where Arlo was.

The spot he had avoided actually telling her about or suggesting they go to and handle whatever was out there. *Together.*

Like partners.

Which made her slam through that back door a surprise when she nearly plowed into a very large form standing in her way.

She sidestepped quickly, but as she caught sight of Arlo on the other side of the large, hulking form, she immediately moved into action.

She quickly followed with another sidestep when Arlo used her surprise arrival to go on the attack with the man. She couldn't see one, but she assumed there was a weapon and used Arlo's quick attack and her position from behind to lock her arms in the man's bent elbows.

The position was awkward and unsustainable, but it was just enough to give Arlo additional leverage and he plowed a fist into the guy's gut, then thrust outward with his right hand, dislodging a blade that went flying to the ground.

The thick form she was hanging on to like a monkey back-stepped—*hard*—slamming her into the door. She saw stars as her head hit the thick wood and Kerrigan felt her grip slipping as the pain took over.

Determined, she knew she needed to fight through it, but felt her grip giving way all the same.

And then it didn't matter because Arlo was barreling forward into the man like a bull, the two men quickly descending into full body fighting.

Abstractly, Kerrigan heard a shout from the direction of the parking lot, and she inched her way back, struggling to get herself to a sitting position and clear the swirly, raging lines staggering through her vision.

Two younger men came rushing over, one she remembered because he'd taken their car earlier when

Arlo had pulled up to the valet stand. They went to work pulling Arlo and the bruiser apart and Kerrigan debated how to play this.

Did they give up their date-night ploy and pull out their badges?

Even though she was mad at him for going off on his own, she was willing to let Arlo see it through and watch how he played it.

But if the thug attacked again, all bets were off.

The skirt she had on didn't allow for particularly decorous movement, but it did give her quite good range of motion, so she braced her feet apart, prepared to leap back in, if needed.

The back of her head still throbbed but the squiggles had cleared from her vision, and she was able to take in the scene.

Arlo wiped blood from his lip off the back of his hand, but he'd stopped fighting and the valet holding him had dropped his arms. The thug was still struggling, and Kerrigan saw the man holding him whisper something in his ear, but she couldn't make out the words.

Whatever it was, they had a calming effect, because the big guy stopped, even if his body still braced like a mad animal ready to strike.

He spit a stream of blood before speaking. "You want to tell me what you're doing back here?"

"Came out to bum a smoke." Arlo stood at his full height, layers of menace telegraphing out of his gaze. That fathomless blue, normally bright with humor or alert with ideas, had gone a flat, cold, icy color that made a shiver run down Kerrigan's spine.

This was Arlo?

It was a side of him she hadn't seen. She should have expected it. He was a cop—an excellent one—but even with that knowledge, she hadn't ever envisioned such a bleak, unyielding visage.

"A cigarette? Yeah, right." The thug's hands were clenched at his side but he made no move to strike again. "You've been asking questions you have no business asking."

"And you've been eyeing my girlfriend and I want to know why."

"I've been eyeing a cop." The guy looked over his shoulder, his slimy gaze settling on her. "Two cops."

Kerrigan feigned surprise at the accusations, but it was Arlo's quiet, steady presence that never wavered. "Prove it."

Those words—part challenge, all threat—hung in the air and Kerrigan nearly pulled out her badge, willing to end it all there, when a loud noise rent the air.

Everyone glanced in the direction of the noise, and in the distance, visible beyond the chain-link fence surrounding the parking lot, a few more blocks down the street, a ball of fire rose up toward the sky.

Chapter 14

Arlo grabbed Kerrigan's hand and the two of them raced back into the building, then out into the street. Whatever had happened, someone needed help, and he and Kerrigan would be the first on scene.

Their cover was already blown so they might as well do something useful.

Not that he'd expected they'd last long nosing around the bars in Brooklyn, but he had estimated they'd get through at least an evening before being fully made as cops.

It wasn't to be.

They'd worry about it later, in the debrief. Right now, someone needed help.

He reached for his phone to call in whatever had happened, but Kerrigan had beat him to it.

"Downtown Sunset Bay," she said into her phone.

"Intersection of Fourth and Bay. Apparent car explosion of some sort."

She matched his quick pace next to him, her long legs eating up the sidewalk, in heels no less. He'd also seen her take that hit when the bar jerk was trying to throw her off and she had to be hurting right now.

"You okay?"

"We'll worry about it later."

And then she put on a burst of speed in the last block as they saw the smoking car, still burning from the front, its hood blown off.

A crowd had already started to form, and Arlo pushed his way through it, his badge in hand. The sound of sirens filled the air, but it was Kerrigan's soft cry that held his attention.

"Arlo! It's our waitress."

The woman was lying oddly positioned in the front seat and he and Kerrigan immediately went to work. He hauled open the driver-side door, using his sport coat to protect his hands from the heated metal, while Kerrigan reached in and unbuckled the woman's seat belt.

"Hello! Can you hear me? We're going to get you out of here."

Blood ran freely from a wound at the woman's hairline and her face was covered in dirt and debris. Shattered glass from the windshield covered the car and lay over her in a scattered pattern that refracted the overhead light shining in, and Kerrigan brushed some of it away as she reached for the woman.

"We're going to get you out of here."

Arlo helped Kerrigan pull the woman fully out of the seat, careful to take her weight into his arms as Kerrigan made sure the lower part of her body didn't hit the ground as they pulled her free.

He'd already assessed her as painfully thin when she'd waited on their table, but as Arlo cradled the woman's body in his arms, he felt how small and slight she really was.

Who had done this to her?

And what, exactly, was going on? He and Kerrigan had asked a few questions, nothing more. Suddenly there were knife-wielding thugs in the back parking lot behind the bar, scared valets and one of McNulty's waitresses had been attacked.

He and Kerrigan had been there a few hours. Who the hell had the wherewithal to put this together?

And this fast?

After verifying she still had a pulse, Kerrigan kept up a steady chatter to the woman. She wasn't getting any response, but blue-veined eyelids did waver and flutter a few times as Kerrigan continued a soft conversation, coaxing her to talk to them.

Just like the sniper's victim, he thought.

It was oddly similar, people in a position to know what was going on suddenly facing death because of it.

The sirens screamed closer and closer, and a few uniforms had already been dispatched to the area as well and were helping with crowd control while also creating a lane for the EMTs to get in.

"What's your name?"

Kerrigan stroked the woman's hand, speaking to her softly. Those eyelids fluttered open. "Tia."

"Tia, we're here to help. You need to hang on."

"Blue skies," Tia murmured, the words slurred and uneven. "Was going to go… Was saving…up."

"I know. We all dream of vacation."

"No." Tia's voice was firm on that. "Moving away. Just—just needed enough…money."

"Why were you moving away?"

"Far away. Want to get away from here. From all of it."

"From all of what?"

"Away." The woman's voice drifted off and Arlo knew they'd lost her.

Kerrigan seemingly did, too, as she looked over at him.

"Another one." Kerrigan said, her voice strained and choked. "All we did was ask a few questions. It's a terror campaign."

"It is."

"But *we* asked the questions. She's on us, Arlo."

He wanted to stop that train of thought immediately, but the EMTs rushed over, inserting themselves between the two of them and taking over with Tia.

"She's gone." Kerrigan moved into full cop mode. "We removed her from the car, laid her down. She was speaking to us."

One of the EMTs barked out a series of questions as they worked over her, and Kerrigan answered them all.

And as he stood there, watching her work, Arlo recognized the truth.

There were cases in a cop's life that left an irrevocable mark.

He'd sensed from the start—so had Captain Reed—that this case was bigger than they expected.

Darker, too.

But as he watched Kerrigan's face and the near-robotic responses she relayed to the medics, he knew this would be a case that would forever leave its mark on Kerrigan Doyle.

Kerrigan stared at the form lying under a sheet on the EMT gurney and replayed the night in her mind. They shouldn't be here.

There shouldn't have been what was inevitably a car bomb in the middle of Sunset Bay.

And the woman under that sheet shouldn't be dead.

Tia Lutz.

They'd identified her prints from a possession charge she'd faced just after turning eighteen. It hadn't necessarily defined her—the ME would confirm, but Kerrigan hadn't gotten the sense the woman was using—but it had likely set her on a course.

One she was looking to escape.

Blue skies.

Was going to go... Was saving...up.

Just—just needed enough...money.

Would those words ever not haunt her?

And why had this woman been targeted?

Kerrigan sat perched on the edge of the EMT's back fender, submitting to various tests to see if she had a concussion. The dull throb of a headache hadn't subsided but it sort of faded in and out of her consciousness as they'd worked the crime scene. She would have forgotten about it altogether if Arlo hadn't insisted the EMTs look her over.

The raw look in his eyes brooked no argument and she knew a checkup was inevitable if she wanted to do her next dive, so she submitted to the quick series of tests.

"You're lucky, Officer. It looks like you're going to have a bad headache that you should baby for a few days is about it. I'm not seeing immediate signs of concussion, but you should be checked again in a couple of days to be absolutely sure."

"Thank you."

And just like that, there went her next dive. The protocols were inarguable and she'd be manning the Zodiac boat or riding a desk until being fully cleared.

She thanked them and headed back to the car and the bomb squad that had been called in to handle the scene. She was just in time to catch the end of the lead's summation to Arlo.

She'd met Lieutenant Rhodes before, when he and his team worked a device she'd brought up off the harbor floor. His dark skin bore the stress and pressure of a big job, with lines around his eyes and across his forehead, but the dark brown gaze that took in the sight before them was rich with empathy and care.

"Crude car bomb but effective. It was placed on the undercarriage and designed to go off once the engine caught."

"Who has the knowledge to do this?" Kerrigan struggled to understand how someone did this on a busy street, full of people at any moment.

"Far too many people, I'm afraid. It's pretty straightforward and can be done with household items."

"We can start checking exterior cameras on the businesses and homes around here," Arlo affirmed.

"Do that. It's a quick job and if someone remained low enough it's not hard to stay unobtrusive." Rhodes dropped into a crouch and pointed out a few points on the car. "They'd be in and out in under thirty seconds if they knew what they were doing. They'd need to stay low and wedge themselves under the front left tire to make the connection."

Rhodes moved off to handle the rest of the cleanup and Arlo turned to Kerrigan. "What did the medics say?"

"They don't think it's a concussion. I need to get checked out in another forty-eight hours but I think I'm fine."

"The doctor will confirm that."

"Yes, Arlo. Others can certainly make the final decision."

The response snapped out, as surly and nasty as she felt, and she knew she'd hit the right chord. His own ire flared, his eyes going dark, before he seemed to catch himself.

"See that you do."

"I'm going to get started on the video footage. I'll see you later."

"Kerrigan—"

He broke off as she turned back to face him. "What, Arlo? We need to get to it as fast as we can. I'll take this side of the block. You take the other. We'll have it done in no time."

Whatever he was about to say, he seemed to think better of it.

And without saying another word, Arlo turned on his heel and headed off across the street.

Kerrigan stripped off the clothes she'd be very happy to never see again and climbed into the shower. She already had a hot mug of tea steeping on the bathroom counter, and she figured it would be the perfect temperature by the time she scrubbed the night off her skin.

Even if there was no scrubbing off the shame and guilt she felt over Tia Lutz's death.

As she'd agreed with Arlo, she'd hit all the businesses on the north side of the street while he'd taken the south. A bodega, a dry cleaner and a national bank branch ATM were the businesses in likely view of Tia's car. The bodega owner was quick to comply, and she'd made notes on the dry cleaner and the bank.

She'd swing by in the morning to get the cleaner's footage and had already left a message for them that she would be coming in. The bank would go through standard information-request protocols, so she hoped like hell that wasn't the lucky shot because it would be another three days, minimum, before they saw any footage.

Who would do this to Tia?

The question haunted her as she scrubbed her hair and then lathered in conditioner before rinsing it all out. The water might have sluiced away the soap of her shampoo, but it did nothing for the guilt that continued to pound beneath her skin.

Had this really happened because of the questions she and Arlo asked?

Even now, she could remember the haunted look in the woman's eyes as she warned Kerrigan away from nosing around when they stood side by side in the bathroom.

What still didn't play for her was the speed with which it all happened. Arlo made one lightly probing ask of the woman as she took their drink order. A question she roundly ignored.

And then there was the conversation in the bathroom, the running water obscuring their words.

Had someone heard, anyway? Was the bathroom bugged? Clearly, Tia had thought so if she'd run the water in two sinks.

Although there was a big part of her that just wanted to curl up and forget the night, she was anxious to look at the footage from the bodega owner. After drying off and giving herself a few minutes to let her tea do its work, she sat down at her computer and loaded up the footage.

The owner had given her a full day's worth of footage and she started in the morning, moving through quickly until she saw Tia park in that space. The footage was grainy and it was hard to make out specific details, but she did have a clear view of the car and Tia as she climbed out of it.

Other cars surrounded Tia's parking spot and the view of the ground wasn't great. Based on Lieutenant Rhodes's description of what they were looking for—someone who had to get down on the ground and go under the front driver-side wheel—Kerrigan figured she was unlikely to get a view to whoever set the bomb. But...

She kept scrolling the footage and realized she might get enough of a view of people walking by or approaching the car to narrow in the data they needed off another camera.

The work was tedious and she kept it on double speed to ensure she didn't miss fine details, but the daytime showed nothing of interest. She was working off the theory that Tia didn't become a victim until she'd spoken with her and Arlo, and it meant the money shot was likely later. Still, she was determined to watch it all.

The timing still bothered her.

They simply hadn't had enough contact with the woman to make her a target that quickly. Right?

Even as she asked herself the question, she knew it was possibly a foolish thought. Whoever was running this deal behind the scenes wanted absolute obedience and compliance. The only way to do that was to make quick decisions.

Impulsive.

That idea flashed back in her mind, one of the assessments the team Arlo had assembled in the conference room a few days ago had landed on.

There was a reckless nature to what was going on that continued to pervade each crime. And it kept coming back to the lack of impulse control.

Own a fancy, unregistered boat? Kill your henchmen, then burn and sink it all?

Set up some guys to follow the cops, then set up a sniper to take them out?

See a waitress handling a standard evening crowd of curious, misplaced questions? Kill her with a bomb?

They were all outsized reactions to the situation. Reactions that kept screaming "look at me" and "see what I can do" and "don't you dare mess with me."

The knock on her door pulled her from her thoughts and her heart leaped in her chest. She knew it was Arlo, despite the anger that still remained over his actions.

He went out to the back lot of the bar on purpose with nothing more than a deliberately vague text.

It hadn't taken her long to piece it together and she'd tossed money on the table to pay their bill, somehow intuitively knowing they weren't coming back inside.

But it had all left her with the sinking feeling that no

matter what she did or how hard she worked, he didn't see her as an equal on this case.

He only focused on the risks to her.

What he didn't seem to understand was that as partners, not trusting her to go through the door with him meant he was putting himself at risk, too.

They had to face this together.

Or she might as well ask for reassignment.

It pained her to think that way, but what other choice did she have? He didn't trust her to have his back and because of it that thug in the bar had gotten the jump on him.

She crossed to the door, looking through the peephole, confirming it was her partner on the other side. She opened the door and stared at him across the threshold.

"What do you want, Arlo?"

What did he want?

That question had haunted him on the drive over to her place. Hell, it had haunted him since that first moment he'd seen her stripping out of her wet suit in the pouring rain on the police boat.

He wanted her.

And it had messed with his head, his logic and, most of all, it had messed with *her*.

Her career and her safety, yes. But on top of it all, her trust.

He'd been a bad partner tonight. Worse, he'd violated her faith in him because he couldn't get out of his head or out of his own way.

"Can I come in?"

She stepped aside and let him into her apartment, and he waited until she'd closed the door behind him.

"I need to talk to you."

"Oh? You need to talk to me now? That's rich. After you've done your lying deeds without informing your partner and avoided me and put yourself in terrible danger? *Now* you need to talk to me?"

"I made a mistake."

"No, Arlo. You keep making the same mistake. Which means it's not a mistake at all. It's deliberate action against me."

"It's not against you."

"Then who the hell is it against? The poor dead woman we pulled out of a car? The thug who tried to shiv you? Who, Arlo?"

She was right.

In every single thing she said, she was right. He'd put them both in danger and he'd betrayed her horribly in the process.

"I wanted to keep you safe."

"That's not your job."

"I'm your partner!"

"Yes. Just like Jayden or Gavin or any number of individuals are my partner when we go down on a dive. We trust each other and we follow the rules set up to keep us both safe. *Both* of us. One of us doesn't go rogue to satisfy some urge to play cowboy."

"It's not about playing cowboy or going rogue."

"Then what's it about?"

"I don't want anything to happen to you!" He ran a hand through his hair, tugging hard on the strands as the old memories rose up, swamping him and nearly stealing his breath. "I've been you, okay? I know the risks to you because I took them."

"Took what risks? And what do you mean *to* me? I'm

a cop, Arlo. The job comes with inherent risk." Her gaze had narrowed but her voice had softened. "So what, exactly, are you talking about?"

"Early on. My first case."

Even now, he could still conjure it up. The cold warehouse. The feel of the duct tape on his wrists. The belief he'd walked into something he wouldn't walk out of.

He'd spent a lot of time over the years putting it behind him. He'd extensively analyzed where he'd gone wrong and had worked methodically to ensure he didn't make the same mistakes again.

It was why he was so good at his job.

Why he'd closed the cases he had and how he kept it all by the book.

He worked harder and smarter than anyone else because there'd been a time, once, when he'd done neither.

"Arlo, what's this about?"

Although he usually avoided alcohol as a way to handle the memories or the nightmares that came with them, it had been a long day.

Too long.

"Do you have anything to drink?"

"Wine or whiskey?"

"Whiskey would be good."

She nodded and went into the kitchen, puttering around in the cabinets before coming back with a glass of amber-colored liquid. She'd seemingly understood his need, the glass not holding much more than about two fingers, but it was enough to wet his throat and give him the extra boost to get through this as they crossed to sit on the couch.

She deserves it.

The thought whispered through his mind, and he

knew it for truth. She deserved it as his partner and as his friend. And even more, in this very room where she'd shared her past. The career problems that had hurt her, but not broken her.

Didn't he owe her the same honesty?

He took a sip of his drink, warm fire coating his throat, and he leaned into that as he launched into his story.

"My first big case was working with Vice to bring down a prostitution and trafficking ring."

"That's quite a case to start on."

"I earned my way onto it with several proactive late nights and some additional questions I managed to ask some of the working girls when I was a beat cop."

"They trusted you? That says a lot."

"A few of them did. They knew I was looking out for them. I'd protected a few when I was off duty and gained some trust."

"That's not exactly protocol, Arlo."

It wasn't. In fact, it was the opposite of proper protocol, using his off duty time to pursue cop work. To look the other way when crimes were being committed just because he wasn't in uniform.

"I know. And I thought it was in service to the bigger cause, so I did it."

"What happened?"

"One of the girls I befriended and offered some protection to. Her name was Gabrielle. She gave me some feedback and details on a new shipment of trafficked women coming in. She didn't have a lot of details, but what she did know matched chatter the lead detective on the case already had and she was able to give us the date. So we set up the op and promised to keep her safe."

Even now, he could see it so clearly in his mind. The hopeful eyes in a face whose beauty had long worn thin. Her belief that he really was working to help her and her friends. And that he would help save those other girls before this horrible phase of their lives even started.

He'd believed it, too.

And in the end had been too confident of the intel and not nearly focused enough on the pimp who'd gotten wind one of his girls was giving out information to the cops.

"Only we didn't keep her safe. I walked straight into a setup. She was already dead after being tortured for information and the traffickers who managed her pimp were waiting for me."

She'd remained quiet through his retelling, her eyes big, solemn oceans of empathy in her face. Despite her anger—fair, righteous fury she was fully entitled to— she leaned forward and laid a hand over his where he still held his glass with both hands.

"How'd you get out?"

"There was enough chatter on what was going down that it got back to someone working undercover at Vice. They weren't directly on the case, but they knew the op we were preparing for and knew enough to call in backup. I figure I had about two hours left."

She nodded at that, her hand tightening over his. "I'm sorry."

"I can still see her. Gabrielle."

He'd long stopped thinking he'd forget what she looked like, splayed out like a piece of discarded garbage on the floor of the warehouse he was held hostage in. He saw her in his dreams, and he saw her on every op he went out on.

"Some cases are harder than others. They take more out of you. They're the ones that haunt us."

"I was responsible for her. I got her to trust me so I could get the big score. Win the big case."

"You didn't do that to her, Arlo."

"You can sit here and tell me you don't feel the same way about Tia?"

It was a low blow, especially knowing how fresh their waitress's death was, but Arlo pushed it anyway.

Because, yeah, there were cases that were harder than others. The ones that haunted you long after they should.

And then there were the ones you felt responsible for.

"Are you weaponizing what happened tonight?"

"I'm making a point. You feel responsible for her."

"I am responsible for her. You are, too."

"No, Kerrigan. The people who did that to her? They're responsible for her. Don't forget it or lose that perspective."

She sat back then, her hands falling away from where she'd held his.

"And here you go, once more, protecting me."

"I'm telling you the truth."

"No, you're not. You're telling me a version of the truth to get me to back off. To get me to stop feeling what I feel when I do this job. To my earlier point, you're weaponizing your pain to make me step away."

She stood at that, whirling on him.

The woman who'd opened the door to him, fresh-faced from a shower with wet hair piled atop her head, had changed. Morphed, really, into an avenging goddess. Color rode high on her cheeks and the hair that had begun to dry as they spoke framed her face in soft, curly waves.

"I haven't weaponized anything."

"Sure you have. You've done it from the start. Protecting me. Hiding the run you did on the Gentry family business. Going out tonight to confront the thug from the bar. You keep doing it, over and over."

She was right.

Arlo knew she was right, to the depths of his soul he knew it. And damn it, he hadn't been able to stop himself.

"I don't want you hurt."

"So what's better? Sabotaging me? Putting me in a position where I'm unaware of danger and walking into it without protection? Without knowing it's happening? How's that protecting me?"

"I was going to handle it. You were never going to be in danger."

"News flash, Arlo! We're both in danger. Each time we put on the badge and go out to do the work, we're targets. The only protection we've got is our training and our minds and our partnership."

He sat there, his empty glass in hand, and could do nothing but stare at her.

Could only look his fill and finally—*finally*—acknowledge what he'd been doing all along. Why he'd been so upside down and why he'd been so insistent on acting in a way that he not only knew was wrong, but also deeply believed was wrong.

"I love you."

Kerrigan had already stalked off toward the fridge

and turned at his words, two bottles of water in her hand. "You what?"

"I'm falling in love with you."

She stared at him for several long moments, the light from the fridge highlighting her features in the dim overhead she had on in her kitchen area.

He got the distinct sense she was working through something, but try as he might, he couldn't pinpoint what it was.

Had he surprised her?

Pissed her off?

Or hurt her because every single one of his actions flew in the face of how you loved someone?

"That's your excuse?"

"Yes. It's a damn poor one, too, for all the reasons you named. If I cared, keeping you in the dark is the worst thing I can do."

"So why have you done it? Worse, why have you continued to do it?"

"This is new territory for me."

"And sabotaging me is the answer?"

"No! It's not like that." How did he make her understand? This bone-jarring fear for her that he'd never felt for anyone. It clouded his judgment and had been doing so from the start of the case.

From the very first moment he'd asked Wyatt if he could take her on as his partner to solve the harbor crime.

Which meant he had to try and explain himself.

Love was a powerful word, but it meant nothing without action. And it meant even less if you weren't willing to speak truth behind it.

He'd spent his entire life living that reality with his family.

Was he really interested in staying on that same path? Worse, was he determined to hurt someone he cared for—truly, deeply cared for—because he refused to chart a new course?

Chapter 15

Kerrigan's head spun from the argument with Arlo.
And she didn't think it had anything to do with the
knock she'd taken against the back door at McNulty's.

He loved her?

Was *in* love with her?

Why was it those few simple words had lodged
like a boulder in the middle of her chest, generating
wild flutters throughout her body even as she felt their
weight like being encased in concrete?

She couldn't let it matter. Not now. Not in this moment, when she was not only entitled to her point of
view, but also where he had to realize that telling her
he loved her wasn't a substitute for his actions.

Even though it did matter.

That he loved her.

"It's not sabotage, Kerrigan."

He'd stood and crossed to her in the kitchen, taking the cold water bottles from her hand and setting them down on her counter space. She knew her studio was small, but it had never felt quite as crowded as it did right now. And that included the time her immediate family, as well as cousins, aunts and uncles, had come over after she'd first moved in.

Arlo crowded her.

It was both delicious and overwhelming and it only served to heighten her anger once more.

"Don't play with my emotions."

"I'm not. I'm trying to get my own under control. I've—"

Just like earlier, when he'd fought the man at the bar, Kerrigan saw yet another facet of Arlo.

Raw emotion limned his face, the small light over the sink reflecting all the heat and need and true confusion in his deep blue eyes.

"I don't know what I'm doing," he finally said.

"I don't know, either."

"But I can promise you, it's not to undermine you. Or make you feel less than. Or to put you in harm's way. It's just that I couldn't see past myself when that guy looked your way. And when he hurt you—"

Arlo reached up, brushing her hair away from her temple before painting the tips of his fingers over the crown of her head. "He hurt you."

"Yes, he did." She reached up, putting a hand on his chest. "And I'm fine. He also nearly hurt you. If I hadn't shown up when I did… I shudder to think what would have happened to you."

"I was working on that."

"Yeah, well, from my view it looked like you were

stuck in the middle of a blade and bad decision." She stopped then, willing him to understand. "I can handle myself. In that situation and in any other my training calls me to."

"I know you can. And I know you do. Hell, you dive the depths of New York Harbor. If that doesn't take a serious amount of mettle and courage, I'm not sure what does."

"Then you'll get out of my way?"

"Yes."

"And you'll stop with this ridiculous need to protect me?"

"I—" He stopped, his hand drifting to cup her shoulder. "I will stop leaving you out of things. I'm not going to apologize for wanting to see you remain safe. It's not ridiculous."

"But you won't stand in my way."

"No."

They stood like that for long moments, wrapped up in each other yet wary to move forward or to move away.

And in the space of a few heartbeats, she knew she loved him, too. It wasn't something she could put to words—she needed time and she needed to process what had happened—but to keep pretending she didn't have feelings or could will away the ones she had was no longer possible.

"Stay."

The request slipped out, as powerful as a bomb detonating in her small apartment.

His eyebrows slashed over those gorgeous eyes, even as she saw the distinct notes of desire in the deep blue. "I didn't come here to sleep with you."

"I know that."

"And I have a lot of bad behavior to make up for."

"You do."

"Then why—" He broke off even as she heard the questions stamped so clearly in the husky timbre of his voice.

"I want you. It has nothing to do with being partners or being mad at you or expecting more from you. I want to be with you and after all we've experienced today, I can't see any reason to keep denying that simple, life-affirming fact."

In the end, Kerrigan acknowledged to herself, it really was that simple.

As she lifted her lips to his, finally meeting in the one place they could wholly agree, she gave in to all that she wanted.

And all the promise that stretched before them.

Arlo wasn't sure how he'd gone from rightfully being taken to task to kissing a beautiful woman, but he was nothing if not an opportunistic bastard and he wasn't letting this moment pass.

He wanted her, with a desperate yearning he'd never felt before in his life.

Never had he met a woman who could make him feel on top of the world and wildly taken to task in a span of moments.

Yet somehow, with Kerrigan, it was all part of the same.

He loved her, that he knew.

But he also respected her. Who she was. Her opinions. And her unwillingness to let him skate by without owning his actions.

He'd done her wrong earlier this evening. He'd put them both in danger with his solo stunt at the bar and he'd nearly paid for it with a knife to the ribs. And still, she could separate her anger at him with her feelings for him. It was a level of generosity he'd never experienced before and it took the base desire that had throbbed between them from the start and moved it to something rare.

Special.

And oh, so sweet.

With their mouths still fused together he moved them into her living room. The love seat where he'd confessed his feelings beckoned, but she stopped him. "I have a Murphy bed. Help me pull it down. It's way more comfortable than a love seat."

He couldn't hold back the smile. "It doesn't look so bad."

"You're not exactly short and neither am I." She nipped a quick kiss at the base of his jaw. "I'd rather have room to spread out."

"When you say it like that..."

She gave him one more quick kiss before directing him to the handles that pulled the bed from the wall. The process was seamless, and in moments she was smoothing the sheets over the bed and placing already-plump pillows at the head.

"That's a nifty trick."

"You've never seen a Murphy bed?"

"Admittedly, not in real life."

"So glad I could offer an education."

She gave him the perfect opening and he wrapped his arms around her waist, pulling her close. "One of many tonight."

A small moan drifted from the back of her throat as he kissed her again, settling one hand at the base of her spine while the other roamed over her body. The thin robe she was wearing, wrapped over a small tank and pajama shorts, was removed in short order and he stepped back to look at her.

He knew what she looked like and knew the innate strength in her lean, lithe body.

And still, staring at those high, firm breasts, nipped-in waist and the long, long legs clad in only those thin shorts had his breath catching. Hard.

"God, you're beautiful."

"I feel beautiful." She leaned in, her fingers seeking the buttons of his shirt. "You make me feel beautiful."

Moment after moment spun out, just the two of them, with the entire world outside the door kept at bay. Arlo felt her hands glide over his chest after she finished with his buttons before dipping lower, over his stomach.

His muscles quivered under her touch, but it was her deft movements, one hand slipping lower beneath his belt, that had him drawing coarse, uneven breaths at her touch.

"Temptress."

"Why, thank you." Her eyes glittered beneath her lashes. "You're quite tempting yourself."

Although he was desperate for her, his body responding with aching need to every single one of her touches, he was determined to make the moments last. To not only make this memorable, but also to know that they'd managed to brand one another before the night was over.

It was nearly feral, this wild, untamed need for her,

and he leaned into that ferocity, allowing himself to feel it all.

To give in to the deep desire instead of holding himself back.

With that foremost in his thoughts, he slipped his hands over her hip before grabbing the material of her tank top, pulling it up her body and over her uplifted arms. He then worked down the thin material of her shorts, dispensing with them equally quickly.

He filled his hands with her breasts, his thumbs caressing each firm nipple. Another deep, low moan drifted from the back of her throat, and he bent his head, trailing kisses over the column of her neck.

A light sheen of sweat coated her skin, and he savored the slightly salty taste of her. A taste that was at subtle odds with the sweet floral notes of her soap.

It was a sensory feast, Arlo realized, as he pushed her down onto the bed, replacing his hands with his mouth. And as he slipped one taut nipple into his mouth, tracing his tongue over the thick, distended tip, he knew a deep satisfaction.

One that filled him wholly, even as there was so much left to explore between them.

Kerrigan writhed beneath him, so responsive, and it spurred him on, continuing a path down her body. He painted his tongue in the dips of her stomach, over the small cavern of her belly button, before moving on. And felt his own body tighten several more degrees in response when he heard her gasps, his mouth closing over the most intimate part of her.

Her thighs tightened slightly against him in subtle resistance before she seemed to go slack as her body simply indulged the pleasure.

And Arlo drank his fill.

This greedy need for her was all-consuming and the sheer openness of her sensuality awed him beyond measure. She was wholly in the moment, her body rising, up, up, up with the increasing pleasure, and he felt the moment she crested, her deep cries the sweetest response.

"Arlo!"

His name was a hard cry on her lips, and he moved up, traveling the return trip over her skin, before wrapping her up in his arms and pulling her close.

And as she smiled up at him, her dark eyes now a fathomless black, he felt a special sort of triumph.

Shared pleasure. And a sort of liquid desire that flowed between them with fiery need.

"I believe you're overdressed, Detective."

He glanced down, where his shirt hung haphazardly off his shoulder, the slacks he'd worn that evening open at the waist. "We'll get to it."

"We most certainly will."

Something sparked in those dark depths, and she rose up beside him, tossing a leg over his waist. "And I believe we'll start now."

Kerrigan was amazed her vision had cleared enough to see Arlo, let alone be able to climb onto his body and begin the delicious act of stripping off his clothes.

But she considered herself an enterprising gal and there was no way she was ready to stop what had started between them with all the power of a tornado.

Even if the man had simply shattered her with that clever, artful mouth.

He sat up beneath her, helping her with the sleeves of his dress shirt, before lying back. She worked her way farther down his body, pulling his slacks the rest of the way off his legs, allowing the heavy material to drop to the floor beside the bed.

The same awe and reverence he'd held as he looked at her hit her in spades as she took in the hard lines of his body. The thick muscles of his chest that tapered into those firm ridges over his stomach.

She was a woman who worked a physical job with nearly all male colleagues. She'd seen them in various states of undress, their chests exposed to the air after a dive or in the practice pool as they swam laps and ran drills.

But none of those physiques she'd seen up close had prepared her for Arlo.

He was magnificent. Hard lines and broad shoulders, a tapered waist and an impressive erection she was doing her level best not to stare at.

But a woman was only so strong, she admitted to herself as she allowed her gaze to roam over him.

Fully.

"Kerrigan." His voice was strained, strangled even, and it had a smile breaking out despite her best efforts to keep her cool.

"Yes, Arlo?"

"You keep looking at me like that and this will be an awfully quick ending."

"Hmm." She flicked a glance up at him before returning her gaze to the delectable lines of his very impressive body. "That would be something to see."

"Honestly, woman." His voice tightened another notch. "I wish I was teasing you."

"I wish you were, too." She reached down and ran the tip of her finger over that length. "But a woman's got to test boundaries, you know. See if she can take a man just to the edge—" She added her palm to the next stroke. "And over it."

He reached up and pulled her down on top of him, crushing his mouth to hers. She wanted to laugh from the sheer joy of the moment, but he captured her mouth, occupying her with far more interesting pursuits than simple laughter. And as their bodies pressed to each other, the increasing urgency of the moment took over.

Hot kisses that electrified matched the glide of hands over sweat-slicked skin.

Tongues that teased and stroked pushed want and need to ever higher heights.

"Give me one minute."

She slipped from his arms, edging off the bed.

"Where are you going?"

"Just need to get something."

She scampered off to the bathroom to get the box of condoms she'd purchased a million years ago. It had been her intention to enjoy what her friends were calling a "hot girl summer" a few years back, but all she'd managed to do was go on a few uninspiring dates from Memorial Day to Labor Day.

And those poor little condoms had remained snug in their box.

She was suddenly grateful she hadn't touched one of them. Especially with the evidence still warm in her bed that the right man was worth waiting for.

And the uninspiring ones…well, they hadn't been worth her time.

"What's this?" Arlo smiled at her as she climbed back into bed.

"A box that promises us both a sexual feast, assum-

ing I haven't had them past their expiration date." She
held the box up to the light, breathing a hard sigh of
relief. "More than a year to go."

Arlo reached for the box in her hand. "Nothing like
a ticking clock to push a man into high gear."

She couldn't help but glance back down at his naked
form. "I think you're already in high gear."

His harsh bark of laughter was infectious, and she
fell into his arms, their lips meeting in an effortless
kiss. It was sweet and funny and more than a little odd
to be talking about expiration dates on condoms and
yet…perfectly normal.

And wasn't that just the oddest—and most won-
derful—thing?

Arlo already had the box open and a small foil packet
in hand, but she took over before he could get it open.
"I'll do the honors."

"And what was that I was saying about you being
a temptress?"

"You ain't seen nothing yet," she whispered in his
ear as she unrolled the condom over his length.

Slowly.

She took great joy from the hard exhale that whispered the hair over her face.

And then the foreplay was over and his hands were
at her waist, guiding her down over his hard length.
Kerrigan took him in, that delicious, aching stretch of
bodies a precursor to the most beautiful movement.

They quickly found a rhythm and as their bodies
met, again and again, pleasure building with each
stroke, Kerrigan felt herself rising again. A seeming
impossibility after the heights he'd already taken her to,
but the pleasure was even more powerful than before.

It was all *more*.

More intense.

More feeling.

More *love*.

She might not be ready to say it, but as the wave broke over her once again, Arlo following immediately on her heels, Kerrigan knew it with all that she was.

She loved him.

In fact, the real question wasn't whether she loved him.

It was whether it would be enough.

Dyson Gentry walked the perimeter of the boat, delivered just that night, inspecting each piece as he walked along the dock. He looked up at his brother, who was standing on the other side of the boat slip. "You think she'll be satisfied?"

"She'll have to be."

"It's not as big as the other one."

"But it's faster. And how much room does she really need?"

Dyson wasn't sure his brother's casual response was quite the right one, but he kept it to himself. Decker had grown increasingly distant and it had taken everything in him not to go to their father.

But what would he say?

Gee, Pop, we've been running some off-market parts?

His father and his grandfather before that had run Brooklyn Yacht with pride, passion and the deepest sense of honor. Was he really thinking of breaking the old man's heart that way?

Especially since they'd run a hell of a lot more than parts.

Which was why he was now resolved. All they had to do was get through this. Give the bitch her boat and move on.

He certainly was ready to.

Because in the end, Dyson had come to realize he wasn't cut out for running off-market and under the table.

And if Decker didn't agree, he'd find a way to convince him.

His brother might have grown oddly distant these past few months, but he needed to see reason. After the favors they'd called in to get this boat delivered, he had to know it was time to cut bait and get out of whatever this all was.

The sound of heels broke him out of his thoughts, and he turned to see Wendy Parker confidently clipping her way down the dock.

"I see you have my boat, gentlemen."

"As agreed. Early, even."

She eyed Dyson, her disdain evident. Despite the fact he'd spoken, she turned toward his brother. "You have delivered."

"In full."

Decker's cool facade never changed, but Dyson didn't miss the way his gaze roamed over the woman.

He was fascinated.

Dyson was fascinated, too, like a person watching a cobra exposing its full hood. But Decker...

In that moment, realization after realization filled him.

Decker didn't want out of this. In fact, he'd built a

program and a supply chain specifically because he wanted *in* on the criminal game.

And he'd pulled Dyson in, too.

He'd preyed on the desire Dyson had to grow the business. To grow his skills and his influence and go beyond the staid, boring business their father ran.

Why hadn't he seen it before? He'd been a pawn, following along like an eager puppy who saw a new toy and not the cliff he had to leap into to get it.

Damn it.

Decker walked up to Wendy, his hands extended to hers. "I'm sure you'll be pleased."

She wrapped her hands in his and pressed a warm kiss to Decker's cheek, lingering there a few extra beats, then pulling back. "You did deliver."

Then she stepped back, and those heels *tap-tap-tapped* as she walked the perimeter of the boat, just as he and Decker had, before she came to stand back beside his brother.

"This is smaller than my last boat."

"Faster, too. This will get you down the coast and back at a speedy seventy-five knots per hour."

"Hmm." Wendy's smile remained in place, but Dyson could see, even from this distance, she wasn't happy.

"I wanted a replacement for my old boat."

"And you have one." Decker kept his smile in place, too, his chest puffed out. "A better one. A faster one."

"A smaller one."

"I appreciate you're growing your business, but this has more than enough space for what you need."

"Yes, but I was clear I wanted a replacement."

No matter how enamored, Decker held his ground. "Which we delivered on."

Dyson thought of the cobra again, its hood extended as it presented itself to its opponent.

Who would blink?

And who would fold up and back down first?

Since it looked like something was needed to break the tension, Dyson stepped forward again. The woman might not have much time for him, but she'd hardly walk away from the celebratory champagne he'd bought for the occasion.

"I think you're going to be quite pleased with the boat. And to celebrate, I've got two bottles of champagne. One to christen the boat and one to toast your new, sweet ride."

Wendy turned to him then, her smile broad. "A lovely idea."

Satisfied the showdown had ended, Dyson crossed over to the small ledge that rimmed the boat dock. They often used the shelf for the same ceremony, with paying customers, of course. But it was a matter of honor and hospitality at Brooklyn Yacht that a new owner got one bottle of champagne to christen their boat and a second to toast it.

For tonight, he'd pulled out the big guns, the green-and-gold label winking in the overhead lights on the dock for the champagne they'd sip. The second was the sort used for this purpose, with a scored bottle in a fine mesh bag.

He'd initially thought the impulse silly, but realized this was just the ice-breaker they needed to get the woman happy with the boat and, frankly, out of their lives.

Then he'd go to work talking some sense into Decker. Assuming, of course, it wasn't too late.

"Thank you, Dyson." Wendy took the bottle he held out to her, her long, slender fingers closing around the neck of the christening bottle. "Where do you want me to stand?"

Dyson picked up the other bottle, then walked her back down the dock. "Right there on the edge of the bow. That should make the perfect spot to officially make the boat yours."

It was a good idea on a few fronts, Dyson admitted to himself as he helped Wendy get into position. The small ceremony defused the current situation. And they hadn't christened her first boat. He was just superstitious enough to believe the troubles that had followed had been because of that fact.

Decker looked vaguely amused by the whole thing, but he crossed around to stand beside Dyson for the ceremony.

"What do you need me to do?" she asked.

"Have you named the boat?" Dyson asked.

"*Speedy Money*," Wendy answered without missing a beat.

It was just the level of crassness Dyson had expected, but he kept his smile in place and nodded all the same. "Then hold up the bottle and as you smash it against the bow, say 'I christen thee the *Speedy Money*.'"

Wendy lifted the bottle, doing as he asked, the distinct sound of breaking glass echoing off the bow of the boat.

Dyson placed the other bottle in the crook of his arm as he clapped, before moving forward to take the now-broken bottle in the mesh bag from her. "Why don't we switch?"

"Yes. Let's."

He took the broken glass and walked to the small trash can they kept for the ceremony. It was only as the glass made a satisfying thunk as it hit the bottom of the can that he heard his brother's shouts. They echoed into the darkened night, followed by a heavy blast of gunfire.

"What?" Dyson whirled around, shock and a slimy layer of panic crowding his throat...

Only to find Wendy standing over the body of his brother, a gun now pointed at him.

"We delivered." The words felt like they were coming from a million miles away as the thick sound of the gun firing still throbbed in his ears.

"I know you did." He read her lips as much as heard the faint sound of her voice through the ringing.

But it was the lift of her gun that had him shrinking back, even as he knew there was nowhere to run.

There was no getting out of this. Not now.

Nor was there going to be another chance.

Dyson briefly eyed the water, thinking he could slip into the cold depths and take his shot, but another gunshot ripped through the air, effectively ending his plans.

The shot had him staggering into the same railing where he'd left the champagne.

It was only as he looked over, the woman's cat eyes narrowed on his, that Dyson felt his knees give way. The last thing he saw was her lift the champagne high.

"Thank you, Mr. Gentry."

Chapter 16

Kerrigan rolled into a hard, warm body and burrowed in, vaguely questioning when her bed had gotten so hot and why she felt so loose and comfortable.

And then she remembered.

Her eyes popped open, right into Arlo's amused blue ones. "Good morning."

"Hi." The word came out in a squeak, so she swallowed hard and tried again. "I mean, good morning. Have you been up long?"

"A few minutes. Did I wake you?"

"I'm an early riser."

"How does your head feel today?"

Since she hadn't given her head a single thought since last night, she almost needed to ask why when her ill-advised monkey-cling-on-a-determined-criminal move came winging back into her thoughts.

"Okay, actually. I feel good."

Good sex must be even more restorative than she'd imagined was all she could come up with. Especially since her monkey-cling move had likely landed her a few more days off the harbor team until she cleared the possible concussion protocols. By all rights, she should be taking it easy, but she and Arlo had done nothing of the sort last night.

And she felt amazing.

"What time is it?"

Arlo reached for his phone on the small end table she kept near the couch. "Just after seven."

"We didn't get much sleep."

"I consider that the highest compliment, Doyle." He punctuated his point by leaning in and nibbling kisses down her neck and into the crook that led to her shoulder, and Kerrigan had the abstract thought that it would be incredible to wake up like this every day.

Which was a dangerous thought to be having after one night of good sex. And yet...

He said he loved her.

The thought didn't fill her with dread, especially knowing she felt the same, but even after sleeping on it, she wasn't entirely sure it was the answer, either.

They still had a lot to work through. And while she appreciated his apology the night before, they also had an open case to solve. One he kept maneuvering her out of.

Yes, he'd apologized.

Would he also change his behavior to match?

Because much as she wanted to believe they were close to solving this, they still had precious few clues. Wrapping it all up felt like a distant milestone.

Who was trying to take over the drug trade?

And there was still the matter of taking care of the thug at McNulty's. A man whose name they didn't know and who'd proven himself to be more than problematic. Arlo hadn't formally addressed himself as a cop last night out behind the bar, but there had to be enough in the man's unprovoked behavior to pick him up for questioning. Especially with Tia Lutz's death.

"Your ambition is spiking."

"Sorry?" She whispered it against his ear. "Because I really would love to stay just like this."

"And I can hear you thinking about all we need to do." Arlo lifted his head, his gaze eminently understanding. "There's a dead body of a young woman in the morgue and a brute keeping watch at a bar who knows far more than he's letting on."

"And don't forget someone who's behind it all."

"That, too."

Arlo rolled over, his impressive back and very naked ass catching her attention. "You really are built, Prescott."

He glanced over his shoulder, his gaze appreciative as he reached behind himself to tug the sheet down her naked body. "Lady, I've got nothing on you."

She lifted herself up on an elbow to kiss him, the moment quickly taking both their good intentions and scattering them to the wind. It was only the ring of one of their cell phones that pulled them apart.

"Yours or mine?"

He glanced at the end table. "Mine."

Arlo disengaged himself and snatched the phone. She'd nearly fallen back onto the pillow, prepared to admire his delectable backside, when she keyed into his side of the conversation.

"What? When?"

Kerrigan sat up, unsure what could possibly have happened but sensing by the immediate stiffening of his back it wasn't good.

"I'll inform my partner and we'll be there within the hour."

He disconnected the call, a string of curses spewing into the air.

"What is it?"

"Dyson and Decker Gentry. They were found about a half hour ago by one of the people who has a boat slip at Brooklyn Yacht."

"Found how?"

"With bullets in their chests."

The words were harsh but the sheer anger and shock in Arlo's gaze mitigated the unforgiving language.

"No way."

"I'm afraid so."

They dressed quickly and within fifteen minutes were in Arlo's car and heading toward Sheepshead Bay.

Although she didn't know Big Will's sons well, she had a clear picture of them in her mind. They'd been part of Brooklyn Yacht for a long time, and she'd talked to them over the years at various events.

"Everyone we've touched. It's uncanny, Arlo."

He glanced over at her as he navigated the morning traffic. "You're not responsible for this and neither am I. The person killing people is responsible for this."

"I know. I do. But hear me out."

When he remained quiet, no obvious arguments, she pressed on. "Each person we've talked to. Each person we questioned. Even those guys who were sent out to follow us. Someone's getting ahead of our investigation. How?"

"You think we're being targeted?"

"I think we're being watched. And taunted." She played it through her mind, that steady impression of impulsiveness continuing to feel like an answer.

Or part of one.

"The waitress certainly feels like a taunt."

"She's sort of solidified the idea for me. There's no way she was targeted until she got our table. Yet, as soon as she did and we ask a few innocuous questions, she's hurt."

"Those aren't innocuous questions to the person who wants to keep this all under wraps."

It might not have been but a few nosy people weren't reason enough to kill someone, either. The fact was a big neighborhood drug bust did go down at the bar. There was no way in hell they were the first people to ask about it or make a comment.

"We still need to go through that footage, too," he added.

"Which reminds me. I started looking last night at what I was able to get from the bodega across the street. There were good clean shots of Tia parking but not much at ground level, where we could see someone tinkering with the undercarriage."

"Something else should come through from the other businesses."

She agreed with that, even as her thoughts about Tia kept spinning out. "Here's the thing. Someone had to have eyes on her talking to us."

"I tried to slip her my card when you went to the ladies' room."

"Did she take it?"

"Nope. Didn't even look at where I had placed it on the table beneath my napkin."

"She tried to warn me off in the bathroom, too."

"Cameras in the bathroom?" Arlo asked. "They certainly have them in the bar."

"Could be. Or they've got it bugged, at minimum. Which takes us back to the ownership of McNulty's."

Arlo shook his head. "We'll run him again. The guy was clean, though. And we looked at him for the drug bust. Over and over we ran him and the financial forensics on his business."

"Is he still there?"

"What do you mean?"

"He didn't know what was going on the first time around. Is he a figurehead somehow?"

"He seemed involved. Knew his business and talked knowledgably to the cops." Arlo zipped in between a few cars. "Who the hell knows anymore? Because something's going on in that place. Again."

Arlo took the exit and traveled the now-familiar path to Brooklyn Yacht. There were several police cars already there when they arrived, as well as the coroner's van, and Kerrigan braced herself for what they would find.

Fifteen minutes later she was still shaken by all they'd discovered.

The bodies of Dyson and Decker Gentry had been covered but they were still in the same position in which they'd been found, shot dead on the deck that surrounded an empty boat slip.

"No video footage at all?" Kerrigan asked the first uniform on scene.

"Nothing. We've spoken to the office manager and

were given access to enter the business office to review the tapes. Nothing was there."

"No footage?"

"Nothing. It stopped around nine o'clock and wasn't started again."

Kerrigan filed that away as the booming voice of Big Will Gentry filled the air. "Where are they?"

The man raced down toward the boat slip, his gaze lasered in tight on the two bodies covered in white tarps, with several officials working around them.

"My boys!"

Kerrigan was already moving in to intercept Big Will, Arlo intent on doing the same.

"What happened?" Will's face was filled with an impossible level of anguish, his movements nearly frantic. "Who did this to my boys?"

Arlo already moved in. Though his own sizable form was dwarfed by Will's, he stood tall, authoritative in the moment.

"Will. Please give us a few minutes. They're being cared for, and we'll take you to them, but we need to talk to you first."

Kerrigan put a hand on Will's arm. "Will, it's me. Kerrigan Doyle. I'm here to help."

"Kerrigan?" Will's gaze brightened as he looked at her. "You came."

"Of course. I'm here to help. We all are."

She and Arlo walked Will through what they knew so far, gently probing him on the business and what he'd believed were his sons' plans the evening before.

"Decker had a date and Dyson had tickets to a concert. Both were heading out straight from here and I said good-night to them around six."

The man's face crumpled at that. "I just said good-night. Didn't even hug them or spend time with them or—" He broke off as the tears came. "I didn't really say goodbye."

"You had no way of knowing, Will. No one could have known."

"Why were they here?"

"Mr. Gentry. Do you keep your security cameras on?"

The vague, disoriented look in Will's eyes faded at the question. "Twenty-four-seven. It's a promise we make to everyone who rents a slip from us."

"The cameras were turned off around nine o'clock last night."

"Impossible. The cameras are never off. We have a backup generator to ensure it."

"They were off last night." Kerrigan kept her voice gentle, but firm. "Which means someone turned them off."

"I don't understand."

"We think it's possible one of your sons turned the cameras off."

"But I—" Will shook his head. "It's impossible. They know the rules. Know how much we focus on a secure environment."

Arlo gave her a quick nod and tilted his head toward the bodies.

She understood his point. Whatever Will might or might not know, his only thought right now was for his sons.

Sons whose deaths had broken his heart.

And sons who would break it again when he realized they were the ones most likely to have shut down the cameras.

* * *

Two hours later, Arlo walked back into the precinct and headed straight for the captain's office. He'd texted Dwayne from Brooklyn Yacht and quickly got the request to check in as soon as he was back at the 86th.

Kerrigan had opted to join the uniforms who'd been first on scene to try and canvass the area after seeing Will got safely home to his wife. She was also keeping watch on the various employees as they arrived at Brooklyn Yacht, gauging their behavior and anyone who seemed to be out of the ordinary.

Or who didn't show up at all.

Although the idea of splitting up to handle the case left him ill at ease, he knew they needed to divide their efforts in hopes of getting to the bottom of the situation quickly.

You have to stop protecting her.

The night before had been beyond anything he'd have ever expected. Because it wasn't like anything he'd ever experienced before.

She was responsive in bed, yes, but she'd artfully separated the attraction between them from the work frustrations that brewed between them. It was a rare skill and more than twelve hours later he was still awed by her emotional generosity.

Even if she hadn't responded to every aspect of last night.

She didn't say she loved you back.

That had been the lone sticking point of an otherwise perfect evening and he wasn't sure how he felt about it.

He'd never said those words to a woman before. Hell,

he was still trying to process why they'd come out so easily with Kerrigan.

And yet they had.

Because he *did* love her.

In the bright light of day, a small part of him wanted to run from it. All while another part wanted to run to her and beg her to tell him she felt the same.

Which left him stuck in the strangest reality.

He had to wait and give her time. She'd certainly been generous and responsive the night before. They'd been in the moment together and he knew she felt something.

But love?

Especially after the way he'd acted, she had every right to be wary.

Had his actions ruined the chance for something more with her?

He wanted to believe they could work through it, but he had a lot to overcome. He'd betrayed her more than once and if the positions were reversed, would he be so quick to leap to declarations?

Resolving to talk to her about it later, he knocked on Dwayne's door.

"Come in, Detective." Dwayne had gotten an early start. His jacket was hanging on a coatrack in the corner and his shirtsleeves were already rolled up. "I looked at the file. Nice, detailed job there, by the way."

"There's a bit more to include after this morning."

"Fill me in."

He walked Dwayne through the events at the bar, the car bomb that killed Tia Lutz and the news of the Gentry brothers.

"What the ever-loving hell, Arlo? We've got three bodies in a matter of hours?"

"Yes."

"You've got more than enough for a warrant at Mc-Nulty's."

"First on my list this morning."

"And you need to get a handle on who the bouncer at the bar is."

He'd gone over that one in his mind and still cursed the fact that he didn't have Kerrigan go check on the car bomb while he dealt with the guy. "I should have dealt with him last night."

Dwayne's tone was grim. "You were a little busy. And saving the woman's life took priority."

"We were a little busy." As the idea hung in his mind, Arlo's thoughts racing through last night, something clicked. "That's it, Dwayne. There's a lot going on. Murders and bombs and snipers. One thing after another, with the wind constantly changing direction. Kerrigan keeps going back to impulse."

"Impulse, how?"

"On the part of the mastermind behind this. Nothing's predictable and we barely have time to catch our breath before the next problem erupts."

"It's erratic, that's for sure. Nothing methodical other than the sheer willingness to cause chaos and loss of life."

"We've been working off the theory that the chaos is designed to keep the criminals in Brooklyn on their back foot. But what if it's also a strategy for the cops? Kerrigan and I have been chasing our tails since we started this case. No time to breathe and certainly no time to sit back and consider all the pieces."

"Then maybe it's time to sit back. You set the pace."

"We need to catch this killer before they hurt some-one else."

That reality was sharp and oh-so stark in his mind.

But Dwayne had a point, too.

Right now, all they were doing was bumbling around. If they didn't slow down and get some direction to fol-low, they weren't of any use to anyone.

And keeping them running in circles only gave the killer more time to hide in the shadows.

Kerrigan accepted a ride back to the 86th with one of the uniforms at Brooklyn Yacht and she'd bought the woman lunch as a thank-you. Their stop at a sub shop on the way back had given her an opportunity to get Officer Ramirez's take on the crime scene and al-lowed Kerrigan to pick up lunch.

With a meatball sub for him and an eggplant parm sandwich for her, she walked back into the precinct with precious little more than the day before.

They had managed to rule out the staff at Brook-lyn Yacht. She'd run everyone's name and looked at them, but no one had missed work and the genuinely shell-shocked faces had suggested grief far more than nefarious dealings by Big Will's employees.

Which brought it all back to the sons.

And the increasingly sad evidence that Dyson and Decker Gentry had been running a secondary business under their father's nose.

It was the theory she'd batted around with Ramirez, and it fit.

The unregistered boat that went down in the har-bor had to come from somewhere. And Big Will's sons would have access and the contacts to facilitate a purchase like that.

So why kill them now?

The boat going down in a storm was hardly their fault as the supplier. And if she circled back to her theories way back at the beginning, owning an unregistered boat would still require maintenance and the contacts to keep it running.

Why go to all the effort to find a supplier to meet your needs and then kill them?

Kerrigan hit the button for the squad room, her mind racing through the problems, when it hit. Without waiting for the elevator to arrive, she took off at a run for the stairs, racing up two stories and into the squad room.

"There's another boat!"

She hollered the realization loud enough that it had Arlo lifting his head, along with everyone else in the room.

Careful not to drop the sandwiches, she set them down on the edge of his desk, even as excitement spilled out faster than she could contain it.

He smiled at her, and she ignored the shot of pure, unadulterated lust that hit her belly at the knowing look in his eyes. She was going to have to get a handle on *that*.

But she'd deal with that later. Right now, she had a line to tug.

"I've got a theory."

"Lunch and a theory? It looks like a banner day, Officer Doyle."

"There's a second boat, Arlo. That's what went down last night at Big Will's place. That's why the cameras were off."

The smile fell, replaced by that determined cop face she had come to admire and respect and yes, *love*.

She tapped the edge of Arlo's desk, already reaching for her phone. "Let's get Wyatt. We need to get out on the water."

The police boat bobbed in the harbor near the site where the drug runners went down in the storm. Kerrigan assessed the calm waters. The harbor had a glassy look that was rare for the waters around New York, and she opted to take it as a good sign.

They'd already notified the Coast Guard and several teams were working the waters up and down the coast. But she and Arlo, along with Wyatt, Gavin, Jayden and Captain Reed, were poring over maps in the boat's wheelhouse.

None of them were convinced this spot just off Governors Island was going to be the path of another drug run, but without anything else to go on, they'd opted to start here and consider various paths from open Atlantic waters into Brooklyn.

"The working theory is they went down coming back into the harbor because they had the drugs on them in the storm. Which means they have a supplier somewhere up or down the coast and they're coming from the Atlantic." Kerrigan tapped various points on the map as she spoke. "They could be working out of Philly or Baltimore or points farther south. Providence or Boston are options, too, but the weather's going to be less favorable as it gets colder. But a boat like that could make the trip distance-wise either direction."

"But it's a haul," Wyatt added, using a ruler to point out the distance, "especially for any attempts much past DC. That's a few days' trip with a lot of cargo at risk of discovery."

Kerrigan tapped the map. "If we operate under the theory the mastermind behind this took possession of the boat last night at Brooklyn Yacht, they have to be gearing up for a run quickly."

"Did they find anything yet in the files in Gentry's offices?" Wyatt asked.

It was Arlo who took the briefing on that piece. Kerrigan had worked with Arlo before they'd headed out to the docks, that process of requesting a warrant new to her.

"The warrant came through this afternoon and the same team that was first on scene went to recover any evidence they could find, as well as take possession of the electronics."

"I've put the data team on it as top priority," Dwayne added. "But it's going to take them a while."

She was of two minds on what they were going to find but knew the digital forensics team needed the space to do their work. There was a big part of her that had to believe the Gentrys kept records of what they were handling.

And the other, bigger part of her knew there was little benefit to them to keep records.

Their cell-phone and text histories were likely going to turn up far more than computer records but they'd take what they could get. Maybe a stray email or log-ins to a personal, private email account.

Even with the potential to dig up something there, they really needed cell phones. But the last report they got from the team doing the warrants was that no cell phones had been found.

"How would you hide a boat?"

The captain's question pulled her from her thoughts. Although it was directed at all of them, Wyatt was the one to answer. "You'd need a slip for keeping it in place."

"What paperwork's needed for that?" Dwayne pressed.

"Insurance. Ownership. Registration." Wyatt ticked off each required element a purveyor of dock space would expect.

"So nowhere respectable," Dwayne added.

"The bar!" Kerrigan thought about McNulty's and Bulldog's and realized there was something there. "McNulty's has the parking lot behind it, but Bulldog's sits on the water. There's a likely chance there's a private slip back there."

"It might have even driven the decision to take the location," Arlo added. "You want to run illegals, you need a place to do it. People won't look quite as close at your boat if it's hidden on your property. No nosy paperwork, either."

Bulldog's made sense, she considered as she imagined the property and where it sat along the water. But so did McNulty's as home base. Especially if you wanted to keep attention off the boat in its hiding place.

It all fit.

It was why they kept coming back to the bar as a base of operations.

And it was also why the employees were at risk.

People might know how to keep their mouths shut for a paycheck, but it didn't mean they were blind to what went on around them.

Tia knew things. Arlo had already gotten the same

impression from the valets. And if they didn't want another one of them ending up like Tia Lutz, they needed to get this whole damn thing dismantled as fast as possible.

"We need to get to Bulldog's." Kerrigan looked at Wyatt, Gavin and Jayden. "We can dive from several yards down the dock, swim in and figure out what's going on. We'll check for serial numbers on the boat while we're at it."

"If it's stolen, we can seize the property without a warrant," Captain Reed added. "But I'm going to request one, anyway, for the dive so no one can slither out of this."

"It's stolen," Kerrigan said, convinced they were finally on the right path. "But we'll do it by the book."

She caught sight of Arlo's face as she and her fellow divers all started mapping out a plan of attack. His expression was blank, but she recognized what was there, roiling beneath the surface.

Hadn't she seen it often enough already?

He'd shut down each time she had to risk herself for this case and it was obvious he was fighting the urge to do it again.

But he'd have to deal with it.

This was something she not only had to do, but she was also the half of their partnership who had the skill to do it.

Chapter 17

Arlo considered the docks around Sunset Bay and reviewed what Kerrigan and Wyatt had worked up on the boat. He could see the dive pattern they'd mapped out. Where they'd drop into the water and where they'd come up to inspect the boat.

It was dark, murky work but they were trained for it.

And Arlo knew he had to let her go.

This was her job. Her skill set.

And it was her shot at solving this case.

She'd earned it.

Even as every fiber of his being fought the reality of what she was about to do.

He sat on stakeout down the street from the front entrance of Bulldog's with another detective he'd worked with several times in the past. Detective Tom Casey was seasoned and he knew Brooklyn like the back of his hand. He'd gotten up to speed quickly when the captain brought him in for the briefing, clear on the layout and the objectives of the dive.

He was equally clear on the protocols to move in and seize the boat once they determined it was stolen.

"Quite an operation," Casey said as he sipped from a take-out cup of coffee. "And the swath of destruction in a matter of months is incredible."

"No mercy seems to be the MO on this one."

"You're not kidding. The Papa left quite a hole." Casey let out a curse. "I'm glad you brought me in on this, but you know damn well we'll cut this node and three more will spring up in its place. It's frustrating."

It was the reality that haunted him, even as Arlo struggled with agreeing with the man.

Casey was a good cop. An honest one, too. But he'd been at it for a long time, and he'd weathered a lot.

And if he was being honest with himself, Arlo knew where the man was coming from. He'd felt that emotion and hopelessness far too keenly after the trafficking job with Vice that had gone sideways. He'd worked through it and vowed after he came out the other side that he wasn't going to give in to that way of thinking.

Not for himself. Not for the job. And not for Gabrielle.

If nothing else, he owed it to her memory to do the work and do it with the belief he was making a difference.

His comm unit crackled with an update and Arlo keyed into Wyatt's voice and off the dismal thoughts that threatened to overwhelm.

"Boat sighted in the slip," Wyatt said through their comm hookup. "Gavin and Jayden are the first team down. Kerrigan and I will go second."

Arlo knew they kept their comm limited, focused only on giving the essentials, so he avoided asking too many questions. In the meantime, he and Casey had to figure out how to get in and get out without any risk to civilians.

It was still early, which worked in their favor, but the lunch crowd would be arriving soon.

Although the plan had come together quickly, they'd all agreed as they mapped out the op that protecting civilian life was essential at all costs. Especially since they knew they were dealing with an adversary who wouldn't hesitate to kill.

"How do you like working with Harbor?" Casey asked.

"Good. Trumball and I get to pair up together often."

"And now you're mentoring Doyle? How's she working out?"

"She's doing well. She and her dive partner found the bodies on the boat mess that kicked off this investigation. She wanted more case time, so Trumball, Captain Reed and I agreed she should see it through."

"Good for her. The kid is ambitious. She's impressive to watch."

"That she is. Her instincts are rock-solid. She's coming along really well."

It felt almost clinical to speak of Kerrigan this way, yet he knew what was expected of him. Knew Detective Casey was assessing Kerrigan as a prospective partner. More, he knew his coworker was assessing Kerrigan as a talent in the department.

His feelings for her—for what they shared—had to remain separate. He owed her nothing less.

And, he realized, he owed himself nothing less.

He'd always struggled with his role in a relationship. How much he wanted to run once things got serious.

Well, what was between him and Kerrigan was serious.

And he wasn't looking to run.

So he'd pump her up and have her back and *believe* in her.

"They're a fearless bunch, that harbor crew," Casey added.

Arlo almost started laughing at Casey's assessment, Kerrigan's words at their first breakfast coming back to him.

The harbor team seems to have a special reputation. But it's like we're held separate somehow. The words are always complimentary, but we're still seen as something other from the department.

But it's also cop work in a city surrounded by water. Somebody's got to do it.

Someone did have to do it. And that special reputation was not only well-earned, but it also came with admiration when you recognized someone was the best.

Casey turned to him, about to say something, when a shot rang out, shattering the windshield and still traveling with enough force to slam into the detective's chest.

Arlo scrambled to get down, reaching over to Casey to pull him to the side and out of the line of fire.

"Tom!" he yelled. When the man didn't respond Arlo remained low, scrambling for his comm unit to call it in.

"Officer down! I repeat, officer down!" He quickly rattled off the directions along with his badge number, even as he waited for another shot to come ringing through the car.

It was only as he looked up, he saw the broad shoulders and even broader grin of the thug he'd fought at McNulty's, standing beside the car.

And a gun was pointed directly at him through the driver-side window.

Kerrigan sat beside Wyatt on the small Zodiac they'd taken to the edge of the docks. They were about three hundred yards from the boat slip at Bulldog's and they'd been monitoring Jayden and Gavin's dive. The captain had equipped them with body cameras for this dive and they'd watched on a small screen what the men saw as they moved around the boat.

"She sure is shiny and new," Wyatt muttered.

"That she is. And in every place they've checked now, unmarked."

It ate at her, the sheer magnitude of what they'd uncovered. The number of people who'd been injured along the way. And the ridiculous loss of life.

And for what?

She'd played the female angle over and over in her mind. It wasn't that she believed a woman incapable. Quite the opposite. Someone with determination and a will to succeed could be any gender. But it was the layer of dark, twisty violence that bothered her.

Because the woman behind this had decided the only way to the top was by removing every single thing that got in her way.

The Gentry brothers.

An innocent waitress.

Even the brainless thugs who should know better, but also didn't deserve to die in some ridiculous game of chicken.

A game with murderous consequences.

They'd all left their comm units open, and she could hear Gavin and Jayden's short, clipped answers to each other as they inspected the boat. Could hear the captain asking for updates where he still sat on the NYPD boat farther off the coast.

And she thought of Arlo, where he sat waiting to move in. Just waiting for the signal that the boat was dirty.

They were going to finish this.

Today.

Which made the sudden scramble on their open line a horrifying punctuation mark to the deep need she had to close this case.

To end it.

"Officer down!" Arlo's voice came through clearly in her ear, along with the resulting instructions for support.

Wyatt gave the instruction to come back to the Zodiac, affirmatives winging back from Gavin and Jayden.

But it was the words that came a short while later that stole her breath.

Arlo left the line open in the undercover vehicle and she heard a new voice. One full of menace and purpose.

"You're with me, *De-tec-tive*." There were mocking notes as the man sang out the word *detective*. "We're going to finish what you can't seem to keep your nose out of."

Although she couldn't be entirely sure, she thought she'd heard the same dark notes in the man's voice as she remembered from the alley behind McNulty's.

Which meant their thug bouncer was a bigger part of this.

"Wyatt, I need to get in there."

Wyatt had heard the same exchange on the line and shook his head at her request. "You can't approach. We'll catch them in open water."

"We can't wait for open water. You heard Jayden's description. This boat's an upgrade over the last one. Sleeker and faster, and there's no way we can let them take Arlo."

When he looked moderately swayed by her argument, she continued. "You and I both know boats. One of us can support him and the other can take out the engine."

"Kerrigan, this isn't—"

"We can't leave him!"

She was already zipping up her wet suit, prepared to ignore a direct order, when Gavin and Jayden surfaced, climbing aboard the Zodiac.

"What'd we miss?" Gavin asked.

"She's going after him," Jayden said, pride shining in his eyes. "You'd better hurry your sleek ass up. They're getting ready to move out. I heard them moving around on the deck."

Kerrigan eyed Wyatt across the Zodiac, even as she continued finalizing her equipment for a dive.

At Wyatt's muttered curse, she knew she had a partner. "I'll take the engine. You go up the side."

"There's a ladder starboard," Jayden said. "The movement all seemed to be coming from port side, where they're coming on and off against the dock entrance."

She reached over and linked hands with Jayden. His gaze was deadly serious when it landed on hers. "You watch yourself. I expect my girl back in one piece."

"That's my plan."

Before she could question the situation further, she attached her waterproof field kit, inclusive of her weapon and her badge. She checked that her bailout bottle was firmly attached and took the second Gavin handed her. "Arlo might need it."

She nodded and hoped like hell they were walking him off the boat, but it paid to be prepared.

And then she pulled down her mask and dropped backward into the water, the only sounds she could focus on coming from her comm unit and the heavy, labored breathing of Arlo's stakeout partner.

Arlo kept his gaze focused on his surroundings as he was perp-walked to the back of Bulldog's. The place looked different in the light—dingier, actually—and he counted off the steps between the front and the back entrance before catching sight of a cavernous structure that looked like a barn-door closure.

It had to be the dock, he quickly calculated, and was proven right when the doors swung open just enough for him to be pushed through from behind.

"Get in there."

Since he'd now faced the guy down twice, Arlo figured they were close enough to get on a first-name basis. "You got a name? Because you've been 'thug' in my head for a week and I figure we should know each other a bit better."

"You don't need to know my name."

"*Thug* it is," Arlo growled, not surprised when the gun at his back dug harder into a kidney.

Although he wasn't complaining, he wasn't sure why the dude hadn't shot him outright. But since he was still free of gunshot wounds, Arlo prepared himself for whatever came next.

Only to find a petite blonde in four-inch heels standing on the deck of a shiny new boat as he and Thug came up beside it.

"Mr. Prescott. Or should I call you Detective?"

A come-hither smile painted in a vibrant shade of red set off her petite features, but the look in her eyes was predatory. "Miss Parker."

"Oh, come now. You're dating my old friend from the neighborhood. You can call me Wendy."

"This is your doing?"

"I'm afraid so."

"The harbor killings and the sniper shots and the poor dead waitress?"

She made a show of glancing down at her nails in boredom before looking back up. "It's so hard to find good help. That's why I'm so lucky I have Mark."

She gestured in the direction of the man behind him and at least Arlo now had a name. It wasn't much, but they could work with it.

He *had* to work with it. There was already one man down, desperately in need of the EMTs on the other side of the building. And if things moved the way he figured they would, there was every chance he wasn't walking out of this one.

He needed to get what he could and hope he figured out a way to stay alive long enough for help to arrive.

To see Kerrigan again.

That thought struck swift and low in the gut and he forced himself to focus because he needed whatever intel he could get.

Locking away thoughts of Kerrigan, Arlo glanced

around at the firepower amassed on the boat deck. He trusted his colleagues and knew he'd had just enough time with the open comm unit in the car for them to have a sense of what happened to him and to Detective Casey, but *Mark* had ripped the one in his ear out before they were five feet away from the car.

Which meant no one knew what was happening right here.

"You've been building quite an empire for yourself." Arlo kept his attention on Wendy, well aware it was her impulsiveness that had driven every outcome so far.

Mark might have a gun pressed to his back, but Wendy held the cards and he needed to keep his full focus on her. Mark might enjoy brandishing the threat, but Arlo knew he was safe until Wendy decided he wasn't.

Which meant he had to talk fast and hope like hell the team fanning out beneath the boat could get here in time.

"This town hasn't seen anything yet," Wendy preened before him. Although he wanted to chalk up her behavior to a feral sort of madness, it was impossible to miss the clear eyes and the woman's sheer determination.

"Brooklyn's got an opening for a new crime boss, and I decided it's going to be me."

Although he hadn't climbed aboard yet, Arlo had taken note of a third person milling around the decking that led to the boat. He had a long-range sniper's rifle in his hand and a spring in his step as he headed for the entrance to the boat.

Wendy smiled at him indulgently, even as her gaze strayed to Arlo to size up his reaction. "Nice work on the cop."

Arlo fought the cold rage that burned low in his gut at the casual assessment.

"I could have taken them both," the man with the sniper's rifle bragged as he crossed to board the boat.

Wendy's smile never wavered but her tone took on a decided edge. "And carelessly leave more shell casings behind on my roof?" She shook her head before producing a gun out of her coat pocket and aiming for the man.

Without missing a beat, she fired, the shot frightfully accurate as the man fell backward.

"Get his gun," Wendy ordered Mark, all while she kept the gun in her own hand level with Arlo's chest.

Impulsive.

Brash.

Determined.

All that he and Kerrigan had puzzled through for the past week suddenly came clear in the woman that stood before him.

Wendy Parker was as lethal as she was determined.

Kerrigan kept her comm line open for everyone else to hear what was going on up on the deck. She'd waited with Wyatt while he found the engine panel, only moving on when he tapped her on the arm to proceed. She'd been careful to surface as quietly as possible, as far away from where Jayden and Gavin heard footsteps above them.

Once she was above the waterline, she moved quietly around the starboard side of the boat. The calm water had made their dive easier than usual, but it also meant there wasn't a lot of lapping water on the boat side, nor was there the cover of thick waves to keep anyone from hearing her.

She maneuvered herself toward the ladder, just where Jayden had said it would be, and heard voices above her.

A sharp spear of joy filled her when she heard Arlo's voice, bordering on insolent as he spoke with the guy that had to be their thug from the bar. The same one she'd heard in the comm unit.

She'd confirm it when she surfaced enough to see the deck, but for now, she was operating on that assumption.

But it was the woman's voice and Arlo's response that had Kerrigan stilling all movement, her fingers digging into the smooth hull.

Wendy Parker was behind this?

Rah-rah Wendy with the big smile and flirty laugh?

Even as she struggled to process that reality, she had to admit it fit. The woman's presence in McNulty's the first night she and Arlo were there.

The subtle insinuation she'd kept up with Kerrigan's life, using the old neighborhood as the excuse for the knowledge.

And the gunshots on the two boat victims, executed by someone shorter than them.

Wendy was petite, even in the heels she favored. And she had a lot of access in town, especially when her fashion business, which would undoubtedly need shipping services, was factored in.

She'd positioned herself well and Kerrigan could only imagine this was the next step for her. One that had been carefully plotted and planned.

And one she'd upended with her obvious bloodlust and uncontrolled actions.

It was a shock and yet it strangely fit.

Reining in her reaction, Kerrigan moved closer to the ladder, the conversation on board filtering over. She had to get Arlo out of there, and with any luck, Wendy and her goons would try to maneuver out of the boat slip before taking any action against him.

A trip that wouldn't be happening when she saw Wyatt surface farther up the hull, his quick thumbs-up a confirmation he'd disabled the engine.

A trip that she suddenly feared was about to turn far more deadly when Wendy's voice echoed off the water and the cavernous, covered area of the boat slip.

Followed by a gunshot.

Arlo watched the entire tableau play out, the sniper down on the deck and Mark's instructions to go after him.

He hadn't forgotten the gun pointed at his midsection—nor had he forgotten the woman who held it and her willingness to shoot fast—but he knew he wasn't getting another chance. On a deep breath, he leaped, rushing Wendy and hoping he had her just enough off guard to tackle her before the gun went off.

Her scream lit up the air and he didn't miss Mark's grunt and string of curses from the deck.

He managed to get a hold of the gun in her hand, still hot to the touch, but he ignored it as he slammed her wrist against the floor of the boat.

She continued to scream, holding tight to the gun and scratching him with her clawlike fingernails with the other hand.

And then it all stopped as one thick rubber foot came

down over Wendy's wrist, crunching hard on the delicate bones there.

"Police. You will cease and desist now."

Arlo glanced over his shoulder to see his avenging angel, water dripping heavily off her wet suit and a gun in hand as she stood over them.

Wyatt stood a few feet away, his own gun pointed at Mark on the deck.

"Wendy Parker. You're under arrest." Arlo stood to help Kerrigan cuff the woman, all while his partner read the woman her rights, followed by the list of her crimes.

Arlo was going to move off and help Wyatt once they had Wendy in cuffs, but their captain, followed by Jayden and Gavin, were already boarding and made the arrest on Mark.

He saw Gavin reach down to check the pulse of the sniper before shaking his head.

One more lost life at the hands of Wendy Parker.

Arlo turned to Kerrigan and while he wanted nothing more than to pull her into his arms, he kept his distance as the two of them dealt with the spitting cat of a criminal. Each of them took an arm and walked her off the boat.

And it was only after they had her settled in the back of a police cruiser that Arlo finally found the time to say what he wanted to say.

"You saved me."

She stared up at him, a smile twitching the corners of her lips. "I saved my partner, yes."

"That's true. You did do that today. But you saved *me*, Kerrigan. Me, Arlo. I didn't realize I needed saving until you came along, but you did."

"Well, when you put it that way, maybe we saved each other."

"You needed saving?" He pulled her close, suddenly not caring who saw them.

"I've spent my life focused on work. On what came next. On who I wanted to be. And while I don't regret a single minute of it, I didn't spend a lot of time thinking about who I wanted to spend it with."

"And now?"

"Now I still want to work hard and be the woman I know I can be. But I want to share it with you. Because I love you, Arlo Prescott."

"I love you, too."

He bent his head to kiss her, only to be interrupted by a muffled screech from the police car they'd bundled Wendy into.

"Is that her screaming?"

"I told you she's sort of a lot."

"Sort of a lot? The woman was trying to single-handedly run the drug trade in Brooklyn. She might have succeeded if she'd learned to be a little less quick with that gun."

Kerrigan nodded, her gaze solemn. "And now we have to investigate it all. How she started. Who she's involved with."

"It'll be a lot of work." He smiled as he pulled her close once more. "You up for it?"

"I think I am."

"You think?"

She wrapped her arms around his neck and pulled his head close for a kiss. "I think I need to get some pancakes first."

Arlo took her mouth in a kiss, and it was the sweetest he'd ever known.

Sweeter, even, than the syrup-laden one he laid on her a few hours later in the middle of a diner full of cops, all eating pancakes for dinner.

* * * * *

Romantic Suspense

Danger. Passion. Drama.

Available Next Month

Colton's Secret Stalker Kimberly Van Meter
Hunted Hotshot Hero Lisa Childs

Deadly Mountain Rescue Tara Taylor Quinn
Undercover Cowboy Protector Kacy Cross

 LOVE INSPIRED

Lethal Mountain Pursuit Christy Barritt
Kidnapping Cold Case Laura Scott

Larger Print

 LOVE INSPIRED

Protecting The Littlest Witness Jaycee Bullard
Undercover Colorado Conspiracy Jodie Bailey

Larger Print

 LOVE INSPIRED

Witness Protrction Breach Karen Krist
Sabotaged Mission Tina Radcliffe

Larger Print

6 brand new stories each month

Romantic Suspense

Danger. Passion. Drama.

MILLS & BOON

Keep reading for an excerpt of a new title
from the Intrigue series,
COLD CASE IDENTITY by Nicole Helm

Chapter One

Palmer Hudson liked to have fun. He'd learned at an early age that life was going to punch you in the nose as often as it could, so you might as well enjoy the ride between blows.

That didn't mean he was irresponsible. Maybe, on occasion, he hit the bottle a little harder than he should, and definitely, on occasion, he was a little careless with women, but always, no matter what, Palmer showed up and did what he was tasked with doing.

Some days, it was ranch chores at the sprawling Hudson Ranch, which had been part of his family for five generations. And sometimes it was stepping in as investigator on one of the cold cases his family investigated as part of Hudson Sibling Solutions—his oldest brother's brainchild after the disappearance of their parents when Palmer had been twelve.

One day they'd been there…and then they'd been gone.

No one had ever figured out what had happened to them. But Jack had stepped up and taken care of the five minor Hudson kids. Jack had been eighteen and had taken on the weight of *everything*.

Had it turned him into an uptight tool most days? In Palmer's estimation, yes. He could hardly hold it against Jack when Jack had kept them together. Driven him to football practices, signed off on his joining the rodeo early, made sure there was food in the fridge and money in the bank.

Jack had been the glue so much so that, even though they'd each tried their hand at off-ranch things—Grant had joined the marines for a time, Cash had gotten married and had a kid, Mary had gone to college and Anna had tried her own brief stint at the rodeo—all these years later, they were all back home. At the Hudson Ranch. Running Hudson Sibling Solutions and living just outside the Sunrise town limits.

Family.

Nearing thirty, Palmer didn't consider his wild days behind him, but he supposed he was starting to understand the adult art of *balance*.

Mostly, he thought darkly when he recognized the raven-haired woman sauntering toward him. He'd been heading for the main house, but now he was seriously considering turning on a heel and beating a hasty retreat.

Louisa O'Brien was the one person, maybe in the whole world, who made Palmer Hudson *uncomfortable*.

Since she was his kid sister's best friend, he'd once enjoyed annoying and torturing Anna and Louisa whenever given the opportunity. It's what big brothers were for.

But ever since Louisa had come home from some fancy college out east a couple of years back, Palmer had done his level best to steer clear.

Because Louisa O'Brien had grown up into a flat-out knockout. Wavy black hair that she almost always hung loose around her shoulders, dark green eyes the color of deep summer and an almost-constant smirk that promised she knew a lot more than you did. Not to mention the way she wore her jeans—which he absolutely refused to notice ever since that *one* time he had very much *not* realized it was Louisa he'd been ogling at the local bar.

He might not have a lot of boundaries when it came to women, but Louisa was one.

"Hey, Palmer," she greeted, coming to a stop in front of him.

He hadn't run away, so he supposed he just had to deal. Much as it pained him. "Afternoon, Louisa. Anna's out of town."

"Yeah, I know. I actually came by to see you."

"What the hell for?" That was another thing about adult Louisa. He was forever saying the wrong thing around her when he'd never had trouble charming a woman in his entire life. From the *cradle*, he'd been able to wrap the female population around his…finger.

Of course, he didn't want to charm Louisa. He wanted to stay the hell away from her at any and all costs.

She grinned at him, green eyes wreaking real havoc

with his system—a system that should absolutely know better.

"I need a favor," she said, and though she tried to keep the grin stretched wide, he saw the shift in her eyes. Something serious lurked behind that attempt at amusement.

"Why don't you ask literally anyone else?"

"Why so grumpy?" she asked, reaching out to poke his chest.

He sidestepped her. He had learned that *nothing* good came from pretending like she didn't affect him. So, he just straight up *avoided*.

"Got things to do, Louisa."

"And people, I assume," she returned with a smirk. A smirk with *just* enough flirtation that he had to very firmly take his imagination to task. No picturing Louisa O'Brien in absolute any kind of state of undress.

Ever.

"I need shady help," she said, as if she didn't know how she affected him when he had the sneaking suspicion she knew and used it against him. Routinely. "And you're the shady one."

"Anna's shady."

"No, Anna's vengeful," she corrected. "There's a difference."

It was true, but Palmer didn't have to like it.

"It's a bit delicate. I'd ask Cash, but he's not taking cases right now. At least, that's what Mary said. And as much as I trust Anna with anything... Well, I need a delicate hand."

It irritated him that she'd want to go to Cash over

him, which wasn't a fair assessment since he didn't want her coming to him. But still. Emotions and facts didn't always line up neatly. So, his response was a little gruffer than it should have been. "Since when is that my department?"

She blew a breath, frowning out over the distant mountains. Something twisted in his stomach. He very much wanted to fix whatever was worrying her. But he could not take that risk.

When she returned her gaze to him, he was sunk. "This is serious, and I need someone I can trust. I'd go to Grant or Jack, but they're just too…straight and narrow. I need someone who's not afraid to bend the law a little. I need answers at literally *any* cost."

"*Any* cost is a dangerous proposition, Louisa. You might want to rethink what you're offering." Because every now and again, the best defense was an obnoxious offense.

She frowned. "No one's paying you to be a jerk."

"Nope, I do it for free since I love it so much."

She laughed. That was another problem with Louisa. Sure, like everyone else, she didn't take him too seriously, but she didn't get bent out of shape. She took things as they came, and since that was his entire life motto, he couldn't help but respect it.

Her laugh died quickly though, and any attempt at humor too. She clasped her hands together, looking up at him imploringly.

Hell and damn.

"I found something that changes my entire life,

Palmer. I need answers. I need help. I don't know who else to go to."

"Like what?"

"Like...I don't think my parents are who they say they are. I don't think I'm theirs. And I don't think any of it was ever legal."

Louisa wouldn't cry in front of Palmer Hudson for a million dollars. She had pride. Some people had told her she had too much.

She didn't mind. Pride got a person places, and it kept them protected from people taking advantage. It protected soft hearts that didn't want to be soft.

So, she had her pride and she forced back every last *drop* of moisture in her eyes that threatened. Even though it was hard.

She'd never said the words she'd just uttered out loud to Palmer or *anyone*. She still didn't want to believe it. But the past six months had her feeling hollowed out and empty. Sad and scared. She couldn't live in denial any longer. She needed answers.

She hoped to *God* she got answers that were comfortable. With every passing month, it felt less and less likely.

"I don't follow," Palmer said, studying her in that careful way of his. Palmer played into his fun-loving, heavy-drinking, serial-dating reputation. He made sure everyone thought there wasn't much substance under that black cowboy hat.

But Louisa knew his family saw the substance underneath, and she knew that under all those bad boy ways he'd learned to cope with his parents' disappearance was a man who was careful with the things that mattered.

She wasn't ashamed to admit, in the privacy of her own mind, that she'd been in love with Palmer Hudson since she was thirteen years old. Who would have been able to resist? He'd been impressive at seventeen. Homecoming king. Football quarterback. Off to the rodeo, always smiling and laughing despite the tragedy that had befallen his family.

She'd believed—hoped—for years she'd grow out of those feelings for him. She knew he'd never, *ever* reciprocate those feelings. But hers stubbornly and religiously stayed, even after her four-year stint in New England for college.

Even if she sometimes entertained the fantasy he might reciprocate *other* things if not feelings.

Regardless, she loved him. And she'd bite her own tongue off before she admitted it to anyone.

That little wrinkle had kept her from asking for his help for months now. She'd tried to think of a way to bring it up to Anna that wouldn't send Anna flying off the handle. She'd considered, over and over again, consulting one of the other Hudsons. *Any* other Hudson.

But if everything she suspected was true, *she* was a cold case. And she needed help. Careful help. Determined help.

Palmer fit the bill. Unfortunately, more than anyone else. He wouldn't want revenge. He wouldn't tell anyone. He wouldn't follow every law to the letter.

He'd find her answers.

Maybe he'd tempt her in the process. Because, damn, the man was enticing. If that was the price she had to pay, then so be it.

"So, this woman found me on Facebook," she said, since starting at the very beginning seemed safer somehow.

"No reasonable story starts with those words, Lou." He looked down at her, so condescending, she almost turned and left right then and there. She didn't need his disdain. She didn't need *him*.

But she did need answers.

"She was a freshman at my alma matter," Louisa continued, trying to keep the snap out of her tone. "And she'd seen my softball team photo in the athletic complex from when we won our championship."

"Still proud of that one, huh?"

"I assume you're still proud of all your buckles?" He didn't respond to that.

"So, she contacts you and says what?"

"That we're identical. And isn't that so weird? She sent me her softball picture."

"You opened an attachment from an unknown source?"

"Yeah, I did, Palmer. So buy me some antivirus software. The point is, she was right. She looked almost exactly the same as I did at eighteen. We decided to try to trace our family trees to see if we...connected somehow. Like long-lost identical cousins."

"And you didn't?"

"No. But then she suggested we do one of those ancestry DNA tests. You know? The ones that tell you where your family came from, and you can connect to other people with the same DNA or whatever."

"Sure."

"I was kind of excited. I thought it would be something cool. Like my great-great-grandma had an affair with some outlaw. I thought it would be fun, maybe funny. I entertained the possibility we weren't related at all and we're just freak doppelgangers too, but dreaming up how we might connect felt... I don't know. It was just *fun*. So I told my parents. I thought we should all do it."

He must have read something in her tone because his frown deepened. "They didn't go for it?"

"They forbid me."

Palmer's eyebrows drew together. "Forbid you? I didn't think your parents forbid you *anything*."

"Well, I wouldn't go *that* far, but no. They've always been lenient. Bent over backward to make me happy. I know that." She wrapped her arms around herself. It was silly. A silly thing to still be upset about, but it was *jarring* when parents got really militantly angry for the first time when you were *twenty-four*.

Even when they'd caught her with a beer after graduation, she'd gotten gentle talking-tos, despite every don't-drink-before-you're-legal lecture known to man. They just...didn't get mad. They were overprotective, but they were careful.

Now she wanted to know why. Why for twenty-four years they'd been so accommodating when all her friends had had more rules, more lectures, angry fights with their parents as they'd experimented with teenage rebellion.

But Louisa had never been able to rebel, even when she'd tried, because her parents did not forbid.

Until, as an adult, she'd asked to do a fun little DNA test. "They threw a whole fit. Said it was dangerous to give your DNA to those places and there was no way any of *our* DNA was going to be sent off to some shady business."

"It's not a bad point, Louisa."

She didn't groan, though she badly wanted to. "No, it wasn't. Still, I wouldn't have thought anything of it. If they'd been rational. If this woman hadn't told me…"

"Told you what?" Palmer asked.

This was the hard part. The part that didn't make any sense. The part that, for months, she had convinced herself wasn't true. Until Kyla Brown from Lakely, Ohio, had sent her picture after picture of family members who looked like Louisa herself.

When she'd never once been told she took after her parents. Never *once*.

"Her older sister was stolen as a baby. Kidnapped. They never found her—not a baby or a body. And they never figured out who did it."

"Louisa. You can't be serious." He didn't sound condescending this time. No, he sounded like he *pitied* her.

That was worse.

"I know it sounds out there. I want it to be a lie. A joke." She had to pause to swallow the emotion that threatened to envelope her whole. She'd been trying to